LAST NIGHT'S STRANGER

One Night Stands & Other Staples of Modern Life

EDITED BY

PAT ROTTER

LAST NIGHT'S STRANGER

One Night Stands & Other Staples of Modern Life

EDITED BY

PAT ROTTER

A & W PUBLISHERS, INC.
NEW YORK

For the stranger who brings stories
For the stranger who brings love

With love and thanks for my father's
support in all my efforts.

Published by
A & W Publishers, Inc.
95 Madison Avenue
New York, NY 10016

Manufactured in the United States of America
Designed by Gloria Adelson/Lulu Graphics

Front cover design by Gloria Adelson/Lulu Graphics
Front cover illustration from Art Deco Posters and Graphics by
Jean Delhaye, copyright © Academy Editions.

1 2 3 4 5 6 7 8 9 10

Library of Congress Cataloging in Publication Data

  Main entry under title:

  Last night's stranger.

    1. Short stories, American.   I. Rotter, Pat.
PS648.S5L3   813'.01'08353   81-70460

  ISBN 0-89479-104-4   AACR2

CONTENTS

INTRODUCTION

IF YOU THINK the subject of one night stands is merely titillating, or really grim, think of this. Last night's stranger could
be tomorrow's husband, wife, lover. On the other hand, last
night's husband, wife, lover could soon become tomorrow's
stranger. That's the way it is in this life. And our kind of life is
set up for it. People pass through. Bars and bar stools, bus
stations and airports. Revolving doors. But isn't passing
through better than passing by? And those *little* sparks do give
off warmth. Better than nothing. And maybe better than the
big sparks, more dangerously catching fire. In love. In husband
or wife. In all that commitment and fear of loss.

Think of Fire Island, or Malibu, ski chalets and lodges. All
those bodies on the ferry, all those bodies on the beach, all
those bodies schussing and falling, and toasting by the fire.
Leisure. And then there's travel, inviting us to stray. 9 to 5,
inviting us to play. And city sidewalks in the summer, full of
sexual display.

Promiscuity isn't just promiscuity these days. We're only out
there looking. Looking, and maybe finding. Maybe every girl
who goes to bed with a man is looking for a husband, that
prince on white charger her pre-Lib mother read her stories
about. She's just trying harder. Think of it that way. Then

again, maybe she's looking to avoid one. We're all looking for something, aren't we? True love? Pie in the sky? Or just Madison Avenue blue-jeaned behinds, and fast food sex? Does anybody really *just* want to get laid? It seems to me more complicated than that.

And those words, "getting laid," or "he laid her." How come they're almost always in the past tense? Done and gone. In and out. Ice cream melts. Your puppy dog dies. And so we all do. Then we get "laid out."

So life, or catching it, is what it's all about. Or is it those "little deaths" that dull our pains in life? The Big O, or small. Multiple orgasms, or one at a time. Of course. It's medicine. Drugs and sex and drink, and loving, dull the pains of life. And bring sweet pain. Grabbing, sweet stroking, or even the back of a hand. To stay and to keep? Or to pass on by?

"Keep moving. Keep moving," the traffic cop says.

Keep moving. Caught in the cold, in the deep snows of life, you've got to keep moving or die of frostbite.

But it isn't just one night stands that we're talking about here. That all of these writers are writing. It's people moving in and out of each other's lives, leaving sometimes something behind. Husbands and wives. Killer and victim. Lovers, and ex-lovers, and those who never will be that. The dead leave the living, passengers passing us by. Though memory will keep them to us, the dead and the gone, leaving us our own short story collection to live on.

Last Night's Stranger started as a short story, my first. But like the relationship with the man who inspired it, that one didn't work. Then there was a manuscript I'd read while I was an agent, called *Singled Out*, about a singles' bar killer. And Judith Rossner's very successful *Looking for Mr. Goodbar*. But mostly, there were the lives of myself and other women I knew, single women who never could seem to build solid connections with men. Men who couldn't tie up with women. The divorces. Like London Bridge, our relationships were all falling down, permanency a seeming thing of the past.

It seemed to me that the short story was the perfect medium to express these relationships. Easy satisfaction. But unlike one night stands, the good ones leave a lasting kick, though both, if we're smart, tell us something of life. *Last Night's Stranger*, though sometimes cruel, is an anthology of short fiction by some of our best writers of contemporary fiction. It is meant to show, in their unique words and tales, the realities, the fantasies more real than reality, of our impermanent lives.

"The shortness of affairs and decrease in permanent relationships is some obscure step in the evolution of man whose purpose cannot yet be determined. . . . " That's what Baldessari thinks in this anthology's story by Paul Kennebeck, *Baldessari's Dead Sea Flights*.

In John Irving's story *Other People's Dreams*, his character Fred, dreams the dreams of those who have left him. His wife, his child, even his old labrador, Bear. Keeping what he's lost, keeping their pain and his, Fred knows more of them than when they were with him:

"Now in the mirror," Irving writes of one dream, "Gail had gone to sleep on the pile of her unloved clothes on the floor. That was the way Fred had found her—the night he came home from his first infidelity.

"He woke up from her dream in the bed alone. He had understood, before, that she had hated him for his infidelity, but this was the first time he realized that his infidelity had made her hate herself."

Fred's dreams reveal the real character in the characters drawn, the truth in Fred's passing marriage. Just so, these stories, the stories here in *Last Night's Stranger*, reveal the damp truths underlying our lives.

But single life is the life most often limned here. Lists and lists of lovers passing through. Gail Godwin's *Indulgences* does just that. Lists, and builds that list, and cruelly forgives that list. Religion and sex, color and blood.

"Why should I be ashamed?" the woman in the story says to

her lover pushing to know her past. "My past has nothing to do with me, with the person I am now." True or false, sins or indulgences, the woman in Godwin's story uses her past to free her from this lover.

Boredom or lust or need push us forward into those sexual enthusiasms we later reject, shudder or yawn on. Randall Reid's *Detritus* and Sybil Claiborne's *Flotsam and Jetsam* list them for us, virtual encyclopedia of sexual events, sex objects. The dictionary is Erik Tarloff's *Flesh, Pleasures of the*. And Don Mitchell's *Celeste, in Camera*, a picture palace of pin pricks on skin, spelling out sin, conquest, and pain.

But fantasy is sometimes the stronger. Stronger even than flesh. Find it in Raymond Carver's *Neighbors*, Robert Coover's *The Elevator*, Hilma Wolitzer's *The Sex Maniac*. Wolitzer's story pulls us into a life stirred by fantasy:

"Everybody said that there was a sex maniac loose in the complex and I thought, It's about time. It had been a long asexual winter." And then, "I wondered who he was, after all, and why he had chosen us. Had he known instinctively that we needed him, that winter had chilled us in our hearts and our beds?"

Raymond Carver, the master of sub-rosa, gives us a couple who are sexually turned on while caring for the cat and the plants in their neighbors' apartment, turned on by the sexuality of lives other than their own. So much happens, even though nothing really happens.

And Coover's *The Elevator*. The very same elevator we take up to our offices every day, run by the same girl in the same color uniform. And foully, raucously, sexily—the same fantasies some of us might have had. One such subway fantasy is developed by Kenneth Bernard in the *Dirty Old Man*. Raunchy turn-ons, as in Lynda Schor's hilarious and shocking, *The Horse*.

Even death and disfigurement limn the dark side of *Last Night's Stranger* in Joyce Carol Oates' *Narcotic*, David Huddle's *Waiting for Carl*, and *Cordials* by David Kranes. Singles' bars and freedom, and city anonymity lead us into a life matching dangers and options. Like a candy store display case full of penny candy, the choices are myriad. Or seem so. The tit man, the ass man, the man with a sweet tooth can find what he wants most anywhere. Or what he thinks he wants.

But though the dangers of these nighttime slidings-by are also myriad, they're less likely to result in physical harm than in psychic and emotional wounds. Most unpleasantness is left to leaving, to those insults we can't quite wipe off our lapels. *A Soldier in Iceland* by Barton Midwood is a brilliant story of two lives passing, of a soldier of fortune wounded by, not understanding why, the girl, for the moment, next to him.

But some comfort comes in medicine. Or does it? In *The Consultation* by Richard Selzer, the doctor's hand strays for pleasure and finds pain. While in *The Consolations of Philosophy* by John L'Heureux, the medical laying on of hands, comfort for the bereaved, becomes simply laying, cheering at least one member of the patient's family.

Living and dying are passing moments. Passing. Hard to accept. The touching story *Elena, Unfaithful* by Gloria Broder shows a widower living, though harshly, with his wife's "infidelity," her affair with that dark stranger, death.

Best of all for being happy—who doesn't like a happy ending?—is *The Ugliest Pilgrim* by Doris Betts, about the girl who goes in search of a cure for her ugliness and, glory be, finds love.

Isn't that what we all hope to find?

> "Henry," she said. "What do I do when he's pushing it to me, pushing it to me?"
> "Get his name."

INDULGENCES

Gail Godwin

"GIVE ME the child until he is seven; after that you may have him.—St. Ignatius of Loyola.

Jack Cooley
Andy Harkins
André————
Rick Yelvington
Sven (Vespa)
"Malibu" Miller
Phil Starnes
"X" (train to Montreal)
Conrad Ten Eyck
Joost————
Dr. Corchran

She sat at her desk by the window, in the fading light of a gloomy November day, writing their names—or the parts she could remember—down a yellow legal pad. At first she had been chronological; it came easy. Yet the first part of the list had been painful, because parts of her earlier vulnerability still clung to those first names. ("Ah, how impressionable I was!" "The tears I cried over him would fill a small reservoir." "What did I ever see in him?" "How happy I was when he told me, 'You seem so uninvolved,' for that was how I wanted him to see me.")

But then the list grew longer and took on a rather sinister quality. The names were only names. They connected her with nothing but . . . anecdotes. So she abandoned chronology and went by free association. Or, sometimes, like Don Giovanni, took them country by country. Was she a female Don Juan, then? She had been to more countries than he had.

The name of one might recall to her his physical opposite: the tall dark remind her of the small light, etc. Or a name might lead to its counterpart in another language. The eminent judge with a Dutch name recalled the young tour guide in Amsterdam who had given her a disease. Or she recalled a missed period that had dogged her afterward, a conveyance upon which one had ridden into her life—and out again. Yet she had touched and been touched by them all. She had chosen them. They had been her "lovers," whatever that word now stood for. "X": an IBM executive, met on the train; too cautious to tell his name. He got off at Poughkeepsie, kissed his wife and children, then followed her to Montreal in his private plane. But what had she felt for "X"? What had he felt for her? They had been, both of them, extraordinarily pleased about their anonymous little adventure. For, of course, she had given a false name, too. After the grubby Dutchman (she remembered most clearly, for some reason, a child's small brown shoe in his messy apartment—his young wife and child had left him), she had flown to London when the rash appeared. The nice Dr. Corchran, at St. Thomas. So suave. "Not to worry," he said, trying to help her control her humiliation. "All the debs have it this season." His name made the list, too, but he had been careful to protect himself.

She had the feeling Don Juan had enjoyed his "conquests" more.

An hour ago, she and a man had a "lovers' quarrel," here in this very room. "Why do you insist on being so elusive about your past?" he said. "I know you've had other lovers. So have I. I talk about my past freely enough. Why must you withhold yours, unless you're ashamed of it."

"Why should I be ashamed? It's just that it means nothing. My 'past' has nothing to do with me, with the person I am now."

"Everything has a meaning," he said. "Every life has a pattern. If you care about someone, you're naturally interested in their patterns. What is it? Surely you aren't afraid I won't 'respect' you if you tell me you've had ten or fifteen lovers."

The figure is nearer to sixty or seventy, she thought. She said: "There are men who coax a woman into telling these things to titillate themselves. Or to use it against her later."

"When are you going to stop confusing me with 'men'? I'm a person who happens to love you," he said.

She had stood facing him. They were both exactly the same height. She remembered the exotic joy she'd gotten from creating him. The day she knelt down at his feet and ran a tape measure from his ankle to his thigh and then turned to her assistant and said: "Our Banquo here has deceptively long legs. I think we should capitalize on the legs, give them a silvery-metallic quality, let them rustle when he walks, in true ghost-style. When he comes back from the dead, let his face be covered, but the stockings be the same. The stockings will be his trademark."

And then the inevitable jokes together when they became "lovers." Wrapping the ghostly legs around her in bed. "Do I scare you?" he asked. "A little," she said. She was still able to superimpose the freshness of their situation upon the real man, an actor now out of work. But when he wasn't acting, his energies dammed up and he turned nasty. He picked quarrels. He pried into her life. She knew what he was up to; she did it herself. When the drama wore off old scenes, you created "scenes" to entice it back.

So, an hour ago, she had screamed at him, "You won't be satisfied till I make you a *list!* Shall I put little stars by the ones who satisfied me the most? What else would you like to know?"

"I'd like to know," he said, drawing himself up to pronounce the sacred sentence she knew was coming, "whether you have it in you to love."

"I don't know. I need to think about it. Maybe I will make the list."

"I'm tired," he said suddenly. "Let's go and eat something."

"No, I'd rather do my list," she said, with a touch of malice.

"Suit yourself, then. Shall I come back later in the evening?"

"Suit yourself."

"I'll check back about seven. See how you're coming with it. Or do you think" with his own little twist, "you'll need more time?"

"I'll have to see how it goes. I wouldn't want to leave anybody out."

Exit ghost, she thought.

Her apartment was high up in a thick-walled old building overlooking the Hudson. Her bathroom had been made over from a butler's pantry, and she took long baths in generous amounts of scented oil, surrounded by wainscoting. She denied herself nothing. She liked to soap her breasts with French soap and sometimes took a bottle of cream sherry and a wineglass, and lay in water hot as she could stand it, sipping the sweet, nutty taste, and rereading praise of herself.

> The true magic of Adriana Trachey's ("Pelagia") designs lies in their unerring revelation of *the latent.* Her costumes zero in on the meaning behind the word, the private obsession of the public figure. A "Pelagia Design" transcends the conventional aspect of "role" and manages to undress the soul. Thus it goes beyond the usual costumer's achievement of merely gilding the persona.

Framed round the pale yellow walls of her living room (fast growing dark on this sunless November day) hung some of her favorite designs: her Edinburgh Lear in his reversible robe of burlap and fake ermine; her Tyrone Guthrie Antigone in leather; her St. Joan, naked except for the invisible body stocking and the delicately striated wire cuirass and the silver-coated goggles to cover her eyes in battle. "You can't love," they said. "There's a leak in you somewhere. No man will ever be able to fill you up. You'll go from man to man. Remember, nobody will ever love you as much as I did."

And, the final poisonous thrust, when they had given up on her: "You are going to end up alone."

How long had she taken that word at full value? "I love you." Going back to the beginning of her list, she recalled herself using the word, holding it back until the last possible moment, terrified any prematurity might lessen her value. Then the glorious feverish capitulation. ("I *love* you." "Oh, I love you, too.") The relief when you found it was a two-way thing! Then the period when you indulged yourself in the word at the slightest stimulus: Oh I love you I love you I love you I love you I love you I love you. Once, as a small girl, she had said the word "pig" aloud, over and over again, until it lost all meaning.

Then came the period when they began to say, "You are so cool, so detached. Somehow, I can't imagine you loving anyone." And she quivered like a huntress behind a tree, watching her prey, her arrow of "coolness" taut in her bow.

The list grew longer. At what point had it become a thing in itself, leading its own life, separated from what she thought of as her "real" life, which, more and more, in the last few years, was her work?

"Everything has a meaning," her last lover had said. "Everything has a pattern."

But lives could be festooned, could they not, with paper streamers of extraneous matter.

But if her lovers were extraneous, why did she go on committing herself to new ones? Many of the men on this list would have been inconceivable on a shorter list, the modest list of "ten or fifteen" he'd had in mind for her. But scattered about on a longer one, they looked merely colorful, like interesting accidents or errors. Was that it? Was she trying to cover up her earlier bad judgments and losses with a "pattern" of randomness? Which names, if you erased them from this list, would make a difference to her life, the way she had developed? Would make her a different Adriana Trachey on this particular November afternoon?

Several she had "loved" in the days before she began to put love in quotation marks; several had obsessed her; one or two had turned away, rejecting her.

But only one, perhaps, had made her some of what she was. And his name, of course, was not on the list. Though maybe it should have been.

Her uncle had raised her. He had informed her tastes. Exacting of himself, he was forbearing, even amused, by the shortcomings of others. He had the constant appearance of trying to conceal from them that they were fools. He was a busy tax lawyer and worked late into the evenings in his warm library filled with books of law and the lives of saints. His hobby was hagiography and he had once labored for a whole year over an essay about St. Clement, which he submitted to *Analecta Bollandiana*. It was sent back with a respectful letter. They had found his theories fascinating, but were unable to publish it because of certain apocryphal elements. If he would care to revise. . . . But of course he would not. He put the letter and the essay away, with his quiet, bemused smile.

There was always a fire in his library at night. His wife, who seldom smiled, lit it each evening and swept away the ashes the next morning, but at night she went into her bedroom, the coldest room in the house, covered her legs with an Army blanket, and mended or crocheted. The uncle, it was said, had been about to become a priest when he met and fell desperately in love with this beautiful woman. Her aunt a beautiful woman? The pinched face and the cold voice that was constantly saying "No"? And the child could not imagine this stern, forbearing uncle "desperately in love" with anyone.

With her, he was stern, exacting—and tender. "I have work to do, sweetheart," he'd announce every evening. "I hope you do, too." The little girl went with her uncle into the cozy library and spun out her homework, copying everything over a second time "for neatness." After that, she was allowed the freedom of his shelves of saints and martyrs. He had several rare block books, from Germany and Holland. She got crayons and paper and copied the crude look-alike woodcuts of smiling martyrs being beheaded by executioners, also smiling. The neck—or other parts of the body—so recently severed, or hacked to pieces, were so strangely dry and clean. She added great quantities of blood. She gave the pictures to her uncle, who raised his eyebrows and smiled. "You are a realistic little soul, aren't you, Adriana? Better not show these to your aunt. She prefers things sapless."

She progressed from these primitive tortures to the more sophisticated variations. Not all martyrs were surprised by the ax, she found when she learned to read better. They often went in search of it, or inflicted it on themselves. In her uncle's little volumes of de Voragine, she found (and illustrated) the rebellious Christina of Tyre, who threw her father's false gods out the window, and threw pieces of her flesh in his face as fast as he could tear them from her body by hooks; when a pagan judge cut out her tongue, she flung it back and blinded him in the eye. It took arrows to still her heart, so zealous for suffering it was. And she drew St. Lawrence, roasting on his pyre and calling out merrily, "Turn me over! I'm done on this side!" And Elizabeth of Hungary, who liked to put on rags at night, after her husband was safely asleep, and leave the castle and go down into the streets and hug lepers and beggars to her breast. Adriana offered the fruits of her work to her uncle, two bright spots of color on her cheeks from the warm fire. He filed each picture away in an old volume of Blackstone. It was their secret.

For his birthday, she did a "comic strip" of the life of St. Pelagia. How the life of this saint fascinated her! Adriana was drawn to the elegance of this young woman, who was first in everything in the town of Antioch: shapeliness, finery, riches. She was even drawn to her drawbacks; she loved the sound of their names as well: *"Vain and variable of courage, and not chaste in body."* It was a joy to costume such a heroine; it was a challenge to illustrate the dramatic chronicle of her life and present it to the person she wanted most in the world to please. But when she came to the last "picture" in the life of Pelagia, she could not illustrate it.

"The last scene's not finished," she told him after he had professed himself delighted, *delighted,* with her gift. "You are nine years old, and you still know what most of us have forgotten," he said. "You know you can do anything you set out to do. I want you always to remember that, Adriana. And now come and sit here on my lap and tell me what it was about the last scene which gave you trouble. The one where the nuns are laying out the body. It looks finished to me."

She was a little too big for his lap, but glad he did not seem to think so. Sitting there, she explained, "What . . . the nuns saw. The thing that made them realize St. Pelagia was . . . one of them. I'm not sure . . . I don't know how it would look."

Her uncle got a very funny look on his face. One she had never seen before, and she was an avid student of her uncle's face. She was in the habit of measuring the increase of his esteem for her there.

At last he said, "You are certainly one for the truth, Adriana. If you're sure you want it, I suppose I could show you what— what I can see—what I have seen—better than you. Do you want that?"

He was trembling slightly, the way he did sometimes when

he was trying to control his temper after her aunt had done something stupid.

"Yes, I want it," she said in a small voice, feeling this was the answer he wanted. She was a little scared.

He kept her on his lap while he drew. He held her tightly by the waist with his left hand and drew with his right. He pressed the crayon down so hard once that it broke in two. He used red and pink and purple and brown—and, at last, black. He breathed like a man exhausted, climbing up to the top of a hill. She was aware of tensions and tremors in him that she could not explain. At last he finished climbing the hill. He put down the black crayon with its blasted tip. He was perspiring and distraught. "There you have it, Adriana. The reason it is so hard to draw . . . the reason you could not draw it . . . is because you could not see it as the contradiction it is. It is"—and he smoothed her hair compulsively with his hand, a strange baptismal gesture that seemed to cleanse her of all implications—"it is both the gate of heaven and the mouth of hell."

Outside her window it grew dark. A tugboat, inching along behind a barge, suddenly turned on its lights. This reminded her of another name, and she switched on her desk lamp and wrote:

Christian Rasmussen

Rasmussen was the Captain of a freighter. She (and he) was bound from Hoboken to Oslo. Her aunt had just died. She had not a single relation left in the world. She had finished art school but had not yet found the art that suited her best. Thus she was miserable, bent on marrying one minute and dissipating herself the next. She had tried and failed to abnegate herself with a man who would have saved her from the uncertainty of a real vocation. And now she was running away to "enjoy herself," determined to fling caution to the winds and become as cheerful and wanton as her aunt had become in that strange metamorphosis of her widowhood. She decided to fall in love with the Captain—why not? This hulking giant of a man who had to stoop to enter cabins, who smoked pipes of a pungent, foreign odor, whose shy English went up and down in an attractive singsong. At meals he wore summer whites and gold bars; charmed everyone with his lore of tonnage and storms. She saw him standing on the bridge, in khaki shorts and sandals, calling orders in a man's language, the language of the sea, through a megaphone. She heard his men refer to him as "the Master." Well, he would be her master, too, on this summer sea journey. But to her the Captain was distant and respectful. When anyone told an off-color story at the table, he frowned nervously her way. He invited the other passengers, in small groups, for drinks in his cabin: the port engineer and his wife; a young scholar from Ann Arbor; two widows traveling together; a loud, raucous middle-aged California couple . . . but not her. She dawdled over her lunches on the days he sat at her table. She slowly consumed salmon, spiced herring, smoked eel in jellied eggs, salami, liver paste, meatballs, and hot potato salad. "You like our Norwegian food, I think," he said, smiling. She told him, looking him boldly in the eye. "I think I have fallen in love with everything Norwegian." But still no invitation. Until, sketching in despair on deck one day, she saw him approach. Could he see? His face brightened when she told him she was an artist. "You mean to say, that is your profession? Your only profession?" And that night she was invited to his cabin for beer and *schnapps*. He had an extralong bunk bed to accommodate his unusual height— but he could not accommodate her that night. "I'm sorry," he said, looking down forlornly at his sad member. "I think what is causing it is for almost a week I believed you to be a nun. Our purser told me you were a nun. You signed yourself that on the passenger list." "I wrote *none* after occupation," she said. "Because I have no job." "Ah," he said, "but in our language, *nonne* means Bride of Christ, do not touch." Then they had laughed. She snuggled her face against those mammoth thighs. "You are master of this ship, steer her anywhere you want," she said. "Oh, oh," he moaned afterward, "how I am sorry that we wasted all our good time!"

His wife came aboard for the Captain's dinner in port. A serious blond woman, a little too heavy, who spoke no English and obviously adored her husband. Adriana sat next to the wife and drank Spanish sherry, two white wines, the first of whose name meant "Reach for Heaven," the Captain told everyone, just grazing her with his humorous eyes. Then she drank two red wines, one bitter and one sweet, and consumed lobster, duck, and a flaming ice cream. And afterward "the Captain's own brandy." The scholar from Ann Arbor, who was doing his thesis on the friendship between George Crabbe and Sir Walter Scott, got drunk and stuck a lobster leg behind his ear. She seduced him that night in her cabin, imagining the Captain and his wife above them. At three in the morning, she woke, utterly disgusted with herself. It seemed she must get him out of her sight at all costs, so she made up a lie about how she was religious and always said early-morning prayers. He was sullen, but he left. The sun was already shining in the Land of the Midnight Sun. "With the Captain I could have been happy," she said to herself, weeping and swallowing gulps of clean air through her open porthole. She knew she was putting on an act for herself, but went on for a while anyway. The ghost of her uncle watched beside her. "You signed me in on this voyage, didn't you, you bastard," she said to him.

She spent three months in Europe before her money ran out. It was the easiest thing in the world, she discovered, to have lovers. By the end of the summer, she had stopped keeping track.

Her uncle had died slowly, sparing himself no pain. But he said, "Adriana, I want you to go on with your school life. I want you to be a normal teen-ager and have fun." As always, she obeyed. She went out with the captain of the football team and wore his monogram sweater, which came below her knees. They danced glued together from cheek to thigh. They planned to be married. She ate supper at his house several evenings a week. How different from her own! His mother made her own pasta and wore swinging hoops in her pierced ears and belted out "Domani" as she washed the dishes. His father drove a bakery truck and smelled like fresh bread, and pounded his fist on the table to make his point. At the table, the family talked openly about Adriana's marriage to Tony; they accepted it as perfectly normal that she had not yet told her aunt and uncle. "All that suffering over there!" said Mrs. Rosa. She gave Adriana little gifts: a pair of shortie pajamas; a little painting of a kitten and a puppy, which her sister in New Jersey had done; a large bottle of Tigress cologne. After the meal, Adriana and Tony would go up to his room, filled with sporting trophies and her own photographs. They would lie on his bed and tempt each other's chastity. "My wife, my wife," Tony would say, and she imagined herself metamorphosed into this utterly new thing, a "wife." Sometimes Tony would stroke her until she truly forgot who she was; she melted away and was nothing.

Then she would walk home, quite herself again, hugging her coat close, hurrying past the lighted windows of neighbors. And she would spend the remainder of the evening reading to her uncle from the lives of the saints, of repentant hearts and startling conversions, and the eager search for a pain large enough to settle the old debt. Her uncle's face grew sterner and holier as it lost flesh. One evening he said, "I want you to take all those pictures we drew out of Blackstone's—it is the volume on the nature of crimes and their punishment—and after your aunt is asleep I want you to burn all of them." At first she had forgotten what pictures he meant.

Soon after, he sent for the local priest, a man he despised. She could not remember her uncle ever setting foot in church. He made her sit holding his thin, cold hand while he confessed to this stranger about how they had "drawn pictures" in the library. The folds of the priest's white lace sleeve brushed her—the moth-touch of death on her hand—as he anointed her uncle with the oils.

She did not marry Tony. Had she ever believed she would? Even when she melted away in raptures, imagining herself a "wife"?

Her aunt became gay and abandoned in her widowhood. Her personality seemed to have done a complete about-face. When Adriana came home on holidays from college, there were clues everywhere that her aunt had a lover. One night she and her aunt went out to a bar. "Tell me, Adriana, have you had a lover yet?" asked her aunt, her freshly-tinted head cocked brightly to one side. "Oh, don't worry, dear, *I'm* not going to censure you. He made me out an ogress, I know that, but I've earned my indulgences. I had a nice lover long ago, Adriana. I feel you should know this. He would never let me tell you. I betrayed him because I fell in love with this man—a handsome young Army officer—and this man and I had sex together. Yes, sex! This man used to lick me all over; he said I tasted like honeysuckle. And then your uncle found out and the young officer killed himself. Yes, it was quite a tragedy. His young wife left him, she was so upset when your uncle told her. She skidded off the road and was killed. A broken neck. And her husband killed himself. He hung himself in the attic of his house. His dear brother had to go and cut his body down. His dear brother, Adriana, was your saintly uncle, and that young couple was your mother and father you were told died together in a car crash. I have not been well lately, and if, God forbid, there is an afterlife, I don't want this on my conscience."

Jacques Ferian

The one who had all those tiny mirrors in his bathroom. Everywhere you looked, from floor to ceiling, a small mirror. "But you can't see all of yourself in any of them," she said to him. "I don't try," he had replied.

She finished the list at a quarter to seven. Under the glow of her green-shaded lamp, she counted them up. If she'd left any out, it was a fault of memory. It couldn't count technically as a sin of omission.

Over a period of fourteen years, it came to five and two-sevenths lovers per year. Not too shocking by contemporary standards. Out of curiosity, she figured up the total of the average housewife. Three times a week, fourteen years, would come to 2,184 times. Beside this figure, Adriana's output seemed quite modest. How much did it really matter whether it was the same man or a different man each time?

The last name on her list was the person who would shortly receive it. She scrawled a short note:

> *I drink to the general joy o' the whole table,*
> *And to our dear friend Banquo, whom we miss.*

Enclosing the list, she left the envelope stuck in the door.

She went to a double-feature film and then checked into the Plaza Hotel. "My water heater's gone on the blink," she told the desk clerk, curious about her lack of luggage. "And I must have a bath." Her face shone out at him, boyishly candid, above the upturned collar of her autumn-haze mink, which matched her eyes.

Early next morning, she walked over to a little restaurant she knew on Broadway, sat down at the counter, and ordered a huge breakfast. She ate eagerly, with gusto.

A man sat down beside her. He ordered coffee and a Danish. He wore a soiled raincoat and had dark circles beneath his eyes. He had crisp reddish hair, rather long. She bent demurely over her hash browns to let him assess her. Then they exchanged a very brief look of mutual understanding. He had the trickster's twinkle in his weary, intelligent eyes. In many ways, this was the moment she always loved best.

"Just visiting in town, are you? What do you think of our fair city? Got anyone to show you around? I'm the barman over at the Tara. Not a bad place. Good jazz. Do you like jazz? You ought to come round. Maybe tonight. Any weeknight after ten. So your rich friend's on a cruise, eh? That's not very nice of her, to go away and leave you alone. Where is her place? Not far from here?"

"I was always the black sheep of our family, back in Omaha," she told him as they walked convivially down the street, toward the river. Her hands thrust deep in her pockets, a bemused smile on her upturned face. She liked the tall ones. "My younger sister is married to a nice doctor in London, and my older sister is a nun, but I guess I have always liked adventure."

"What kind of a name is Pelagia?" he asked her as they rode up in the elevator. His fingers traced the shape of her face lightly.

"It's an old family name. The first Pelagia was a beautiful young woman from Antioch—"

"I'd rather know more about the beautiful young woman from Omaha," he said.

"She had lots of lovers." They had reached her floor. She pressed up against him and touched the tip of her tongue to his cold stubbly cheek. "She was known for the splendor of her attire and for her lewdness of mind and body."

"And her love of adventure?"

She unlocked the door. The envelope was gone. She led him into the lovely room, filled with morning sun. The well-kept plants and bright fabrics and the elegantly framed costumes made their impression on him. "My friend is so talented," she said. "She is a successful costume designer."

"I don't go to many plays. But it must be nice to live in a place like this. Does your friend have a bedroom? I want to hear more about this Pelagia."

"Well, one day Pelagia was walking through the city in her latest clothes . . . . "

She began to remove her own clothes, a fixed dreamy look in

her eye. "And followed by many young men and women, all of whom were her lovers. When suddenly she met the Holy Veronus, Bishop of Heliopolis. When he saw her, do you know what he did?

"Not this."

"No, though perhaps he wanted to. No, he beat his brow and wept. He felt that God had sent him a sign in the sight of this elegantly dressed woman with her lovers. 'Look,' he said, 'how studiously this woman has clothed herself to give pleasure to her earthly lovers, while I—Veronus—have given so little care to pleasing my Heavenly Spouse.' "

"Weird guy. Oh, what nice sheets your friend has. We mustn't spoil them."

"We won't. If we do, there's a good Chinese laundry right around the corner. Don't you like my story?"

"I like you better . . . . "

"Oh, but," and she laughed and tickled him, "I am my story. Funny, I've just seen it."

"Well, let's hear it, then. But don't make it too long, huh?"

"So Pelagia was impressed by this Holy Veronus. She sent word to him she wanted to be converted and could she see him alone. He sent word back that if she was serious, she would have to bring a chaperone."

"Dumb guy."

"She went to him—with the chaperone—and Veronus baptized her, and she cast herself at his feet and denounced herself as a quagmire of wickedness and so on. Then she went home and settled her affairs with the devil, spent a couple of nights with him for old times' sake, and after that she dressed as a monk and spent the rest of her days as a holy man in a monastery."

"Very interesting story. You're quite a girl, Pelagia."

"No, wait. There's a bit more. She passed herself off so well as a holy man that in time she was made superior at a nearby convent of nuns. But then one of the nuns got pregnant and 'Brother Pelagius' was blamed. The nuns imprisoned him in a cave till he died. When they came to lay out his corpse, they discovered—tell me the honest truth, now: does this look like the gate of heaven to you or the mouth of hell?"

"Neither," he said. "But you talk too damn much, Pelagia. I'm sorry, I can't."

He began to dress again at once. He sat on the edge of the bed, sullenly drawing on a sock. "What kind of a freak are you, anyway? Christ, I'm tired. If I wasn't so tired, I'd kill you. Girls get murdered every day for less than you've done, Pelagia, or whatever the hell your name is."

"I'm sorry—" She, too, began to dress. The whole thing seemed suddenly shabby.

"Well," he said, putting on his raincoat, "so long, you mixed-up girl. Take my advice and don't try your game on just any stranger. I happened to be harmless, but the next one might not be."

She sat at her desk by the window. The morning was clear and beautiful. The pure winter sun glittered in little spangles on the river. Everything so clean and lovely: no one would guess the filth beneath its spangled sheen. She made rapid, feathery sketches on a watercolor pad, and her mouth actually watered at the thought of the colored washes she would stroke on, later today. As she worked, she began to feel less awful about this morning. The sketches were for a new play, *Eve's Girls*, about a house of prostitution in the year 2000. For a week, she had been unsuccessful in coming up with anything. Having exhausted the shock of nudity on St. Joan of Arc, what was left in her repertoire for prostitutes? But, lying briefly beside the strange red-haired man, she had begun to see a design.

The phone rang. Banquo. "I've got to see you," he said. "Darling, this incredible list. You're mistaken if you think I wanted this . . . all these names and numbers. Darling, let's stop hurting each other. Let me come and see you now . . . ."

"I can't," she said. "I'm working. And also, there's someone here. He's asleep."

A long silence.

"You bloody whore," he said, and hung up.

She unplugged the telephone and went back to her desk. She sketched lawn sleeves, caftans, talmas; experimented with high-necked vestal gowns; drew feminine versions of cassocks, surplices, albes, and soutanes. Was that what came next, then: the costume of chastity? It seemed so, the way the rhythms of her pencil swung back, creating a counter current, balancing with paradox this new need in her soul.

From outside her window came three thrilling blasts. She looked down at the sparkling river and saw—like her own portent—a large ship putting out to sea, flags flying, the cheeky tugs nudging the great white stern. Adriana felt the fervor and excitement of the ship's crew, the throb of mission in the great engines. She knew the captain was standing on the bridge, calling out orders to shake off the casual entanglements and the market dust of shore, to trim ballast down to a scary minimum, to train eyes, heart, hands on the lonely prospect.

The economy of the human soul amazed her. Why, her own childish hand had pounced upon and blocked out, in early drawings, the pattern she would follow, and she had the rest of her lifetime to make the individual alterations and apply the personal shades of meaning.

"You can do anything you set out to do," her uncle had said. Regardless of whatever else he showed her, he had also taught her that.

THE SEX MANIAC

Hilma Wolitzer

EVERYBODY SAID that there was a sex maniac loose in the complex and I thought, It's about time. It had been a long asexual winter. The steam heat seemed to dry all of the body's moistures and shrivel the fantasies of the mind. From the nineteenth floor of Building A, I watched snow fall on the deserted geometry of the playground. The colors of the world were lustless, forbidding. White fell on gray. Gray shadows drew over the white.

He was first seen in the laundry room of Building C, but it was not clear just how he had presented himself. Was his attack verbal, physical, visual? The police came and they wrote down in books the fiction of the housewives. He was next seen near the incinerator shaft on the sixth floor of our building. He was seen twice by elderly widows, whose thin shrieks seemed to pierce the brain. There had been an invasion of those widows lately as if old men were dying off in job lots. The widows marched behind the moving men, fluttering, birdlike. Their sons and daughters were there to supervise, looking sleek and modern next to the belongings, chairs with curved legs, massive headboards of marriage beds trembling on the backs of the movers. The widows smiled shyly as if their survival embarrassed them.

Now two of them had encountered a sex maniac. Help, they had shrilled. Help and help, and he had been frightened off by their cries. I wondered where he waited now in ambush and if I would meet him on a loveless February night.

There were plenty of men in my life that winter, not one of them a sex maniac. The children developed coughs that made them sound like seals barking and the health plan sent a doctor. He was thin, mustachioed, and bowed with the burden of house calls. Bad boys in bad neighborhoods slashed his tires and snapped his aerial in two. Angry children bit his fingers as he pried open the hinges of their jaws. I clasped a flower pin to the bosom of my best housedress, the children jumped on the bed intoning nursery rhymes, but the doctor snapped his bag shut with the finality of the last word. His mustache thin and mean, he looked just like the doctors of my childhood. We trailed after him to the door but he didn't turn around. Never mind. There were policemen to ask us leading questions. There was the usual parade of repairmen and plumbers.

There was the delivery boy from the market. His name is Earl. We coaxed him into the apartment. Just put it there, Earl. Just wait a minute while I get my purse, Earl. Is it still as cold out there? we asked. Is it going to snow again? Do you think the price-level index will rise? Will I meet the man of my dreams? Will I take a long voyage? But he was a boy without vision or imagination. He counted out the change and hurried to leave.

That night I said to Howard, "Love has left this land." When the children were tucked in behind veils of steam from the vaporizer, he tried to disprove it. We turned to each other in that chorus of coughing and whispering radiators. The smell of Vick's was there, eaten into my hand, into the bedclothes, and the lovemaking was only ritual. It was no one's fault. It was the fault of the atmosphere, the barometric pressure, the wind velocity. We comforted each other in the winter night.

The next day the whole complex was thrumming with excitement. The sex maniac had been seen by a very reliable source. The superintendent's wife came from a mining area in Pennsylvania, a place not noted for frivolity. She had gazed at a constant landscape and she had known men who had suffocated in sealed mines. Her word was to be honored; she had no more imagination than the grocer's boy. After the police were finished, the women of the building fell on her with questions. Did he just—you know—show himself? Did he touch her? What did he say?

She answered with humorless patience. Contrary to rumor, he was merely a white man, not very tall, and young, like her own son. But not really like her own son, she was quick to add. He had said terrible, filthy things to her in a funny, quiet way, as if he were praying, and I saw him in my mind's eye, reedy and pale, saying his string of obscenities like a litany in a reverent and quaking voice.

I wondered who he was, after all, and why he had chosen us. Had he known instinctively that we needed him, that winter had chilled us in our hearts and our beds?

But the superintendent's wife said that he hadn't touched at all, only longed to touch, promised, threatened to touch.

Ahhhhh, cried the women. Ahhhhhh. The old widows ran to the locksmith for new bolts and chains.

The men in the building began to do the laundry for their wives. They went in groups with their friends. Did the sound of their voices diminishing in the elevators remind the superintendent's wife of men going down to the mines?

Did you see him? the wives asked later, and, flinging the laundry bags down, some of the husbands laughed and said, Yes, he asked for you, and told me to give you this and *this*, and the wives shrieked with pleasure.

Howard ruined our clothes, mixing dark and white things,

using too much bleach. But when he came back from the laundry room it was as if he had returned from a crusade.

"Have you heard anything?" I asked, and he smiled and said, "*You* don't need a sex maniac."

But you *were*, I thought. Your eyes and your hands used to be wild and your breath came in desperate gulps. You used to mumble your own tender obscenities against my skin and tell me that I drove you crazy. I looked at Howard, his hand poised now on the rim of the laundry basket, and I knew that I was being unfair. But whose love is not unfair? When is it ever reasonable?

Perhaps whatever I needed was outside the confines of the building, farther than the outer edges of the complex where I could see the grocer's boy on his bicycle turning in concentric circles toward our building. Artfully, he raised the front wheel as he rode on the rear one, and then the bicycle became level again like a prancing pony. "Whoa," I said against the window pane, and then I waited for him to come up.

His ears were red from the cold wind. He snuffled and put the bag of groceries on the kitchen counter. He is the sort of boy who won't meet your eyes. His own, half-lidded and secret, seemed to look at my feet. And because I didn't want him to go yet and didn't know what else to do, I said, "Have you heard about the sex maniac, Earl?"

The red of his ears flamed to his face and I thought he would be consumed by his own heat. He answered from the depths of his throat in a voice that might have been silent for weeks. "Whaaa?" he asked.

There was no way to retreat. "The sex maniac," I said. "He stays in the complex. He molests women. *You* know."

Perhaps he did. But, if he didn't then a match had been set to his fantasy. His eyes opened wide and for the first time I saw that they were a bovine brown. Sex maniac, he was thinking, and I watched his face change as the picture rolled inside his head. Sex maniac! A grocery bag slid across the counter and into the bowl of the sink. But he stood there, his hand paused at the pocket of his vinyl jacket. Half-nude housewives lay in stairwells pleading for their release. Please don't, they begged. For God's sake, have mercy. His lips were moving, shaping melodies.

I pulled on the sleeve of his jacket. "Listen, did you bring the chow-chow?" I asked. "Look, Earl, the oranges are all in the sink."

Slowly the light dimmed in his face. He looked at me with new recognition. "I always take good care of you, don't I?" he asked.

"Yes, you do," I assured him. "You're a very reliable person."

"What does this here guy do?"

"Who?"

"The whachamacallit—the maniac."

I began to put the oranges back into the bag. "Oh, gosh, I don't know. I never saw him. Who knows? Rumors build up. You know how they snowball."

"Yeah," he said, dreamy, distant.

"Well, so long," I said. I pressed the money into his relaxed hand.

"Yeah," he said again.

I guided him down the hallway and out through the door.

That evening the superintendent came to fix the leaking faucet in the bathtub. "Keeping to yourself?" he asked as he knelt on the bathroom tile.

I was surprised. He usually avoided conversation. "More or less," I said cautiously.

"You women better stick close to home," he advised.

"Oh, I *do*, I *do*," I said.

"You know what that guy said to the Mrs.? You know the kind of language he used?" His eyes were a cruel and burning blue. He unscrewed a washer and let it fall into the tub. He raised his hand. "Do you know what I'll do if I catch that guy? Whop! Whop!" His hand became a honed razor, a machete, a cleaver. "Whop! Whop!"

I blinked, feeling slightly faint. I sat down on the edge of the closed toilet seat.

The superintendent replaced the washer and stood up. "You ever see him?" he asked.

I shook my head.

His long horny forefinger shot out and pushed against my left nipple as if he were ringing a doorbell. "Maybe he don't go for a big woman," he said, and lumbered through the doorway.

I sat there for a few minutes and then I went into the kitchen to start supper.

Several days went by and gradually people stopped talking about the sex maniac. He seemed to have abandoned the complex. It was as if he hadn't been potent enough to penetrate the icy crusts of our hearts. Poor harmless thing, I thought, but at least he had tried.

The children's coughs abated and I took them to the doctor's office for a final checkup. He examined them and scribbled something on their health records. "Did they ever catch that fellow?" he asked suddenly.

"I don't think so," I said.

"Did he actually attempt *assault?*" the doctor asked. I must have seemed surprised because he poked at his mustache and said, "I've always had an interest in crimes of a sexual nature."

I dropped my eyes.

"I'm concerned with the psychodynamic origin of their obsession," he persisted.

Aha, I said to myself. I stood up, smoothing the skirt of my dress. His eyes followed my gesture, lingering, and I thought, So here's my chance if I want one. Here's unlicensed desire. Was this where the sex maniac had led me?

"Oedipal complex, all that jazz," said the doctor, but his gaze stayed on my hips and his hands became restless on the desk.

But this wasn't what I had meant at all, not those clinical hands that tapped, tapped their nervous message. I could see the cool competence in his eyes, the first-class mechanic at home in his element, but it wasn't what I needed. He had nothing to do with old longings and the adolescent rise and plunge of the heart. He had no remedies for the madness of dreams or the wistful sanity of what was familiar and dear.

"I once considered a residency in psychiatry," he said, and he laughed nervously and glanced up at his wall of diplomas as if for reassurance.

Nothing doing, I thought, not a chance. But I laughed back just to show no hard feelings. I walked to the door and the doctor followed. "So long," I told him in a voice as firm and friendly as a handshake.

"Keep an eye on those tonsils," he said, just to change the subject.

The children and I went out into the pale sunshine. Filthy patches of snow melted into the pavement.

Home, I thought, home, as if it were my life's goal to get there. We walked toward the bus stop. Everywhere color was beginning to bleed through the grayness and I felt a little sadness. I had never seen him. Not once crouched in the corner of the laundry room, not once moaning his demands on the basement ramp, not once cutting footprints across the fresh snow in the courtyard. It was as if he had never existed. The winter was almost over and I was willing to wait for summer to come again.

Pulling the children along, although there was no one waiting for me, I began to run.

NEIGHBORS

Raymond Carver

BILL AND ARLENE MILLER were a happy couple. But now and then they felt they alone among their circle had been passed by somehow, leaving Bill to attend to his bookkeeping duties and Arlene occupied with secretarial chores. They talked about it sometimes, mostly in comparison with the lives of their neighbors, Harriet and Jim Stone. It seemed to the Millers that the Stones lived a fuller and brighter life. The Stones were always going out for dinner, or entertaining at home, or traveling about the country somewhere in connection with Jim's work.

The Stones lived across the hall from the Millers. Jim was a salesman for a machine-parts firm and often managed to combine business with pleasure trips, and on this occasion the Stones would be away for ten days, first to Cheyenne, then on to St. Louis to visit relatives. In their absence, the Millers would look after the Stones' apartment, feed Kitty, and water the plants.

Bill and Jim shook hands beside the car. Harriet and Arlene held each other by the elbows and kissed lightly on the lips.

"Have fun," Bill said to Harriet.

"We will," said Harriet. "You kids have fun too."

Arlene nodded.

Jim winked at her. "Bye, Arlene. Take good care of the old man."

"I will," Arlene said.

"Have fun," Bill said.

"You bet," Jim said, clipping Bill lightly on the arm. "And thanks again, you guys."

The Stones waved as they drove away, and the Millers waved too.

"Well, I wish it was us," Bill said.

"God knows, we could use a vacation," Arlene said. She took his arm and put it around her waist as they climbed the stairs to their apartment.

After dinner Arlene said, "Don't forget. Kitty gets liver flavor the first night." She stood in the kitchen doorway folding the handmade tablecloth that Harriet had bought for her last year in Santa Fe.

Bill took a deep breath as he entered the Stones' apartment. The air was already heavy and it was vaguely sweet. The sunburst clock over the television said half past eight. He remembered when Harriet had come home with the clock, how she had crossed the hall to show it to Arlene, cradling the brass case in her arms and talking to it through the tissue paper as if it were an infant.

Kitty rubbed her face against his slippers and then turned onto her side, but jumped up quickly as Bill moved to the kitchen and selected one of the stacked cans from the gleaming drainboard. Leaving the cat to pick at her food, he headed for the bathroom. He looked at himself in the mirror and then closed his eyes and then looked again. He opened the medicine chest. He found a container of pills and read the label—*Harriet Stone. One each day as directed*—and slipped it into his pocket. He went back to the kitchen, drew a pitcher of water, and returned to the living room. He finished watering, set the pitcher on the rug, and opened the liquor cabinet. He reached in back for the bottle of Chivas Regal. He took two drinks from the bottle, wiped his lips on his sleeve, and replaced the bottle in the cabinet.

Kitty was on the couch sleeping. He switched off the lights, slowly closing and checking the door. He had the feeling he had left something.

"What kept you?" Arlene said. She sat with her legs turned under her, watching television.

"Nothing. Playing with Kitty," he said, and went over to her and touched her breasts.

"Let's go to bed, honey," he said.

The next day Bill took only ten minutes of the twenty-minute break allotted for the afternoon and left at fifteen minutes before five. He parked the car in the lot just as Arlene hopped down from the bus. He waited until she entered the building, then ran up the stairs to catch her as she stepped out of the elevator.

"Bill! God, you scared me. You're early," she said.

He shrugged. "Nothing to do at work," he said.

She let him use her key to open the door. He looked at the door across the hall before following her inside.

"Let's go to bed," he said.

"Now?" She laughed. "What's gotten into you?"

"Nothing. Take your dress off." He grabbed for her awkwardly, and she said, "Good God, Bill."

He unfastened his belt.

Later they sent out for Chinese food, and when it arrived they ate hungrily, without speaking, and listened to records.

"Let's not forget to feed Kitty," she said.

"I was just thinking about that," he said, "I'll go right over."

He selected a can of fish flavor for the cat, then filled the pitcher and went to water. When he returned to the kitchen, the cat was scratching in her box. She looked at him steadily before she turned back to the litter. He opened all the cupboards and examined the canned goods, the cereals, the packaged foods, the cocktail and wine glasses, the china, the pots and pans. He opened the refrigerator. He sniffed some celery, took two bites of cheddar cheese, and chewed on an apple as he walked into the bedroom. The bed seemed enormous, with a fluffy white bedspread draped to the floor. He pulled out a nightstand drawer, found a half-empty package of cigarets and stuffed them into his pocket. Then he stepped to the closet and was opening it when the knock sounded at the front door.

He stopped by the bathroom and flushed the toilet on his way.

"What's been keeping you?" Arlene said. "You've been over here more than an hour."

"Have I really?" he said.

"Yes, you have," she said.

"I had to go to the toilet," he said.

"You have your own toilet," she said.

"I couldn't wait," he said.

That night they made love again.

In the morning he had Arlene call in for him. He showered, dressed, and made a light breakfast. He tried to start a book. He went out for a walk and felt better. But after a while, hands still in his pockets, he returned to the apartment. He stopped at the Stones' door on the chance he might hear the cat moving about. Then he let himself in at his own door and went to the kitchen for the key.

Inside it seemed cooler than his apartment, and darker too. He wondered if the plants had something to do with the temperature of the air. He looked out the window, and then he moved slowly through each room considering everything that fell under his gaze, carefully, one object at a time. He saw ashtrays, items of furniture, kitchen utensils, the clock. He saw everything. At last he entered the bedroom, and the cat appeared at his feet. He stroked her once, carried her into the bathroom, and shut the door.

He lay down on the bed and stared at the ceiling. He lay for a while with his eyes closed, and then he moved his hand under his belt. He tried to recall what day it was. He tried to remember when the Stones were due back, and then he wondered if they would ever return. He could not remember their faces or the way they talked and dressed. He sighed and with effort rolled off the bed to lean over the dresser and look at himself in the mirror.

He opened the closet and selected a Hawaiian shirt. He looked until he found Bermudas, neatly pressed and hanging over a pair of brown twill slacks. He shed his own clothes and slipped into the shorts and the shirt. He looked in the mirror again. He went to the living room and poured himself a drink and sipped it on his way back to the bedroom. He put on a blue shirt, a dark suit, a blue and white tie, black wing-tip shoes. The glass was empty and he went for another drink.

In the bedroom again, he sat on a chair, crossed his legs, and smiled, observing himself in the mirror. The telephone rang twice and fell silent. He finished the drink and took off the suit. He rummaged through the top drawers until he found a pair of panties and a brassiere. He stepped into the panties and fastened the brassiere, then looked through the closet for an outfit. He put on a black and white checkered skirt and tried to zip it up. He put on a burgundy blouse that buttoned up the front. He considered her shoes, but understood they would not fit. For a long time he looked out the livingroom window from behind the curtain. Then he returned to the bedroom and put everything away.

He was not hungry. She did not eat much, either. They looked at each other shyly and smiled. She got up from the table and checked that the key was on the shelf and then she quickly cleared the dishes.

He stood in the kitchen doorway and smoked a cigaret and watched her pick up the key.

"Make yourself comfortable while I go across the hall," she said. "Read the paper or something." She closed her fingers over the key. He was, she said, looking tired.

He tried to concentrate on the news. He read the paper and turned on the television. Finally he went across the hall. The door was locked.

"It's me. Are you still there, honey?" he called.

After a time the lock released and Arlene stepped outside and shut the door. "Was I gone so long?" she said.

"Well, you were," he said.

"Was I?" she said "I guess I must have been playing with Kitty."

He studied her, and she looked away, her hand still resting on the doorknob.

"It's funny," she said. "You know—to go in someone's place like that."

He nodded, took her hand from the knob, and guided her toward their own door. He let them into their apartment.

"It *is* funny," he said.

He noticed white lint clinging to the back of her sweater, and the color was high in her cheeks. He began kissing her on the neck and hair and she turned and kissed him back.

"Oh, damn," she said. "Damn, damn," she sang, girlishly clapping her hands. "I just remembered. I really and truly forgot to do what I went over there to do. I didn't feed Kitty or do any watering." She looked at him. "Isn't that stupid?"

"I don't think so," he said. "Just a minute. I'll get my cigarets and go back with you."

She waited until he had closed and locked their door, and then she took his arm at the muscle and said, "I guess I should tell you. I found some pictures."

He stopped in the middle of the hall. "What kind of pictures?"

"You can see for yourself," she said, and she watched him.

"No kidding." He grinned. "Where?"

"In a drawer," she said.

"No kidding," he said.

And then she said, "Maybe they won't come back," and was at once astonished at her words.

"It could happen," he said. "Anything could happen."

"Or maybe they'll come back and . . . " but she did not finish.

They held hands for the short walk across the hall, and when he spoke she could barely hear his voice.

"The key," he said. "Give it to me."

"What?" she said. She gazed at the door.

"The key," he said. "You have the key."

"My God," she said, "I left the key inside."

He tried the knob. It was locked. Then she tried the knob. It would not turn. Her lips were parted, and her breathing was hard, expectant. He opened his arms and she moved into them.

"Don't worry," he said into her ear. "For God's sake, don't worry."

They stayed there. They held each other. They leaned into the door as if against a wind, and braced themselves.

DETRITUS

Randall Reid

I SUPPOSE I'M BORED. That is an affectation, of course. And as a way to begin it is as banal as *Once upon a time.* But it doesn't matter, I don't aspire to novelty. Just memory and malice. And vanity. Portrait of a man alone with a mirror, making faces in the glass.

What next?

Wives are the best. Their purity has already gone to market, and they need not guard it anymore.

"But my husband, my children, my responsibilities—"

"You are too good for all that."

Secretly, at least, she will of course agree. And security palls. You appeal to her sense of freedom, her desire to be rid of it all. A little flattery, a little wicked titillation, and then the unanswerable question: "Why not?"

Well, why not?

Stopped for cigarettes at a newsstand and found myself staring at a magazine nude tacked to the wall. Another commodity. They have rouged and retouched her skin until it looks made of orange fudge. Enticing, of course—and her breasts are magnificent, or at least huge. But her groin is just another armpit, shaven and scented and sexless. Our modern mermaid, the girl with no way in. All her cleavage is above the belt.

I gathered my change. Her nipples watched me like fleshy pink eyes, her eyes saw nothing but the camera.

P.M.: Philip was here, talking of betrayal and heedlessness in his tormented voice. I tried to calm him. Useless. He is right, of course, but it doesn't matter.

I fell in love with Laura because her shoes did not fit. They made her totter when she walked, and her huge round eyes had a terror in them, as if she were always about to fall. It was comic in its way. There she was, with arms like thighs and breasts the size of cabbages. She could have given birth to an army and scarcely felt the pain. Yet she reminded me of a child. I pitied her, I wanted to touch her and tell her not to be afraid of the dark.

My sympathy made her cry. And tears made her helpless. She thought it very good of me to console her, in my way.

Treat a big woman as if she were very frail. Usually she is.

When Harriet left, I lived with two girls named Anne and Suzanne whom I fucked endlessly, separately and together, until they became for me a composite body with mouths everywhere, and too many nipples, and soft, superfluous thighs. They proposed a "real" orgy. I should do everything possible to each of them, and they would do everything to each other, and we would all watch. We did. And it excited me, even profoundly excited me. All those tongues and thighs and breasts, endlessly duplicated by the mirrors and our eyes. But at last something seemed to get stuck. Images repeated themselves: mouths sucking, hands grasping, orifices being plugged. It went on and on, like some dreaful labor we were condemned eternally to perform.

The next day I received a letter with an invitation—an old

friend had purchased a house with forty acres of woods and meadow. I went into the country for the sake of my health and the good of my soul.

Curiously enough, it worked. My senses blossomed, I discovered smells that were not recognizably female—oak leaves, hot dust at the edge of the road, the sweet, boggy smell of horses and meadow grass. Very trite, of course, but very pleasant. And my friend turned out better than I expected. The years had worn away his illusions without damaging his heart; he was that rare creature, a nice man who was not a fool. It pleased me to pat his dogs, admire his view, compliment his wife. I even acquired a remote and sentimental love for his daughter, home from her first year at college. She was such a little thing. Her clear gray eyes grew wide whenever you spoke to her, and she smelled as clean and pink as a new eraser. I felt strangely protective; it was a pleasure not to touch her, to leave her fragile and intact beside me.

We rode together sometimes, or drove into town for the papers and stopped for a picnic on the way home. Once we found a quiet place near the river, a grove of trees where a path led down to a pasture and a little spring. The day was still, hot. We ate our sandwiches in the shade and shared our silence. I had a pleasant regret to nurse, born of my approaching departure. Later, she wandered down to the spring and I went back to the car for cigarettes. I returned to find her stretched naked on a beach towel, asleep. There was no breeze, only the pure and soundless heat; her firm young buttocks glowed in the sun. I touched her, and her lips came apart. She whispered something I could not hear. But her arms reached for me, and we rolled together on the grass. Again and again, until the sweat stung my eyes. At last she slept, while I sat dazed and trembling in the sun.

That was ecstasy, if you like. Of course the sequel was not so pretty—tears, confessions, my friend compelled to act the outraged father, but too aware of his comic position and too confused in his outrage to be impressive. Instead of indignation, it produced only confused shame, as if we had all dirtied our-selves publicly. I left amid mutually averted eyes.

I saw Shriver today. He looked dried up, made of dandruff and parchment. Still very dapper, of course, but his eyes are fever-ridden. Those spiderish lusts of his. He loves delirium, fantasy, orgy—in his dreams, convent girls squirm in perpetual coition with monks and Great Danes.

I despise all voyeurs of the forbidden.

And the gourmet of handsome flesh, too. You know the type; he is found wherever luxury can be purchased—a fat, balding man with the mouth of a carp. To him, the flesh of young girls is a sensuous pleasure, like cigars and vintage wines, and a material solace, like money.

I am a seducer, not a satanist. A semiretired roué.

Dreams again, that drastic vaporous light. The sea is made of glass and the beach is patrolled by aging fairies with orange hair and purplish tans.

I seem to have settled at last. Here, on my unfashionable hill, with a view of freeway loops and a glimpse of the bridge, I sit like some bit of debris beached by the tide.

I do no work, but I have an income—now, like other things, rather drastically reduced. My career? Thirty years a lover—until one night I humped MacGregor's wife on a borrowed bed, and caught a chill.

Blue veins and congealed fat. Pubic hair like dead moss. And an awful, sourceless cold like an emanation. The sheets smelled of it—snot-cold, fog-cold. She tried so hard to feel some plea-sure. And I pumped and stared at that flat face, stupid with effort, until the spasm came. Then nothing. A seeping cold that made me shiver in her arms. She cried a little. When I with-drew, I saw it hanging there, weak and cold and small, like a shriveled teat. And the cold has proved ineradicable.

But I see a question quivering on your tongue.

"Are you still . . . I mean, can you?

The answer, madam, is yes—yes to the question as you meant it, though perhaps I should say no. When the moment of revelation came, I was not visited by a penitential impotence. No, the machinery still works, obeying some law of its own. It works in spite of me. My orgasm is like a gun going off in another room; I scarcely hear the report.

Banal idea: Every desire breeds its opposite. To love is to hate, to hate is to love, ambivalence is the law of life, et cetera. And it doesn't stop there. Pleasure calls for pain. To desire success is to lust after failure. If freedom lures us, so does slavery—not just also, but *because:* desiring freedom makes us desire slavery. Hence vacillation, frustration, despair. A man cannot act without betraying a part of himself.

Antitheses are like sexes that blindly seek to couple and complete themselves—the secret love of vice for virtue and of virtue for vice.

Mara was not pretty, but she had a certain sluttish elegance. Her shoulders were always bare and round and buttery soft, cut by two little straps. When she bent down, her breasts would spill like water over the top of her dress.

Those were the days when every girl had a mouth like a whore's. Lipstick so red and thick you could see it shine. She had a whore's laugh, too. I hated her laugh.

It excited me.

I was a pale and delicate child. My school pictures would amuse you—I sit like a little seraph amidst the grosser substance of my classmates. Beware the delicate child. Beware anyone who wears his sensitivity like a suit of clothes.

Women should always dress so that they can be gracefully undressed. The process, not the mere result of nakedness, is what matters; it is an art to be performed and prolonged.

And suspense is its soul. To be almost seduced, with the final act imminent but still unperformed, is to be deliciously helpless with anticipation. So I always let the final garment stay for a moment. I kiss her throat and breasts, brush my lips against the muscles of her spine, until at last my hands slide beneath the elastic and begin to draw her panties down. But slowly, slowly, so that she feels herself being exposed. Voluptuous sensation! The gliding silk against her skin, my eyes and hands caressing her—even the air whispers her nakedness. A little hesitation to savor it. Then down, all the way down, and that lovely mound is revealed, so warm and swollen, so exquisitely wet with her surrender.

And so it goes. Memories, little pictures from the past. Sometimes only the nerves remember. Whoever she was, she remains nameless. I am aware only of her freckled shoulders, the special flavor of her mouth.

They seem to be increasing, these phantoms of the senses. And all mixed up with the women are smells of forgotten rooms, the taste of some breakfast food I had as a child. Symptomatic, I suppose, the efflorescence of decay.

Things wear out, but not quite. Something is left, something meaningless but sufficient. I am quite safe.

Philip accused me of his mother's death. She is dead, I said, what does it matter? Take the guilt if you want it, mine or hers. And of course he has. You can see death in him. He has that terrible bodiless rage—white face, pinched nostrils, a screaming horror in the voice. It is a convulsion of the nerves, with no flesh or bone to sustain it.

In one of those treacherously serene states which follows a debauch, I found myself paired at a dinner party with a girl who said she knew of me through friends. She was small, very plain, past thirty—one of those colorless little virgins who can be found aging in every library, every school. She bored me, but I didn't mind. In such a mood, to be bored seems virtuous, both charitable and ascetic. Some whim of gallantry even made me offer to see her home.

Whatever we talked about, it must have charmed her. She invited me in for coffee. I was inattentive; caresses were a reflex, and so were words.

But not for her. Soon she was half-undressed and quivering beneath me on the couch.

Her eyes were so helpless. I felt a qualm, or something, and I did a strange thing—I stopped. A pretty scene. There she was, with her skirt up and her dignity down, and I began to talk. I moralized, apologized, stalled. And every moment her bare loins grew more ugly in my eyes and in hers. The moment prolonged itself unbearably. She could not move, could not even cover herself. She just shriveled up until there was not enough left of her to cry.

There was destruction for you, admirably thorough. I leave it to those who have a taste for it.

I am troubled by dreams. Amuse yourselves with this one. A woman with no mouth and huge breasts—mottled, sausage-colored breasts. When I squeeze them, they pop like boils.

Conventional bric-a-brac. Roués exude triteness, even in their dreams.

"But don't you really believe a married woman should be chaste?"

"No." My denial was as abrupt and titillating as a slap in the face. She found it irresistible.

Radical ideas induce tumescence of the brain.

I write by fits and starts, flirting with subjects as promiscuously as if they were women.
Scriptus interruptus.

Women are attractive only when they are frightened or aroused. Left to themselves, they run to teacups and little hats and fat—not woman fat, but steer fat: sluggish, neutered flesh. One torments them out of love and pity; one cannot bear to see them be so dull.

Carolyn was rich. And cultured and passionate and sensitive—one of those women whose appetites are insatiable but exquisitely refined. We had to make love to Mozart, or watch the evening darken while a flute sang in another room. Very pure it was, and very pretty, and it made me ill.

I despise serious music; it is ashamed to let its vulgarity show. Give me drums that pound and saxophones that wallow in their own ooze. Or moonlight and sweet dreams—lies too old and artless to conceal the truth.

The truth, indeed, as if I could tell it.

I try to speak, but my tongue misquotes me, my hands gesture blandly of themselves. I have the mannerisms of a veteran salesman or a veteran whore.

Rain today, cold and damp. I sit and watch the blue flames of my stove, huddled close, with memories wrapped like a shawl around me.

And I have been rereading what I have written. I do not like it; it smells as withered and faintly rotten as an old apple. It is false, too; memories are only retrospective fantasies, not to be trusted. And why tell them? To write one's memoirs is only a complicated form of self-abuse.

I have begun to leak aphorisms. Onanism and morality. In his old age, Don Juan becomes just another sententiously nasty old man.

My dotage: I shall acquire kidney stones and prostate trouble, affect a cane and wear a flower in my lapel. Perhaps I shall even find a wife—a middle-aged practical nurse who believes in laxatives and the power of prayer, or one of those dowagers whose bosoms emit little geysers of lavender scent at every breath.

No, those dowagers no longer exist. Grandma wears stretch pants and rubber breasts and an orange wig.

An aphorism on aphorisms: they are the mark of a promiscuous mind. An aphorist avoids philosophy as a roué avoids marriage; he is afraid to commit himself.

Certain lies speak to us more powerfully than any truth. Therefore they are the truth. About us.

I became a seducer because I could not bear to lie. So flattery, betrayal, the violation of all my anguished candor. On principle. Like the gratuitous cruelty of the tenderhearted, with the vicious little pleasure such a violation always brings.
. . . Another lie.

Now every magazine has its flawless nudes. They are worse than travel posters, those assertions of ideal flesh. Like visions of Rhine valleys and castles and happy picturesque folk. Somewhere that never was.

It isn't just the magazines. Ideals are nasty things no matter where they come from. All that dirty Greek marble—petrified daydreams, the destroyers of life.

That little white-haired man was in the papers again, still cackling out pronouncements at ninety. He is a living reproach, I suppose. Rationality, the strenuous pleasures of the mind, *mens sana in corpore sano*, the public self—one of those who strut around in the light of reason like sun-worshipers at a beach.

Well, reason *is* a light. And like any light it blinds while it illuminates. Stay in the sun too long and you can't see in the dark at all.

You cannot make love with your eyes; close them. Our loves should be as private as our dreams.

I could feel her presence beside me in the bus. A curious intimacy: the night heavy with sleep and motion, two strangers traveling together in the dark. I knew nothing about her except the smell of her hair and skin, the texture of her dress, the whisper of her stockings as she crossed her legs. And I wanted her. The aura which enclosed us was as palpable as any touch.

We romanticize our urgency and make it the measure of our desire, and that is nonsense. I have never been less urgent, and I have never desired anyone more. The soft pressure of her thigh stirred me. I wanted to touch it—not possess it or violate it, just touch it—the way one touches animals or smooth stones.

She accepted a cigarette. Her hand touched mine, and in the flaring match I saw her eyes and knew. So we spoke, kissed. Whispering a little, we made what love we could.

As we neared San Francisco, the lights came on and we were confronted by the absurdity of other people. She withdrew, straightening her skirt. I put my lips against her ear. "Get off with me," I said. "Here."

She nodded at last, not looking at me. "I must make a call."

The depot was full of that peculiar smell that public places have—rest rooms, buses, lunch counters—a smell composed of too many strangenesses mingled and cancelled.

She made her call and we found a room two blocks from Market. The fading prints of elastic at her waist and thighs were like the marks left by fetters. I smoothed them with my lips.

And then for once I forgot myself and her, and made nothing but love. The dark was full of it.

I woke at noon and found her curled in sleep against me. Against my chest, the faint suspiration of her breath—a rhythm I could enter. My thrust was as deep and slow and effortless as her sleep.

In that long tranquillity of desire, there is ease, not frenzy—a perfect closeness in which sensations flow back and forth like tides.

Then sleep again. At last I dressed, went down to the cafeteria on the corner, and brought back coffee in lidded paper cups.

She had put on my discarded shirt and was sitting up in bed. The shirt queerly accented her femininity. In that mannish collar, her neck looked frail and bare, and the dark circles of her nipples showed against the cloth. We sipped the coffee and did not talk. Outside: streetcar bells, traffic, the vague noises of the street. They were better than bird songs.

Soon it was time. I watched her resume the constrictions of bra and girdle, bend to the mirror and redraw her mask. When she had gathered her self about her, she touched my lips and eyes and disappeared. Where? To the depot, I suppose, and another bus, something which would carry her back to whatever she had left.

The ring she wore proclaimed that she was married. And there were signs of children—faint stretch marks on the abdomen, nipples that looked as if they had given suck. But I did not ask. We shared an intimacy that only the anonymous can ever know. Without identities, we could be ourselves.

I have spoiled it. It smells of my aphoristic smut. Yet I remember that time with pleasure, and there are not many such times.

Real abandonment is rare. Our selves, our moralities, our constraints seldom slip away. Instead, we nerve ourselves to violate them, and the result is hysteria, not release.

It is like sleep, the ability to slip quietly into another self and be restored. But few can do it. Most are like insomniacs, our waking dead. I have heard them cry out in their pleasure as they cry out in their sleep.

Never mind all that. What about the smut?

Excuse me, I have neglected a duty. Certain things are expected when a roué tells all.

Anatomical secrets: Chinese girls are crosswise. If niggers don't get it twice a day, their glands swell up and they go crazy. I knew a girl in New Jersey who could pick up pennies with her pussy.

Novelty: French ticklers. The sixty-nine secret positions of a Tibetan goatherd. Do it under water if you really want a thrill.

Satisfied?

No, tell me more.

They are all lies. All the novelty there is lurks hidden in the familiar gesture, the customary act.

Novelty is a pimp's invention, a fraud.

Forbidden glimpses. Dreams. They are made for the solitary one, the little masturbator in his soiled sheets. Alone, with flushed cheeks and furtive hand, he pursues his phantoms: black stockings, the pale gleam of flesh swollen around a garter; a nighttime world where nipples glow and wink like neon lights. His pleasure ends in the smell of his own semen, cold as snot against the skin.

And what about you, buddy? You and the wife read any good dirty books lately? The bedside shelf, Marriage Manuals and Erotic Classics. How-to-do-it books. Before long, someone will be selling blueprints for orgies, and the guests can fit themselves together like prefabricated pieces in the latest erector set.

Philip again, looking worse. A hemophiliac, he is forced quite literally to live on the blood of others, and he would rather die. So he wears that look of ghastly suffering, like a vampire Christ.

Pills seem to stick in the throat even after swallowing. They have a taste, too, no matter what they're made of. Bitter, chalky things. They made me take them every morning as a child.

Enemas, syringes, syrups, pills. The smell of rubber sheets and vaseline. All those implements they use. Cold, passionless fingers that probe into you, proud of their indifference. There is no violation worse than that impersonal touch.

They told me witches were not real, but I knew they were; I had seen them. I had seen Hansel, too, and Gretel, and that sweet hideous house. It tasted like the candy flowers on birthday cakes . . . .

Hand in hand the lost boy and girl stand together in the darkness. The house lures them, frightens them. It is forbidden, they know, all sweetness is. They taste, and the vision of sweetness turns to stale confectionary sugar on the tongue. And then the witch's voice, with its unspeakable invitation.

On the day before my seventh birthday, I found a mouse fresh caught in a trap. It was squeezed flat in the middle, like a pinched sack full of something soft, but it was still alive. And it would not die. The mouth gaped and closed, gaped and closed, until I screamed and old Maria came and smashed its head with a bookend.

Then she dried my tears. "You are a very tenderhearted boy," she said. "But why don't you every cry for yourself?"

My first love was the sun-warmed trunk of a dead eucalyptus tree. It lay in a tangle of morning glories and mallow weeds behind the garage—a narrow, forgotten place where no one ever went. I used to crawl in there and lie hidden in the sun. Hidden and naked. I liked to stretch on my belly, feeling the sun on my back and the warm smooth wood against my loins. And I would begin to rock, gently. I thought of nothing—only the warmth and the smell of weeds and hot tar paper roofs, and the pleasure of my secret flesh.

I never told anyone and no one ever found me, so I felt no shame.

When I was nine, she came to live in the duplex on the corner. Her name was Lucille, though I never called her that. I never spoke her name, except to myself. She was young, married but still childless, a thin girl with pale cheeks and long white hands. She let me sit in her kitchen and talk to her while she worked. Her white hands looked cool and soft, and when she bent over me, I could see the little shadow between her breasts. I wanted to put my lips there.

I was teased, of course—by parents and playmates. But it did not matter. Each evening I watched her come out on the step to greet her husband, lifting her lips and her pale hands to his face. A beautiful gesture. If I was jealous, I do not remember it. I simply wanted her; it did not occur to me to want her all to myself.

She kissed me once, laughing, while I stood like a stricken fool beneath the Christmas mistletoe. I could only look at her until she saw my eyes and something in them made her laughter stop.

And then she was gone. They moved away and had a baby and I did not see her again.

Childhood memories are all lies. We condescend to them, we posture, we affect to be amused, we formulate official autobiographies which we tell ourselves and others—and all to forget the wounds that never heal. We cannot forgive ourselves for having suffered; it is a weakness and we despise it. We like to pretend that the child grew up.

Recess. A numbed girl with pimples and breasts sleepwalks through the corridors. Her eyes, behind the rimless glasses, are watery and pale, and her flesh tries to shrink up and conceal itself within her clothes. Whispers buzz like flies around her. Jackal laughter—all the bastards snicker and rub themselves through their pants.

It was her husband's idea, the portrait. He was young and rather stupid, therefore impressed by me. I knew books, could sketch a little—a man of many talents, all of them small.

But my pencil lied as easily as my tongue, so the portrait pleased her. I suggested a nude. She blushed, looked vaguely frightened. No, she couldn't do that.

"But you have a lovely body."

We settled on another portrait, this time in oils. She would sit for it in my apartment where the light was right.

And all the time she sat I talked quite shamelessly about myself and women, sometimes adding praises of her eyes and the voluptuous curve of her neck. She was fascinated, of course. To a virtuous woman, nothing is more exciting than the attentions of a roué.

I asked her to sleep with me, and she refused. A day or two later, I asked again. No. When I took her in my arms and kissed her hair and eyes, she trembled, went rigid, then broke away. Her speech was what you might expect. She said I had made her trust me and tried to take advantage of it. She said she loved her husband. She was not the sort. I had no right.

I agreed, apologized, and promised not to bother her again. Her disappointment was visible. Within a few days she called me and virtually begged me to resume my siege. And I did, with predictable results—despite her tears, fears, and equivocations.

But why laugh? She wanted intensely to remain chaste and she wanted intensely to succumb. What was she to do? The little drama I had launched was very exciting—it aroused both of her desires—but dramas, like syllogisms, require conclusions. There must be a final act.

And then what? The drama is over, but life isn't. One must somehow fabricate another play, one in which there is something precious to be lost, something alluring to be gained . . . .

A curious point. Have you ever noticed that a seducer always ends his triumph by intimating that it wasn't a triumph at all? All he did was offer a pretext; his victim, he suggests, was really dying to fall.

The rapist: I made her do what I wanted her to.

The seducer: I made her do what *she* wanted to.

A true gentleman, the rapist exonerates the lady and takes full responsibility for his act. Not exactly. There is sovereign contempt in him, but no courtesy. He would no more grant her the right to say yes than to say no. He is the conqueror, the violator, the bloody lord.

The seducer, however, persuades the lady to violate herself.

The bully versus the cad, eternal opposites. They were all together in the Garden: the lordly rapist, the seductive serpent, the woman—and Adam, your eternal husband, placid, steady, dull, cheated.

It was Paradise, ruled by the inventor and sole proprietor, Old Omnipotence himself. Adam and Eve were his prize serfs. They didn't know they were naked, but God did. His little joke. Made for his pleasure, they were as innocent as animals, and as easily used.

But Paradise can never last, even for God. The serpent coils and waits. He has already had his encounter with Omnipotence—and is its victim, doomed and knowing it, a weakling who cannot fight but will not fawn. God, the lordly bully, strides the Garden as if it were a manor or a playground. Adam tugs his forelock, Eve spreads her thighs obediently at God's approach.

The serpent feels the tremor of those heavy boots. Sounds reach him: Eve's little shudder, the smack of flesh on flesh, that dreadful thrust. At last the lordly one is done. Sated, he rises and buttons his pants, while she lies disregarded in the dust.

The footsteps fade. In the streaming sun, she lies dazed and helpless, soiled. The serpent glides nearer. Her eyes wound him. He too has known what it means to squirm for God.

Goddess, he calls her, immortal beauty, adored by all creation. He positively seethes with desire—and with love, that unclean thing, born of his wounds. Caressing her, he takes pity upon himself.

Eve feels his words like a touch. His eyes, too, and the radiance of that supple insinuating form, so perilously erect.

In all those glittering scales, the same image is reflected, clothed in opalescent shimmers and nothing else. She has always been beautiful, but now she knows it. She is inflamed with visions: her mouth, her pomegranate breasts, her soft, dissolving thighs. Surrender is triumph, the consummation of herself.

So in exquisite apprehension she reaches for the apple.

The usual ecstasy. But as usual it subsides. Forbidden fruit, once eaten, tastes like everything else.

Yet something is ominously different. Though the visions fade, sight doesn't. She is still aware of herself. And the self she sees is not a goddess but a woman, a woman exposed, vulgar and vulgarly betrayed. By what? That limp little thing in the dust, the worm in the apple. It lies there, too spent even to wriggle, with nothing but malice left in its eyes.

And everyone knows. The serpent sees to that. It is his revenge for having betrayed himself to Eve. The final humiliation is his—the moment when she understands his impotence, that having seduced her he doesn't know what to do with her now.

Now she must endure Adam's stupid tears. And God isn't even jealous. He simply discards her—a trivial plaything that someone else has soiled.

She is no longer pretty. Her face is dull and her body feels heavy and unclean. She spends her days in hating—herself, the serpent for what he has done to her, Adam for what she has done to him. It is of course the rapist she really desires. If only God cared a little, or if only Adam would stand up to God.

But God doesn't want her. And Adam will submit to anything—his God, his fate, his wife. Numb shock followed by helpless self-pity—that is his only response. Then stupid submission, acceptance. Even of her beauty. He does not understand it, just as he does not understand the motive for her shame. To live with him, she must become as dull as he is, breeding and suffering with stupid equanimity. That is her final lot. After violation and betrayal, she must mutilate herself. She performs it. She lets everything go—her looks, her desires, her dreams. She becomes at last Adam's wife.

A happy ending, as stories go.

Ladies, I give you your choice: the rapist, the seducer, or the eternal husband? That's all there is, in or out of Eden.

And where did he come from, that poor fool on the cross? He was the serpent's brother, a younger son.

Philip on crutches, flanked by his fiancée, her eyes aglow with the trivial fanaticism of sacrifice. A lovely pair.

But it didn't work. I could see hatred growing in him, and she, sweet stupid girl, she didn't understand. She tried to be even more devoted. He called her a smothering bitch and left her crying in my rooms.

"But I love him. What can I do?"

"Get sick," I said. "Go blind or lose a leg. Let him immolate himself for you."

She didn't, of course. And so it ended, as it should. We want no heirs.

At Bilstein's house, I turned from the bar and saw Harriet looking at me. Her eyes glazed quickly, but it was too late, I had seen. I crossed the room like a man walking toward a cliff. And I asked her to dance. While our bodies touched, we did not have to look at each other.

I have always been afraid of eyes. They ask too much, betray too much. They embarrass me like the nakedness of a woman I do not desire. But there are moments, of course. Eyes look at us, and we glimpse something incurable in them, something which is also incurable in us.

If I could have met her in the night, always in the night, with no face to look at, no face of my own to be seen.

This arranging of faces, this smoothing of hair, this conversation at breakfast when every word makes it more impossible to talk. We soon despise each other.

In the twilight of that summer, Harriet sits in the porch swing, watching the sky fade and darken. Her bare legs glow in a patch of light. They are classic legs: full thighs, long slender calves, thin ankles with the bone white against the skin. But now they are marred with dark sores, mosquito bites which she scratches until the blood comes, then scratches again, tearing at the scabs that form.

Harriet betrayed me and lied about it. And I understood why she betrayed me and why she lied.

Definition of a pervert: the rabbit who empathized with the dog who ate him.

Destroy sympathy. It is a disease. Cruelty and indifference are better.

With that tremor of the eyelids, that faint crouch of the body, Harriet seemed always to be trying to shrink, as if every touch were painful. Yet her most disquieting tendency was a total absence of reserve. She would tell anything: her morbidities, fears, humiliations—the time a teacher yelled at her and she wet herself in front of the class. And these same things would make her writhe in anguish. So she fascinated the vulgar souls, those who were flattered or titillated by so much intimacy. But it was not trust and it was not perverse self-advertisement. For her, confession was a desperate strategy. She reminded me of those sea creatures who eviscerate themselves when threatened, leaving their guts to fascinate the pursuer while they escape and grow new ones.

We had beer and cold crab and tacos, and we danced all that afternoon. Something came alive in her eyes, something I had not seen before. She arched her back and stuck her butt out in a proud little strut; her skirt whipped and swirled about her thighs. While the song sustained her, she was not afraid of anything, even herself.

Stillbirth: ominously appropriate. The next day I found her dressed and sitting in the corridor, making perfectly audible comments on the nurses as they passed. Then it stopped; her face went dead as suddenly as if someone had blown out the light. I led her in silence back to her room. No tears—she just sat there, her breasts swollen, the useless milk staining her blouse.

A year later there was Philip.

Real love is terrifying, unflattering, ugly. It is a violation.

To be loved is to have your nakedness exposed, to the lover's eyes and to your own. Unbearable. To be seduced is to be given a flattering version of yourself, cosmetically clothed and unreal, incapable of being hurt.

And now a document:

> Dear Joe,
>
> I tried not to write because I knew you'd despise me for begging, and you're right, but here I am.
>
> I want you to come back, Joe. I always knew I'd lose you and now I have, only come back to me please. I did that thing so you'd hate me, because I hated me and you should too. That makes no sense but that's why I did it. When you first came to me, I didn't believe it, it was too good, you made me so happy, and I wouldn't show how I felt because I didn't dare, because if they know how you're happy they know how to hurt you.
>
> So I wrecked it, but please. It's not your fault, but I'm no good alone, I don't know what to do or think and I get frightened. Joe, Joe, I'm so mixed up. This baby, too, it cries and I can't help it. I'm no good at loving, I never was.
>
> Oh God, Joe. I'll be whatever you want if you want me. Please come.
>
> *Harriet*

Perhaps betrayal is the most intimate of all acts, the one in which complicity is the most secret and most shared.

She stands brushing her hair while I lie in bed beside her. Her face is averted, her bare thighs an inch or two from my lips. And all the curving lines of belly and thigh converge on that little mound, there where her flesh opens in folds as smooth and intricate as the involutions of a shell.

I am married to that, even now.

I do not believe in divorce. I do not believe it is possible.

The fire began in her apartment they said. A careless cigarette, probably—something which smouldered in the couch and then burst and ran up the walls. It happened in the middle of the day and she was home, but she gave no alarm. When someone above noticed the smoke, the stairway was already in flames.

They said she must have been drunk or doped, but I know she wasn't. She was just afraid—afraid to sound the alarm because they would know the fire was her fault and blame her. It was easier to die.

So she burned. And so did the others who lived in that house—a widow, a retired couple, three children who were home alone because their mother worked.

She lived alone, said the newspapers. Her one child, Philip, had resided with his grandmother in San Jose since the separation of his parents.

My son who looks like a ghoul, who bleeds if you touch him.

And so it happens. A new love—as sudden as an apparition. My neighbor, she says, she had "noticed" me before. Perhaps "recognized" says it better. And whatever the signs were, they must have been unmistakable. They brought her to my door, with perfect confidence, at two in the afternoon.

She has all the equipment of youth—firm breasts, firm thighs, a blue-white milky skin. But her eyes are the color of a bruise, her mouth limp and stretched like old elastic.

Please God, her name is Sharon.

I don't want her. I didn't want any of them. I wanted to be alone and quiet, and I never was.

Love affairs: a dismally expressive phrase, self-cancelling. Words soon couple and exhaust themselves. Caresses turn into gestures. Whatever it was becomes a charade, a game, a dance.

And the alternatives? Hysteria or habit. Blow your mind, as they say—and a lovely saying it is: cerebral self-fellatio, the beatific transport of the young. Or take the sanative fucking of the decently married, who void their lusts as they void their stools. Or take nothing at all.

I am tired of it. The flavor of lies and cleverness, epigrams.

My little Sharon again, as regular as any fate, But why? She does not talk. If irritation makes me speak, she smiles and murmurs something. When I mention my age, she says she prefers an older man.

She has a peculiar voice. It is echoless, unreasonantly empty.

Now Sharon comes every day and fixes lunch. Her own idea. She is very efficient, too, even garnishing the plates with little sprays of carrot curl and parsley.

When the meal is done, she sits beside me. The afternoon wanes. There being nothing else to do, I pull down the blinds and we lie together on my couch. Her thighs part with the ease of many accommodations, her mouth releases little pleasure sounds. Yet even then that mild, dead voice never quickens. It is vibrationless, spent.

And that is our love. Perhaps we shall marry. She could accommodate herself to that.

Sat in the park among the pigeon-feeders. As usual, I watched the women—mothers, mostly, out with the tots for an airing. In front of me, a dark-haired girl with a blurred mouth laying dozing on the grass. She had that slack, stupid look. But her skirt twisted as she rolled over, and I saw plump white thighs, a curve of buttocks swelling out of her panties. It made me hot and faint. Walking home, I was actually trembling with desire, but when Sharon came, it vanished, and I was cold again.

A.M.: Dreamed about the woman in the park.

Went to see Philip at the County Hospital. He has been there a week, it seems, but I was not informed until today. Acute internal hemorrhages, prognosis reserved.

I have my own prognosis. His face has begun to collapse, and his arm have great yellow-green bruises from intravenous feeding. There was nothing to say. He lay in that ward and stared at me as if I were part of the wall.

I decided to walk back. The morning was appropriately gray, cold, and oppressive. Coming up the hill, I crossed the street to avoid a little tableau—a man and woman in sullen confrontation against the wall. He held her wrist in one hand and had the other raised as if to strike her, but he never did. Perhaps he enjoyed the suspense of that threatening hand. He cursed her, too, methodically. She stood with her head down, limp, as if she did not care enough even to cringe. A trivial scene. But as I passed, I felt a novel chill. It looked like Sharon.

Was it? I don't know. If it was, she did not see me, and I did not look back. Let secrets remain secrets. I don't want to know them.

Can one graph a recurring point in all the spiral wandering of the self? Perhaps. And that recurring point, of course, would be the stake to which one is tethered, and one's spiritual voyages then would be the futile dashes and retreats of a dog on a chain.

I do not know what a recurring zero is, but I like the taste of the phrase. It is descriptive.

Sharon was here. She was as willing as ever, but afterwards, as she stooped and washed herself, she looked at me with her clotted eyes. "It's not much fun," she said. "Is it?"

At Grencher's party, we all stood around in the den, surveying our host's collection of trivial pornography. Someone gave me a little peep show telescope and told me to look into it. They said I would see something very special, and I did. I saw my own eye, hideously distorted and magnified by the mirror in the tube. It stared back at me, fat, with a fried-egg look, obscene. My face betrayed something, I suppose—enough to detonate their laughter. I excused myself and went outside to be sick on my host's lawn.

There is a child in the yard next door—a pale child with pale hair and bloated flesh. His eyes look like bits of celluloid left too long in the sun.

Philip falling on the steps, cutting his chin. He bled like some dreadful fountain.

Every animal suffers, we are told, the post-coital blues. But what about that peculiar desolation and resentment, that sense of irrelevance? We don't like to admit it. Instead, we claim the weariness of too much bliss. And we graceful lovers cover our retreat with kisses and endearments, withdrawal poetry. We lie our way out as we lie our way in.

I know all about exhaustion, the sag of spirits with the flesh, and I say it doesn't matter. The point is: something is not exhausted, something has been tricked.

Ladies, after all our ecstasies, I have but one honest thing to say: "I'm sorry. That isn't what I meant."

A.M.: Services for Philip.

Fog now, many days of fog. You can smell it in the curtains and the rug. I have not seen Sharon for more than a week. I should inquire, I suppose, but I prefer not to know where she has gone. I am alone again, and that is enough—an old man, a liar still, with no self but my own to betray.

OTHER PEOPLE'S DREAMS

John Irving

FRED HAD NO RECOLLECTION of having had a dreamlife until his wife left him. Then he remembered some vague nightmares from his childhood, and some specific, lustful dreams from what seemed to him to be the absurdly short period of time between his arrival at puberty and his marrying Gail (he had married young). The ten dreamless years he had been married were too tender wounds for him to probe them very deeply, but he knew that in that time Gail had dreamed like a demon—one adventure after another—and he'd woken each morning feeling baffled and dull, searching her alert, nervous face for evidence of her nighttime secrets. She never told him her dreams, only that she had them—and that she found it very peculiar that he didn't dream. "Either you *do* dream, Fred," Gail told him, "and your dreams are so sick that you prefer to forget them, or you're really dead. People who don't dream at all are quite dead."

In the last few years of their marriage, Fred found neither theory so farfetched.

After Gail left, he felt "quite dead." Even his girl friend, who had been Gail's "last straw," couldn't revive him. He thought that everything that had happened to his marriage had been his own fault: Gail had appeared to be happy and faithful—until he'd created some mess and she'd been forced to "pay him back." Finally, after he had repeated himself too many times, she had given up on him. "Old fall-in-love Fred," she called him. He seemed to fall in love with someone almost once a year. Gail said: "I could possibly tolerate it, Fred, if you just went off and got laid, but why do you have to get so stupidly involved?"

He didn't know. After Gail's leaving, his girl friend appeared so foolish, sexless and foul to him that he couldn't imagine what had inspired his last, alarming affair. Gail had abused him so much for this one that he was actually relieved when Gail was gone, but he missed the child—they had just one child in ten years—a nine-year-old boy named Nigel. They'd both felt their own names were so ordinary that they had stuck their poor son with this label. Nigel now lay in a considerable portion of Fred's fat heart like an arrested case of cancer. Fred could bear not seeing the boy (in fact, they hadn't gotten along together since Nigel was five), but he could not stand the thought of the boy hating him, and he was sure Nigel hated him—or, in time, would learn to. Gail had learned to.

Sometimes Fred thought that if he'd only had dreams of his own, he wouldn't have had to act out his terrible love affairs with someone almost once a year.

For weeks after the settlement he couldn't sleep in the bed they'd shared for ten years. Gail settled for cash and Nigel. Fred kept the house. He slept on the couch, bothered by restless nights of blurry discomfort—too disjointed for dreams. He thrashed on the couch, his groaning disturbed the dog (he had settled for the dog, too), and his mouth in the morning was the mouth of a hangover—though he hadn't been drinking. One night he imagined he was throwing up in a car; the passenger in the car was Mrs. Beal, and she was beating him with her purse while he retched and spilled over the steering wheel. "Get us home! Get us home!" Mrs. Beal cried at him. Fred didn't know then, of course, that he was having *Mr. Beal's* dream. Mr. Beal had passed out on Fred and Gail's couch many times; he had no doubt had that terrible dream there and had left it behind for the next troubled sleeper.

Fred simply gave up on the couch and sought the slim, hard bed in Nigel's room—a child's captain's bed, with little drawers built under it for underwear and six-guns. The couch had given Fred a backache, but he was not ready to resume his life in the bed he'd shared with Gail.

The first night he slept in Nigel's bed he understood what strange ability he suddenly possessed—or, what a strange ability had suddenly possessed him. He had a nine-year-old's dream—Nigel's dream. It was not frightening to Fred, but Fred knew it must have been pure terror for Nigel. In a field Fred-as-Nigel was trapped by a large snake. The snake was immediately comic to Fred-as-Fred, because it was finned like a serpent and breathed fire. The snake struck repeatedly at Fred-as-Nigel's chest; he was so stunned he couldn't scream. Far across the field Fred saw Fred the way Nigel would have seen him. "Dad!" Fred-as-Nigel whispered. But the real Fred was standing over a smoldering fire-pit; they had just had a barbecue, apparently. Fred was pissing into the pit—a strong stream of urine rising around him—and he didn't hear his son crying.

In the morning Fred decided that the dreams of nine-year-olds were obvious and trite. He had no fear of further dreams when he sought his own bed that night; at least, while he slept with Gail, he had never had a dream in that bed—and although Gail had been a steady dreamer, Fred hadn't had any of *her* dreams in that bed before. But sleeping alone is different from sleeping with someone else.

He crept into the cold bed in the room reft of the curtains Gail had sewn. Of course he had one of Gail's dreams. He was looking in a floor-length mirror, but he was seeing Gail. She was naked, and for only a second he thought he was having a dream of his own—possibly missing her, an erotic memory, a desirous agonizing for her to return. But the Gail in the mirror was not a Gail he had ever seen. She was old, ugly, and seeing her nakedness was like seeing a laceration you wished someone would quickly close. She was sobbing, her hands soaring beside her like gulls—holding up this and that garment, each more of a violation to her color and her features than the last. The clothes piled up at her feet and she finally sagged down on them, hiding her face from herself; in the mirror, the bumped vertebrae along her backbone looked to him (to her) like some back-alley staircase they had once discovered on their honeymoon in Austria. In an onion-doomed village, this alley was the only dirty, suspicious path they had found. And the staircase which crooked out of sight had struck them both as ominous; it was the only way out of the alley, unless they retraced their steps, and Gail had suddenly said, "Let's go back." He immediately agreed. But before they turned away, an old woman reeled round the topmost part of the staircase and, appearing to lose her balance, fell heavily down the stairs. She'd been carrying some things: carrots, a bag of gnarled potatoes and a live goose whose paddle-feet were hobbled together. The woman struck her face when she fell and lay with her eyes open and her black dress bunched above her knees. The carrots spread like a bouquet on her flat, still chest. The potatoes were everywhere. And the goose, still hobbled, gabbled and struggled to fly. Fred, without once touching the woman, went straight to the goose, although—excepting dogs and cats—he had never touched a live animal before. He tried to untie the leather thong which bound the goose's feet together, but he was clumsy and the goose hissed at him and pecked him fiercely, painfully, on the cheek. He dropped the bird and ran after Gail, who was running out of the alley—the way they had come.

Now in the mirror Gail had gone to sleep on the pile of her unloved clothes on the floor. That was they way Fred had found her—the night he came home from his first infidelity.

He woke up from her dream in the bed alone. He had understood, before, that she had hated him for his infidelity, but this was the first time he realized that his infidelity had made her hate herself.

Was there no place in his own house he could sleep without someone else's dream? Where was it possible to develop a dream of his own? There was another couch, in the TV room, but the dog—an old male Labrador—usually slept there. "Bear?" he called. "Here Bear." Nigel had named the dog "Bear." But then Fred remembered how often he had seen Bear in the fits of his own dreams—woofling in his sleep, his hackles curled, his webbed feet running in place, his pink hard-on slapping his belly—and he thought that surely he had not sunk so low as to submit to dreams of rabbit-chasing, fighting the neighborhood weimaraner, humping the Beals' sad bloodhound bitch. Of course, baby-sitters had slept on that couch, and might he not expect some savory dream of *theirs?* Was it worth risking one of Bear's dreams for some sweet impression of that lacy little Janey Hobbs?

Pondering dog hair and recalling many unattractive baby-sitters, Fred fell asleep in a chair—a dreamless chair; he was lucky. He was learning that his new-found miracle-ability was a gift that was as harrowing as it was exciting. It's frequently true that we have offered to us much of the insecurity of sleeping with strangers, and little of the pleasure.

When his father died, he spent a week with his mother. To Fred's horror, she slept on the couch and offered him the master bedroom with its vastly historical bed. Fred could sympathize with his mother's reluctance to sleep there, but the bed and its potential for epic dreaming terrified him. His parents had always lived in this house, had always—since he could remember—slept on that bed. Both his mother and father had been dancers—slim, graceful people even in their retirement. Fred could remember their morning exercises, slow and yoga-like movements on the sun-room rug, always to Mozart. Fred viewed their old bed with dread. What embarrassing dreams, and *whose*, would enmesh him there?

He could tell, with some relief, that it was his mother's dream. Like most people, Fred sought rules in the chaos, and he thought he had found one: impossible to dream a dead person's dream. At least his mother was alive. But Fred had expected some elderly sentiment for his father, some fond re-membrance which he imagined old people had; he was not prepared for the lustiness of his mother's dream. He saw his father gamboling in the shower, soapy in the underarms and soapy and erect below. This was not an especially young dream, either; his father was already old, the hair white on his chest, his breasts distended in that old man's way—like the pouches appearing around a young girl's nipples. Fred dreamed his mother's hot, wet affection for the goatishness he'd never seen in his father. Appalled at their inventive, agile, even acrobatic lovemaking, Fred woke with a sense of his own dull sexuality, his clumsy straightforwardness. It was Fred's first sex dream as a woman; he felt so stupid to be learning now—a man in his thirties, and from his *mother*—precisely how women liked to be touched. He had dreamed how his mother came. How she quite cheerfully *worked* at it.

Too embarrassed to look in her eyes in the morning, Fred felt ashamed that he had not bothered to imagine this of her—that he'd assumed too *little* of her, and too little of Gail. Fred was still condescending enough, in the way a son is to his mother, to assume that if his mother's appetite was so rich, his wife's would surely have been richer. That this was perhaps not the case didn't occur to him.

He was sadly aware that his mother could not make herself do the morning exercises alone, and in the week he stayed with her—an unlikely comfort he felt himself to be—she seemed to be growing stiffer, less athletic, even gaining weight. He wanted to offer to accompany her with the exercises; to insist that she continue her good physical habits, but he had seen her *other* physical habits and his inferiority had left him speechless.

He was also bewildered to find that his instincts as a voyeur were actually stronger than his instincts as a proper son. Though he knew he would suffer his mother's erotic memories, each night, he would not abandon the bed for what he thought to be the dreamless floor. Had he slept there he would have encountered at least one of his father's dreams from the occasional nights that his father had slept on the floor. He would have disproven his easy theory that dead persons' dreams don't transfer to the living. His mother's dreams were simply stronger than his father's, so her dreams dominated the bed. Fred could, for example, have discovered his father's real feelings for his Aunt Blanche on the floor. But we are not known for our ability to follow through on our unearned discoveries. We are top-of-the-water adventurers who limit our opinions of the icebergs to what we can see.

Fred was learning something about dreams, but there was more that he was missing. Why, for instance, did he usually dream *historical* dreams?—that is, dreams which are really memories, or exaggerated memories of real events in our past, or secondhand dreams. There are other kinds of dreams— dreams of things that haven't happened. Fred did not know much about those. He didn't even consider that the dreams he was having *could* be his own—that they were simply as close to him as he dared to approach.

He returned to his divorced home, no longer intrepid. He was a man who'd glimpsed in himself a wound of terminal vulnerability. There are many unintentionally cruel talents that the world, indiscriminately, hands out to us. Whether we can use these gifts we never asked for is not the world's concern.

FLOTSAM AND JETSAM

Sybil Claiborne

A PICTURE OF A NUDE tacked to the wall of the newspaper stand reminds me of Johnny. Same jaunty tilt to the penis, same-size shapely balls. The pubic hair is the color of sand, suggesting Anglo-Saxon origins. The circumcision is neat. The model is holding his sexual parts between his hands as if they were too weighty to hang unsupported. Or perhaps he is making an offering or, in a sudden access of shame, attempting to cover his nudity. As you can see, it is not an easy picture to understand.

I move off still studying the model. In a certain light he reminds me of Percy; in another, Harry, Steve. I have known so many men, shared so many delights, secrets, passions, pleasures. But the face of the nude tacked to the wall of the newspaper stand bears no resemblance to the faces of any of my lovers. It is full of cupidity. This man is a schemer if I ever saw one, a plotter of small, tedious cons. Yet, strangely enough, there is the suggestion of an erection in the massive sexuality he holds. Actually it isn't strange. If I have learned anything in a long and misspent life it is this: the unlikeliest man can get it up.

I move away still thinking of the nude, and of the many men the picture evokes. I remember how I taunted Charlie, ignited Mark, drove Donald up the wall. Was it Charlie who ate standing at the fridge because of greed, incompetence, and sloth? Or was that Michael? No, Michael was the frightened one. He carried a rear-view mirror in his lapel, embraced posts in the subway lest some black man, maddened by three hundred years of intolerance, should push him into the path of an oncoming train. Poor Michael.

Where are the lovers of yesteryear? Scattered like leaves, discarded like no-deposit bottles. Where are Harry, Percy, Connors, David, etc? Each one different from the one before, with his own history, illusions, tastes. Some were paranoid, a few melancholy, many had faults. When disappointed, their nervous systems went out of synch. Men are delicate. They die early, put on weight, obsessions seize them, they drink. Many find it difficult to make friends.

The ideal lover: should be neat and clean at all times, self-reliant and tactful. He should know when to talk, when to be still, and avoid foolish questions at all costs. How explain a dropped stitch, bias skirt, a dart? The men I have loved best have known how to occupy themselves.

The ideal lover: should dress simply, zippers oiled, buttonholes neither too loose nor too tight. Nothing kills desire faster then complicated fastening, pants that refuse to yield their treasure. Yet sometimes the opposite is true.

A man lies on my bed. His name is Jock or perhaps Basil. He is young, handsome, modest. His eyes are closed, his pants bulge with lust. "Hurry," he whispers as I start to disrobe him. But the zipper will not move. Loins dripping, I work over it with trembling hands. "Oh, please hurry," he moans. "The fucking zipper is jammed," I say. I oil it with 3-in-one, get my doctor zipper kit. Nothing works. Finally I grab by dressmaking shears. "Oh, no," he screams, covering his crotch. But I am already cutting away his pants, along the outseam, across the fly.

Freed! I gaze upon his treasures, fling myself upon him. A complicated sexual game ensues. I press his nipples, he presses mine. He screams, I moan. We come to the ringing of bells.

Later I find some jeans for him, give him a token, pat his behind, send him on his way, savoring his firm thighs, small ass, sprightly walk. Drained of sex, my pleasure is aesthetic, based on certain principles.

Another man walks down the street. I fall in love with him instantly because of his loose pants. Nervous, self-conscious, obviously fearful of exposure and ridicule (those twin bogies that haunt our dreams), he sidles along, gripping his pants with white-knuckled, nervous hands, a metaphor for man's plight. Tenderly, protectively, I followed him across Seventh. He pauses at the curb, to stretch the stiff fingers first of one hand, then the other. "Come home with me and I'll take a tuck or two," I say.

He lies down on my bed. In one easy motion, I yank off the pants. But this disrobing is too easy. It kills desire. I study his body, searching its folds and convolutions for some blueprint to a bang. A roll of fat conceals his waist; his buttocks are on the heavy side. His chest is flaccid; his pubic hair has lost its curl. "You've had a busy life," I say.

"You guessed it," he says, falling in love with me for my perceptivity. "Do whatever you want," he begs. I force myself to begin, a little foreplay, a finger aft. But it is all sham. During coitus, I think about the universe. He senses my preoccupation. "I'm not attractive, am I?" he says. I deny it, of course— but he is not convinced. His parts shrivel, his eyes mist. And when he leaves his nerveless hands allow the perimeter of his pants to droop below his navel. He has lost the will to hold them up.

I recall my feelings vividly—my callousness, indifference, ennui. But who is he? What's his name? Where did he come from? Names, faces, histories are as insubstantial as headlines, as mysterious as a scrap torn from an unidentified garment. All that remains is a sexual memory, an index of penises, scrotums, balls; a feral imprint that goes back beyond the dawn of history to that long dark night when everyone looked alike.

Man is a miracle, the fruit of a million years of evolution, descendants, tax shelters. Nobody knows how many men there are. Some say four hundred, others a billion. I have known quite a few.

Morris is a man. He is very rich, very primitive. He thinks about sex, the stock market, and what he will wear to the races. While we make love, his manservant Bradley stands above us reading the ticker tape. "Anaconda 60, up 2½." We come on a rising market to a crescendo of gains. How pleasant are the ways of the rich.

In the years of my youth, I mothered a child, a son, a strange but lovable boy, given to odd foods, unusual longings. I planned to mother another, searched for a man genetically sound, took measurements, gave tests. I looked for someone who would cancel out my flaws, negate my tendencies. In my search for a perfect mate, I balled with this one and that one. The years passed. For a while I lived with two men, Joseph and Cary. Although we did not reproduce we devised new ways of being together, patented them, grew rich. At the board meetings, we exchanged reports on techniques. Past performances were constantly reviewed.

I taught Cary how to make mocha icing, Joseph how to clean the oven. "I never knew it was so easy," they said. They were smiling, the evening was soft and quiet. Tears of pride trembled in their dark eyes. We shared an inner glow. "At times like this possibilities seem infinite," they said. It is easy to make a man happy.

Time passes. Their giddy chatter begins to weary me. They grow mustaches to revive my interest but desire is dead. Bored and restless, I leave my lovers for a stay in the country with traditional friends. Their names are Martha and Barry.

They live on a dirt road. Because of their isolation they have preserved customs and conventions that have disappeared from other places. For instance, they embrace a socioeconomic explanation of history that long ago was discredited in all the academies. They believe in the possibilities of change, the efficacy of analysis, the benefits of self-expression. They bake their own bread. They look at me incredulously when I tell them about the self-sharpening knife.

Their simple ways renew me, my stale senses grow fresh. I inventory the assets in their freezer, take dips in their limpid pool. Each day succeeds the day before, a miracle of continuity. The nights are quiet. We go to bed early.

The summer wanes. Their son, Raul, returns from camp, loaded with badges, medals, accolades. "He's cresting too early," Martha tells me. "Talk to him," Barry says. "He'll listen to you. Tell him to slow down."

Raul lies under the house studying his accolades. I stand beside the pilings looking down at him. His firm young buttocks glow in the gloom. "Hello," I say. "Hello," he says. We study each other, smile. "Would you like to see my accolades?" he says. "Very much." I crawl under the house. "This is my best," he says. He holds up something square and shiny. "I got it for the loudest primal scream."

"Impressive," I whisper. We hold hands, discuss things, polemics, praiseworthy reforms. I lean toward him, brush his mouth. His lips part, his tongue meets mine, his chest heaves, his sweet parts expand. "I am too old," I protest, but we are already coupling in the dirt.

Things sticks to us, discarded window screens, a pair of nylons so ancient they have seams, a New School catalogue, spring '52, a prototype of the instant pudding, a can of prehybrid corn. All the flotsam and jetsam of modern life cut our backs, our buttocks, sting our souls.

Later I find Martha studying me suspiciously, for a piece of flotsam is clinging to me. A heavy silence blankets the cocktail hour. I tell a joke. Raul laughs, Barry stares at the sunset. Martha picks a fashion fight. She sneers at the patches on my jeans, criticizes my tight sweater. I question her sincerity. She castigates my life style. "No wonder you're unhappy," she says, "the way you live. But I know a doctor who can help you."

"I'm not unhappy," I say.

"He uses a combination of repulsion therapy and reason."

"I'm a bundle of health," I say.

"Transference takes place in a matter of weeks."

"Think about all my good qualities," I say.

"Many patients become nurses or social workers."

"I'm leaving," I say.

Raul weeps. "What about my brief encounter with genital maturity?" he says.

"See what you've done," Martha says. "You've given him a phallic fixation."

"Not to worry," I say. "He will soon regress." I kiss Raul and leave.

Men make the best soldiers. Their needs are simple; they don't feel pain the way the rest of us do. Still this does not entirely explain their propensity to fight. A recent survey revealed the following: 33 percent, a childlike need to shine; 12 percent, a love of machinery; 14 percent, liked the uniform; one man had an inner rage. "Actually only 10 percent like to fight. The rest are drafted," a vocational counselor explained. There were other contributing factors.

A figure waits at my door. It is Perry, my only begotten son. I let myself in and he follows me, a sheaf of papers clutched in his hand. He writes sayings for a fortune-cookie syndicate, worries constantly about their quality. "Listen," he says. " 'The winds of change blow cold.' 'The earth is dying.' "

"I thought they warned you against bleakness," I say.

"They did," he groans. "What's the matter with me? I used to be funnier than I am now. Remember the time I recited an entire preamble in dialect?"

"That was a long time ago," I say. I think back to when his father lived with us, for it was then that it started. He was a plumber, a dreamer. "Beyond the perimeters of possibility lies the solution to pollution abatement," he used to say as he pondered equations, drew up blueprints, made plastic models of his dreams. He wanted nothing less than to revolutionize the disposal of waste.

Unfortunately his vision exceeded his grasp. His connections were bad, his pipes dripped. Hot water often ran cold.

One day an unstable client appeared and threw a bucketful of waste over him. "The toilet is flushing upward," she sobbed.

He showered and shaved and picked up his tool kit. "I'm going for a walk," he said. We never saw him again.

He left behind an entire set of pipes which Perry stored on the floor of his room. "Someday he might need them," he said. Years passed. The pipes rusted under mounds of debris, mildewed teddy bears, umbrella skeletons, and other things. One day in a fit of cleaning, I threw the entire lot out. Perry never mentioned the lost pipes but a change came over him. He grew solitary, spent many hours studying himself in the three-way mirror, muttering, "What is the meaning of life?" Sometimes I would see him on the street below rummaging in garbage cans as though looking for a lost object.

"Remember the pipes?" I say.

"I don't remember," he says.

"They were lying under mildewed teddy bears."

"I remember the mildewed teddy bears but I cannot remember the pipes," he says. But his voice is tinny with repressed feeling, blighted hopes. I stay up half the night writing fortune-cookie sayings that will amuse and entertain.

On the street, a smörgasbord of flesh confronts me. Bare shoulders, hairy chests, biceps. I walk along in a sexual haze. Male deodorant and hair spray perfume the city air. Pants bulge opulently. Thighs quiver, buttocks twitch, balls are delineated against tight jeans.

I savor, taste, sample. Each coupling is unlike the coupling before. Danny, deriding the Protestant ethic, ejaculates prematurely. Bill is a spy, penis wired for transmitting code. We couple carefully lest a loose wire tip off the enemy. Then he is sent off on a dangerous mission to Ankara or Athens. The fear of geography runs through my family like a smirch.

On certain days every man has a pimpish look. They exude an air of menace that has an indefinable charm.

I lunch with the girls. We discuss the high crime rate, fear of the vertical, lips moving, deserted streets. We show each other weapons. Sylvia complains because it is too hot to wear her bullet-proof vest. Hilda wears a .38-caliber Smith and Wesson. Maria's son gave her a hand grenade for her forty-second birthday. Perry gave me a plumber's wrench. Over dessert we talk philosophically on whether it is better to maim or kill.

High in my eyrie, I watch the old women below carrying paper shopping bags filled with neatly folded paper bags. They are the last savers left in the world.

Thoughts on a day when the air quality is unsatisfactory. Masculinity has been an influence among men for some time, resulting in nervousness and indigestion. Their inability to have a good time leads many of them to a life of crime. Yet, because they are able to withstand monotony for hours on end, they are good at repetitive tasks. Did you know the director of intelligence for the entire state of New York is a man?

As a child I devised tests that would measure my sensitivity. Each night for twelve nights, I secreted a pea beneath my mattress in the hope of being rubbed raw. But pain eluded me. I said to my mother, "Though thirteen mattresses separated the princess from the pea, she could not sleep. I had only one mattress but I didn't feel a thing. What's the matter with me?"

"The technology of bedmaking has changed," my mother said. But I didn't believe her.

In a tiny room, Cabot and I become lovers. He reads me quotations from Chairman Mao on the correct handling of contradictions among the people. "I wish I'd known this earlier," I say. We study revolutionary-flag recognition, test each other, pray for backlash. Cabot calls the Austrian Embassy daily to demand the release of all political prisoners. "We do not have any political prisoners," the embassy says. Cabot doesn't believe them.

Forced out of their own territory by enemies, men migrated into this area about eleven hundred years ago. With a rise in security, they became adept at tennis and other competitive games. In their age-old yearning for immortality, they developed a complicated afterlife. But the Day-Glo spray can had not yet been invented and most men died without a trace.

Naked and exhausted, we lie on the floor. Due to early childhood deprivation, Neil cannot come. His mother was hit by a volleyball when he was five. The part of her brain where recipes were stored was knocked out. While other children were learning how to interact, Neil was busy making melted-cheese sandwiches.

To comfort him I read aloud. " 'I am going to move out and get the contingency sample,' Edgar said.

" 'I am going to point this thing at you,' Connors said.

" 'No, no, no,' Edgar screamed. 'It has fragments around it.' But Connors pressed the trigger and soon Edgar was pulverized."

The excitement gets to Neil. Lusting, trembling, he points his penis at me.

We tell each other our dreams. Each dream I have is like the one before. I am on the street, surrounded by people I know, not friends exactly, but leaders, opinion makers, captains of industry. Perry is there too, but he looks right through me. Perhaps he is only pretending not to recognize me. If so, I cannot blame him. My hair is uncombed, my face is greasy with anti-wrinkle cream. My eyes are puffy for I have just awakened. The front of my housecoat is dirty, two buttons are missing and beneath you can see everything I own. I smell a little.

I am talking to a captain of industry. We are discussing Bergman. I say, "His reality always admits of distortions."

He says, "Not necessarily." Although he pretends not to notice the state I am in, I can tell by his patronizing tone that he is thinking of little else.

"My dreams are much worse than your dreams," Neil says. "For instance I am being loaded onto a fighter-bomber and they are going to drop me over enemy territory at forty thousand feet."

I analyze this dream. "It indicates a blurred sense of identity."

Neil disputes this. "It indicates anxiety over our defense posture. If we end up second best, I don't know what I'll do."

A loathing for centrists keeps us together. "Give me a right winger or a left winger any day of the week," Neil says.

"Me too," I say.

We discover other shared abhorrences. We both hate Hawaii, convenience foods, dirty sidewalks, death. We marvel at our compatibility, fall in love.

"I abominate music that makes you weep," Neil says.

"I rather like it," I say.

An inability to reconcile our differences tears us apart.

It is late at night. Perry knocks at the door. "I have eaten all my fortune cookies," he says. His eyes are glazed, his speech is thick.

"Sayings and all?" I say.

He nods. I help him to a chair. "I am looking for something." he says. "The meaning of life. It is this long, this thick, this—" He closes his eyes and sleeps. Will it ever end?

I share an ecstasy, tell a secret, savor, taste, tease. John looks at me, I look at him, we touch. He undoes his shirt. I take off my sweater. Slowly he drops his pants. I unhook my bra. His penis unfurls. We march toward each other.

BALDESSARI'S DEAD SEA FLIGHTS

Paul Kennebeck

ON THE FLATLANDS BETWEEN DENVER AND OKLA-
HOMA CITY there is an airstrip built in the early Fifties that is
unused now except by an air charter service named Ciafu Flying, which attempts to fly a fairly regular route between the
two cities, carrying, for the most part, vegetable and meat pre-
servatives, tenderizers, emulsifiers, and food stabilizers, Ciafu
Flying's clients being a loose collection of the taco, roast beef,
hamburger, and fish-and-chip franchises of either city.

Off to one side of the abandoned airstrip were the remains of
a hangar. An old man sat beside the hangar and stared silently
across the dirt airstrip overgrown with weed, prairie grass, and
cannabis that moved and shifted in the random winds of the
place. The man straightened up against the hangar, tilted up
the straw hat he wore, and gazed at a baby-blue 310 that hung
over the far end of the airstrip, faltering, sinking, settling finally to the earth. The port engine emitted graceless wisps of
smoke and oil; both engines coughed and sputtered. The plane
taxied with a list. The old man watched the pilot, Baldessari,
bring the plane to a halt, climb to the ground, pull out a hand-

kerchief, hack into the dust. Then the old man watched Baldessari stare curiously at him across the field. Baldessari was unshaven, fat, wore a T-shirt; a slight southwestern wind ruffled the shirt. Dust powdered the bottom of his cords. He lit a cigarette, cupping the match against the wind, and smoked in short, cheerless puffs. It was not very long before a Piper Apache appeared low over the grass strip, settled smoothly to the earth, and taxied next to the 310. The pilot cut the motors, climbed out of the Apache, and hurried into the 310. Baldessari headed toward the new plane, flipping the other pilot the bird as he hurried past him. Baldessari started the engines of the Apache, and the other pilot, after some effort, started the engines of the 310. They taxied to the end of the airstrip and took off in the direction from which they had come.

The old man watched carefully. He nodded to himself, stood up, tilted his hat low over his head, and shuffled off to his home. The gentleman walked through the yard, up the steps, into the house, and took off his hat and laid it on the sofa.

"Two planes landed. One good, one bad. The pilot from the bad plane flew the good one away. The pilot from the good plane flew the bad one away."

The woman looked up suspiciously. "What's it mean?"

The gentleman settled into the sofa, looked away, closed both eyes: "It means some people get good stuff and some people get bad stuff. The people that get bad stuff get screwed."

There is a great flat plain of dust out there, dust that the moon affects like the tides, pulling and tugging, causing great waves of it to sweep silently from Texas to Oklahoma to Colorado and back, great silent unstoppable dry movements that are a secret between the white hovering moon and the earth. Baldessari can see it, *feel* it, when he flies over the abandoned landscape of eastern Colorado. The dust: it washes and wears against the edges of the cities that are built upon the plains. At the farthest edge of the last suburb of any prairie city, at the last row of houses, at the last fence, is the dust that stretches to the horizon.

At the western edge of the plains is Denver, port city to this long-dead sea. And as weight lifters thank God that things are heavy, so too do the horny thank Him for this oasis. In Denver on East Colfax, between a Ski-Doo dealer and a tackle shop, is a dating bar called the Sperm and Ova that is frequented by the first-generation dental assistants, receptionists, key-punch operators, beauticians, secretaries, manicurists, and barmaids who have come in off the plains to live beyond their emotional means. Next door to the tackle shop that borders the Sperm and Ova is the Enola Gay, raffish hangout of charter pilots, mechanics, ground crews, crop dusters, ex-Air Force people.

One night Christopher Baldessari, drunk on Coors, the local product, crude in some old corduroys and Hawaiian shirt, came ricocheting out of the Enola Gay, past the tackle shop, and stumbled blindly into the Sperm and Ova. That was where he met Didi, first-generation stew.

Some affinities can be touchstones: perhaps Stewardess is subconsciously pointed in the direction of Pilot. If Diedre was her Christian name, then Didi was a cabalistic one. She was mysterious and subtle-seeming, a prime-looking lady who hid herself in a hundred looks: coming on foxy in bell-bottoms and pout; or showing up innocent in pigtails and knee socks; or appearing in stockings and heels, looking quite prepared for a sexual event of the highest caliber. Baldessari, never sure if he would be seduced or up for rape, wondered why he deliberately cultivated schizophrenia.

She lived in a townhouse complex, a place of generally bad resonance close to the airport built when the sun was in Gemini and the moon in Aries and filled with other stews and airport personnel. And Baldessari, after several nights of casually hanging around the Sperm and Ova playing various minor roles, mostly that of pilot, which he found he had to play even though he was one, found himself one evening standing on the balcony outside Didi's apartment, holding a drink and staring down at the tennis courts, game areas, and swimming pool, his witty line being, "Let me take you away from all this." Which got from Didi only a look.

Intimacy between the two did not come with a gentle touch or with some shared embarrassment, but with the simple step of Baldessari entering the girl's bedroom: on her bed, as bold as any cliché, sat a worn toy animal of indeterminate species, remainder of girlhood; taped to a mirror were snapshots of people Baldessari'd never know; on a desk was a collection of letters postmarked Los Angeles; next to a dresser covered with face creams, brushes, and sprays was a fishbowl barren except for a single angelfish that Didi fed twice during the night (sex made Didi hungry, so the fish got fed?): Didi's possessions. They drank and listened to records. Baldessari's eye fell upon a night table and an incredible collection of pills there: bottles of wheat germ, iron tablets, prescriptions. Didi picked up a bottle, deadpanned: "These are the pills I take to keep from becoming a hypochondriac." She turned off the light.

Maybe it was the vitamins: some unconscious realization that she had in a bottle what you used to have to eat a whole wheat field for. Maybe it was her job; the realization that time and distance were now nothing. All of this giving a new sense of capabilities. Whatever the reason, in the long arrogant sweep of emotion Didi was part of a contribution to the careful parceling of fervor. This was new; except for the history of actors and whores and politicos, calculated emotion had never been enjoyed on a wide scale. Didi was both curiously uninhibited and curiously cautious with Baldessari, any felt emotion heightened by the knowledge that no part of it would hang around malingering and bothersome.

"I hope you finish everything you start."

"Well begun is half-done, my dear." This in Baldessari's best W.C. Fields voice.

Baldessari could almost feel the structure of health in her firm flesh. He imagined strong veins hurrying Vitamin A and iron to weaker parts of her body, shoring up some dent or discoloration he had caused in his cloddish assault. They moved about; caught each other smiling; spoke quietly. Satisfaction loomed around the corner. After a moment, it came.

They talked in the dark, joked, told long stories, drank some. He told her about his life.

"Hey, Deidre. There's this strange old man out there. He watches me."

Didi, hair spread like angel dust on the pillow, lit a cigarette, sympathized. She smiled; and then, after a moment, she frowned. "Can't you get a real job?"

The old man stared across the airfield. He coughed slightly, hand over mouth, but the sound escaped, went tumbling southward toward the Gulf of Mexico. He watched Baldessari step out of the plane and into the dust. He watched Baldessari stare curiously at him across the airstrip, Baldessari thinking that being on the ground in western Kansas is almost the same as being in the air. Baldessari shuffled his feet in the dirt and wished he were waiting alone.

Bennett, which was the name the FAA put on its maps for the place, was 280 miles from Denver, 330 from Oklahoma City. The other pilot, one Compton Sheats, necessarily arrived in Bennett after Baldessari, since they both left at ten every morning, Ciafu Flying supposedly establishing some regularity of schedule to qualify for a federal mail contract between the two cities. Sheats' perpetual lateness gnawed at Baldessari. Waiting at Bennett had become a focal point of Baldessari's day. He woke each morning knowing he was flying into a minor vacuum over which he had no control. Baldessari was not sure how the vacuum had come into existence; he did not know what to do about it.

Maybe on other planets, other galaxies, there are other Oklahomas, other Denvers, with two beings flying madly between them. Baldessari hoped so: the redundancy would offer unity, completeness; certain absurdities might be lessened by the sheer number of participants. Otherwise Baldessari was one of only two men in the entire universe who landed at Bennett and changed planes. The thought was not appealing.

Sheats had the Apache again. Baldessari heard the faint buzz of it, the only noise at Bennett. He saw it appear, saw it come in low to land, and then watched awestruck as it began to climb toward the sun, Baldessari suddenly running after it across the flat face of Kansas screaming at the plane to get the fuck down here. Sheats dove, banked tightly, and came in low over the airstrip, and Baldessari could see Sheats staring down at him with disapproval. Then Sheats smiled at Baldessari: he stayed low over the earth, circled off to the south, and became a dot. Baldessari stared.

Sheats sat out there in the far sky playing with perspective, coming hesitantly into middle distance, noodling about in the foreground, then retreating again an inch or two above the horizon, a small mark, waiting to be erased. He disappeared from the scene entirely, leaving only a noise. He puttered about the countryside, generally using up fuel, and then he sneaked back over the horizon and put the thing down upon the earth, taxied to Baldessari, cut the engines, climbed out, and with a large Oklahoma smile on his red face hurried into the waiting 310. Baldessari, hurrying by him, flipped him the bird, got into the plane, and started the engines. The two planes taxied, took off, and the pilots headed back to where they had come from.

It was quiet, the sky and earth abandoned. The old man leaned against the hangar and stared across the field: the impression of Baldessari flipping the bird remained mysteriously in the air, a sign, a gesture, the very finger, maybe, pointing to the beating heart of God. It carried on a tradition whose origins reach back to the singular times when insult first appeared in the lexicon of emotions, when the first oblique knowledge lodged in some primal consciousness that some poor fool of an anthropoid had not risen to the expectations anticipated of him, that, as a result, anger flashed and dour wit came exploding out in gesture, word, whatever, and, yes, accompanying it was the first dim wrenching knowledge that, jesus god, there are going to be expectations, criteria, a code, for this long stay here on earth.

Baldessari flew low over the prairie town that had an airstrip and a hangar or two and a ragged row of parked planes; he slowed, circled, seeing if he recognized any of the planes. People from the Enola Gay flew out this way: crop dusters in biplanes, ex-Vietnam pilots on random charter flights, amateurs in P51s and P48s, pilots of varying degrees of flakiness who made unscheduled flights over the Mexican border and back.

Baldessari, like most of the pilots who flew the area, had at one time or another put down on nearly every airstrip someone had taken the trouble to lay down, filling up with fuel, having a sandwich and coffee, then taking off. There were queer places out there, places Baldessari'd dropped into and never visited again, maybe couldn't even find again if he'd wanted: small isolated towns whose populace was inbred, Baldessari catching glimpses of the same gesture, the same facial characteristic, in everyone: towns whose anonymity was sought by the deformed and cast-off; towns of the old, that smelled like the blue hair of near-dead ladies. Baldessari had landed in towns that had no discernible reason for existence, towns where sometimes he'd see a look, a cast, that he had last seen in a town fifty miles to the east. Strange tides of genes and private madnesses flowed and dispersed to the rhythms of some unknown law: Baldessari coming upon whole towns that were sunk into a black catatonic depression, life at a standstill: all these towns whose only link (if there was any link at all) was the traveling cockfighters or the five-tent carnivals with their Oklahoma flatland prairie girls who did their thing in the back tent or the fourteen-and fifteen-year-olds who married and settled in another part of the plains, returning home only to attend funerals, births, basic life/death events worth the trouble of traveling for.

Baldessari showed Didi some of this: the two of them flew low over the earth toward Kansas, suspended over a large flat brown manila envelope for which no amount of postage would suffice. Didi frowned: small precise wrinkles appeared momentarily above her nose, disappeared. The land took on more than it offered thanks to granny glasses of a purplish/rosy tint. She was in her stewardess uniform: wry humor for this excursion; she had packed a picnic hamper of United Air Lines food—finger sandwiches, cocktail nuts, artful little cakes, a rattling collection of basic airline liquor, ten or fifteen 1/10-pint bottles of bourbon, Scotch, and whiskey.

Didi, slightly white against the primary colors of her lipstick, makeup, and uniform, sat poised, back straight, remembering some lesson of posture and decorum taught in girlhood, Baldessari realizing she had probably never seen anyone actually *fly* before, that she was maybe apprehensive at the ease with which he had lifted them from earth, no flight crew, navigators, computerized flight patterns, just he, Baldessari, who was now maybe rubbing it in a bit, flying low, catching every thermal updraft, tacking this way and that over the flat earth. A general aura of wind, vibration, and engine noise surrounded them, intruded upon only by static and by a voice Didi said she knew, the cool, low-key voice of Denver control tower granting permission for someone to come to earth, a voice smooth, unruffled, cultivated, it seemed, off some free-form FM radio.

At Bennett Didi climbed out of the plane and stepped into the dust and scrub grass and stood still for a moment staring at what was Kansas. Baldessari brought out the hamper and a blanket.

"There's the old man."

Didi laughed, had thought maybe Baldessari had been making him up. Didi invited the old man to join them in lunch, and, after he sat down on a corner of the blanket, he made himself comfortable and drank two small bottles of bourbon. The deep wrinkles of his face held midday shadows. His eyes were watery blue, glaucomatous, and Baldessari wondered if for all his staring at him he had seen anything. The man removed his straw hat, laid it beside him on the blanket, and accepted his lunch as if Baldessari should have brought it long ago. They ate quietly, small winds scuttling dust across the blanket, and Baldessari listened for the sound of the Apache. When Sheats landed, Didi, Baldessari, and the old man watched without speaking. Sheats climbed out of the plane, looked at the blanket and the bottles and the food without expression, and hurried into the 310.

"Thank God we don't have to go to Oklahoma City," Didi said.

"Precisely," Baldessari said.

The old man nodded.

They finished eating and Didi and Baldessari stood up, folded the blanket, and put their things in the hamper.

Baldessari looked at the old man. "See you tomorrow."

The man nodded.

Baldessari and Didi taxied by the old man in the Apache, Baldessari gunning it, Didi looking back at the gentleman, standing alone, casting a small noon shadow upon the dust.

The shortness of affairs and decrease in permanent relationships is some obscure step in the evolution of man whose purpose cannot yet be determined, was Baldessari's theory. Baldessari would be gone for hours at a time on his flights and Didi would be gone for days on hers. Sometimes she would switch schedules, or be shunted onto other flights, and return at curious hours carried beyond exhaustion on nerves hyped by time changes, speed, pressurization, and the cities she'd touched down in, her nervous system kindled beyond reason by its odd touches with America and forty-three cups of coffee.

Didi took Baldessari on one of her routes, to places Baldessari had never been before: St. Paul, Minneapolis, Chicago, Moline, Kansas City. He got on board through some low-air fare scheme of Didi's and, once airborn, felt a vague despair at having given up his destiny to pilots and crew he didn't know.

Didi walked up and down the aisle, looking good in heels and black stockings, dressed to please a nation of traveling fetishists. Stews hustled back and forth and liquor flowed. Didi hurried by, winked, Baldessari smiled. Or *was* that Didi? They all dressed the same. The passengers were brought bottle after bottle of booze. The fear was communal, came free with the purchase of every 727.

They spent the evening in Minneapolis or Chicago, Didi, laughing at Baldessari's sense of displacement, refusing to tell him which. They visited three or four clubs where Didi knew people: other stewardesses, pilots, airline people, some of whom Baldessari had met in Denver, the clubs identical to ones in Denver, the parking lots filled with the same cars, the kind all of Didi's girlfriends owned: Mustangs, Mavericks, Colts, Pintos, sprightly little automobiles named after the first warm thing American womanhood had wrapped its thighs around. Detroit being no fool.

The night was passed in a stew's apartment who, yes, was in Denver that night, a fact leading Baldessari to suspect he was receiving an ill-focused picture of some vast complicated linkage he was not a part of, something he was being allowed to glimpse the outer edge of, with perhaps more revelations to follow, if only certain steps were successfully passed. He returned with Didi to Denver the next day via Kansas City, Moline, Omaha, or some such, and he felt better than he had in ages. He wondered why: Didi? the booze? the force-fed oxygen? A damned fine way to feel. Which was probably exactly what Didi wanted to show him. Get him out of Bennett while there was still time.

Thus, once home: "Jesus, what a bummer you are. Fly halfway to Oklahoma City and back. You get up, eat a Danish, fly half as far as any sane man would, and you're back for dinner."

"Sheats knows this barmaid in Oklahoma. He doesn't want to spend every other night in Denver."

"Sheats," Didi said. "God . . . "

"I don't want to spend every other night in Oklahoma."

Didi glared. She had a set of gestures, facial expressions, blinking of eyes, pouts, frowns, casual smiles that she had acquired over the years during various sexual situations (which the present argument was). The coyness she sometimes used still brought the same reaction it had eight years before in junior high in West L.A.

"Don't you know Ciafu's making an ass out of you and Sheats?"

Baldessari said nothing: Ciafu being the one who figured that a simple solution to many problems would be to have his pilots change planes halfway between points of destination.

"Christ," Didi said. "I bet Ciafu had to hunt all over, give psychology tests, mental tests, IQ tests until he found two people that *failed* them. Two people who *want* to underachieve. You have to *lack* something to fly only halfway to a place day after day."

There being some truth to what Didi was saying, Baldessari was thinking: maybe they could move. Go east. Maybe Didi could just transfer to another airline, merely change uniforms, stews probably being free from those difficulties encountered by Jesuits jumping to the Dominican Order, Dominicans to the Capuchins.

"Most people would want to go all the way."

"Bennett *is* all the way."

"For you."

She was getting dressed. Their arguments came whenever she had to leave; proceeding out the door before any conclusion was reached. She was putting a small hat on her head, topping off a very neat package. Nothing messy; you knew she was going to work at someplace clean. And Baldessari, unshaven, hairs protruding from the area of his belly, with eyes that seemed not to look at things, could be going only to Bennett.

Didi looked at him. "Something's missing. Don't you feel something's missing?"

Baldessari shrugged. "You be home tonight?"

Hands on hips, her mouth a moue, standing by the door, Hollywood exit, she slowly shook her head no.

Baldessari started his fat, decrepit Olds. A small blue-white ball of smoke appeared from the exhaust, lingered, caught the hot weak wind, stretched and thinned, and moved across the road. It hung there, alone, conspicuous, cloudlike, sitting half-way between the grass and the skein of smog over the city it'd soon join. Denver was filled with a yellow-brown cloud that held the thin sunlight and diminished any clarity. The vague dark fingers of the stuff reached into the canyons of the mountains, the thick heavy palm of it lay over the city. The city was hypertense, as if the flickering of the stoplights and mercury lamps was causing vibrations other than those that caused waves to enter the visible spectrum.

The haze had been upon the city for days, flat and brown like the plains to the east: the haze contained its own heat, its own maneuverings, its private winds; it dictated life-styles, demanded obeisance from lungs and hearts. Psyches warped, changed shapes, curled at their farthest ends, withdrew upon themselves, and then became irritable when even this small portion was stepped on.

Baldessari taxied the 310 to the end of the runway, the plane partaking in slight, graceful bounces over cracks in the cement. Didi. God: Didi. More initials. FAA, VHF, ETA, DD. She couldn't see him for a while; her gynecologist said, she said. What did Baldessari know? There were people in cities all over the United States she told everything to. Doctors, analysts, lawyers, dentists, stews, girl friends, pilots, and ground crews knew more of her secrets and problems than Baldessari: a great underground of people who knew Baldessari secondhand. Once, twice, several times Baldessari thought he heard mention of his name come over carelessly left-open microphones, random voices pierced by static, comments emanating from cockpits and control towers discussing Baldessari's habits and his odd flights halfway to any decent destination. He was positive he caught the names of the Sperm and Ova, of various clubs around the country. Didi's name was spoken continuously. He heard the names of Didi's friends he had met. Again he heard his own name. He felt he had stumbled onto some vast inner core of America, a great web whose strands stretched across the country, interwoven voices and static-pierced broadcasts of wants, desires, greeds, and simple communications. Then, abruptly, Baldessari ceased to hear his name at all, and he wondered if he had imagined it. He listened intently. He decided, after much thought, that his name had just stopped being spoken.

Baldessari peered eastward, could see the lip of smog that ended not far from Denver. The tower finally gave him clearance, but he waited still longer before leaving, careful to avoid the turbulence and wash of the 727 that had preceded him, waiting extra minutes until it was gone, a speck in the sky, before beginning his takeoff down the long runway.

IN DESERT WATERS

Richard Ford

HE LOOKED to see if someone were standing back up on the shoulder behind the Buick, but there was no one, only the black imprint of Santa Rosa quavering on the low table of the desert.

When he stopped, the woman quit waving and rested her hand on her hip but kept her eyes shielded with her fingers. He got out and walked along the car, looked down in the back seat and saw it strewn with beer cans, some of the beer spilling out.

"Sun's real bad for your features," the woman said, removing her hand so he could see her small face.

"What'd you do to it?" He motioned toward the car.

"He says the pump's busted, but I don't know nothing about it. I know it stopped." She pinched up a piece of her blouse and pulled it away from her skin.

"So where's he gone?" he said.

"Variadero. Building a hamburger palace." She shaded her eyes again and studied him as if she had heard something she hadn't liked. He slid in and waggled the key.

"It wouldn't do *me* no good to go turnin nothin." She stepped into the shade of the car and pushed her hair up.

He tried the key. The motor turned over but quit short of starting. He held the accelerator and twiddled the key back and forth trying to spark it, but it wouldn't fire, and he finally stopped and squinted at her standing outside in the heat. She stiffened her mouth. "Half them's Larry's," she said, flicking her eyes away. "He drinks his breakfast on the way to work—I drink mine on the way home." She laughed. "I don't pick up no hitchhikers, though."

"Nobody said you did," he said.

"I don't, either," she said.

"That's good," he said, and climbed out. "I can't get your boat fired up." He flicked the sweat off his chin. "I'll take you down the road," he said.

"Curvo," she said, raveling her mouth up into a smirk.

"How far is it?"

"What difference does it make if you're going that direction?"

"None," he said.

She reached inside, yanked up a split package of beer, and came behind him. "I got my valuables out," she said.

"You going to leave it like that?" he said, looking at the beer and back at the car.

"Hell with it," she said, and climbed in the truck.

She sat high up on the seat, her hand flounced out the window letting the breeze flit through her fingers. She was different the first moment she got in the truck, a little more fragile a framework, he thought, and she had a small round bruise underneath her ear that she worried with her fingers, and every time the wind stripped her hair back against her temples he got another look at it.

"Air temp makes a difference," she said, watching the hot air through her fingers. "They put 'em in trucks."

"Is that right?"

She looked at him, then turned her face into the breeze.

"What is it your husband does?" he said.

She cranked the window up and gave him a stern look. "Hod

carrier. He's eight years younger than I am." She reached forward, ripped the package a little more and set a can on the armrest. "You think I look old?" she said.

He looked at her short neck and tried to make out he was estimating. "How old are you?" he said.

"That ain't the point," she said, pulling on her beer and setting the can back on the armrest. "That ain't the goddamned point. Point is, how old do I *look*? Old? You think I look old?" She watched him carefully to see if he were thinking over telling a lie.

"No," he said.

She raised her head slightly and widened her eyes. "I'm thirty-one. Do I look it?"

"No," he said. "That means the old man's twenty-three."

She gave him a surprised look. "I ain't worried about that," she said.

"Nobody said so."

She took another drink of her beer. "I take him to work in the morning and come get him in the evening. Them little town bitches come wherever he's at and switch their asses in his face, but they know I'll be pulling up there in my white Buick at six o'clock, holding a sack of beer in one hand and something better in the other, so he don't have to go nowhere to have fun but with me. I'm the goddamn fun."

"Where is it you live?" he said, snuffing his cigarette.

"Rag-land." She pointed off into the desert, where he could see the gauzy pancake hills to the south.

"How far you drive every day?"

"Seventy there, sixty back," she said. "I mix it up."

He started figuring miles and looked at her and added it up again and looked forlornly down the highway. She took a last long swallow of beer and let the can drop between her legs, pinching her mouth into a hard little prune as if she had just decided something.

"That's a hell of a ways," he said. "I'd let them switch their ass if it was me."

"You worry about you," she said. "I own the Buick. If I want to drive it to the moon, I will." She turned away and stared at the desert and then back at the man. "I just don't want to lose him," she said slowly, speaking so softly he had to look at her to see if she were talking to him. "I've had about as much trouble as I can stand," she said. "I'd just like to have things easier, you know?"

"Yeah," he said.

She pulled another beer out of the sack and peeled off the top. "We ain't been married but four months," she said, taking a tiny sip. "I had a husband to *die* on me seven months ago. TB of the brain." She looked at him appraisingly. "We knew he had it but didn't figure it would kill quick as it did." She smacked her lips, looked at him again and wrinkled her nose. "Flesh started falling off, and I had him in the ground in a month. In Salt Lake, see?" She was getting engrossed and tapping her beer against the window post. "We was in the L.D.S., you know?"

He nodded.

"I was the picture the whole time we was married." Her face got stony. "And after he died they all come around and brought me food and cakes and fruit, you know? But when I tried to get a little loan to buy me a car so I could go to work, they all started acting like somebody was callin them to supper. And I had been the *picture.* I let them have their meetings right in my house." She drew her mouth up tight again. "Raymond was born one, see? But I was raised on a horse farm outside of Logan."

She took another sip of beer and held the can in front of her teeth and stared at the desert. It was past midday. The sun had turned the desert pasty all the way to where the mountains stuck up. He watched her while she looked away and maneuvered himself so as to see the white luff of fabric between her blouse and her shoulder showing the curve of her breast.

"I had a friend that had that Buick just sitting in his garage." She kept looking at the desert. "I told him if he'd let me pay it off a little bit every month, I'd buy it. I always wanted a Buick, and it never seemed like I'd get one. It's queer to have to get down before all your dreams start coming true." She looked at him. "Anyway, I quit the L.D.S. right there," she said. "Got the hell out of that Salt Lake City. Let me tell you, don't be fooled by them. They're cheap-ass, I swear to God."

He looked at her blouse again to see in the little space, but she had swiveled head on to him and the little space was gone.

She tapped the can against her teeth. "I think I'm better now," she said. "Less quick to judge. It ain't easy to have a window on yourself." She slid back in the seat with her arms folded. "Where you going?"

"Arkansas," he said.

"Where's your wife at? Did you leave her home to take care of your babies?"

"I didn't say I was married," he said.

"I know it." She sighed. "You ain't hid nothing, have you? You're right up on top with everything."

"I guess not," he said.

"I ain't getting after you," she said.

"Ain't nothin to get after," he said. "How come you to get married so quick?"

"Bad luck," she said, and laughed and made her shoulders jerk. "Why don't you drink a beer? I'd feel better if you drank one."

He looked in the mirror and saw nothing but markers flashing. "I'm fine," he said.

She pushed a ring top out the ventilator. "Let me slide over—don't nobody know me at Curvo anyway."

She shoved across the seat and socked her head against his shoulder and put her heels on the dashboard. She let the can of beer rest on her stomach and arced her fingers around his thigh. Then she held the can up to his face and rolled it back and forth. "Larry likes that," she said, smiling.

He looked at her, hiding up under his shoulder, and reached around her so her cheek was drawn up against his chest.

"Do I look thirty-five?" she said.

"God, no," he said. "You think I look thirty-four?"

"You're married," she said.

"So are you."

"That's right," she said. "Let's don't talk about that now." Tears broke out of her eyes.

"I want to know how you got married again so fast," he said, holding the truck to the road.

She hugged him so that the tears got wiped off. "Life rushes, is all," she said, and eased her hand up, unzipped his trousers, and went touring around inside as if she were after something that wouldn't keep still.

"I'm tired of talking," she said.

Curvo was off the highway ten miles on a gravel track that made a giant curve east, then north, and marooned the town, which was only a red clapboard store building, two glass-bulb pumps, and a file of butchered outbuildings, with the desert open all around to every direction. He could see that all the outbuildings were cages of sorts, patched in with coiled chicken wire to permit inspection from the outside. The largest coop, a square built of two-by-fours with chicken wire basted over, had a stenciled sign that read zoo.

He stopped by the pumps and looked out the woman's window, waiting to see someone come out. The building had a plate window flocked with red fishing bobbers and line plaquettes. A rooster crowed from down among the cages, and he heard it flap its wings as though it were trying to get away from something.

"Where is everybody?" the woman said, lifting her hair off her neck. "Some kid works here—I seen his old flatbed last week. Beep the horn." She grabbed at the wheel, but he caught her.

"I'll get out," he said, taking a look back at the cages. "What's your name?" he said.

"Jimmye," she said, aiming her chin out at him. "What's yours?"

"Robard."

"What is it?"

"Robard."

"That's a damn poor name."

"You're real sweet," he said, shoving the door to.

He walked down the row of cages, looking in each one to see if someone were squatting inside tending to whatever was locked up. In the zoo pen there was nothing but a few scraps of wrinkled cellophane and a gamy smell, as if something had died inside. The second cage was a high four-poster frame built of creosote posts covered with chicken wire, and it was full of climbing raccoons. All the raccoons stopped and stood looking at him, then all at once went back to climbing the cage. In the third cage, a rooster had removed himself to the top branch of a fresno bole that had been dragged in from outside and gouged in the ground on the side farthest from the raccoons. It looked to him as if the coons were avid to get at the rooster and were only waiting to find some tiny fault in the mesh that would turn the tide in their favor. The rooster was eyeing everything guardedly, his beaky head snapping from one little coon face to the next.

The woman all of sudden honked the horn and held it a long time, exploding the quiet, and he grabbed a piece of dirt and flung it at the truck.

"What in the shit!" the woman yelled, her head erupting out of the side window, her mouth open. "Who's bombing me?"

"Cut out that blowin! You ain't helpin nothin!"

"I'm hot as shit!" she yelled.

"We're all hot," he said.

She ducked her head back in the truck and disappeared below the back window.

A latch snapped at the end of the row and a little girl in jeans let herself out of the last cage and walked up squinting in the sunlight. She drew her hair away from her ears, catching it high up with a rubber band, making her face look bald and round.

"You got a mechanic?" he said, looking behind her to see if anyone else were coming up out of the cage.

The girl was wearing a shirt with arrow pockets and mother-of-pearl buttons that belonged to someone bigger than she was. "What's the matter?" she said, her face arranging itself into a little frown.

"I don't know," she said, looking back at the truck, hoping the woman wouldn't lay down on the horn again. "These here your animals?"

The girl surveyed down the row of cages as if she were trying to make up her mind. "That's right," she said.

"They're nice," he said, taking another uneasy look at the truck and trying to think how to bring up getting the Buick worked on.

"You want to see Leo?" She cocked her head into the sunlight and squinted one eye.

"I seen him if that's him," the man said, pointing at the rooster.

"That ain't him," the girl said, smiling. "He's back yonder." She motioned him to follow.

In the cage at the end of the line a big rufous-colored bobcat sat lounging in the dust, staring at nothing. The girl looked at the bobcat and then at the man as if she were expecting a compliment. He studied the bobcat, feeling a little cold commotion inside that had to do with wild animals and the suspicion of what one could do to you before you got turned around. At the bottom of the cage, almost at the man's feet, there was a big long-boned jackrabbit resting on his haunches, eyeing the cat quietly, the jack's ribs shoved against the wire so that tufts of fur poked through the tiny hexagons. The man stood back and stared at the rabbit and said nothing, though after a minute he noticed something about Leo he hadn't noticed before. The right back paw was missing at the low joint, the stub matted with hair and sprawled behind as if it ended in a big padded paw.

"What come of his leg?" the man said, catching his knees and staring at the cat's empty leg.

"Borned bad," the girl said. "Hillbilly give him to my dad in Missouri. Found him in a hollow log, starving." She squatted on her heels and wriggled her fingers through the wires and called the cat, who rolled over and squirmed in the dust and stretched his forelegs straight in the air. "Com'ere, Leo," she said, and the cat looked at her with his head upside down, his eyes half open. The rabbit looked at her and squeezed back into the corner where she was.

"Rabbit thinks I'm callin *him*," she giggled. "Don't he wish."

"I don't doubt it," the man said.

The rabbit went back to measuring distance.

"You see my coons?" she said, walking up the row to where the coons were decorating the wires.

"I saw 'em," he said.

He looked back at the rabbit and had an impulse to kick open the gate, but the cat bothered him, dozing in the dust, waiting for somebody to make a move. He followed the girl back up the row.

"I'll sell you one for sixty cents," she said.

"Don't think so," he said.

"Yes I will," she said, looking at him professionally.

"I'll buy that rabbit," he said.

"Ain't for sale," she said, and looked out across the empty road and slowly bent her line of vision to the truck sitting in the dead sunlight. "That your truck?"

He studied the truck. It looked like a thing dropped out of a passing airplane.

"That's right," he said.

"Can't you fix your own truck?"

"Lady's car needs fixin. Ain't the truck."

"Lonnie won't be back here before tonight," she said. "But

he won't work on nothin. Be too dark. He won't have the right light."

"Who else is here?" he said.

"Nobody," she said. "Lonnie's in Tucumcari. Be roarin drunk when he comes back. Won't work on nothin."

The man looked at the sun, cerise and perfectly round, and thought it might be two-thirty.

"Is that the woman in the truck?" the girl said.

The back of the woman's head was visible in the oval window. She was working on her face in the rearview.

"That's her," he said.

"You'll have to spend the night, then, or go to Tucumcari," the girl said, turning back to the cages. "There ain't no mechanic from here to there." She pointed up the road into the desert. "Lonnie'll be good in the morning. He ain't but twenty-two, but he ain't a fool."

"Where's your daddy?" he said, looking up at the desolated back side of the building. A white tub washer was set outside in the dirt.

"Gone," she said, and pursed her lips.

"Are they dead?" he said.

"Gone to Las Vegas. They ain't come back."

"Do you expect them?"

"I guess," she said.

"What time is it?" he said.

The girl consulted her wristwatch, a thin silver strippet with a face as small as her shirt buttons.

"Three o'clock," she said. "We got a room. Got a fan in it."

A breeze lifted off the desert and passed through the cages and carried the raccoon foulness back into his nostrils.

"I got to clean that empty cage," the girl said, wrinkling her nose to let him know she could smell it.

"What was in there?" he said.

"That there rabbit," she said, moving a strand of her yellow hair from across her temple where the breeze had left it.

The man looked back at the rabbit hied up against the wire, studying the bobcat. A tiny vein of panic opened inside him.

"Lemme buy that rabbit," he said quickly.

The girl frowned. "Leo gets hungry when it gets cool," she said. "That rabbit don't know that, though."

"I bet he's figured it," the man said.

The girl giggled and let him know it didn't make any difference what a rabbit knew.

"What's your name?" he said.

"Mona Nell," she said, wagging her shoulders and forcing her hands down inside her pants pockets. "What's that woman's name?"

"I believe she said Jimmye."

"That's my daddy's name," the girl said, and laughed.

"Where the hell is everybody?" the woman said, scowling out the window, her hair plumped up.

"Gone," he said softly. "Won't be back till night." He leaned on the windowsill and looked back at the girl squatting in the dust.

"That's the shits," the woman said. "What the hell am I supposed to do if I got to get Larry at six?" She fattened the corners of her mouth.

"Looks like two things," he said, staring down at the ground. "Ride to Tucumcari. That kid said there's mechanics there. Or stay put and call somebody. You can get Larry to come get you."

She frowned at him as if she didn't like hearing the name. "They got a telephone?"

"I guess," he said.

"Son of a bitch," she said. "He'll be off with his pissant brother drinking beer quick as he sees I ain't coming. That's the trash he is."

She lowered her brow, and he understood she could see all that was coming.

The first truck to pass the station hissed through the curves and ground out into the road—a tandem hauling diesel smoke into the desert. There was large writing on the sides through the dust and grease—WHACK MY OLD DOODLE and TAKE ANOTHER LITTLE PIECE OF MY HEART—as though one line followed on the other and made good sense. The man looked at the writing and wondered what that might mean and thought of asking the woman to tell him, but she looked mean.

"What time is it?" she said.

"Something till," he said.

The girl was down at the far end of the row of cages, cooing to the bobcat, saying his name over and over.

"Let's get out of here," the woman said.

"Where we going?" he said.

"A tourist court out at Conchas. You and me is staying in it. Let's git."

He looked at her to let her know he was considering it. "What about the car?"

"Let's get out of here, all right?" she said. "Worry about that Buick tomorrow. You just leave my business to me. If I need any advice, I'll ask your little cooze you're so hot about."

He sealed his forehead on his wrist and spit down into the dust. "I ain't hot," he said.

"I'm waitin," she said.

"What're you waitin on?" he said.

She sat staring out at the long curve in the road. The breeze switched and came up from behind the building. The little girl was sitting on her haunches, making a high-pitched hooting sound.

"Ain't no need being mad," he said into the hollow of his arm.

She looked away.

"Ain't no need to go somewhere else."

"I'm past the point of carin," she said.

"They got a room right here," he said. "That boy can look after the car in the morning."

She caught a corner of her lip between her teeth and drummed her fingers. "They got a air temp?" she said.

"Fan," he said.

Her face looked like coarse pale cloth held to the sun.

"Might as well," she said, sighing. "We ain't going to dance in this heat."

The girl led them inside the house, where it was murky and cool, and stood behind a counter before a kind of ledger book. The room was lit by whatever light could angle through the flocked window and by a mint-colored bulb in a cold case at the back of the store. He had to get near the page to see to sign, and when she pointed out the place, he looked at the book a moment and signed Mr. & Mrs. S. Tim Winder. The only other registration was at the top of the page, written in squared pencil letters: RAMONA ANELIDA WHEAT, THE QUEEN.

The girl led them between two steepled rows of Vienna sausages and Wheat Chex and up two flights of stairs to where it was quiet and hotter, and where it smelled like an icebox locked up and left. Sunlight brightened a square of green linoleum, and the little room the girl opened drew together inside like a kiln. There was a brown metal bed, a serpentine commode with a doily, a chair, and a string-pull ceiling fan with one blade removed.

"You better open up a window," the girl said, holding her ponytail up to let off the heat. "It'll cool off when the sun moves. You'll be hollerin for a blanket."

"Ain't there no toilet?" the woman said.

"That fan works." The girl reached on her toes and yanked the string. The motor hummed, but the blades stayed still. "Pot's downstairs," she said. "We got two."

He went to the window, pried it up and stood back to allow in the breeze, but there was no air moving. The truck looked abandoned in the yard, sunshine baked on the hood. He tried to think about what had gotten him up this far, up into the room when he should have been on the highway halfway to somewhere.

"Ain't there no sinks?" the woman said.

"In the pot," the girl said. "I'll put a glass in there. Lonnie'll be back tonight. You'll hear him cause it'll be a noise when he does."

"I can't wait," the woman said, flouncing on the bed. "What else does he do?"

"Nothin," the girl said, and let her jaw fall open and shift back and forth while she stared at the woman. "Checkout's eight-thirty. You get charged another day." She threw the key on the dresser and slammed the door before the woman could speak.

"A.m. or p.m.?" the woman yelled, but the words got slammed in the door. "Little split-ass. A kid pimp—ain't that the shits," she said.

He stood staring down at the truck.

"I know you," she said, laughing and bouncing lightly on the bed. "You got the eye for that little twat."

He walked across and stood in front of the bureau and looked at her and sighed, his hands in his pockets, wondering whether it would do just to leave her sitting, go off for a Grap-ette and never show back.

"What're you lookin at?" she said.

He shook his head.

"What're you shakin your ugly head at?"

"Not anything," he said.

"You think you're some hot stuff, don't you?" she said. "You thought you were too good to screw me, but I got some bad news for you. You're right to my level. It may of took you a while to get here, but you're here, by God." She retired to her elbows.

"Where'd you get that mark on your neck?" he said.

"He give it to me," she said proudly. "It ain't no *mark*, either. Don't you know what a hickey is, Robert? Did you think some-body'd been beatin up on me?"

"I didn't think about it," he said.

"I guess not." She poked around after the mark, as if she thought she could feel it.

The fan had begun circling. He picked up the chair and brought it to the side of the bed. He sat with his elbows on his knees and his face collapsed in his hands. She smiled at him and he knew she knew everything.

"You gonna stay mad at me?" he said quietly.

"I ain't mad," she said. "You ain't nobody."

"That's right." He listened to his breath escaping between his fingers.

"You ain't hidin nothin—are you, Robert?"

"No," he said.

Her smile sweetened and flesh collected in a little pouch under her chin. "How come you're up here with me? I'm a married woman," she said. "You're married, ain't you?"

"I guess," he said.

"Ain't you got no sense of right?"

"I guess not," he said.

"This here's adultery, boy," she said, leering. "Who's paying the bill?"

"Whoever wakes up second, I reckon," he said.

She pressed in his direction. "You going to strand me, are you, Robert?" She let her calves touch his knees, pushing her pants above her ankles.

"What's his name'll be to get you," he said.

"Sure will," she said. "You better hope he don't find you here or there'll be shit to fly."

She pushed off her elbows and straddled him, her pants squeezed up on her knees, her eyes widened. He set his hands along her calves and wedged them in the material and felt the cords down in her thighs. She lay on the spread, letting her head go back side to side.

"He won't find me," he said, his mouth dry.

She hummed in her throat somewhere, turned her face so she stared at the metal bedrights. He unbuttoned her pants and slid them around her thighs. Her skin was bluish. She hissed through her teeth as though it were a pain commencing. He laid her pants over the chair and pushed up her legs. She bridged back into the ticking. "Robert?" she said, her arms laid out, her hands made into fists.

"What?" The linoleum buckled. He tried to get himself up onto the bed and pay attention to what she was saying all at the same time.

"Do you think I look thirty—I mean with you looking at me?"

"No, sweet," he said softly. "You don't look twenty where I'm at."

She drew her legs up and eased his hand. "I ain't mad at you no more," she said, her voice lost in her throat.

"That's sweet," he said. "That's real sweet."

It had turned grey down in the east. The coons were up on the wires, staring at the sun sagging by degrees. Leo lay quietly, eyeing the rabbit, who had dozed as the day cooled and was awake now, the breeze pushing back against the hatch of his fur.

The man lay beside the woman in the brown light, feeling the breeze draw on the room, pulling the curtains and plucking the flesh on his arms. The screen door slammed and he could hear the girl move out in the yard, cooing at the animals. The woman shuddered and he looked at her, expecting her eyes to open, but she lay still, breathing as if barely alive. He could smell the sage, a faint burning aroma, and he could hear the raccoons clicking up and down the wires.

"You make me feel kinder to the world," the woman had said, and he couldn't figure why and lay with his chin in the pillow.

"Don't you feel that way all the time?"

"No." Her lips were to his ear. "I get contrary, get people in trouble."

"Don't he make you feel good?"

"Larry does. Sometimes. But I don't trust him." She had turned on her side and crossed her arms beneath her chin.

"You're up there every day," he said.

"If I wasn't, he'd be humpin some bar bitch like he is right now."

"But you *are* up there," he said.

"You're sweet," she said, and gave him a kiss on the shoulder. "I love him. But I can't trust him not to wipe me out. I got to cheat on him a little so it balances, see? He can't feel like he's put nothin on me, cause he knows I'm probably puttin something on him already. You got to stay balanced."

She ran her fingers through the hair on his belly. "I want you," she said in a queer high voice.

"Wait now," he said, picturing Larry bricking in Variadero, wondering where his wife was while the sun was going, whether she was stopping over in some tonk bar and not making it until tomorrow. "Does he know that's how you're playing it?"

"Let's us don't talk," she said, grabbing him in her fist.

When she had gone to sleep, he lay and stared at the ceiling, spattered with the gold tinsel of water seepage. When it rained, it rained until the boards soaked and the water shot the walls and set the house floating. He dozed and felt himself drawn to a powerful locomotion, the sky driving through cages, drowning the animals, filling the truck bed and buoying him inside until it was necessary to hold the bed rails to save from going under. There were lights in the yard, flashing through the panes across the wall in his room, revolving rectangles across the wall, and he had sat up startled and faced them and heard the groan of someone's pickup and doors slamming and lilting voices in the yard. He walked out on the plank porch and stood where his mother was watching the two men while they talked one at a time to get the story told and gone. They stood large in the night, the truck light fanning the grassy spider webs, and for a while she stared past them into the high beams, and then the men finished and left. The way the woman had told it, the man, his father, had gone up into the hills to attend a service and took the woman with him, and three-quarters of the way up the grade full of roots and chucks, the old car failed where they forded a creek, a ribbon of spring-water squirreling down the mountain to the Illinois. The woman said she got out and went into the bushes while his father stayed and monkeyed with the dashboard wires, trying to get the car going before it got night. And when the woman came back from the bushes, it had begun "an unimaginable rain," she said, that smacked the side of the car, and the water rose over the bottoms of the doors and swirled and sped past the car so that a strong man couldn't have walked through it without falling. And she said she could see him inside humped over the dashboard studying the wires and not knowing, she guessed, that the creek was up or that it might not do to be out in it. She herself, a plump, slope-eyed woman from Tonitown, said she never imagined what the outcome would be and went up and squatted underneath a plum bush to wait for the rain to stop and the creek to subside so they could go on to church. And as she sat, the water got dark and creamy, and rose, and pieces of split-off timber came down the chute, and she got wringing-wet watching the limbs batter the car and the water rise to the door locks. She said she believed the man did sense something was not right, because he opened the window and said something to her that she couldn't hear and tried to open the door, but the water was against it and the other side was busted from before she knew him. And she said that he closed the window and looked out, laughing and grinning and making funny signals with his hand, signals she said she couldn't make out any better than what he'd said. She said for a long time the two of them sat and looked at each other, she on the bank under the plum bush, wet, and he shut inside the car with the water gyring around, smiling and making signals, perfectly dry. Until, she said, the water seemed to go over the car all at once, and without a wave or a tree limb to hit it or any inkling that it was losing purchase, it just suddenly, rolling, rolled over and the water over it and it was gone.

Behind the house the clouds had piled against the sky. The sun had gone and left the sky indistinct. In the east it had been dark a long time. He lay still in the smoky light. There was a chill in the room, and he could hear the girl outside teasing the raccoons onto the rungs of the cage. He rose quietly, dressed in the corner and carried his shoes out the door. On the floor outside, the girl had laid a blanket, and he carried it inside and spread it over the woman, covering her until her fingers clutched the basting and she drew it around herself and slept on. He slipped down the stairs to where the cold box glowed and the compressor hummed in the gloom. He took a candy bar out of a plastic jar and a soda from the cooler and stepped into the lot, where the air was slow with sage.

The little girl looked up when she heard the screen slap and went back to tempting the raccoons. "You got a Butterfinger?" she said, keeping her eyes averted.

"And a Grapette," he said, squeezing candy out of his teeth and taking a look down the cages.

"Seventeen cents," she said. Her hair was full of fine gold threads mingled with what was almost white. "I set you a blanket out," she said without looking up. "I knocked, but didn't nobody answer."

"We must've dozed," the man said. "What about your rabbit?" he said, stuffing the candy paper in his pocket and glancing down the list of cages. "His time must be about up."

She giggled and pulled a cellophane bag of peanut hulls out of her shirt and began feeding them to the coons one at a time. "His time came and went," she said.

He looked at the girl quickly, suddenly feeling bested. "I thought you said he don't get hungry till the sun went down."

"Light can't tell Leo when to get hungry," the girl said.

"I didn't hear nothin," he said, looking up at the window, the chintz curtains flagging limply outside.

"Leo don't make no noise," she said.

He felt an awful anguish and looked back at the girl watching

him from where she squatted in the dirt. He felt maybe somebody ought to sit down and talk to her, tell her she wasn't
doing things right, give her an idea on how things ought to be.

"What time is it?" he said.

She looked at her wristwatch. "Seven-forty. Dark by eight."

The sky was steely down to the horizon. A flicker of bat
slipped through the air and disappeared.

"Lonnie won't be back till late," she said.

"Do me a favor." He rubbed his fingers through his hair.

"Depends," she said.

"Tell that lady," he eyed the window, "I had to leave."

The girl got up and dusted her jeans and put the cellophane
in her shirt pocket. "Who's payin it?" she said.

He got out his wallet and took out four bills.

"Three dollars and seventeen cents," she said, letting him
know she saw the empty bottle dangle off his finger.

"Keep the rest for the favor," he said.

"She ain't sick, is she?"

"Tell her I had to take off."

"She ain't going to like it," the girl said, confident, rocking
on her heels.

"She won't care."

"What you say," the girl said. "You ain't foolin nobody."

"I know it," he said, backing toward the truck.

He could see the stippets of white in the girl's hair. He took a
look at the window and saw the curtains swell with air, turned,
and started fast for the truck. He dropped the bottle in the oil
can between the pumps and heard the screen door whack shut,
heard the girl's boots hit the inside stairs. He let the truck idle,
watching the door, watching for the woman and the girl to
come boiling out like bloodhounds. But no one came, and he
let the truck roll into the road. Adream, he watched the window in the mirror while it sank, and it satisfied him to think
that when the woman awoke she could as soon feel kinder to
the world as not.

FLESH, PLEASURES OF THE

Erik Tarloff

WHY DID PAUL FLANNERY prefer to play the field?

Paul liked variety, savored what he vulgarly called "a mixed grill."

Why vulgarly?

Because mixed grill is the name given to a dish, popular in Europe, of a wide choice of meats cooked together in the same pot.

Could you briefly describe Mr. Flannery's appearance?

He was five feet eleven inches tall, one hundred fifty pounds or so. Dark hair. Regular features. In recent years he has sported a moustache.

Could you describe the moustache?

Just a regular moustache.

Handlebars?

No, I'd say the ends were inclined to droop.

Was it bushy?

Not particularly.

The same color as his hair?

Perhaps somewhat lighter.

Continue.

He dressed well. Conservatively, but with flair.

Did he have a tailor?

No, he got his suits off the rack.

Would you, then, to sum up, describe his appearance as attractive?

Yes sir, I would, He was not an Adonis, but he presented an attractive appearance. He was quite presentable.

What was his age?

Thirty-one.

And could you tell us his occupation?

He was an investment counselor.

I beg your pardon?

An investment counselor.

That pays well, doesn't it?

Yes, quite well. Paul made approximately $50,000 a year, which, as a bachelor, he found more than ample.

Good. Now, let's see. To return to the subject. The women Mr. Flannery had his alliances with . . . did they come from a distinctive social stratum?

Oh, it varied.

There was no pattern?

Well . . .

No preponderance?

Well, I suppose there were quite a few secretaries. But also teachers, salesgirls, editorial assistants, script girls, students, women engaged in diverse managerial tasks, researchers, writers (including a remarkable number of poets), musicians, waitresses, topless dancers and other artistes, accountants, computer programmers, and many representatives of the chronically unemployed.

Does this represent a more or less complete list?

No sir. By no means.

Would you be willing to assemble a complete list and submit it to me at your convenience?

Certainly sir, if you wish.

Fine. Now, how about appearance?

I'm sorry?
Appearance.
The women?
Yes. Were they generally attractive?
Generally.
But not exclusively?
No sir.
Preponderantly?
That might be a fair characterization.
How about June Cabot, the woman in question? Was she attractive?
No sir, she was not.
She was not?
That is correct.
Would you describe her, please?
She was about five foot three or four inches. I don't really know how to estimate a woman's weight, but she was on the heavy side.
How far on the heavy side?
Not grossly fat.
Pleasingly plump?
No, I don't think that would be an accurate description. It wasn't her overweight, however, so much as a general . . . shapelessness, you'd have to call it.
And her visage?
Her what?
Her features. Her facial characteristics.
She was not pretty.
Was she ugly?
That might be a little strong. She wasn't pretty.
All right. I'm a little bothered . . . it would seem . . . Am I wrong in inferring from what you've said that looks were not important to Mr. Flannery?
He was very conscious of appearance.
That's not exactly what I'm asking.
I don't mean to be evasive. Feminine beauty was important to Mr. Flannery. He had a very sharp eye for, a very healthy

appreciation of, beautiful eyes, a pert nose, high cheekbones, full and sensuous lips, a shapely neck line, a full or beautifully shaped bust, a slim waist, a striking pair of buttocks (either saucily large or provocatively tight and smooth), long lean legs, a well-turned ankle, a graceful instep. But he was usually willing to settle for less.

If pretty girls were not available, he would compromise his ideals. Is that what you're trying to say?

Well sir, it's not that simple. I'm sure that's part of it. It may have been that way for Paul once upon a time. But . . . well, that would imply he experienced disappointment if he did not secure the company of a beautiful woman, and this is simply not the case. He was delighted with virtually any woman whose acquaintance he happened to make.

But what about the beautiful jugs and all the rest of it?

Generally he found compensations.

Such as . . . ?

Sir, it's necessary that you understand that Mr. Flannery viewed fucking as an exploration; if you will, an existential exploration.

Is that his phrase?

No, it's my own.

Proceed.

And so, if nothing else, fucking an ugly woman taught him how an ugly woman fucks. But further, it suggested to him what effect the ugliness had on the fucking.

Could you explain further?

Certainly. Some women, to compensate for their ugliness, or as a result of extended deprivation, fucked like demons. Others were so conscious of themselves they were unable to enjoy their good luck.

This sort of thing could also apply to attractive women, could it not?

Oh yes indeed, sir, I'm sure it's never absent. But Mr. Flannery found the effect particularly piquant with the less fortunate. He once spoke to me of the Benjamin Franklin essay "On Choosing a Mistress." He said, "Ben didn't really know the half of it, or maybe he was more interested in a good joke than the truth. Maybe some older women will be grateful, but there are plenty of others who will never forgive you."

That's very interesting.

Isn't it?

Yes. Hmm . . . Did Mr. Flannery regard himself as a good lover?

Yes sir, I believe he did.

Did he ever expatiate upon the subject?

He was not a particularly boastful man. I think, if pressed, he would have said simply that he enjoyed sex so much he believed his pleasure to be infectious.

A rather unhappy choice of words.

Indeed. My apologies.

But I believe I take your point. Did he ever experience difficulties or problems?

Sexually?

Sexually.

Oh yes.

For example . . . ?

Temporary impotence.

Temporary?

It almost never lasted more than fifteen minutes or a half hour or so.

How rare was this?

Not rare at all. Quite common, as a matter of fact.

Didn't he find this . . . embarrassing?

Sometimes. He became rather adept at dealing with the problem.

Any other difficulties?

After several acts of intercourse in an evening, he sometimes couldn't come.

Anything else?

He sometimes had the opposite problem, coming too quickly.

Anything else?

I can't think of anything off-hand, no sir. What else is there?

How did he deal with the problem of coming too quickly?
It varied.
Well, tell me one way.
I believe he sometimes said, "I'm sorry, baby, you got me too excited."
That's not bad. However, to proceed. Miss June Cabot. Where did Mr. Flannery make her acquaintance, if I may ask?
Certainly. At a bar.
A bar?
A so-called "singles' bar." Where people go to meet other people.
You mean there are places where unaccompanied women actually go to . . . to get picked up?
Yes sir. Many. It's quite a thriving industry.
And no one feels embarrassed about entering such establishments?
They are regarded as quite respectable.
Is admission granted only to unaccompanied persons?
Oh no. You see, sir, for one thing, often two members of the same sex go together, perhaps to bolster each other's confidence or to help pass the time pleasantly in case nothing develops. And for another . . . well . . .
Yes?
Well, many couples also frequent singles' bars to meet other couples or to find a third partner.
And these places are legal?
Oh yes.
And have liquor licenses?
Most of them.
When I was in the first flush of youth—well, never mind that. So he met her in a singles' bar?
Yes sir.
What first drew him to her?
She was drawn to him, to be precise. She approached him and asked if she could buy him a drink.
Is such a gesture common at these places?

Not uncommon.

And he accepted?

There was no gracious way to refuse.

All right. What were his first impressions of Miss Cabot?

He noted she was unattractive. He found her voice pleasant. Something in her manner—a kind of confidence or presence normally lacking in unattractive women—indicated to him she was probably very intelligent.

How much time did they spend together in the bar?

Just over a hour.

What was the substance of their conversation?

They discussed their backgrounds, their geographical origins, their respective modes of employment—

Excuse me for interrupting, but what was Miss Cabot's mode of employment?

She was a graduate student at UCLA in English literature.

All right. Go on.

They discussed politics, current books, current films, the possibility of common acquaintances.

Did they have any?

They did not. They discussed the bar in which they found themselves. They discussed Los Angeles. They discussed sex.

Who raised the subject of sex?

Miss Cabot.

What exactly did she say?

She said, "Would you like me to suck your cock?"

Out of the blue?

Yes sir, virtually out of the blue. Following a lull in the conversation.

My my. How did Mr. Flannery respond?

He said, "Yes, I'd like that very much."

He did not manifest surprise?

He did not.

Did he feel surprise?

Oh yes sir. Miss Cabot's timing was unexpected.

Had he been preparing to make a proposal of his own?

He had suspected it wouldn't be necessary. And of course it wasn't.

To whose domicile did they repair?

Miss Cabot suggested her apartment. As they had come in separate cars, she wrote down her address for Mr. Flannery.

Did he ever suspect she had written down a false address as a cruel jest?

No sir.

Did Mr. Flannery counter with a suggestion they use his own apartment?

No sir. Miss Cabot seemed eager they go to hers. He suspected she had some reason.

Such as?

Such as possibly pride in its appearance. Such as possibly a collection of . . . of sex devices, or something of that kind.

Was either suspicion justified?

Both.

Could you be more specific?

It was immediately apparent that she had taken great pains to' decorate her apartment distinctively. Movie posters, great leafy plants, and exotic pieces of sculpture adorned every available wall, nook, and cranny.

Did Mr. Flannery find the effect pleasing?

He found the effect amusing, yes sir, he found it an imaginative expression of Miss Cabot's personality.

Which he found congenial?

Yes sir.

You mentioned sex devices.

I used the term rather loosely. A king-sized water bed with heater and vibrator, and electronic cordless battery-run plastic vibrator, a collection of glossy color pornographic photographs, and a jar of musk-scented lubricating gel.

Did she show him these all at once as soon as they arrived?

No sir.

What did happen?

She arrived some minutes before Mr. Flannery. When he knocked on her door, she called, "Come in, it's open." He entered the apartment. Miss Cabot was undressed, seated in an easy chair with each leg draped over an arm of the chair.

The effect being to expose her private parts to Mr. Flannery?

Yes sir. Not merely to expose . . . the effect was . . . she seemed to *offer* her private parts to Mr. Flannery.

What was Mr. Flannery's reaction?

He was touched, excited, repelled, attracted, and embarrassed.

What did he do?

He kissed Miss Cabot's proffered genitals.

For an extended period of time?

A minute or so. Then he stood up again. Upon which, Miss Cabot pulled him to her and opened his pants.

Was Mr. Flannery wearing boxer shorts?

Jockey shorts.

White?

Blue. And then she began to fellate Mr. Flannery.

Did he have an erection at this time? Prior to the fellating?

Semi, sir.

Semi?

The process of tumescence had begun, but was not yet completed. Mr. Flannery restrained Miss Cabot and suggested they retire to the bedroom. Miss Cabot did not seem entirely pleased at the interruption, but agreed and led him down the corridor to her bedroom.

Where the act of fellatio continued?

Yes sir.

Did Mr. Flannery undress before they resumed?

Yes.

Did he fold his clothes neatly?

Yes sir. Across the back of a chair.

And then joined Miss Cabot on her heated vibrating water bed?

That is correct.

Did he passively enjoy this experience, or did he reciprocate in some way?

He did not reciprocate. Except . . .

Yes?

Except he stroked her hair and breasts. In order to be doing *something*. You understand, sir.

Did she . . . did she bring him to climax?

Yes sir.

Did he give her a warning that his climax was imminent?

Yes sir.

In what manner?

I believe he said, "Whoops."

Did she thereupon withdraw her mouth?

No, she did not.

She swallowed, then?

Yes sir.

Did Mr. Flannery at any time comment upon her skill at this activity?

Yes sir, he had occasion to praise her expertise.

Was this praise sincere?

From the bottom of his heart.

I see. And then?

She suggested Mr. Flannery satisfy her with the plastic vibrator while he waited for his erection to return. To facilitate this latter, she gave him some pornographic photographs to examine.

She had them handy?

Yes. In a drawer in a small chest by her bed.

And he complied with her suggestion?

Yes.

Willingly?

I suppose one could say so.

Enthusiastically, would you say?

Yes. Enthusiastically.

Did he enjoy the experience?

Not entirely.

Why is that?

He developed a painful muscle cramp in the calf of his left leg. He stopped what he was doing and told her about it, and she massaged his calf until the cramp subsided.

She had not yet had an orgasm?

Not yet.

Was she still excited?

Oh yes. Very much so.

And Mr. Flannery?

His erection returned as the cramp relaxed. A coincidence they both remarked upon with amusement.

Did they therefore engage in sexual intercourse?

No, he resumed stimulating her with the vibrator.

Why?

I'm not really certain. To finish what they had already begun, I suspect. Neither of them, in any event, was surprised.

And this time she did achieve a climax?

Yes sir.

Was this event manifestly evident?

Oh yes sir, manifestly.

I see. What happened then?

Miss Cabot requested that Mr. Flannery kiss her.

Which he did?

Which he did not. He still found her unattractive, and he was additionally repelled by the presence of his own semen in her mouth.

They had not yet in fact kissed all evening, is that right?

That's right.

And how did he manage to avoid kissing her now?

By diverting her attention elsewhere.

Could you please be more specific?

He showed her one of the photographs she had given him that he found particularly interesting and asked her, "Have you ever tried that?"

And what did the photograph represent?

A woman engaged in normal and anal intercourse with two men simultaneously.

And what did she reply?

She said she had not. Then he asked her if the idea appealed to her.

And did it?

Yes sir, so she said.

I see. Was this followed by . . . by a proposal?

No sir, it was followed by an awkward pause.

Which signified?

Which signified . . . this would have to be speculation on my part.

I am willing to accept it as such.

Which signified the uncertainty about whether a proposal should be made—and, I suppose, who should make it.

I'm still not sure I understand . . .

Well, it's rather difficult for me to explain. It's just—well, it's just that all the peculiar ambiguities of their position seemed underlined by that awkward pause. Would they see each other again? Probably not. Upon what foundation was their physical intimacy based? Upon quicksand. And yet they were discussing and presumably considering . . . well, I guess I'm still not really making myself clear, sir, but it's the unusual juxtaposition of the almost adolescent concern on the first date of whether there will be a second coupled with the contemplation of engaging in an advanced and very intimate sexual aberration. Do you see what I mean?

Not exactly. But I'm willing to pass on to other matters. Now that the specter of anal intercourse had been raised, did they engage in it?

No sir. Miss Cabot fetched her lubricating gel and began to apply it to Mr. Flannery's penis.

A propos of anything in particular?

She just told him it would feel good.

Did it?

Yes sir. Aside from its oily consistency, it heated up upon contact with the skin.

Ah.

Yes sir.

Did you happen to know how full the jar . . . it did come in a jar, didn't it?

Yes.

Did you know how full the jar was?

No sir, I'm afraid I don't.

All right. So she applied the gel to Mr. Flannery's penis?

And scrotum.

Really?

Yes sir. And then she applied it to herself.

To herself?

Yes. Mr. Flannery offered to help, but she instructed him to lean back and watch her.

Where exactly did she apply it?

To her nipples, her clitoris, and the general area of her vulva.

Was any applied internally?

Yes sir, some.

Did they then have intercourse?

No sir.

Why not, for heaven's sake?

Mr. Flannery leaned over toward her with that unambiguous purpose, but Miss Cabot stopped him, suggesting they smoke some marijuana first.

She was in possession of marijuana?

Yes sir.

Did Mr. Flannery agree?

Reluctantly. He was already quite aroused, and besides, he was not himself a particularly avid marijuana user.

Was this perhaps a function of his age?

Quite possibly. His age and social orientation.

Did he disapprove of its use?

He would never have said so.

Does marijuana have an effect on sexual performance or experience?

So it is reported.

Could it be considered an aphrodisiac?

I'm not an expert, but I suspect it could.
Did she have the marijuana handy as well?
No sir, not literally at hand. It was in another room.
So she went to fetch it?
Yes sir.
She went to fetch it. Did Mr. Flannery just lie there waiting?
Not exactly, sir.
Could you speak up?
Not exactly, sir.
Well?
He began to masturbate, sir.
To masturbate?
Not in earnest . . . he just . . . it was just a matter of casually
touching himself, you see.
With the intention of bringing himself to climax?
No sir, I'm sure not. It was more a matter of . . . of idling his
engine. What musicians call "vamping till ready."
And then Miss Cabot returned?
Yes sir. Quietly. Without his being aware of it. Until she
yelled, "Say cheese!"
"Say cheese"?
She had a Polaroid camera, you see. He looked up, rather
startled, and a flash bulb suddenly seared his vision.
"Seared his vision"?
I am quoting Mr. Flannery.
*In other words, she had taken a photograph of him masturbating, is
that what you're saying?*
Yes sir.
Was he pleased?
No sir.
Was he extremely displeased?
Not extremely. She had an album, a picture album, which
she showed him when she noticed his displeasure. It appeared
to be a collection of candid photographs of her other lovers,
also lying on her water bed.
Also masturbating?

A few of them.

And this mollified him?

I don't know whether "mollified" is the exact word. It interested him sufficiently so that he allowed his displeasure to lapse.

Approximately how many photographs were there?

Many.

A hundred, would you say?

Perhaps not quite so many.

Seventy-five?

That would be a fair estimate.

And I believe a Polaroid camera develops pictures in a matter of minutes, is that not right? So did she therefore show Mr. Flannery his portrait?

Yes sir. And mounted it in the album.

What was his reaction to this?

He experienced an unfamiliar emotional response which he was unable to name or explain, either at the time or subsequently.

Was it pleasant or unpleasant?

He was unable to say.

Did he examine any of the other pictures?

Yes sir.

In detail?

Some of them.

All right. Now something really puzzles me. In Mr. Flannery's experience, was Miss Cabot's behavior common? By behavior, I mean all of it: the sexual aggressiveness, the devices, the marijuana, the camera, the entire business?

No sir, at least in degree, in intensity, it was not common.

It was rare?

It was almost unique.

Okay, good. Now, Mr. Flannery must have had some opinion of all this, some reaction to it.

Well yes, of course. He considered himself very lucky.

Very lucky? That's all?

Yes sir. But you have to understand that Miss Cabot's uniqueness was purely a question of degree. It was not at all rare for a woman to offer marijuana to Mr. Flannery. It was not rare for a woman to own a water bed. It wasn't rare for a woman to express her sexual interest in him. The only thing rare about Miss Cabot was the apparently obsessive, driven quality of her attitude, not its tendency, nor any of its specific manifestations.

He regarded her as merely sexually liberated?

Yes sir.

That doesn't seem to jibe with the words, "obsessive, driven quality," that you just used.

No, well . . . perhaps I am projecting my own present opinion onto Mr. Flannery. I think he simply felt he had struck gold.

"Struck gold"?

Found the perfect one-night stand. Found a woman who shared his drives, and perhaps carried them even farther than he himself.

Okay. Did they then smoke the marijuana?

Yes sir.

Was it already rolled into cigarettes? If not, who performed this task?

They used a water-filled hooka pipe, sir.

Miss Cabot seems to have been fond of gadgets.

Yes sir.

Did they smoke very much?

Yes sir. Several bowls full.

And it was of good quality?

Yes sir, excellent.

And they became quite intoxicated?

Very much so.

Stoned?

That is the term, yes sir.

Turned on?

Turned on, yes, I suppose so.

And then they had sex?

And then Miss Cabot put a record on the phonograph.

She had a phonograph in her bedroom?
Yes sir. She put on a Fred Astaire and Ginger Rogers record.
A record of dancing?
Of singing. Songs from their movies. By Jerome Kern, George Gershwin, Richard Rodgers, etc. I believe it was a rather rare recording, rather precious to Miss Cabot.
And then they had sex?
And then Miss Cabot talked to Mr. Flannery about the songs and the period they represented.
What was his reaction?
He wasn't interested in the songs. He became impatient.
I should say so. Did he express his impatience?
Physically.
You mean he struck her?
Oh no sir. I mean he fondled her.
In order to get things rolling?
Yes sir.
And did she respond?
She told him he had no soul.
Is that a quotation?
Yes sir. "You have no soul" is precisely what she said.
Did he take umbrage?
He continued to fondle her. She became excited.
And then they had sex?
And then she removed the record from the phonograph. She said, "All right, all right, but not in front of Fred and Ginger." And she got up to remove the record. In the process of lifting the needle—remember, she had smoked a large quantity of marijuana and was also rather aroused—she scratched the record badly. It made a terrible grating sound. She cried "Oh no!" and lifted the record off the turntable very delicately and examined the scratch.
It was bad?
The record was ruined, sir. At least the side she had been playing.
What was Mr. Flannery's reaction?

He said, "Never mind, never mind, come to bed."
Soothingly?
Gruffly.
And what did Miss Cabot do then?
She joined Mr. Flannery on the bed. First she put the record back in its sleeve and then she joined Mr. Flannery on the bed.
I see.
And then Miss Cabot began to cry.
Began to cry?
Yes sir. On Mr. Flannery's chest.
Did he try to console her?
In a manner of speaking.
You mean he resumed fondling her?
Yes sir.
And how did she respond?
Well, it's a curious thing. She became very powerfully aroused, but she continued to sob.
And then they had sex?
Yes sir.
Male superior?
Yes sir.
And Miss Cabot cried during the entire act?
Yes sir.
With tears and everything?
The whole works.
How long did the act last?
Approximately fifteen minutes.
Would you characterize it as passionate and vigorous?
Yes sir.
On both sides?
Yes sir.
Mr. Flannery did not find Miss Cabot's weeping to any extent dampened his ardor?
Apparently not.
Did both partners achieve satisfaction?
Orgasm.

I beg your pardon.

Both partners achieved orgasm.

Are you drawing a distinction between orgasm and satisfaction?

I . . . I'm not really sure, sir.

Well, all right. Then to be phenomenologically precise, both partners achieved orgasm?

Yes sir, they did.

Simultaneously?

Miss Cabot was a few seconds ahead of Mr. Flannery.

Did she then stop weeping?

No sir.

She continued to weep?

Yes sir.

What were Mr. Flannery's feelings about this?

He was perplexed.

But he was not at all moved?

Oh yes, of course.

He was moved?

That is correct.

Well, that's reassuring. Did he seek to console Miss Cabot?

He didn't know how to. He told her he was certain the phonograph record could be replaced, but this didn't seem to help. In fact, the very opposite. After that, he was afraid to say much of anything.

But she did eventually stop weeping?

Oh yes sir.

How long after?

How long after they had sex, do you mean?

All right.

I would estimate an hour.

An hour! She was crying for an hour?

Yes sir.

What happened during that time? Did they both remain on the bed?

Mr. Flannery left the room once to urinate.

But other than that?

Yes sir.

Did they both just lie there?

Miss Cabot just lay there. Mr. Flannery passed the time re-examining Miss Cabot's photograph album.

He did not say anything to her?

At one point he asked if there was anything he could do.

How did she reply?

She simply shook her head.

What happened when she stopped weeping?

She left the room. She was gone about fifteen minutes. When she returned, her eyes were still rather puffy, but she seemed much better.

Did Mr. Flannery contemplate leaving at any time?

Yes sir.

I thought he might have. What stopped him?

Well sir, it was after two o'clock in the morning, the bars were all closed, and he didn't like to go home to an empty bed.

All right. What happened after Miss Cabot returned to the bed?

He asked her how she felt. She said she felt fine and apologized for her emotional display. Then she leaned over and began to lick Mr. Flannery's penis.

She what?

She began to—

All right, I heard you, I heard you. Did this cause him to have another erection?

He already had one.

He already had one?

Yes, he had been studying her album, and for some reason . . . I don't mean to imply latent homosexuality; I think it was more the *idea* of the book . . .

And so they had sex again?

Yes sir.

Male superior?

Rear entry.

How long did it last this time?

About twenty minutes.

Did they both achieve—?

No sir, neither of them. At some point during the act it became evident to them both that that certain . . . germ of something that makes sex pleasurable was no longer present.

Are you referring to a psychological attitude?

No sir, I'm referring to a specific, localized, physical sensation. At any rate, Mr. Flannery was inclined to keep plugging—it was his experience that that feeling sometimes could be induced to return—but Miss Cabot finally grew impatient or disgusted or exhausted, and she said, "Are you close?' And he said, "Not too much." And she wrenched herself away from him and collapsed on the bed. They both went to sleep soon after.

Was there any further conversation between them?

Not that night.

Not even to say good-night?

No sir.

Was there any further physical contact?

No sir.

And at what time the next morning did Mr. Flannery awake?

Approximately ten-thirty.

Was Miss Cabot beside him?

No sir. She was not in the room. He found her in the kitchen, in a "rather dumpy" housecoat as he described it, brewing coffee. She asked him if he wanted breakfast, he said no, but asked if he could use her shower. She naturally said yes.

How did he feel at this time?

Slightly groggy, slightly flatulent, slightly sore, with a very bad taste in his mouth. But he also felt rather . . . rather exultant in his body. It's a difficult feeling to describe. He enjoyed walking around the apartment naked. He liked looking down at his distended albeit detumescent penis.

And so he showered?

First he urinated and brushed his teeth.

Brushed his teeth?

He generally carried a little collapsible tooth brush around with him for just such an eventuality as this. After showering, he dressed, leaving off his jacket and tie, and joined Miss Cabot in the kitchen for coffee.

How much longer did he stay?

About twenty minutes.

Did any conversation take place?

He asked for and wrote down her phone number.

Did he actually intend to see her again?

No, it was a matter of etiquette.

And then—?

After finishing his coffee—she made very good coffee, he told me—he said he had to be going. They both rose, and she accompanied him to the door.

How did he take his leave of her?

He thanked her for a wonderful evening.

Did she respond in any way?

She said, "You're welcome." And then he kissed her.

On the lips?

On the cheek.

And then he left?

Yes sir, he got into his car and drove home.

And that was his last contact with Miss Cabot?

Yes sir, his last and his only.

How would you say he rated the experience?

He said it was pleasant, but in terms of its potential slightly disappointing.

That was all?

Yes sir.

He had absolutely nothing further to say?

Not that I can think of.

Well, I don't have any further questions at this time. Needless to say, you are as usual subject to recall should that become necessary.

Yes sir, as usual. And you always know where you can find me.

Yes indeed. Well, thank you for your cooperation. You've been most helpful.

I've tried to do my best, sir.

And we appreciate it. We appreciate it very much.

DIRTY OLD MAN

Kenneth Bernard

LET ME TELL YOU about a strange thing I saw on the subway last week. I am a very regular rider of the subway. I find that it fits reasonably well into the routine of my life, and I take its difficulties in my stride. Sometimes I get a seat, sometimes I do not; sometimes its air blowers work, sometimes they do not; and usually I get where I want when I want. There is also reasonable diversion for an alert mind. The advertisements, for example, which are a fascinating study of our society. One can even perform certain inconspicuous exercises to keep trim, such as tightening and loosening one's buttocks. Most of all there are the people. I am an inveterate observer of people, a Peeping Tom on humanity, if you like. Sometimes I think I must be a little excessive because I do not merely look, I *feast* myself on people. Other riders read their newspapers passionately or retreat nimbly inside themselves or sleep. Very few look. And no one looks as greedily as I do. It is as if there were a great secret I must uncover. My looking is usually connected with fantasy. With women, I strip them naked and dwell on their possibilities of pleasure. How large their nipples, for example, or the thickness of their pubic hair. I look right through the clothing and come to my conclusions. With men, I mostly compare. Are they more self-assured than I, more successful in love, more impressive? Are they men of power and brilliance? Would they be hostile to me? Or are they obviously lesser creatures than I? Can I safely pity them for their shabby lives and shabby souls? Sometimes I go over the edge into violence and mutilate men for their arrogance, their total lack of humility. It is insufferable that any man would dare to belittle me, or laugh at me, or fail to take note of me. It is not even beyond me to kill with the proper provocation. I have wondered whether any of this ever showed on my face, whether my sighs or grunts were more than vividly imagined. It is difficult to say, for although I have great control over my facial expression, finding a bland look the least troublesome in most situations, were my fantasies to break through, no one would tell me. I once saw a teenage boy suddenly begin barking and snapping at people like a wolf. He was very serious about it. But he was totally ignored. A few people found a way to change their position very inconspicuously. But no one challenged him directly with his state. Had he urinated or defecated on them it would have been the same. Anyway, as I said, I feast on humanity; I gorge myself. And one day last week I was staring at an attractive girl in her early twenties. She was not ravishingly beautiful in her face, though its serenity and classic features made it most acceptable. But her body was irresistible. All the more so because she seemed so unaware of its irresistibility. It was, so to speak, waiting (quite selflessly) for sensual recognition; and I was ravaging it. Her face had the same quality. It was quiet, quiescent, but with full soft lips waiting to be touched, pressed, tasted, sucked, bitten. And one knew they would come alive, for their tranquility was not the result of stupidity, nor neurosis. They were simply something that had somehow ripened, like the rest of her, far too much without anyone seeing. And now all of her hung there, lusciously, maddeningly, for me. Yes, for me. In all truth, it should have been unsafe for her to appear in public in that condition. My absorption was total. But it was not, I soon discovered, uncontaminated. Sitting next to the girl was an old man. His mouth was freshly stained; from tobacco, possibly wine, I suppose. His head was sweaty, he needed a shave, he was unclean. On his face was the fat, silly grin of a senile man, and in his lap his left hand quivered from some disease. It was the hand that interfered with my concentration and pleasure. It seemed to have a life of its own. I could not ignore its insistent quivering. In fact, I saw the hand before I saw that its owner was staring at the girl with gross lust. And his eyes were not silly at all. They were hard, direct, and cold. I could see him inhaling all her smells, from the slightly stale perfume to the sweet sweaty flesh of her clinging thighs. He was obviously a connoisseur (still), despite the jelly brains in his head. Once or twice he looked at me; in derision, I thought. But I looked away. I hated him immediately, both because of what he was doing and because of his image, which to me was that of an end product to a lifetime of self-indulgence and debauchery. That he should be violating her was so ugly, so unsuitable, so grotesque. All I can say in mitigation was that she was oblivious of him and his stench also. We rode like that for several stations, people coming and going, the steady rumble of the train beneath me. I still sucked her in, but now self-consciously, with an eye also for the old man lest he catch me at my pleasure. I was aware somehow that it was a strangely unresolved situation. Several things bothered me. For example, if I got off before either of them, I would never know what happened. Of course, *nothing*, but the point was I would never know. If either he or the girl got off first, things would not be so bad. And if they both got off together before I did, well . . . . But no one got off at all, and I confess I became anxious, for my station was coming up soon. The old man himself gave our situation a definite configuration, the very thing that has been troubling me since. Just as the train was leaving one station, he lifted his trembling hand from his lap and put it on her thigh. I hate clichés, but quite literally I could not believe my eyes. My heart pounded and I held my breath. Never in all my experience had such a thing happened.

The girl at first semed not to notice, and I thought that, typically, she was going to avoid this unpleasantness by refusing to recognize it. But then, as he slowly moved his hand up under her dress, she turned to him with something like shock and disbelief in her face. It was rather like a rude and unexpected awakening. I have to give him credit for courage. He was looking straight at her with his hard eyes. And though his face had dissolved into a face of youthful idiocy, his eyes had a bizarre power in them. I could tell she was affected. I was not sure whether she did not do anything immediately because she was afraid, confused, or whatever. It is even possible that in some remote way she recognized him. I thought, very briefly, perhaps he is a crazy relative from the old country, and then realized how ridiculous the idea was. All I can say definitely is that she met his gaze, recognized the power there, and was silent. And during all these *seconds* he continued to move his hand upward. I became quite excited. I could see her undergarment (pale blue), see his fingers slide under and reach in. And at the same time, her legs going perceptibly slack, the look of shock was blended into a look of awkward but not unwelcome pleasure. She had gorgeous legs. Slim as they had seemed below (and shapely), up near her undergarment they were incredibly full and fleshy and white. And there where his hand, now no longer trembling, was clutching and opening rhythmically, there it seemed an unbelievable nest of sweetness and joy. At some point (unperceived by me) I had ceased to hate the old man and had begun to share with him a pleasure I could never have instigated myself. For even though I was a poor second, still I was getting so much more than I had ever imagined. I was supremely thrilled. If only, I thought, he would *rip off her pants.* I realized that at any moment I would have to leave because the next stop was mine. What could possibly justify my remaining? Surely it would be apparent to everyone why I was lingering. The girl's legs were now quite obviously spread. She had slid down in her seat and leaned to one side as the old man worked away with ferocious concentration. She was drooling, and with a lazy smile she muttered, "Dirty old man, *kiss me!*" Words that have been burned into me and shock me unbearably. She began to squeeze her breast, and I saw a hard nipple pressing against her garment. As the train pulled into the station the old man reached over with his other hand and began pulling down her pants. I was furious that it was my stop, and just as I exited I saw a breathtaking expanse of soft white belly with a dark fringe on the bottom. It was sheer madness, and I clutched myself painfully in the groin as I shouldered my way onto the platform. I walked slowly so as to peek in when the train left. But I saw little. It was already going too fast, and he was far too hunched over her. And he laughed, a weird, piercing goatlike laugh, almost of triumph, as he passed me.· I was certain he was laughing at me. I thought of various expedients, such as getting a cab and racing two or three stops ahead and getting back of the train. But it was all very problematical. I didn't know how much money I had. There would be no cab handy, or there would be too many red lights, or there would be a line at the token booth and I would miss the train, or they would already have gotten off. I can safely say that I was quite confused as I walked up into the street. The memory of that ride has caused me great discomfort. I find I am regularly getting on the same train at the same time, hoping to see her again. But what good would it do? Would I even recognize her? And if I did and sat next to her and put my hand on her thigh she would scream or slap me. I should be arrested and exposed in the newspapers. I therefore keep returning to the specific occasion itself. What if *that* day I had put my hand on her thigh (How beautiful if was!)? What if *that* day I had not gotten off at my stop? What if I had taken advantage of her *with* the old man? . . . What *did* happen? *What did happen?* I cannot escape that question. Who was that old man and what was his disease that made his hand tremble so? I feel profoundly cheated and profoundly mutilated in my soul. I have been robbed of the sweetest of mysteries. *She should have let me know I could touch her! She didn't have to put up with a senile dirty old man. God damn him to hell!*

THE ELEVATOR

Robert Coover

1

EVERY MORNING without exception and without so much as relecting upon it, Martin takes the self-service elevator to the fourteenth floor, where he works. He will do so today. When he first arrives, however, he finds the lobby empty, the old building still possessed of its feinting shadows and silences, desolate though mutely expectant, and he wonders if today it might not turn out differently.

It is 7:30 A.M.: Martin is early and therefore has the elevator entirely to himself. He steps inside: this tight cell! he thinks with a kind of unsettling shock, and confronts the panel of numbered buttons. One to fourteen, plus "B" for basement. Impulsively, he presses the "B"—seven years and yet to visit the basement! He snorts at his timidity.

After a silent moment, the doors rumble shut. All night alert waiting for this moment! The elevator sinks slowly into the earth. The stale gloomy odors of the old building having aroused in him an unreasonable sense of dread and loss, Martin imagines suddenly he is descending into hell. *Tra la perduta gente*, yes! A mild shudder shakes him. Yet, Martin decides firmly, would that it were so. The old carrier halts with a quiver. The automatic doors yawn open. Nothing, only a basement. It is empty and nearly dark. It is silent and meaningless.

Martin smiles inwardly at himself, presses the number "14." "Come on, old Charon," he declaims broadly, "Hell's the other way!"

2

Martin waited miserably for the stench of intestinal gas to reach his nostrils. Always the same. He supposed it was Carruther, but he could never prove it. Not so much as a telltale squeak. But it was Carruther who always led them, and though the other faces changed, Carruther was always among them.

There were seven in the elevator: six men and the young girl who operated it. The girl did not participate. She was surely offended, but she never gave a hint of it. She possessed a surface detachment that not even Carruther's crude proposals could penetrate. Much less did she involve herself in the coarse interplay of men. Yet certainly, Martin supposed, they were a torment to her.

And, yes, he was right—there it was, faint at first, almost sweet, then slowly thickening, sickening, crowding up on him—

"Hey! Who fahred thet shot?" cried Carruther, starting it.

"Mart fahred-it!" came the inexorable reply. And then the crush of loud laughter.

"*What!* Is that Martin fartin' again?" bellowed another, as their toothy thicklipped howling congealed around him.

"Aw *please*, Mart! *don't fart!*" cried yet another. It would go on until they left the elevator. The elevator was small: their laughter packed it, jammed at the walls. "Have a heart, Mart! don't *part* that fart!"

It's not me, *it's not me*, Martin insisted. But only to himself. It was no use. It was fate. Fate and Carruther. (More laughter, more brute jabs.) A couple times he had protested. "Aw, Marty, you're just modest!" Carruther had thundered. Booming voice, big man. Martin hated him.

One by one, the other men filed out of the elevator at different floors, holding their noses. "Old farty Marty!" they would shout to anyone they met on their way out, and it always got a laugh, up and down the floor. The air cleared slightly each time the door opened.

In the end, Martin was always left alone with the girl who operated the elevator. His floor, the fourteenth, was the top one. When it all began, long ago, he had attempted apologetic glances toward the girl on exiting, but she had always turned her shoulder to him. Maybe she thought he was making a play for her. Finally he was forced to adopt the custom of simply ducking out as quickly as possible. She would in any case assume his guilt.

Of course, there was an answer to Carruther. Yes, Martin knew it, had rehearsed it countless times. The only way to meet that man was on his home ground. And he'd do it, too. When the time came.

3

Martin is alone on the elevator with the operator, a young girl. She is neither slender nor plump, but fills charmingly her orchid-colored uniform. Martin greets her in his usual friendly manner and she returns his greeting with a smile. Their eyes meet momentarily. Hers are brown.

When Martin enters the elevator, there are actually several other people crowded in, but as the elevator climbs through the musky old building, the others, singly or in groups, step out. Finally, Martin is left alone with the girl who operates the elevator. She grasps the lever, leans against it, and the cage sighs upward. He speaks to her, makes a lighthearted joke about elevators. She laughs and

Alone on the elevator with the girl, Martin thinks: if this

elevator should crash, I would sacrifice my life to save her. Her back is straight and subtle. Her orchid uniform skirt is tight, tucks tautly under her blossoming hips, describes a kind of cavity there. Perhaps it is night. Her calves are muscular and strong. She grasps the lever.

The girl and Martin are alone on the elevator, which is rising. He concentrates on her round hips until she is forced to turn and look at him. His gaze coolly courses her belly, her pinched and belted waist, past her taut breasts, meets her excited stare. She breathes deeply, her lips parted. They embrace. Her breasts plunge softly against him. Her mouth is sweet. Martin has forgotten whether the elevator is climbing or not.

4

Perhaps Martin will meet Death on the elevator. Yes, going out for lunch one afternoon. Or to the drugstore for cigarettes. He will press the button in the hall on the fourteenth floor, the doors will open, a dark smile will beckon. The shaft is deep. It is dark and silent. Martin will recognize Death by His silence. He will not protest.

> He *will* protest! oh God! no matter what the
> the sense of emptiness underneath breath lurching out
> The shaft is long and narrow. The shaft is dark.
> He will not protest.

5

Martin, as always and without so much as reflecting upon it, takes the self-service elevator to the fourteenth floor, where he works. He is early, but only by a few minutes. Five others join him, greetings are exchanged. Though tempted, he is not able to risk the "B," but presses the "14" instead. Seven years!

As the automatic doors press together and the elevator begins its slow complaining ascent, Martin muses absently on the categories. This small room, so commonplace and so compressed, he observes with a certain melancholic satisfaction, this elevator contains them all: space, time, cause, motion, magnitude, class. Left to our own devices, we would probably discover them. The other passengers chatter with self-righteous smiles (after all, they are on time) about the weather, the elections, the work that awaits them today. They stand, apparently motionless, yet moving. Motion: perhaps that's all there is to it after all. Motion and the medium. Energy and weighted particles. Force and matter. The image grips him purely. Ascent and the passive reorganization of atoms.

At the seventh floor, the elevator stops and a woman departs it. Only a trace of her perfume remains. Martin alone remarks—to himself, of course—her absence, as the climb begins again. Reduced by one. But the totality of the universe is suffused: each man contains all of it, loss is inconceivable. Yet, if that is so—and a tremor shudders coolly through Martin's body—then the totality is as nothing. Martin gazes around at his four remaining fellow passengers, a flush of compassion washing in behind the tremor. One must always be alert to the possibility of action, he reminds himself. But none apparently need him. If he could do the work for them today, give them the grace of a day's contemplation . . . .

The elevator halts, suspended and vibrant, at the tenth floor. Two men leave. Two more intermediate stops, and Martin is alone. He has seen them safely through. Although caged as ever in his inexorable melancholy, Martin nonetheless smiles as he steps out of the self-service elevator on the fourteenth floor. "I am pleased to participate," he announces in full voice. But, as the elevator doors close behind him and he hears the voided descent, he wonders: Wherein now is the elevator's totality?

6

The cable snaps at the thirteenth floor. There is a moment's deadly motionlessness—then a sudden breathless plunge! The girl, terrified, turns to Martin. They are alone. Though inside his heart is bursting its chambers in terror, he remains outwardly composed. "I think it is safer lying on your back," he says. He squats to the floor, but the girl remains transfixed with shock. Her thighs are round and sleek under the orchid skirt, and in the shadowed—"Come," he says. "You may lie on me. My body will absorb part of the impact." Her hair caresses his cheek, her buttocks press like a sponge into his groin. In love, moved by his sacrifice, she weeps. To calm her, he clasps her heaving abdomen, strokes her soothingly. The elevator whistles as it drops.

7

Martin worked late in the office, clearing up the things that needed to be done before the next day, routine matters, yet part of the uninterrupted necessity that governed his daily life. Not a large office, Martin's, though he needed no larger, essentially neat except for the modest clutter on top of his desk. The room was equipped only with that desk and a couple chairs, bookcases lining one wall, calendar posted on another. The overhead lamp was off, the only light in the office being provided by the fluorescent lamp on Martin's desk.

Martin signed one last form, sighed, smiled. He retrieved a cigarette, half-burned but still lit, from the ashtray, drew heavily on it, then, as he exhaled with another prolonged sigh, doubled the butt firmly in the black bowl of the ashtray. Still extinguishing it, twisting it among the heap of crumpled filters in the ashtray, he glanced idly at his watch. He was astonished to discover that the watch said twelve-thirty—and had stopped! Already after midnight!

He jumped up, rolled down his sleeves, buttoned them, whipped his suit jacket off the back of his chair, shoved his arms into it. Bad enough twelve-thirty—but my God! how much *later* was it? The jacket still only three-quarters of the way up his back, tie askew, he hastily stacked the loose papers on his desk and switched off the lamp. He stumbled through the dark room out into the hallway, lit by one dull yellow bulb, pulled his office door to behind him. The thick solid catch knocked hollowly in the vacant corridor.

He buttoned his shirt collar, straightened his tie and the collar of his jacket, which was doubled under on his right shoulder, as he hurried down the passageway past the other closed office doors of the fourteenth floor to the self-service elevator, his heels hammering away the stillness on the marble floor. He trembled, inexplicably. The profound silence of the old building disturbed him. Relax, he urged himself: we'll know what time it is soon enough. He pushed the button for the elevator, but nothing happened. Don't tell me I have to walk down! he muttered bitterly to himself. He poked the button again, harder, and this time he heard below a solemn rumble, a muffled thump, and an indistinct grinding plaint that grieved progressively nearer. It stopped and the doors of the elevator opened to receive him. Entering, Martin felt a sudden need to glance back over his shoulder, but he suppressed it.

Once inside, he punched the number "1" button on the self-service panel. The doors closed, but the elevator, instead of descending, continued to climb. Goddamn this old wreck! Martin swore irritably, and he jiggled the "1" button over and over. Just this night! The elevator stopped, the doors opened, Martin stepped out. Later, he wondered why he had done so. The doors slid shut behind him, he heard the elevator descend, its amused rumble fading distantly. Although here it was utterly dark, shapes seemed to form. Though he could see nothing distinctly, he was fully aware that he was not alone. His hand fumbled on the wall for the elevator button. Cold wind gnawed at his ankles, the back of his neck. Fool! wretched fool! he wept, there *is* no fifteenth floor! Pressed himself against the wall, couldn't find the button, couldn't even find the elevator door, and even the very wall was only

8

Carruther's big voice boomed in the small cage.

"Mart fahred-it!" came the certain reply. The five men laughed. Martin flushed. The girl feigned indifference. The fetor of fart vapours reeked in the tight elevator.

"Martin, damn it, cut the fartin'!"

Martin fixed his cool gaze on them. "Carruther fucks his mother," he said firmly. Carruther hit him full in the face, his glasses splintered and fell, Martin staggered back against the wall. He waited for the second blow, but it didn't come. Someone elbowed him, and he slipped to the floor. He knelt there, weeping softly, searched with his hands for his glasses. Martin tasted the blood from his nose, trickling into his mouth. He couldn't find his glasses, couldn't even see.

"Look out, baby!" Carruther thundered. "Farty Marty's jist tryin' to git a free peek up at your pretty drawers!" Crash of laughter. Martin felt the girl shrink from him.

9

Her soft belly presses like a sponge into his groin. No, safer on your back, love, he thinks, but pushes the thought away. She weeps in terror, presses her hot wet mouth against his. To calm her, he clasps her soft buttocks, strokes them soothingly. So sudden is the plunge, they seem suspended in air. She has removed her skirt. How will it feel? he wonders.

10

Martin, without so much as reflecting on it, automatically takes the self-service elevator to the fourteenth floor, where he works. The systematizing, that's what's wrong, he concludes, that's what cracks them up. He is late, but only by a few minutes. Seven others join him, anxious, sweating. They glance nervously at their watches. None of them presses the "B" button. Civilities are hurriedly interchanged.

Their foolish anxiety seeps out like a bad spirit, enters Martin. He finds himself looking often at his watch, grows impatient with the elevator. Take it easy, he cautions himself. Their blank faces oppress him. Bleak. Haunted. Tyrannized by their own arbitrary regimentation of time. Torture self-imposed, yet in all probability inescapable. The elevator halts jerkily at the third floor, quivering their sallow face-flesh. The frown. No one has pushed the three. A woman enters. They all nod, harumph, make jittery little hand motions to incite the doors to close. They are all more or less aware of the woman (she has delayed them, damn her!), but only Martin truly remarks—to himself—her whole presence, as the elevator resumes its upward struggle. The accretion of tragedy. It goes on, ever giving birth to itself. Up and down, up and down. Where will it end? he wonders. Her perfume floats gloomily in the stale air. These deformed browbeaten mind-animals. Suffering and insufferable. Up and down. He closes his eyes. One by one, they leave him.

He arrives, alone, at the fourteenth floor. He steps out of the old elevator, stares back into its spent emptiness. There, only there, is peace, he concludes wearily. The elevator doors press shut.

11

Here on this elevator, my elevator, created by me, moved by me, doomed by me, I, Martin, proclaim my omnipotence! In the end, doom touches all! MY doom! I impose it TREMBLE!

12

The elevator shrieks insanely as it drops. Their naked bellies slap together, hands grasp, her vaginal mouth closes sponge-like on his rigid organ. Their lips lock, tongues knot. The bodies: how will they find them? Inwardly, he laughs. He thrusts up off the plummeting floor. Her eyes are brown and, with tears, love him.

13

But—ah!—the doomed, old man, the DOOMED! What are they to us, to ME? ALL! We, I love! Let their flesh sag and dewlaps tremble, let their odors offend, let their cruelty mutilate, their stupidity enchain—but let them laugh, father! FOREVER! let them cry!

14

but hey! theres this guy see he gets on the goddamn elevator and its famous how hes got him a doodang about five feet long Im not kidin you none five feet and he gets on the—yeah! can you imagine a bastard like that boardin a friggin pubic I mean public elevator? hoohah! no I dont know his name Mert I think or Mort but the crux is he is possessed of this motherin digit biggern ole Rahab see—do with it? I dont know I think he wraps it around his leg or carries it over his shoulder or somethin jee*zuss!* what a problem! why I bet hes *killt* more poor bawdies than I ever dipped my poor worm in! once he was even a—listen! Carruther tells this as the goddamn truth I mean he *respects* that bastard—he was even one a them jackoff gods I forget how you call them over there with them Eyetalians after the big war see them dumb types when they seen him furl out this here five foot hose of his one day—he was just trying to get the goddamn knots out Carruther says—why they thought he musta been a goddamn jackoff god or somethin and wanted to like employ him or whatever you do with a god and well Mort he figgered it to be a not so miserable occupation dont you know better anyhow than oildrillin with it in Arabia or stoppin holes in Dutch dikes like hes been doin so the bastard he stays on there a time and them little quiff there in that Eyetalian place they grease him up with hogfat or olive oil and all workin together like vested virgins they pull him off out there in the fields and spray the crops and well Mort he says *he* says its the closest hes ever got to the real mccoy jeezuss! hes worth a thousand laughs! and they bring him all the old aunts and grannies and he splits them open a kinda stupendous euthanasia for the old ladies and he blesses all their friggin procreations with a swat of his doodang and even does a little welldiggin on the side but he gets in trouble with the Roman churchers on accounta not bein circumcised and they wanta whack it off but Mort says no and they cant get close to him with so prodigious a batterin ram as hes got so they work a few miracles on him and wrinkle up his old pud with holy water and heat up his semen so it burns up the fields and even one day ignites a goddamn volcano and *jeezuss!* he wastes no time throwin that thing over his shoulder and hightailin it *outa* there I can tell you! but now like Im sayin them pastoral days is dead and gone and hes goin up and down in elevators like the rest of us and so here he is boardin the damn cage and theys a bunch of us bastards clownin around with the little piece who operates that deathtrap kinda brushin her swell butt like a occasional accident and sweet jeezus her gettin fidgety and hot and half fightin us off and half pullin us on and playin with that lever *zoom!* wingin up through that scraper and just then ole Carruther jeezuss he really breaks you up sometimes that crazy bastard he hefts up her little purple skirt and whaddaya know! the little quiff aint wearin no skivvies! its somethin *beautiful* man I mean a sweet cleft peach right outa some foreign orchard and poor ole Mort he is kinda part gigglin and part hurtin and for a minute the rest of us dont see the pointa the whole agitation but then that there incredible thing suddenly pops up quivery right under his chin like the friggin eye of god for crissake and then theres this big wild rip and man! it rears up and splits outa there like a goddamn redwood topplin *gawdamighty!* and knocks old Carruther *kapow!* right to the deck! his best buddy and that poor little cunt she takes one glim of that impossible rod wheelin around in there and whammin the walls and she faints dead away and *jeezusss!* she tumbles right on that elevator lever and man! I thought for a minute we was *all* dead

15 . . .

They plunge, their damp bodies fused, pounding furiously, in terror, in joy, the impact is

I, Martin, proclaim against all dooms the indestructible seed

Martin does not take the self-service elevator to the fourteenth floor, as is his custom, but, reflecting upon it for once and out of a strange premonition, determines instead to walk the fourteen flights. Halfway up, he hears the elevator hurtle by him and then the splintering crash from below. He hesitates, poised on the stair. Inscrutable is the word he finally settles upon. He pronounces it aloud, smiles faintly, sadly, somewhat wearily, then continues his tedious climb, pausing from time to time to stare back down the stairs behind him.

A SOLDIER IN ICELAND

Barton Midwood

HE ENTERED NOISILY. I hoped that he would take a seat far away but he took the aisle seat in my row.

A stewardess, a dark-haired Icelandic woman, came up to him.

"Are you going to behave yourself today?" she said.

"I'm sober this time," he said.

"Congratulations." She smiled.

He turned to me. "I was drunk yesterday and they kicked me off ten minutes before takeoff. You can't blame them. I was singing and I can't carry a tune."

The stewardess laughed.

"Icelanders are a musical people, you see," he continued. "They kicked me off very musically. I've got no complaint. The airline even paid the hotel bill in Luxembourg. That was hos*pit*able, don't you think?"

He repeated the word "hospitable" and roared with laughter.

The stewardess smiled at the top of his head with maternal superiority and walked away.

He leaned into the aisle to watch her. "She has hair all over her legs," he said. He meditated for a moment. "I can't stand that," he concluded with a scowl, and meditated for another moment. Then he turned to me and said cheerfully, "My name is Hans. Hans Welleck."

I told him my name and we shook hands. He had a two- or three-day growth of beard and his eyes were red and swollen and there was a scar from a recent wound just over his left cheekbone. His clothes, a light brown gabardine suit and a white shirt open at the collar, were wrinkled and stained as though he had been sleeping in them.

We were on an Icelandic flight from Luxembourg to New York, a twelve- or thirteen-hour trip with a one-hour stopover in Iceland at Keflavik Airport. Between us was an empty seat that was occupied a few minutes before takeoff by a thin, attractive woman, about twenty-four years old, who became talkative as soon as we were in the air.

Her name was Mary. She told us she had been working as a secretary for an English executive in Belgium and was now returning to New York to marry a man she hadn't seen in two years. They had been corresponding. He had been a law student when they first met. Last month he had passed his New York bar examination and had written a letter proposing marriage.

"So I accepted," she said. "Life in Belgium was all right, but empty. It was just smooth sailing in shallow waters."

"That's the sort of sailing I'd like to try some day," said Welleck. He laughed with derision and then muttered something under his breath, looking as though he wanted to plunge into her shallow waters and shout.

In fact, he alarmed her and she was put off. She took up a magazine and leafed through it, and he ordered a gin and tonic from the stewardess.

I pushed back the top of my chair, shut my eyes, and managed to fall asleep.

When I woke about an hour later. Welleck's face was flushed and he was talking to Mary.

He was pointing at the scar on his cheekbone. "I got this in a fight in bar in Saigon. This idiot of a sergeant didn't like my face or something. 'How come you don't have any insignias on your uniform?' he says. 'I'm an engineer,' I tell him. So he starts to make fun of engineers. I just laugh. What do I care about the engineers? But he won't quit, you see. I try to keep my mouth shut—but he won't quit! Finally when he says why don't I get a gun like him and all his buddies and do some *real* work in this war, I can't take it any longer. 'Listen, friend,' I say, 'yesterday in fifteen minutes I killed more men than you have bubbles in your beer.' Then I beat the hell out of him and left."

He paused, apparently expecting an encouraging reply, but Mary stared at him in bewilderment.

He was ill at ease. "Some world, eh?" he said.

"I don't understand," she said. "Why didn't you have insignias?"

Welleck noticed that I was awake and he seemed relieved. He winked at me, as though he and I shared a secret. "Because we don't wear insignias," he said.

"Who do you mean by 'we'?" said Mary sternly.

"Professionals. I'm a professional."

"In plain words, you're a mercenary."

Welleck smiled at her and then again winked at me, but did not answer.

"Who do you fight for?" she continued.

He laughed. "Myself."

"But who *pays* you?"

"The American government."

"That's interesting," I said. "What's you job?"

"Two thousand dollars a month," he said.

"No, I meant what do you do?"

"Automatic weapons. I've been in Vietnam for nearly two years. Look, I'll show you something."

He reached under his seat and came up with a brown leather case that was full of photographs. He leafed through them, then handed one to me. "That's my monkey," he said.

It was a photograph of a monkey perched on the hood of a jeep. Standing beside the jeep was a man about thirty-five years old. He was wearing Army fatigues and was smiling at the camera.

"Who's the man?" I said.

"Jensen. He's a Dane. We've been everywhere together. The Congo, the Dominican Republic, Korea. He's taking care of Raffles for me."

"Raffles is your monkey."

"Yes."

"Where are they?"

"Right there." He pointed at the photograph. "Just near the Cambodian border. I've had all kinds of pets."

"Are you going back?"

"I'll stay a couple of days in New York first. I ship out from San Francisco next week." He began to leaf through the photographs again. "Here, look at this one. She got hit by a car in Wiesbaden."

It was a photograph of two small children and an Afghan hound.

"Who are the children?" said Mary.

"My son and my daughter. I had a lion cub when I was in Africa. One day him go. I have a picture of him somewhere."

He began to look for it, but Mary interrupted him. "Do you have any more pictures of your children?"

He studied her a moment suspiciously.

"They're fine-looking children," she added.

"Thanks," he said.

"When was the last time you saw them?"

"Three days ago. They're in Munich with my mother."

"What's she doing in Munich?"

"She was born there. So was I."

Mary looked at him with interest. "I thought you were American."

"I went to school in Philadelphia. I grew up there. My step-father was American. When he died, my mother moved back to

Germany. That was about three years ago. Here, look at this. That's Daisy." Welleck handed me another photograph of Jensen smiling at the camera, now with a parrot perched on his shoulder. "And here's another picture of the children." This he gave to Mary.

"Is that your wife with them?" she said.

"Yes."

"That's Jensen again," I said.

"Yes, in the Dominican Republic."

"Isn't your wife with the children in Munich?" said Mary.

"I don't know where she is. We just divorced." Welleck took the photograph from her and handed it to me. "Beautiful woman, eh?"

"Yes," I said.

"I gave her everything she asked for. A forty-thousand-dollar house in Wiesbaden, a Mercedes, a nurse for the children, two fur coats, everything. Two months ago I get leave. I figure I'll surprise her. I get to my house about ten o'clock at night and a guy answers the door. It looks like I woke him up and he's wearing my pajamas. He wants to know who I am and what I want. 'I am the person who owns this house,' I say, 'and I want my pajamas back.' Then I beat the hell out of him. He was a captain in the Air Force. An American." Welleck paused, preoccupied.

"So you divorced her," said Mary, unashamedly prodding him.

Welleck seemed not to mind. "Not that time," he said. "I just worked her over a bit. She said she was sorry, and I forgave her. Like a fool. I hadn't had any in six months. I wouldn't touch the street girls in Saigon. We had five days together just like old times. Then I took a trip to Munich to see my mother. Three days later I come home and the same guy answers the door in my pajamas. This time I put him in the hospital. *Then* I divorced her." He leaned toward Mary. "It drives me wild. One minute she lies in my arms and tell me she loves me forever and the next minute some idiot is wearing my pajamas. I can't put the two minutes together. Do you see?"

Mary lowered her eyes. "Yes."

"Anyway, the court gave me custody of the children. She can't see them without my permission."

"What happened to the captain?" I said.

"I fixed him good. I got him shipped out to Saigon. I know a colonel in Wiesbaden. Good friend of mine. Hey, do you want to see something special? Look at this."

He began to leaf through the photographs in his leather case again and brought out a picture of Joan Baez, the singer. She was standing in an alley near the back door of a theater and was caught in the middle of an admiring crowd. She was signing an autograph book and smiling.

"I took that picture myself," said Welleck. He had tears in his eyes from talking about his wife and it was painfully apparent that he was making an attempt to get a grip on himself by changing the subject. "You don't see a picture like that every day," he added. "Only professionals get pictures like that."

"It's a good picture," I agreed.

"I'm just nuts about Joan Baez," he said.

"That's ironical," said Mary.

"What do you mean?" said Welleck.

"I mean, she's a peacemonger. I should think you'd hate her politics."

"Why? I don't. I *like* her politics."

"Well, I'm sure she wouldn't like yours."

Welleck's face reddened; he was hurt. "Why? What do you know about my politics?"

Mary shrugged her shoulders and kept silent.

"Who's talking about politics anyway?" continued Welleck. "I'm talking about *mu*sic not politics. I don't give a damn about politics."

Sulking, he started to put the photograph back in the leather case, but then an idea seemed to occur to him and he turned to

Mary. "Look, I'd like you to have this photograph. I mean, it would be nice if you took it. I've got about fifteen prints of it."

"No, no, really," said Mary. "It's kind of you but I couldn't—

Prepared for the rebuff, Welleck promptly closed the leather case and interrupted her. "Look, can I buy you two a drink?"

Mary glanced at me.

"Sure," I said. "Let's all get drunk."

Welleck was delighted. '*That's* the spirit! Stewardess!"

The stewardess, who was just a few yards down the aisle, signaled that she would be with him in a minute.

"What about you, Mary?" he said.

She smiled at him. "All right. Gin and tonic?"

"That's *my* drink too!" He was excited as a schoolboy.

The stewardess appeared. He smiled up at her and there were still tears in his eyes. "We'd like some drinks, miss."

"Gin and tonic for the lady and myself." He turned to me. "What about you?"

"Vodka and tomato juice."

"Bloody Mary for the gentleman," he said.

Mary winced and glared at him sharply, but he was looking elsewhere.

The stewardess walked away.

Welleck turned to Mary. "Did you notice her legs?"

"No," said Mary.

"Hair. You never see that on an American woman."

Mary was embarrassed. "Oh?"

"What's your opinion?"

"Of what?"

"This business."

"Which business."

"Women with hair on their legs."

"I don't know. Will you excuse me for a minute?"

He stood up to let her pass. She went down the aisle toward the front of the plane and disappeared into the ladies' room.

"Did I say something wrong?" he said.

"I think you insulted her when you called my drink a Bloody Mary," I said.

He slapped his forehead and shut his eyes. "I'm an idiot."

"Don't worry about it."

"I just didn't think! I *always* call it a Bloody Mary."

"She thinks you said it deliberately."

"But I didn't!"

"I know."

"I just didn't put the two together."

When she reappeared in the aisle, Welleck looked up anxiously. She had gathered her hair into a severe ponytail and had applied mascara on her eyelashes and fresh lipstick.

Welleck leaned toward me. "War paint," he whispered. He stood up to let her pass.

She bestowed a smile upon him, a tolerant smile, and sat down, quite erect, and folded her hands in her lap. "Tell us how you learned this curious profession of yours, Mr. Welleck," she said abruptly.

Welleck was taken aback. He blushed and looked at his hands; he took a breath, holding it a moment, preparing to appease her. "I joined the Legion when I was seventeen. You can call me Hans."

"The French *For*eign Legion?"

"Yes."

She laughed condescendingly. "I thought that was done only in prewar movies."

"In my time a lot of guys joined the Legion," he said, good-naturedly. "Nowadays they let their hair grow and go to San Francisco. If I were born twenty years later, maybe I'd have gone to San Francisco myself."

"Tell us, Mr. Welleck, was it some fascinating heartless woman, some *femme fatale*, that drove you to make such a dramatic move?"

"No, it was my stepfather. Are you making fun of me?"

Mary fluttered her eyelids mockingly at him and smiled.

"My stepfather and me, we didn't get along," he continued, choking back his pride. "One day I cut him with a knife. In the right shoulder. I left that day and never went back. I had a friend who'd joined the Legion a couple of weeks before, so I knew how to go about it. The Legion trained me. I was with them four years, mainly in Algiers. After that, I could fight where I liked and name my own price."

"You've murdered people in many countries then," said Mary. "How fascinating."

"I suppose you could put it that way," he said softly.

"You'd put it another way, I'm sure."

"Look," he said, "if you're upset that I called his drink a Bloody Mary, I want you to know I didn't mean anything by it. I always call it a Bloody Mary."

Her face reddened. "So do I."

"Then why are you upset?"

"I'm not upset, Mr. Welleck, and I don't care what you call your drink."

"*His* drink."

"*Any*one's drink."

"You've got me wrong, Mary. I'm not a murderer. I'm a soldier."

"He's right," I said. "He's a soldier."

Welleck was glad of the support. Suddenly he became excited. "Did you read the story in *Newsweek* last year? They had three pages on mercenaries."

"No," said Mary.

"*He's* read it, I'll bet." He turned to me. "Did you?"

"Yes," I lied.

"See? He reads."

"What did *Newsweek* say?" said Mary.

"They said that we are the most highly skilled soldiers in the world, that's what they said."

"You must be very proud of yourself."

"You look up that story in *Newsweek*. You'll learn something."

"What will I learn?"

"Lots of things. Like about Leopoldville. We went into Leopoldville four hundred strong. Do you know how many men we lost? Out of four hundred, how many do you think we lost?"

"I don't know and I don't care."

"Guess."

"Two hundred and fifty," she said.

Welleck slapped his knees and roared with laughter. Mary stared at him in horror. Suddenly he stopped laughing, looked her in the eye, and held four fingers in front of her face.

"Four men," he said. Then he winked knowingly at me and leaned back in his seat. "*Newsweek* was right: very *highly skilled soldiers*. There are only a handful of us, you know. Mainly Danes, Norwegians, and Swedes. Not too many Germans like me."

"Yes, it's always the same old boys," he added with pride and nostalgia. "Wherever I go, the same old faces."

"Why are you fighting in Vietnam?" said Mary.

"I told you: the money."

"I don't remember your telling me that."

"That's because you don't listen."

"Would you fight for the other side if they paid more?"

"I don't like the Communists."

"Why not?"

"If you'd seen what I've seen, you'd understand."

"Like what?"

"I've seen a few things that I wouldn't care to talk about."

"Just give us an example."

"Communists have no respect for human life," he said with exasperation.

To illustrate his point he told a story about a massacre in the Congo. An immense body of half-naked men charged his unit, most of them armed with sticks. They rushed into a wall of machine gun fire and kept coming until all of them were dead.

"These people are insane," he concluded. "Human life

doesn't mean a thing to them. I don't know how many I killed in half an hour. Hundreds, thousands maybe."

There was a pause. Welleck rubbed his eyes. Mary's hands were trembling.

After a few minutes she spoke. "Mr. Welleck?" she said.

"Yes?"

"I don't either."

"You don't what?" he said, puzzled.

"I don't have respect for human life."

"Oh?"

"Yes." Then she leaned toward him and spat in his face.

Then she stood up and said, "Please let me pass."

Welleck turned pale and he gaped at her. According to convention, if you are sitting in the aisle seat on an airplane and a woman beside you asks permission to pass, you should rise from your seat and step aside into the aisle. But Mary had just spat in Welleck's face and he was trembling. What should he do, and why did she spit at him?

"Please let me pass," she repeated impatiently.

The stewardess appeared with our drinks on a white plastic tray.

"Sorry I took so long," she said.

"I'm changing my seat," said Mary.

The stewardess glanced at the top of Welleck's head and clicked her tongue in an expression of disapproval. Then she smiled sympathetically at Mary. "That's all right, dear. There are some empty seats up front. I'll bring your drink in a minute."

"Will you *please* let me pass?" said Mary.

Welleck just sat there gazing dumbly at her and trembling.

"The lady is talking to you," said the stewardess.

Welleck stood up and stepped into the aisle. He took a white handkerchief from his pocket and wiped his face. Mary sidestepped out of the seat, hurried toward the front of the plane, and slipped into a seat just behind the cockpit.

A passenger, a rather fat boy about eleven or twelve years

old, came down the aisle and tapped Welleck's shoulder. He wanted to pass. Welleck, after staring confusedly at him for a moment, slid back into the seat to make way.

Then the stewardess offered me my drink and I took it. Welleck made no move to take his, however. The stewardess irritably let down the little table attached to the back of the seat in front of him. Then she put his drink on it and walked away.

The man in the seat across the aisle—an old man who had been putting together a complicated balsa-wood model of a nineteenth-century whaling schooner since takeoff—leaned toward Welleck and said, "If I were you, I wouldn't let her get away with that." He spoke with a Midwestern American drawl.

Welleck glared at him.

"Spitting's a disgusting habit," continued the old man. "She your wife?"

Welleck turned away and closed his fist around the bottle of tonic in front of him.

"People are scumbags," he said.

This was not said to anyone in particular, but the old man understood that it was directed partly at him. He shrugged his shoulders and went back to his whaling schooner.

Welleck stared at the bottle of tonic for a while.

"Are you all right?" I said.

He kept silent and would not look at me, so I let him alone.

Eventually he took a small bottle from his jacket pocket. He emptied three large white pills into his palm, tossed all of them into his mouth at once, and washed them down with the tonic. Ten minutes later he was fast asleep.

He was still asleep when the plane landed at Keflavik Airport four hours later. I saw the stewardess shaking his shoulder as I was making my way to the exit.

When he appeared in the terminal, he went straight for Mary, who was looking at a magazine at the newsstand. He began talking to her with anxious exaggerated gestures. I was about fifty yards off near the coffee bar and couldn't hear what he was saying. Mary just looked at him dumbly and two minutes later she turned her back on him and went into the ladies' room.

I wanted to avoid Welleck myself. I stepped out of the terminal building on the side facing the runways and lit a cigarette.

It was about forty degrees and there was no snow on the ground. There was a light breeze. From here the country looked as flat as a tabletop, though in the distance one could see some hills shrouded in mist. Behind me were the terminal's large glass windows, which were opaque because the sky was reflected in them.

I stood in silence for about ten minutes until I heard a voice behind me. It was Welleck.

"I was waving at you through the window," he said. "But you just looked right through me. Something wrong?" There was a low-keyed threat in his question.

"I didn't see you," I said.

He turned to look at the window. "You can't see a *thing* through those windows, can you!" He laughed in relief. "Really, I'm becoming a paranoiac-type nut," he added.

I offered him a cigarette.

"I don't smoke," he said. "But sometimes I like to take a cigarette from a friend."

He took the cigarette gingerly and I lit it for him, cupping my hands around the match, against the wind.

"That girl hates me," he said.

"She's just upset."

"I ought to keep my mouth shut."

"You've been through a bad time," I said. "Talking helps."

"Talking don't help. Talking hurts."

"Then why do you talk?"

"Beats me," he said, shrugging his shoulders. "You know, sometimes I expect that when I look in the mirror, I'm going to see a monster or something, a real beast with blood dripping out of his mouth. But what do I see? A face not too different from the one I had when I was twenty-one. How old do you think I am?"

"It's hard to say."

"Guess."

"Thirty-six," I said.

He looked at me suspiciously. "You're kidding. Most people guess much lower. If you could see me after I've slept and cleaned myself up, you'd think I was a kid or something."

"How old are you actually?"

"Thirty-five."

He fell silent, reflecting perhaps on the fact that he was thirty-five.

"Some place, this Iceland," he said after a while. "No army here, you know. No navy either. Nothing. A peaceful lot, the Icelanders. Funny, isn't it? I mean, these people used to be great warriors. They have stories in rhyme to prove it, too! If you'd have come here fifteen hundred years ago, you wouldn't have found such a nice little democratic ant-pile with women at the voting polls. You'd have seen big hairy bastards stalking about the place with axes in their hands. Sailors and hunters. A fighting race. The only fighters in Iceland nowadays are the Americans. But the citizens don't like the American bases mucking up their precious little island, I can tell you that for free. They even lock up their daughters at night. That's a fact. You never see any of these hairy-legged Icelandic broads walking about with a GI. I'll tell you something else about Iceland. Somebody got the name mixed up with Greenland. Greenland was the place that was supposed to be called Iceland. It was colder back in Luxembourg, did you notice?"

"Yes."

"People don't know *any*thing. Iceland's not icy, for chrissakes! Iceland is *green*. *Nice* climate. Temperate. I think I ought to have been born here, really. About fifteen hundred years ago. In those days people wouldn't look at me like I was Dracula or something. I'd be a hero. They'd write sagas and all kinds of crap about me."

"That's probably true," I said.

"Maybe I'll write a book myself someday. I have a lot of

stories to tell. *True* stories. Things that don't get into newspapers. I'd get into trouble if I wrote them now. But my contract's up in seven months. I have a nice pile put away in a bank in Belgium. Close to one hundred and forty thousand dollars."

"Will you have to pay taxes on it?"

"No. Of course, I can't touch a penny till my contract's up. But after that I'm free and clear. I'll buy a little bar in Munich and a house near my mother so I can see my children, and I'll write my book. I'll have a nice life. Smooth sailing in shallow waters. The only thing I'd like to do before I quit is fight for the Israelis. As far as I'm concerned, Israel has the best army in the world. That's because they have something to fight for."

"No doubt about it," I said.

"You're looking at me like you think I'm a bullshit artist. You think I won't quit. Well, it's true that it's hard to quit. War is the only trade I know and I'm an expert. But after Israel, believe me, that's it."

I parted company with Welleck. A quarter of an hour before we were supposed to reboard I decided to spend the night in Reykjavik and take a plane the following morning. I had been seduced by the ridiculous brochures stuffed in the pockets behind the seats in the airplane—color photographs of sinful night life in the capital city. Besides, the prospect of getting back into the plane with both Welleck and Mary put me on edge.

Welleck was disappointed. At bottom I think he understood that I wanted to get away from him. As we were saying goodbye, he asked a favor. He asked if I would send him the next Joan Baez album when it was released. He said he would reimburse me for the album and the postage.

"You'll get a bill all right, including travel expenses to the record shop."

At this he laughed. "I'll miss you up there," he said, pointing at the sky, and he laughed again. Then we shook hands and parted.

A new Joan Baez album was released that year and I sent one to him in care of a Saigon address he had given me. Six weeks later I received a letter from Saigon. It wasn't from Hans Welleck, though, but from his friend, Jensen. This is the letter:

Dear R. Anderson,

I am sorry to be someone who brings you sad news. Our friend Hans Welleck was killed by a hand grenade this week. I think it was thrown from behind. He lived in a coma twelve hours after he was hit and he died in the hospital three days ago. It was very kind that you sent the record. Many times he told me about a friend in America who promises to send a record. He would have been very happy. I know. He was my best friend. He was always telling me about Joan Baez.

I have a problem that maybe you can give advice. I have a monkey called Raffles that used to belong to Hans. Once he said that if he was killed I should send to his wife the monkey. But that was last year, and this year he divorced his wife, and I never ask again what I should do with the monkey. It didn't seem right that I should ask. So, now he has no wife. Also I don't know where to find the one who used to be his wife. I don't think she would want the monkey anyway. Also I cannot send it to his children. They would love this monkey, because it is very friendly, but they live with Hans's mother and she is afraid of animals.

Maybe you would like to have the monkey. I think Hans would like you to have it. I don't know your opinion of monkeys but this is a good one. It would be very complicated. There are so many rules about animals and airplanes. But I know some people on the inside, and I think I could fix it. I would keep the monkey myself, but I am shipping out in three months, and where I am going I cannot take monkeys.

Hoping to hear from you,

T. Jensen

CELESTE, IN CAMERA

Don Mitchell

THE FIRST TIME I SAW CELESTE, on the port, in the wind, I turned around and discreetly followed her a block. Her walk, her round hips' neat sway was schooled. *Trained* nonchalance. I guessed this must be Celeste because her hand gripped a Minolta, though she was clearly not a tourist on this tourist island floating, sun-drenched, in the Greek Mediterranean. Like her yellow nylon jacket, half zipped, billowed with fall breezes, so the woman's reputation had sailed forth before her—had even reached me in New York, some few days but lightyears ago, drunk in Dickie's warehouse after hours, waiting for the dawn. "Kid," he told me, "there are girls there that you'd best steer clear of."

I had laughed. "Not man enough, you're saying?"

"There is one, Celeste," he told me. "She takes pictures of men's, uh, privates."

"Dick, don't euphemize with me!" I hollered, staggering with whisky. Then my friend, my night watchman extraordinaire, led me by faint flashlight up a grimy staircase to the roof. On the pink northeast horizon we could see the dawn airport's purple lights, its vapor trails, shadows of its wheeling jets.

"So today you fly—yes, kid? You think that you'll escape now—New York, foxy New York bitches, this evil age, our time. Purist! But the world is smaller. Your Greece is an Illusion. The dull whores have fled before you, they have found my little island. So be careful. Luck," he wished me. "*Sto kalo.*"

But was he less drunk than I was? No, and we'd sent that empty quart careening gaily streetward. I went home, collapsed, and barely woke in time to catch my flight.

Now the bright windbreaker before me slipped into a shop. A bakery. Coming up outside, I stood peering through the window with its shelves of steaming loaves. There is a kind of beauty I can nod to from a distance—pay my respects painlessly—and there is another, a more urgent kind. This latter beauty nibbles at me, then bites deep and chews, sucks me down—and where's the difference? Mere atmospherics, gimmicks: like the bump or wrinkle in this woman's straight hard nose; like the queer downsweeping rake of her narrow eyes. Like the sorrel hair-mane fastened back in thick barrettes of leather. Past all this, within it, I saw desperate control. Counting out her change in drachmas, she raised her eyes once to nail me through the window where I stood staring: her gunmetal eyes. I moved off down the port.

I had made scant friends in my few days here, in my night-long revels. Mainly I'd met Greeks who spoke no English, but who danced with feeling in the dingy firetrap *tavernas* where no tourists go, dancing with retsina glasses smashing all around their feet. My Greek was a frantic flipping pages of a dictionary, piecing nouns and verbs together in a way that kept them howling. Still I say there was a nightly bond between us; I preferred this entertainment to the pricey dockside clubs that catered to the foreigners. It was with surprise, then, that I watched my drinking pals turn sullen when, that night, I read aloud the sentence I'd composed at dinner, sitting in the little house that Dick was renting me till Christmas. I read, Tell me please about the young woman called Celeste.

They found no fault with my Greek. I was ushered to the door.

Thus I came unto the Club Felix with its garish lights, its raucous guests, its alternating tapes of Western rock and Greek bouzouki music shattering the port's night stillness. Here beers were an outrageous two bucks in any money, here the slit-eyed bartender made change in six currencies. I found a dark corner and sat against hard whitewashed stones, nursing *koniacs* while men and women met and laughed and danced before me, praying for youth.

Celeste entered late, alone—at first I didn't recognize her. Now the lithe, windswept body I had followed on the port was bundled out of view: an extended weather forecast, bulletin of winter coming. No one had yet told me sunny Greece was to turn damp and cold. Celeste's clothes were gray, gunmetal, the color of winter skies after the clear light of autumn. I can see the fabrics hanging cold and heavy on her frame: a wide, floor-length skirt; a turtleneck with tight ribbed cuffs; a sweater draped across her back and tied around her neck by its sleeves. Her hair was darker, lively, combed across her willful forehead. And in her hand I saw the shiny black-and-chrome Minolta.

She took a stool at the bar and crossed her legs and faced the dance floor, laughing with superb white teeth at an unspoken joke. She ordered ouzo, the cheapest drink at fifty drachmas, and paid with a single blue note tucked up inside her cuff. Watching, I desired those fine thin wrists. Someone else would have to buy her next drink; she tapped booted feet now, searching for a mark. I eyed her boldly. But before her gaze reached mine, a German crossed the room and stood before her. She rose up to dance.

Oddly, Celeste did not dance well. Not that she danced poorly—but I was primed for something more than standard disco moves, that international body-catechism. This was before I learned that she was from Australia. The German danced harder, sweating at his gray blond temples and grinning at his partner lasciviously. From time to time Celeste would throw her pelvis hard against him. Or her breasts. Those seated round me noticed this and tittered, pleased. After one more drink they left; I stayed on though, getting loaded, and before an hour had passed the German stumbled in again. Alone, with a long cigar. He bought a full fifth of whisky and sat swigging from it, angry.

When it was plain that she'd left him, I made my way to his table. *"Bitte,"* I pronounced. *"Pardon."* "What? I speak English. Sit! Drink?"

I held out my glass. "The girl that you—I was watching. you left here with . . . "

"That bitch? Tease! You know her?"

"Sorry, no," I said. "She is quite wild, though. A beauty, don't you think?"

At this he looked through me. He began to chortle, then coughed until his eyes were red and phlegm was dribbling down his chin. Suddenly he grabbed his bottle, stood uncertainly, and shouted "Yes!" coughing violently. Then he pushed rudely through the crowd between him and the door.

Next night it was my turn.

Dancing with Celeste disturbed me, so I offered at the first chance to escort her someplace else. She asked where my house was, and I warned her it was quite a walk—seven hundred steps uphill, but with sweeping views to match. She said that her rooms were closer, but all her Greek neighbors spied. Twice the Tourist Police had threatened to expel her. For what? I asked. She pouted. "Prurience. I am bad."

"Let's do leave here, though," I said, and steered her toward the night. This afternoon had brought squalls—the first rain since May, I heard—and now the paved stone thoroughfares were washed clean of summer dirt. It was chilly, no mistaking.

"How long will you stay here?" she asked.

"Christmas."

"You'll need something warmer." Saying this she dug her

fingers in the pocket of my jacket, showing me how flimsy was the denim between me and winter. "There is no bad weather," she said. "Only improper dress."

"Thanks," I said. "Will you climb to my house? There is ouzo, wine."

"Yes."

"But first—look, what's that camera for?" I asked directly. "You always seem to have it. Like a prop, a crutch."

"I take photographs."

"Yes—you photographed the balls of my friend and landlord, Dickie."

"Who?"

"Richard Stronson. The importer."

Celeste laughed sharply. "Did I?"

"Yes, you did. Last year. I am not reproaching. He warned me about you, though. That's all."

She mulled this over as we reached the steps and started climbing, winding up a vertical cliff that walled the harbor's edge. "So. What do you do here—paint?" she demanded. "Write?"

"No. I came for living. Purely."

"Are you rich then?"

"Sorry."

"But you do not like photography. Snob."

"I'm no snob, Celeste. Cameras interfere, though—with my seeing. Why have it so easy? With no camera, I look with more care. What I forget is lost."

She climbed with me quietly now, up the glistening wet stone stair-street, breathing hard by my side. How I wished her wrap would come undone, wished I'd see her round breasts heaving! Celeste's supple waist was belted tonight with a brass chain, and the slack links past its clasp sang in rhythm with our walking. Pure—yes, I was a purist, and this struck me as pure living. I could hear this beauty thinking: how to get her shot, then run. For she preyed on new arrivals, men who had not heard about her. What a rare and fine obsession!—leading men to bed to snap them, then getting the hell out. Chaste—more fun for her than sex, no doubt. These modern women! Dick was right, they'd conquered the whole world.

I asked: "These crotch shots of yours—how many are there?"

She stopped walking. "Hey fella, I don't need this crap. Later."

But I knew she wouldn't leave me yet. Not if it were true obsession. I caught her arm. "Relax, listen. You can have me too. But I want to see the others."

"You're sick!"

But I only smiled, and then she said: "Follow me."

Retracing our steps, against the wind now, I reached for her waist. She trembled: we were on to something, the two of us. She led me around the harbor to the clustered little homes of fishermen, perched on ledges by the still wine-dark sea. One of these, set back, was hers: low rent. She swung the courtyard gate in. "Go now. Come back in ten minutes."

"No."

"We are being watched!" But as she tried to close the gate on me, deftly my fingers picked the Minolta from her distracted hands. She fought down a cry. She whispered, "Come in then, you bastard."

So I crossed her courtyard with its grapes, its blooming bougainvillea, then we entered her stone cottage. To my right there was a humble kitchen; to my left, a bedroom. She waved me into this latter, fussing with a kerosene lamp, anger—but anticipation too—written on her face. The light came up. I saw now that she kept her curtains drawn, behind latched wooden shutters. I smelled the first of winter's damp there in Celeste's small bedroom.

Now she drew herself erect. "Strip," she demanded.

"Not yet. Show me first." Truth be told, though, I was astonished at my fortitude. I could have found pleasure now in taking orders. But I stood my ground. I wore the pants. I held the camera.

"Okay." She crossed the room casually—*deliberately* casual—

and with a sweep of her arm drew back the heavy tufted bed-spread. I sucked for breath—to its underside were pinned one hundred, no two hundred little snapshots, each one the same study, but with always different subjects. I approached the bed and made a long (though, believe me! shamed) examination. I mean here was a life's work. When I couldn't stand it, I asked softly, "Do you ever . . . "

"Fuck?" Her voice came from behind me and, turning, I discovered her stepping out of her skirt. "No." I watched her head disappear into her sweater as she pulled it over her long neck, her arms. Then it bobbed back, hair akimbo. "I never do this, either." In the kerosene lamp's glimmer now I saw the pin-pricks—millions of them, red and quite at home as pores—caused by writhing, gownless, underneath that trophy coverlet. "Strip," she said.

"I want to fuck." Oh, I wanted to.

"No—I've shown you everything now. *Much* more than I showed the others! Now give me my camera."

I did. And, slowly, I unbuttoned. Immediately Celeste drew the camera to face, unwilling to behold a man except through her View Finder. Then she clicked away in total satisfaction.

"You must not tell anyone," she said. "Button up now."

"Ha! I'll tell everyone!"

"I will hurt you."

"Threats, now? Just Fuck me. Fuck, and I'll keep quiet."

She considered this, her eyes still hidden behind the shiny Minolta. Then she strode to a small cupboard full of photographic gear. In a flash she changed her roll of film, then loaded alongside it a handsome dark Yashica. Testing with a light meter, she opened wide it's aperture; then she placed it in my hands. "My way," she said, falling on the bed and crouching there like some savage beauty. "You have twenty-one shots. Twenty-two, if you wind the film well. Come."

"But—I don't know how to use this."

"Learn!"

I climbed atop her, learning. Thus I came to give up my

illusions of some mental Greece. Seeing myself, herself through the thick ground lenses, framing views and clicking madly—this was just the opposite of vaunted "pure experience." This was fucking in the third person! For this I had planned and saved, I'd crossed an ocean dreaming of clear light: and here I was, a fleshy object among dim flesh, machines and prickly fabric, *click! Snap!* And the *whir* of thin film spindles winding, winding. Worst of all, I cannot but admit I took pleasure in this. Certainly I postponed my last shot as long as possible. Only the next morning, in the shaving mirror at Dick's place, did I find the grid of red trails crisscrossing my back where Celeste had pushed and drawn the blanket of her obsession round me. Then I groaned and swore for having capitulated eyes, feeling, self, *all* to photography.

Yet I dreamed of her for many nights. And who knows? My sleep may yet again be troubled by her, by her dark face, dark lenses on gunmetal eyes.

Celeste spoke no more with me, not in my remaining month there. But passing where I sat before a portside ouzo one day, waiting for the mail boat, she dropped an envelope of prints onto my little table. Without taking so much as a peek, I sent them off to Dickie.

MAMA'S TURN

Beverly Lowry

HIS NAME WAS RAY but I called him Max: he ate that up. I hadn't known him an hour when I said you don't look like a Ray, I'm calling you Max. . . . And you should have heard the bellow. God he was loud. I think it comes from growing up in California. His last name was Maxwell . . . so, Max. . . . He was twenty-six and he *looked* like a Max right down to curly hair and big shoulders and muscles in his jaw. I remember the first day he came through our apartment . . . like a roaring subway, you couldn't have ignored him if you tried. . . . Stomping and shouting, laughing loud enough to rouse the dead . . . or at the very least Ralph upstairs who works nights . . . And I watched him and I thought well good. We hadn't been around a stomper in a long time and I knew he would give us a lift because, being apartment people, we have always assumed that *nobody* could just go around being as loud as he or she might feel like. It's the walls, you know, and people on the other side of them. We never feel free to let go, not really; there are always people over us, and under us and next to us. . . . Even, Jesus, when we're out on the street, it even comes to that after a while. Max, however . . . who was used to having an *ocean* for God's sake on the other side of him . . . Max couldn't have cared less what people thought; he did what he did, at the volume of his own choice, and they could like it or stick it for all he cared, an attitude which was like fresh air to us and a big asset to him as a salesman and, when I think of it, a definite contribution to the fact that no wonder he made such a ruckus in our lives, no fucking wonder. I'm thirty-eight.

Which I mention right off not because it was the deciding factor in our relationship because it wasn't or at least didn't have to be, it wasn't inevitable, but because it did have a significant effect, one I wasn't prepared for: it made me think I ought to be paying it more attention than I actually was. The *fact* of that hung in the back of my mind constantly. I'm not an unaggressive person normally when it comes to . . . love affairs, I guess, but my awareness of the age difference in this case did take an edge off my usual boldness and create another edge someplace else. It made me hesitant. I didn't want to impose myself on Max or try to be possessive in any way; I mean after all he was a young single man and I was, Jesus let me go ahead and say this though I never did back then not once, an *older woman*, yes with three young children and who was I, I said to myself, to make demands? (Which, by the way, was a mistake; you'll never again catch me saying who am I to . . . anything.)

But as I said *after all* . . .

When he was with me he was with me and that was that. I never asked where he was other times or when he would be back when he left. I just kissed him and smiled and said See you Max, as sweet as a fresh-bathed baby's ass, as pink as cotton candy, as soft as a jet-puffed marshmallow. . . . Bye Max.

Meanwhile. The other edge.

A gut knotted in pretzels, lungs drained of wind, a blood-red boiling behind the eyes. Outraged with fury, with helpless anger, with a need so strong I could taste it long after he was gone, like a sour onion belch that doesn't turn up until dessert. The need to ask. To demand. TO KNOW: Where are you going, when will you be back, *where do I stand?*

But wait I'd tell myself, don't. Don't push or be too heavy or he'll leave, you don't want that and I didn't, none of us did. I remember one time he was supposed to call, he had said he would, and I waited all day. I wouldn't even take the garbage to the incinerator despite the gathering roaches for fear the phone would ring while I was out and I might not hear. All day. It was midnight when he finally called without offering explanation or apology, and the back of my mouth was nearly exploding from wanting to yell and scream, all the time that my head was saying, it's only a call, don't get excited, a dumb phone call. And you should have heard me, I never said a word, never asked, never complained.

What I did was the dishes.

Which is a thing not altogether without its advantages because if there's one thing in the world you can count on it's that people will leave you alone while you're at it. It's automatic, just like when somebody sees somebody else getting mugged on the street, he says to himself: stay away, don't interfere, don't get involved, you'll only make trouble for yourself. Same way with dishwashing. . . . They turn their heads and don't see a thing. So, because you certainly aren't thinking about *dishes*. . . what's to think? . . . You get a little space of time alone in your head to mull things through and that's what I did. I call my sink my wailing wall. Standing over the Joy, the Golden Fleece, the Comet and the Twinkle, swabbing glasses, rubbing plates and scraping pots, I make an absolute spectacle of myself. I let go. I give out with such lamentations . . . such bawlings . . . such heartfelt moanings and howlings . . . that eventually whatever pain I feel for whatever I have let hurt me comes out with the sounds and I get well. (And usually of course it is because of a you-know-what beginning with the letter *m* followed by *an,* I'm stuck on the bastards, they murder me, I can't figure them but Jesus I crave them; I feel instantly better when one comes into my life, no matter how low a son-of-a-bitch he is or how lacking in character and personality . . . . I don't know why but I'm always looking for one; it's just like a match needs a rough surface to strike on, I need something to work against, something that is not the same as me . . . anyway . . . .) It works, that wailing. The time I didn't ask Max why he didn't call until midnight wasn't easy because Max meant a lot, it took two and a half washings to do it, but I did finally get rid of it. Now of course that two and a half included one pot with boiled-over cream of wheat crust inside and out, but still . . . .

And if Max tried to account for his actions . . . rare, very rare . . . I always did this: put up my hand like a traffic cop and heroically stopped him. I wasn't his wife and (I said, as a matter of fact, I *thought*) I didn't want to act like one. Doing that, I told him, made me feel like Ralph's wife upstairs when she hollers out the window. "RAA-UL-PH!" she says. "You said you was going bowling and I called and you wasn't and here's your bowling shirt still ironed. *Where were you, Ralph, if you wasn't at the bowling alley?*" We laughed a lot about Ralph and his wife and when Max laughs he throws back his big head and lets out such a bellow so outrageous and loud, from so deep down, that windows rattle, I surrender, and children . . . thunderstruck with dumb love . . . run to be a part of him, like they do to anything that outsized.

The children's father's been gone now four and a half years, since just before Ricky's birth, and while I can't say I've missed him . . . the man he was at the last anyway . . . . I have wished for some relief at times, someone I could count on. The children need a lot, and it's hard trying to provide it alone and I don't mean just clothes and food. But if he's gone he's gone and anyway, whatever happens, we'll survive. He sends a check every month . . . that's more than some others do and I can depend on it . . . but nothing more. The two older children miss him a lot especially Robby, and every birthday that comes up they insist on believing, this time he'll remember . . .

they're stubborn, I've told them forget him, but they insist . . . then when he doesn't they cry in their beds and hate me for his being gone. Especially Robby the middle one, he suffers most. He thinks it's some kind of *sin*, like robbing a bank or spitting on Jesus, for a mama and children not to have a father in the house. But Robby's strict.

Still we have good times. Playing kick each other off the bed, where we all put feet-bottoms against one another and push until one falls off then another until the last battle which is usually between Caroline and me, Caroline's my oldest, though lately Robby's been pushing me off and it ends up him and Caroline. We kiss a lot and fight and yell at each other and run from one of our three rooms to the other acting like we're trying to find a place to get away but we aren't really, we never go far. We're together . . . however disconnectd we may feel at times . . . we are a group, we're together. I work weekends running a hotel elevator and week mornings making telephone calls for a vacuum cleaner company and . . . it works, works pretty well. I sometimes start feeling sorry for myself sleeping with just old Caroline but then I think, where would I be if it wasn't for them, and since I've never yet come up with any-thing even close to as good as now, much less anything better, I figure it works out okay.

Max goes door to door to try to sell cleaners to the people I, and others like me, make appointments with and usually he succeeds, as you can well imagine, Max being a Max. He's one of the company's consistent top twenty, nationwide; before I even met him I'd heard about him from the bulletin board and the cashier . . . who Max later told me was constantly after him, he said she practically offered him the moon and stars just to take her home and as she called it, have tea with her: bitch, she's forty-five if she's a day. Anyway, the cashier said he was awful . . . brash and obnoxious and horribly egotistic . . . so naturally I was curious.

And I knew as well as I knew my own name what I'd do when I met him and eventually of course I had to. I'd come on strong to him, I knew it, and he'd respond and I'd ask him over, just like that. As I say, I don't always understand *why* but I do know *what* I'm likely to do.

We met picking up our checks and, as predicted, I invited him over for coffee, the cashier glared, he said yes and that was that. Next night there he was again at the door asking for more coffee. Really, I left it up to him at first, I let him carry the original ball and he never fumbled or punted but kept on keeping on, so who was I to call time?

We didn't do much really. We'd just eat dinner the five of us together and fool around, watch television, play cards or dominoes. Max can juggle, of all things, which the kids of course loved and begged for; we always kept oranges in the house in case he said yes, and that was a treat, the nights he did. I knew the cashier was right about Max but, as I said, we are people who tend to draw in our heads, like turtles on a freeway, and his brashness and ego were just what we needed to give us a boost and make us laugh. That was what was so good, the laughing; it was worth a lot. And of course Robby thought it was all set, that Max was his new father. He's usually so glum and serious we call him Sobby Robby, but now he came home from school everyday proud, looking forward to later when Max got there.

I wondered sometimes if Max shouldn't be going out with younger girls more . . . *dating*, I guess, if people still call it that . . . which he couldn't have much opportunity to do, as much time as he was spending with us. But again, that was his business and none of mine. And if . . . because Caroline and I shared the bedroom and the boys slept on a pull-out couch in the living room and Richy was still home during the day . . . Max and I had to take the bathroom to make love on the john seat . . . well, you can get used to anything, and I must say I've had less on a king-size bed.

So. We'd been going along steady and fine for about eight months . . . which is a long time to my thinking and certainly to the kids to whom the norm is more like two weeks which is about as long as a guy can usually take the racket . . . when Caroline came down with the mumps, which Max had never had. Then Robby did too, then Ricky. And after the mumps each of them one by one got the three-day measles which was going around. *Then* . . . God, I felt like Job, the locusts were closing in . . . a chest virus. So the whole place was off limits to Max for almost two months. Also a long time. The first week he called everyday at least once a day, usually twice, and said, "When, baby, WHEN?" (He said nobody but *nobody* brought him off the way I did, particularly with the mouth, he said I knew how to hold on and not stop and keep my teeth covered . . . well, I wouldn't know about that of course, though I've been told it before and I wouldn't tell him but I picked up most of my tricks from the *Homosexual Handbook,* which spells out minute by minute how to do it, there's a how-to chapter on it; and it helps, you know, to find out what it *feels* like to a guy, what he likes that you don't, and how to do it. . . .)

I teased him when he called and said provocative things about what I was going to do to him when we got back on the toilet seat such as sucking his mumps and he laughed his beautiful laugh and I'd almost be content. Neither of us ever mentioned the age difference. I knew about how old he was from things he said and I imagine he'd figured it out the same way about me, but we didn't mention it. One other thing, Max is also an orphan. Which at first I also worried about, that because I was older he might be looking for his dead mother's long lost tit to suck on . . . which I barely managed to do for my own kids . . . . I mean, that's the kind of thing you worry about, but eventually as things progressed I put that fear aside and when after we'd been together so long I told him what I'd thought, Max grabbed one out of my shirt and when the kids were otherwise occupied sucked it to prove he wasn't afraid to and to let me know how silly it was. So I said to myself forget it, he's not looking for a mother; things are good, better then they have been in a long time, so shut up and take it.

During the illnesses I was so busy I hardly had time to think about Max or myself . . . . I barely had time and head leftover to make some sales calls everyday . . . until late, maybe two in the morning, when I'd lie awake and realize he hadn't called that day. I hardly ever called him. He lived with some other guys I didn't know and what with his hours being so irregular and me not wanting to be a clutchy Ralph's wife . . . well it just wasn't part of the deal that I would call him; he did the calling. But he wasn't, not as often.

Then he would . . . and say when, when, when, and you and me and you and me, and I'd live on it again for a few more days.

And when it was finally over and all three were well and I told Max so, he said two words. That's all. "What time?"

The four of us worked all day on the meal. We made a big pot of chili, no beans. Max called twice, said he could hardly wait, and talked to Robby and told him he had a bat and baseball for him. Naturally, we were near-hysterical with excitement. We made cornbread with cheese in it; Caroline sliced tomatoes and onions, and I made a gorgeous lemon pie with hand-squeezed lemon juice in it, lemons squeezed by yours truly. I bought cold beer, Heinekens, please, and made coffee in advance. I mean I had it all in the pot ready to fire up when we wanted it. We even stuck candles in old wine bottles for decoration, and Robby sprayed Lysol around to take care of any remaining mump dregs.

When he didn't call by five as he had said he would, I waited until ten minutes to six and went ahead and called him . . . scared as shit, like a kid. When there was no answer, I called again thinking I had the wrong number and let it ring six, seven, eight times in case he was in the shower, but there was still no answer. I called again at 6:10, 6:20, 6:30 . . . obsessed by now, after all it was important and something could have happened to him . . . and then every fifteen minutes, by the clock, until finally at 9:45 there was an answer, a girl. She sounded young, like a child, and she said, "No, I'm sorry but Ray's not here." (Knowing nobody called him Max but me, I'd asked for him by his full name; still, it sounded strange hearing him called *Ray,* as if we were talking about somebody else, somebody not Max.) Then she said, "Would you like to leave a message?" I managed to say no and hung up. Waited until ten thirty, to avoid speaking with her again . . . no answer. At eleven I gave up. Or anyway I stopped calling. The children by then had eaten and gone to bed, not terribly disappointed surprisingly enough. Except Robby because of course he wanted that bat and ball. They probably have a better idea of the risks involved in trusting an adult's word when it comes to dates and time and being someplace as promised, than I do. Myself, I sat up and stared out the window half the night, eaten up inside, wishing with all my heart we were married so I could have the pleasure of saying what I felt like which was, "Where the hell were you, Ralph?"

I didn't sleep much. I kept thinking I'd heard the phone ring. Then when he still didn't call the next morning, I couldn't help phoning him at the office.

"Oh . . . listen," he said, "I'm really sorry I missed you last night. . . ."

And that was all. Really sorry.

Then he went into a long story about a cleaner sale that when the husband got home turned into a party and so on and so on and he couldn't leave because it was a $300 sale and God he was sorry, he sure did want to see me and meet me on the john seat. I mean it was all so *casual;* like, another lady another appointment another deal to close. I was totally choked up, I said I didn't know if I even wanted to see him anymore and hung up; sat a minute and thought now what have I done, I've let him go, which I couldn't do, he meant too much, so I called him back. Quickly, before he left.

"Hey," I said, "I really sounded like Ralph's wife then, didn't I?" And I apologized and we made up and he told me more about his cleaner sale and how it knocked him out so he was in bed asleep by ten . . . no, he corrected himself, eleven-thirty. We made a date at my place for that night after I got off working the elevator and I felt happy when I hung up until I looked over at the kitchen table and saw that black cast-iron pot of chili all crusted over with a layer of hardened red grease; and half a stick of real butter melted into a pie on its plate, and tomatoes congealing in oil, and the table still set, with those candles . . . I mean, *candles!* . . . like me, leaning, waiting to be lit. Okay, I said, it's only a dinner, it's only food. But deep inside something else was contradicting that because it was love not food I wanted to serve him. I, not the chili, was the main course, and rejecting my food turned into rejecting me. I thought I'd better clean up and then on second thought, thought better of it.

Not the dishes, not the wailing wall, not yet . . . hold on a minute. (Which may have been a mistake.)

Because suddenly the light dawned. It was like being hit over the head with the baseball bat Robby didn't get. I had a vision. I saw . . . of all people . . . Mama. Not my mama, particularly, or his, not anybody's particularly, but just mama-in-general, *the* mama. My idea of her and yours. The one Caroline's dolls cry for. With her hand up a turkey's ass, stuffing.

She looked happy, Mama did. (And when I say *saw* her, I saw her all right, not with eyes but with everything; I saw what was right in front of me that I'd been closing my eyes to before . . . and that's seeing.) Humming a tune as she pushed and packed. (Adds resonance, says the *Handbook*, humming does.)

I saw her cranberries simmering, smelled her pie roasting; I watched as she stirred her giblet pot and I knew what she was thinking: will they say it again? that my turkey's always moist and my dressing never dry? will they? (The most important thing to remember, according to the *Handbook*, is to keep things *wet.*) The telephone rings. She wipes her hands. (And to avoid hepatitis: wash wash wash.) It's Bubba, or Junior, maybe Sonny, from college. He's got an invitation he says to go to a friend's place for the holidays, a three-day party; he knows she understands but will refuse the invitation . . . he says . . . un-less she promises to freeze him some dressing and a second joint. And she knows why. Because hers is moister than what anybody else fixes him. Because . . . Mama . . . knows . . . *how.* (The teeth, Mama, *draw in the teeth.*) And Mama says sure, Sonny, you just go ahead and have a good time, Mama'll freeze what you want, then turns from the telephone as I did. What she wanted to serve him *won't* freeze. (And thawed just ain't the same: *HH.*)

Well, shit.

I don't know why I'm so dense sometimes.

I was right all along, I should have known, all I had to do was go one step farther. I *was* Max's mother-substitute all right, only I had misread his motivations. Max didn't need mama's milk, he had that; his mama didn't die until he was ten so he got his nipple gratification and nourishment. But he didn't get to make that phone call, like Junior, the one that would enable him to say that's it, Mama, I've had it with you and your second joints *and* your dressing, I'm after my own now even if it's dry . . . so stick yours. he *had* to step on me; he never had another choice. I was astounded that I hadn't seen it sooner. Me, the big smartie who gives the best always moist, no-teeth blow job in town; me, playing the Mama scene full-out, whole hog without ever having even seen the script. Me, eating up humiliation like candy. Apparently loving it. I was confused still but not rattled. I didn't do the dishes.

I went to work.

Working the elevator, like washing dishes, has its good points, the biggest being I don't have to think about the job so when I'm alone in it . . . going up to the twentieth floor, say, to pick up passengers or having let them out at the top and on the way back down again . . . I feel clean and detached and in control; set off in my own cool cubicle of space and time I can see things clearly in there. There is something about being in that absolutely contained path, limited to straight-up, straight-down, all angles and straight lines, no curves, no forks, no decisions to make about direction, that helps me think straight about things. One thought leads directly to another and another without obstruction and I can focus and zero in and find answers. I'm like a fucking monk in his casket.

It was on a trip from sixteen that I realized Max was home the night before the whole time, listening to the telephone ring, knowing it was me calling but not answering. He *was* in bed at ten as he let slip and before ten, but not alone. That was who answered at 9:45, the poor girl, she probably couldn't stand hearing it ring any more. "Christ," I could hear old Max saying . . . not missing a beat meanwhile . . . "she doesn't give up easily, does she?" Old Mom. Easier to leave than anything. And on the way to seven, after having carried down a loud drunk group of pharmacists and fending off a goose from one of them, I figured out what Mama had to do.

Max was waiting outside the building when I got there, grinning like a kid. I know he didn't want to give me up, I know I was important to him, it wasn't that. He needed Mama as much as he needed that little girl, but I had to do what I had to do (I suppose). The children were asleep. I paid the babysitter, closed the door and turned to him. He looked . . . wary? Guilty? Maybe something in my eyes. Maybe he saw Mama there, her hand deep in turkey. But Mama couldn't retaliate the way I could, she simply was not at liberty to.

Without a word, I led him to the bathroom and didn't bother locking the door.

My dressing was never moister. No son was ever treated better. Matter of fact, I thought for a minute he was going to let go and die, right there on the toilet, with an erection up to his navel yet. I licked his ass and sucked his balls and held his cock way back in my mouth . . . past the back of it actually, down *in* the throat, that's what he likes and after some practice you stop gagging . . . until the very pupils of his blue blue eyes gave up; they just let go and rolled on down through it and out . . . into me, waiting to swallow it up. (Barely tastes, you know, salty kind of . . . but it does hang in the throat.) When I think of it, I was without mercy that night. Of course he loved it . . . I gave him the works and I do mean the works . . . but I kept on keeping on maybe more and farther than he wanted to. I was demanding then, all right, until I had more of him than he knew he had to give. I got, in a way, *Max.*

He had his head all laid back on the tank lid. moaning, smiling, frowning, sighing, slobbering, reaching for me then clutching the toilet-paper holder with one hand and the sink with the other to keep from falling (the toilet seat was getting to his tailbone by then, I knew the feeling). I was astride. I slid up the sweat on his chest to his ear and whispered, sweet as Mama promising to freeze her baby boy a second joint, "Now. Go blow your*self* . . . " and I paused a little then returning to him his name . . . "*Ray.*"

Then I slid down and sat on the tub, letting my belly hang like the thirty-eight-year-old mother of three I am. He smiled at first. He wasn't sure what I meant. The message crept slowly into Max's awareness, what with his reactions being so sucked down, smoothed over and wiped out, but he got it all right, he's quick . . . the message came through and he could handle it, he was getting ready to go into a Max act. Shit, I think he could handle anything. But not this time, I wouldn't have it. I got up, sucked in my belly fat and walked out, holding my ass muscles as tight as I could to keep from jiggling. (I may be thirty-eight but I'm still vain and have got a better figure than most my age . . . and anyway I thought I'd give him a nice parting shot, which wasn't easy, as ice-cold as the floor was.)

I went to bed and he left and that . . . was that.

That was over a month ago.

And wouldn't you know it, the children now blame me for the absence of *two* men! Robby hardly even speaks to me any more, he's so mad, and in a way I don't blame him because it's true, things are not as good here without Max around. The walls don't shake, the food lasts too long, we don't laugh like we did . . . and who else in the world will ever *juggle* for us again! I don't know, as I said, maybe I shouldn't have stopped to think that morning, maybe I should have gone on and washed the dishes and kept what I had. But at the time I couldn't and I still think I was right, I had to turn myself around and get my fist out of that turkey's ass.

And, well, it would have been different if I'd have been like Ralph's wife and could have at least *yelled* at him; could have said to him: WHERE THE FUCK DO YOU THINK YOU'RE GOING NOW or JUST WHO DO YOU THINK YOU'RE FOOLING WITH . . . ANYBODY?

But look at me, wailing at the sink all this time instead, my arms still immersed to the elbow . . . would you say I'm better off? Robby says no, and I must admit I do sometimes long for the feel of it . . . cool and damp with the pocked and wrinkled skin folding over my fingers . . . as I hum . . . and pack . . . and stir . . . and taste . . .

The *Handbook* says deep breathing is essential and that you should keep a tight steady grip, creating as you go a vacuum between your lips and your epiglottis so that if you were to let go, or he were to withdraw . . . if the two of you were to, so to speak, disengage . . . . you would hear a soft, wet *pop* . . .

A MATTER OF ACQUIESCENCE

Don Hendrie Jr.

A MAN LIVED IN A SMALL NEW ENGLAND TOWN with his family and his things. Though he was a college teacher, a novelist, and a lover to his wife, he had no friends. This had not always been the case, but now he found his life and things and wife and children sufficient unto himself; and he did not worry that his arrogance and pride and protective scales had made of him a bitter and lonely man, for he did not know it.

Christopher Blount believed in the truth of the lie called silence, and in keeping silent he thought himself benevolent, wise and fair. And because he believed he knew himself as well as he knew his books, he brooked no challenges to his right to remain mute. While his wife Sara had not challenged him once in the seven years of their marriage, other men and women had tried him time and again, but Blount always won.

On Saturday mornings during the summer Blount made a point of playing catchball with his oldest son Oliver. A frail, strung boy of six, Oliver's habit was to make a fierce run for the ball as it arced toward him through the air, and though he sometimes collided with and embraced it, more often than not the ball went on by him and struck the grass at the moment he seized his father's knees with a cry of "Jesus, Daddy!" When Sara Leary Blount heard, from her lawn chair perspective, the climax of this liturgy, she invariably cast anxious glances for the whereabouts of the other son, Tom.

In June a new babysitter was chosen. One film night she met Blount in the kitchen.

"Mr. Blount."

"Hello there."

"I—I . . . may I."

"My wife is in the shower."

"I'll come in, I'm early, I love your kitchen, your wife's pans. Are those *artichokes?*"

"I'll show you the children's bathroom. That's where they are, and the aspirin."

"Thank you. I'm glad to meet you finally, my friend says you exude something . . . refreshing in your writing classes."

"What was your name? Come through here, that's the telephone."

"It's Monica."

"Yes. Well, this is the living room . . . and the stairway, the children's rooms are off the balcony-thing there. It's like toothpicks, please don't let them lean."

"I won't."

"SARA!"

"It's exciting to be here. What's this?"

"Proofs, book proofs. Sara, don't come . . . Monica's here."

But already Sara was posed above them, behind the balcony rail. From below, for Blount, she appeared a pale elongation of nude damp flesh, her adept face crowning his immediate apprehension of lustrous crotch hair, fleshed navel, and the water-shrunk nipples. "Hello," she said to Monica, and placed one hand atop the railing, the other on a thrusting hip. As Blount watched her bend from the waist, shifting a portion of her weight to the railing hand, he quashed the impulse to shout maledictions, and only then realized that Monica's up-turned face was an agog study.

"Hi," Monica said. "I think your house is fabulous, Mrs. Blount."

"Sara, hurry up, you're *dripping* on us."

"Oh Chris . . . . Monica, come and help me with the kids."

Monica ascended.

Blount owned a 10–speed French bicycle as light as a suit-case. When he wasn't writing or teaching or moving about his house he rode the town's hills with a ferocity not seen in games with Oliver, or any of his dealings with Sara. As soon as the snow melted he put on greying tee shirt and shorts, a pair of wizened leather cross-country shoes, and pumped and geared the machine over macadam, dirt, gravel, until his thick body sweat enough to ward off the spring cold. In time, the bicycle's racing tires wore to flattened ribbons, and he replaced them with a type more suited to the crude surfaces over which he covered such great distances. Distance was the challenge, and his sweat a victory over space and the involuted beats of his heart. Dogs did not chase him, but Blount feared automobiles, their fickle drivers, more than he liked to admit. He never cycled at night.

Eight miles from town was a crossroads of clapboard houses and a boxy Congregational Church, a point on the map called Bristol East. On any summer morning, after a breakfast of yogurt laced with honey—his best pedaling fodder—Blount could reach Bristol East in fifty–five minutes. It happened that his habit of drinking water from the tap behind the church, water which also served to dilute his sweat, caused him one morning to meet Pablo Eaton, whose duck pond, backyard dale and house adjoined the church cemetery. Blount, who had turned from the faucet with a sense of being watched, wiped his lips and permitted the bicycle to rest against his groin as the man came from among the jumbled headstones, trod barefoot over the clipped grass, until it was possible for him to speak to Blount without raising his voice. His hair was tied back with a red bandana, and he wore a bathing suit, a wooly Mexican vest without sleeves, and a blond beard which the bright sun could fairly disappear. His smile, a lip-curve and a grimace of pale crowsfeet eyes, contradicted both his costume and the pear swoop of his soft torso as it fell outwards to his waist; a thin man's careful smile.

"You're Blount," he said, and in the silence put forward his right hand. "Pablo Eaton. I've seen you from my pond."

Blount touched the hand briefly. It was very dry, and hollow. He allowed the pause to lengthen until he felt sure Eaton would break off this barren meeting, but the man seemed determined to outwait Blount's rudeness. Eaton's blue eyes harbored neither guile nor amusement; they merely waited, in complete opposition to the bathing trunks and the lax belly flesh. Resigned to chat, Blount gripped the bicycle's saddle and rolled it ahead a foot. "Do you ride?" he asked.

The honest bellicosity of the response quickened Blount's heart. "No . . . I don't write shitty books either," Pablo Eaton had said.

Later, Sara Blount handed her husband a colander of their garden's Kos lettuce. "Wash this, love."

"Is Monica coming tonight?" The tapwater fell onto the fresh leaves, skittering soil grains, an ant, mulch debris not unlike Eaton's dead blond hair.

"Yep." Sara turned from the stove in the act of caressing with a forefinger the tip of her tongue. "Will you get her?"

"Sure."

Lifting the colander from the sink, Blount shook through excess water, wrapped the lettuce in a dishtowel, placed the bundle on the counter, and made one stop in the direction of the refrigerator before a clot of cottage cheese thrown by high-chaired Tom curded across the front of his grey cycling shorts.

"Tom! . . . sonofabitch." And the child's shrieks would not cease for his whispered comfort. "Daddy's sorry, honey."

From her darkroom in the basement Sara brought three fresh prints. Blount put aside his rum&tonic, put aside the bulk of his page proofs, and carefully took the photographs in hand. Each glossed a portion of Monica.

"They're nice," he said.

"Do you like the one in the leaves?"

"Yes. She looks like you."

"What do you mean?"

"Look . . . miles of leg, roadhouse ass, short back, shoulder blades like wings."

Sara laughed. "It is me, love. Monica took it from up in a tree at Eaton's."

Blount sipped from his drink, gazing with what he considered matter-of-factness at the next bleached-out photograph of Monica's thrust hip bones, which bracketed a groin thatch vaguely marred by a negative scratch, or piece of straw. "Eaton's," he murmured. Only in the third photograph could he see Monica's face: the camera peered upward from the area of her navel, so that while even the tiniest corrugations of her nipples were agonizingly sharp, her face framed above was slightly out of focus. "Where she lives," Sara said, taking her photographs from his extended hand.

At seven, Blount fetched Monica. He propelled his sedan into Paul Eaton's yard and halted it in the $\mathcal{L}$ formed by the ramshackle house and tumbled barn attached. At the bleat of his horn a thick-torsoed woman stepped from the dusk of the barn and squinted at him. Blount fluttered his hand against the windshield. The woman put down the bucket she was holding, the squint relaxed into what struck Blount as wide-eyed scorn, and she disappeared, sucked backward by the innards of the bar.

Monica entered the car.

"Hello, Chris."

The jocose lilt of the babysitter's voice set Blount's stomach to trembling; somehow, somewhere, he was being toyed with, and he supposed that if it had anything to do with Paul Eaton, or the photographs, or the bucket woman, then the dangers were closing upon him at bicyclist speed.

In the bedroom Sara caressed his cheek. "Oh, lovey, would you shave," she said in her imperious way.

Blount, who following a nightcap had skipped rope for ten glorious minutes, decided he would also take a shower. "All right," he said.

"And don't use any of that damned witch hazel."

To Blount, shaving was as sensual as, and certainly more private than sexual intercourse. The smooth glide of the blade over the lathered cheek gave him the momentary illusion that his tawny skin was not filagreed with pock and enlarged pore. He stepped from the shower, performed the act, slapped on the witch hazel, and went outside to allow the July night to evaporate his small rebellion.

The Blount bed rested on thick stilts and reached, Blount knew in the darkness, to the level of his diaphragm. He placed both hands upon the mattress frame, hopped, and in the air rolled horizontal, so that he settled gracefully if heavily just parallel to his wife's long body. Sightless, he saw in his mind the smile of anticipation spread the width of her wide Irish mouth. He slowly filled his lungs with air, and heard the ratchet sound—his inner ear—of his bicycle's main sprocket pedaled in reverse. He awaited the initiation of the act, the game, the match; and was not afraid because he knew there would be no words impinging on him, as if for Sara and Blount the contract of conjugal rights had indeed been written for mutes. Sara had agreed, had finally conceded when he left a written message beneath her pillow: *Talk not in bed and I will fuck thee silly.*

He knew her shape was risen over him. The hand, two slender fingers, encircled his cock mid-way, like a wedding ring of bone. Motion occurred, layers of flesh moved against each other, and the dark mass of her bent to him as he watched from his vantage point above. Always this preliminary of hers had seemed to him a kind of anesthetized mime, as if he were a dummy to be stroked and mouthed into proper animation; but he had, of course, never said a word. And to be sure, there was

A MATTER OF ACQUIESCENCE **189**

pleasure in her craft. As the warm perpetual motion of her head bobbed below his abdomen he forgot himself and grabbed in his fists a hold on her fine brown hair.

Habit and rhythm of her mouth told him, yes, it was time to reverse, to go quickly to the apex of her wondrous legs, to take his smoothed face there, to be at work in the outpost for a while. But when he went to go she violated all habit (and his own pronouncement) by saying, in a most ordinary way, "No, not particularly," and so he did not go down, but rolled instead on top of her, and in between those cinching legs. With a deft hand and a tilted pelvis she aided in the abrupt transition.

For a while it was the usual. He knew what came when: the furious, the calm, the steady, a touch, a bite, a need for pain just so. Yet a haste was upon her. The fingers that spread over his buttocks seized and pushed and seemed to signal that she had gone far ahead of her usual self, that her skimming above the heady maw of her pleasures was far beyond even her muted breath-intakes, which rose in his left ear like a musical scale. And it was all over: the rhetorical thrashing of her head: the legs that would seem to snap his femur bones; the fingers that sought to mark his flesh . . . as he so carefully held himself in check, above her, determined not to crush or hurt, only to give pleasure when needed.

And only then did his semen go into her lax body, like words onto one of his pages.

Monica laughed at him, not because he was drunk and driving badly, but because his refusal to answer her silly questions about fiction had apparently irked her to the point of what Blount considered impudent, 19-year-old teasing.

"But every character can't be as intelligent as you are, Chris," she prodded.

"You're crazy!"

Paul Eaton says the novel is dead . . . useless."

Blount maintained the car in third gear, the better to negotiate the strange carbuncles on the road's night surface. Were his glasses—night glasses—fogged?

"Eaton wouldn't know good fiction if it grabbed him upside the balls," he said thickly.

Monica giggled. "He's very competitive."

"He can't even read."

"Maybe he wants to be a character in one of your novels."

Blount groaned, downshifted, coasted into Bristol East, curious about Eaton despite himself. "What does he do, this competitor?" he mumbled, intended sarcasm slurring into parody of his own pompous self.

Monica leaned on the dash, the better to see her sodden employer. "He's a photographer."

"Oh."

"Sara thinks he's careless," Monica offered, "but she thinks his images are very . . . *direct*."

Before Blount could query this opinion of Sara's he had not ever heard, the Eaton driveway loomed in front of him; he determined to stop the car, allow Monica to walk the distance to those shaded windows, softly lit from behind with evil kerosene. His foot bypassed the brake pedal, the car continued; a fear of being sucked upwards to the Eaton house overcame him, and he brought back his foot for a good sock to the brake, this time successful. The seizure propelled Monica's head into the windshield with a smart thud. "Excuse me," he said, the car still rocking on its springs. "What do I owe you?"

Monica said nothing. Blount was able to peer through his glasses with sufficient clarity to conclude that he had somehow offended the now-haggard girl. That at the moment she was perhaps hating his sloshing guts. Enough wisdom remained to allow her to go without payment for the night's services.

"See you," he called.

The next morning, Saturday, Blount fell out of bed, and made, because of his hangover-stupor, only a child's heartbreaking whap when he struck the floor. His flesh burned at sternum, belly and knee as he attempted the kind of orthodox push-up his reason gave as the purpose for his being cold-cocked on the floorboards. But when he discovered his reflexes were no good, and that the cells of his brain were aswim with fusel oil, he let himself lie in the pulsing thump of his misery.

"Was it you, that noise?" Oliver's fast, earnest soprano. "It was a very peculiar—"

"Where's your mother?"

"Outside. She's mulching."

"What?"

"The hairs on your fanny look like it."

"Don't tell me—"

"Just like black mulch. Did you roll off the bed? Sometimes Tom does and sounds like a soccer ball."

Blount winced and turned his head toward his son's blackened bare feet. "I dreamed I was getting up," he said.

"You stink. It's nearly time to play ball."

"God! . . . okay, just go away."

In the bathroom, in the shower, he adjusted the water to a heavy stream on the back of his neck. To clear his brain of a certain regret—when he had come home the night before he boorishly refused to accompany Sara to bed—it was necessary to con it into ticking properly. *Lord Jesus Christ, have mercy on my soul,* he recited until the sub-vocal words got one with his heartbeat and the steady battering of the water on his lolling neck. Once the meaningless litany was established, it lasted through the toothpaste, the shaving cream, the water, the blade, and the final slap and tickle of the witch hazel . . . when he found himself thinking not of the past, but the day ahead: food, sunlight, sweat, writing. Blount left the bathroom with his pain very much to the rear of his head.

From the kitchen window he could see Sara bowed over the garden's crooked aisles, Tom digging beside her in the unplanted dirt. Twelve o'clock. The coffee sat cold on the stove, the refrigerator yielded no yogurt. He buttered a wad of bread and kept it moving down his throat with a glass of bitter orange juice. Rather than heat the coffee he elected to wash the crowd of dishes from the morning and the night before, and thus he continued unbroken a habit as old as Tom.

Oliver's lovely brown eyes rose above the window sill in front of the sink. "Daddy, look!"

"You're standing on the sandbox."

"How'd you know?"

"X-ray vision."

The eyes went wide. "Mommy says there's no yogurt, go get some, and hamburgers too."

Blount wiped his hands. "Anything else?" But the boy had disappeared.

As a bicycle ride, the trip to the grocery store and back was a mere two miles, but Blount, by choosing to remain in the highest gear, made a hard, muscle-pulling game of the journey. He rode correctly, his shoulders almost touching the reversed handlebars, and with some pride in the ability of his ass to cleave to the polished saddle blade. On the way back, his knapsack hefty with meat, butter, bottles of wine, and the hamburger buns Sara had called for as he rolled out of the driveway, Blount came near to dying.

By accident most absurd. At the crest of the hill above Fellow's Orchard the blacktop narrowed in recognition of the state's jurisdiction over the road from that point on. A stretch where he habitually slowed in anticipation of the squeeze situation that could result from a coincidence of cars going both ways, plus himself. Now, he looked over his left shoulder, and above the knapsack caught a quick glimpse of a maroon pickup cab. Squeeze right. Coast. In front, coming uphill in the left lane, a cream Land Rover at a high rate of speed. No problem. He would listen to sprocket clicks until the shock of air from the passing vehicles signalled him free and clear. But the pickup, gunning and caterwauling decided to pass him just as the Land Rover drew even with Blount's front tire. The result had been in his dreams; with the pickup's hot nose in his periphery, surely about to touch him, he wrenched the handlebars to the right, as if he were opening a stubborn valve, and was immediately upon the loamy shoulder, the bicycle bucking but controlled until its momentum fetched it up against the concrete edge of the Fellow's driveway. And he lost to the driveway and the weight of his knapsack. The concrete smacked Blount far more effectively than the morning's bare oak floor. *Lord Jesus Christ, have mercy on my soul . . .*

"You're all right?"

"Yes, thank you."

Jeffrey Fellows lifted the bicycle from his station wagon's tailgate and allowed it to lean against Blount, who held the wine-soaked knapsack by one strap. In order to show Fellows that he was indeed recovered, Blount turned and extracted the mail from his roadside mailbox. The bicycle, without his support, fell to the gravel, the sound meeting Blount's ears only after he had seized the packet of letter.

"Shit," he said.

"I'll be going."

"Yes, thank you."

In a crocheted bathing suit Sara lay with her bare stomach in the grass. She was reading his proofs, staring at his words through enormous black sunglasses. "You get faster every time," she said, without looking up.

"It's a matter of fanaticism."

"Ummm . . . . Chris, the women in this book are unreal."

Blount wasn't listening.

She glanced up. "What happened to your shirt?"

"I fell. Look at this."

"What is it? You've got blood in your ear."

"Your friend Eaton has sent us a photographic invitation," he said, attempting to minimize with his voice both the seriousness of the bloody ear, and his peevish feelings about the small photograph he held, an object he had found among the day's mail; an image of—what?—stained languor. A woman lying at ease on her damask couch, wearing coolie pajamas of unbleached cotton, smiled invitingly at the camera with a set of black-edged teeth, these beneath darkened wench eyes and a thick clout of Gibson-girl hair.

In the hot sun Blount hunkered by Sara's head to point out the tiny nipple that blemished the woman's studiously arranged pajama top.

"I can see it," Sara said.

Blount chose the diplomatic. "I thought you'd miss it in the glare. It's an engaging nipple."

"Well, I've seen it before," she said. "It's 'The Photographer's Wife,' made by Corsen in 1914." With a dismissive shrug she looked away.

"Then you know the message?" Blount asked, irritated at her apparent lack of interest.

Sara pushed the sunglasses to the tip of her nose. "You said it was an invitation."

He flipped the photograph and read her felt-tip scrawl. "Come cook with us Saturday afternoon. Paul-Lucia-Isolda-Monica."

` Sara smiled at the pissed-off tone Blount failed to keep out of his reading voice.

He withdrew in order to lave his ear and sort out his preposterous thoughts as to what the Eaton household was trying to do to his, to his own guarded well-being, but Sara trailed him to the bathroom. He felt that her very navel watched him as he douched the encrusted blood from his wretchedly scraped and cauliflowered ear.

"You fall a lot," she noted wryly. Why was he being goaded? "Are you starting to bumble like one of your book protags?"

He tried a baleful look but his newly opened wounds disallowed it. *"Protags?"* he countered weakly, clutching a sanguine washcloth. Did Sara smile a fraction too soon? Suddenly he wanted desperately to work, wanted to go alone to his workroom and write the sentence that had just now bled into his abused brain: *I've never told you this, but she had to taste herself before she could come.*

Sara interrupted. "No, he doesn't. Why?"

"Why what?"

And that wasn't the only crazy thing about her.

From upstairs, Tom shrieked the end of his nap. And Sara was no longer with Blount. But she called out from the stairway, "I'm going to the Eaton's are you?"

No kidding, one taste and she'd be gone.

"No! No!" Blount cried. "I've got work to do."

In the workroom. *There was nothing ambiguous about her; she was more or less a complete lie. I told you there were other lunacies. She read Nin, all of it, and went around saying, "I have to discover my lesbian self." I couldn't stand it, the wondering just where she'd meet up with it; it drove me up the wall. Finally I had to follow her, wherever she went, and when—*

"Daddy, open the door."

"No."

"You said we could play ball."

"You're going to a goddamn picnic."

"But . . . can't I stay here, can't I?"

"Oliver, for Christ's sake!"

"That girl Issy Eaton kills ducks."

"No . . . no, she does not kill ducks. You go with your mother. Tomorrow we'll play catch."

"Promise."

"Yes!"

Blount knew something was amiss with his bicycle's derailleur before he had got one mile from the house. The chain would not hold on the high sprocket, kept slipping down with a rude clunk. He would lever it up, only to have the same cursed slippage occur again and again. He finally settled for the lowest gear of all, the hill-climber, and had to spend vast energies to transport himself the first four miles to Bristol East. The sweat was on him. So much so that despite his angry haste he stopped halfway up Dummer's Hill, dismounted, and walked the ailing bicycle the remainder of the grade.

At the hilltop, after leaning the bicycle against a scabby maple, Blount finally asked himself what the fuck he was doing. He had needed at least a look at that very picnic he had denied himself; wished for a real tableau of hotdogs and children to replace the confusion of photographs and photographers in his head. But now, sub-vocalizing at bicyclist speed, he knew himself to be on a fool's errand of mistrust; Sara could do what she pleased. And Blount was damned if he'd seek to ferret out a secret that he might nurse like a congenital defect which would someday kill him.

So he took up his bicycle again, crossed to the opposite side of the road, and prepared for the effortless coast back down the hill. To the workroom, where he properly belonged. As he poised, about to push off, he was delighted to see the maroon pickup take the curve a quarter mile below him. He heard the engine cough with the grade, and he knew then that the truck was senile enough to be stopped, if he, Blount, desired it. And he did; his body tuned for the kind of solid confrontation he never would have found at Eaton's picnic. He chose to sit and simply observe what would happen when the pickup's driver realized whose will commanded the heights. It came on, to the point where Blount could make out the general thickness of the man, an impression of swart—in hair, skin, clothes. Perhaps ten feet in front of him the pickup halted with a heavy frontal dip and a hollow tapping of slowed valves, which ceased even as Blount saw the driver lean from the cab with his clumsy and pitted face arranged in a country-confidence smile, as if he were about to render aid.

"Hello there," he said, pushing at a black forelock.

Blount nodded, politely, but had already measured his opponent; had observed his hands to be as short and unwieldy as dill pickles.

"Will it be acrimony? or will you let me apologize for putting you on your ass?" He spoke in such clipped and bitten syllables that Blount scarcely captured the words.

"What?"

"I said I'm sorry you ride that thing so ineptly."

Blount, who had the odd sensation he was looking at an older, hulking version of himself, decided both that the apology was genuine, and the man likeable. Blount nipped at a thumb nail, spat gently, and fixed his eyes on a point dead-center the fellow's low and smile-wrinkled forehead.

"Do any sports?" Blount asked.

A hoot. "I watch."

"I wrestle."

"I know all about you, Blount. I *like* watching my body rot. Name's Nick Winnoe. We were supposed to meet down to Eaton's, but you seem to be heading the wrong way."

Blount allowed the bicycle to roll forward until he was even with the pickup.

"Look, buddy, I'm only out for a spin, and you don't know a fucking thing about me."

"You look peaked."

By now Winnoe looked as pleased as punch. "Come on then, come to Eaton's for some nasty gin and hamburgers."

"My wife is there," Blount said thinly.

"No shit. Prove you're not the misanthrope you're reputed to be."

"You're irritating enough to make me do it."

"Ha! I've scored with the great writer. Come on then!"

Moving down the road to Bristol East, in the cab with cheerful Winnoe, nervous of his bicycle loose in the pickup's bed, determined to protect himself from whatever the picnic might offer, Blount accepted a Camel cigarette from Winnoe's crimped pack. They smoked, jiggled. Winnoe, in a pair of dirt-shine jeans, smelled like a bear of ill-repute, and not to say unpleasantly.

"How do you like Monica?" Winnoe finally said, as if Blount were a hitchhiker to be queried about the weather.

"She's a good babysitter."

Winnoe delivered himself of another friendly hoot. "Caution it is, eh, Blount? I'm especially fond of her melony ass."

"That, too," Blount said, and smiled despite himself. "Are you married?"

Winnoe frowned. "Shit, you really don't know me, do you? I've lived here fifteen years."

"Nope."

"I'm no culture-fucker." A serious declaration, apparently. "I mean, there are people around here who keep *score* of who famous they've had in their living rooms . . . bunch of sycophants and trucklers. And Pablo Eaton doesn't collect *novelists* either."

"No doubt," Blount said, "but are you married?" Should he be embarrassed by this running at the mouth?

"Ofttimes, yes, Sylvia will arrive for a portion of marriage, a diddle among the plate. But generally she stays in New York."

"Oh."

Because Blount did not at all believe in pulling teeth, he allowed the pause to lengthen until the subject of Sylvia Winnoe became lost somewhere in the engine noises; Winnoe himself used the time to stuff out his cigarette before bringing the conversation back to Monica's backside. A more or less one-sided, fleshy banter occurred until they reached the church and made the left-hand turn onto the dirt road that cut up to Eaton's, and nowhere else.

Beside the house a yard of shaggy grass sloped down and away to the sudsy duck pond, and the cemetery beyond. Children, including Blount's own, stood about the pond. No adults in evidence as Winnoe maneuvered the pickup between Blount's sedan and what was probably the Eaton's splattered van, all three vehicles arrayed before the barn door where Blount had glimpsed the bucket woman . . . Lucia Eaton, no doubt.

Not surprisingly, Monica debouched from the house before they could alight from the pickup. She moved quickly to Blount's door, joggled it open, gripped his elbow, and said, as if identifying some kind of edible root, "You, Christopher." A finger of hers dug shamelessly at his ulnar nerve, so that he was drawn out onto the ground in order to alleviate the odd balance of pleasure and pain. "It's great you came, fantastic." Rubbing his elbow, Blount was not inclined to believe her, yet she did seem genuinely pleased to see them both. And Winnoe appeared to know her well enough to leer with heavy eagerness as he came around the truck to receive her chaste kiss. "And Nicholas, you hunk, welcome," she cried, in a way Blount had never been party to. She herded them toward the side door of the house like children being babysat, nattering more phrases, which Blount failed to comprehend in his growing belief that he was being manhandled into a situation more chaotic than he deserved.

Yet the unperturbed Winnoe seemed to suck some of Monica's gay mood for his own; he fell to a steady bantering, a stream of dubious wit involving essence of juniper berries and the joy of bleeding meat. Blount—as they fumbled in tandem through the door—decided he really ought not mind that he was trapped between his culture-fucking lout and the beautiful youth, Monica; he was, after all, here, and perhaps had something to learn of the folkways of this house and its uncomprehended, only photographed inhabitants. He'd ride the noise as if it were a strange music.

They entered a drop-all foyer: plaster board minus paint or paper, linoleum bulging and waving over the floor, broken-down toys; and they almost fell over a crudded child's swimming pool just in front of the kitchen mouth. Through which they stumbled and, sure enough, discovered the bucket-woman slicing a bulbous onion in the midst of the most incredible mess Blount had ever seen.

"Hello," she said, the tears carpeting her high cheeks like sweat. "I'm sorry," and she offered a whole-body shrug for commentary on the living kitchen. She had no breasts, nothing swelled, but sturdy nipples set her chartreuse tanktop a pointing. "I'm Lucia, you're Chris, your Sara is here."

"I know," said Blount, pulling from Monica's grasp, and wishing the tears did not boil so from this Lucia's poor eyes. Winnoe traipsed through the debris on curiously graceful legs, not thick trunks as Blount would have supposed, but narrow stems topped by flapping folds of blue jean over a non-existent ass. Winnoe waded around the obstacles—the chairs and garbage bags and miniature tea table—to reach a counter on which whiskey bottles stood like shiny tools.

"Blount, what will you have?"

But before he could answer, Monica turned on him, a forefinger just coming away from her tongue. "Why'd you change your mind? We thought you weren't coming."

"Winnoe got me." Lucia Eaton giggled. Nervously? "I'll have a beer," he called.

"My God, a beer!"

"Pablo's outside," Lucia said, approaching the refrigerator, opening it to what Blount first saw as an underwater mass of seaweed and greenish creatures—all tucked, pushed helter-skelter into the suffering box. A bottle of beer fell onto the floor, a phenomenon Lucia seemed to accept as quite ordinary. Monica went for the bottle, had it opened and into Blount's hand before he could move. Behind him, Winnoe cracked a quart of tonic, and then moved to discover a probable lemon among the bright vegetable droppings of the kitchen worktable.

"We must go outside," Monica said. "The children are probably drowned."

Blount's stomach enveloped his heart. "Is that where Sara is?"

"The kids are all right," Lucia said. "Issy's a big girl."

Relieved, Blount quaffed a good portion of the beer, and as his eyes came down from the ceiling in tune with the bottle, he noticed that Monica's long soft throat was covered with a pink flush that extended in amoeba patches even to the fair expanse of sternum showing above her halter; the sort of gentle discoloration the books claimed as the markings of successful sexual intercourse, but which Sara's body stubbornly refused to exhibit. "But where's Sara?"

Monica smiled, put a hand to her throat to cover what surely was no more than selective blushing, Blount decided.

Lucia moved on heavy legs back to her vegetable table. "She must be outside," she said.

"Let's go there then," Blount declared.

Winnoe rattled his gin&tonic, Monica's fingers glided over her splotches, Lucia sliced a tomato with a knife like a razor. A reluctance among all of them to respond to his practical suggestion.

"We need a fire," Lucia said.

Monica said, "Christopher is good at that."

"Outside then, the outside is where you go," Winnoe pronounced, leading them—all but Lucia—through a battered dining room, a hallway hung with impeccably mounted photographs of what struck Blount in passing as a series of grotesque, leathery mummies; and on over a doorless stoop into the sunlight. Where, with the exception of the children by the distant pond, they encountered no person. A black, lumpish habachi squatted in the grass, beside it a fresh bag of charcoal and can of naptha. Now the shouts of the children came clear over the length of the ragged lawn, and Blount suddenly startled himself with a perfect, logical milli-second of image: the faceless, swollen form of Pablo Eaton simultaneously—triple exposure—screwing all three women in residence. Of course! All explained, conjecture erased, the problem solved. All that remained was quick violence to Eaton, a wink of victory to Winnoe, and he could take Sara and his children home from this slough of flesh and mummery.

Sara stood beside him. She had come from the house, and bore a platter of livid meat patties. "Hello, love," she smiled. "Couldn't work?" Her breezy assertiveness, the very mundaneness of it, drove the absurd epiphany from Blount's head, reduced him then to merely Sara's husband, nodding at his wife . . . as if he had been discovered storing his nosepickings beneath the arm of her favorite chair. *Her* neck displayed no amoebic blushes.

Sara greeted Winnoe, and brushing past Monica laid the meat platter beside the habachi. "Let's get the fire started. I thought Pablo was doing it." She gazed in the direction of the pond, where Blount could see Tom beginning the trek up the hill to his mother.

From behind them, from the doorway, Lucia said, "Pablo must be walking, looking for the goddamn dog or something."

Monica moved downhill to intercept Tom, who had chugged close enough to yell words Blount could not understand. Monica picked him up and brought him to Sara. He looked not at Blount, his face flushed, words piling over one another as they plopped from his mouth.

"Oliver shooting ducks." Sara laughed. "They're hunt-ers."

Blount, watching the two women and the child between them, decided that what he wanted most was to talk with Oliver; perhaps make amends for their failure to play catch-ball, and his closed-door shouting at the boy; in fact, make amends for the entire bang-headed day. He gave his empty beer bottle to Winnoe and strolled away from the adults, hearing Lucia say to no one in particular, "Don't let the dog get those hamburgers."

Oliver and the girl Isolda had a long bent stick, which they were using to fend off one fierce and plump duck. Both of them laughing with glee.

"Oliver!"

He turned quickly, eyes wide and glistening, poised with the stick, about to run with the girl, perhaps, from Blount's unjust intrusion. "Daddy, look at this, this duck's crazy!"

"Leave him alone. You're hurting—"

"But it's fun."

Isolda smiled, gap-toothed, sweet as a TV child.

"Where's your father?" She shrugged like her mother, grabbed Oliver's stick, and scampered away through the mud, yelling, the stick held erect.

"She's crazy," Oliver said, watching her disappear over the hillock on the left side of the pond. "She gave Tom a dog turd." His giggling made Blount's teeth ache.

Pablo Eaton stood across the water. Same bathing trunks,

vest, same beard disappearing in the sunlight. "Blount!" he called out, and waved his arm in casual salute. "Have you got a drink?"

Blount nodded, exaggerating the motion for the sake of distance, and unwilling to begin some yelling conversation over the brackish waters.

"He swims in that stuff, Daddy, did you know that?"

"Why don't you go up and have a hotdog?"

"Should I find Issy? . . .

"No, just go up."

Eaton was ambling the perimeter of his pond, blond head down, possibly watching the jactitation of his stomach. Blount went to meet him halfway; thinking to give the bastard a chance to redeem his "shitty books" remark by playing the host . . . or perhaps Eaton would discover the symbolic language necessary to tell Blount that his needs stopped with the two women who inhabited his house.

Once again, they shook hands, and again Eaton's hand struck dry and hollow.

"I'm glad you could come. We were thinking Sara a widow."

"You can thank your friend Winnoe." Puzzlement surrounded Eaton's pale eyes and thin nostrils. "He plucked me off the road," Blount said. "I was going home."

"Yeah? Let's walk by the cemetery. That fire'll take a while."

Blount glanced up to the house and saw that Winnoe and Monica stood distorted by the habachi flames.

They walked through a stand of maples bordering the gathering of worn tombstones.

Eaton said, "My idiot dog likes to eat rocks. He once bit a chunk out of Elmer Jessup's stone. A thing for granite."

Blount snorted politely. He wanted to return to the house, another beer, the safety of the children, people, the Eaton mess. In him there existed no desire to chat; anything but to be alone with this relaxed, soft-bellied enigma.

"My property ends here," Eaton said, the emphasis upon the word "my." He stamped his bare foot down hard on an invisible line that only he saw in the grass. "I'm going to tell you something, Blount. Unsolicited information. Maybe you'll put it in a book when you get home."

Blount stared at the man. The face was composed, even gentle, yet did the nostrils not seem pinched, even whiter than the rest of his skin? And solemn blue holes for eyes.

"Man, Monica is balling your wife."

In the silence that followed Christopher Blount knew he had indeed got the unwanted knowledge that was part of coming to this place. And while his brain went about the necessary adjustments, it saw fit to produce frozen, tender images of the two women in all of their attitudes. And, finally, Blount knew that he would never utter about it a solitary word. *I've never told you this, but . . .*

HAT TRICK: HER WESTERN DREAM

Don Hendrie Jr.

A MAN of little repute came to town. In the town, but for her, his repute fell to worthlessness. Before sunrise he came scuttling to her place. She felt *something* about him must have value. He hemmed and hawed during the beginning of their private audience, and finally he blurted if you could jack me off I would be happy. No arguments against it came to her. It could do no harm. And why not? The need was there. He dropped his trousers to the floor and she began. His shirttails were the color of wet brown soap. She worked. Outside, the sun showed itself. In the distance horseshoes clacked and clattered on pavement. Grew louder. He gasped. She thought to finish, but his panic wouldn't allow it. At least four horses and their riders were before her stoop. Without pulling up his trousers he scuffled to the door, and out. She walked after and was in the doorway when the shot came like a window slam in the night. On the pavement he lay in a twist of trousers; his shirttails were neatly folded over his erection. The horses had schlepped on up the highway. She had done her best.

CORDIALS

David Kranes

IT WASN'T UNTIL the waitress brought her Benedictine and she felt her first contraction that Lynn even thought of herself as being pregnant. She was anatomically thin and had managed to conceal the fact for well over seven months, with a regimen of boiled turnips and cold consommé—and the reminder was badly timed to say the least. She had wanted to sleep with David Marker from the moment she and Jack had spent a Saturday with the Markers sailfishing three months ago out at Wildwood, but there'd been interferences at just about every point. She had called him; he had called her; they had tried one afternoon at her apartment only to find her son Adam home from Hotchkiss as a surprise. Fall in New York is a difficult time to have an affair: everything starting up, schedules overcrowded again; and so this evening was to have been an island for both of them.

"Something the matter?" David asked her.

She smiled. "No."

"You winced."

"Just anxious, I guess."

"As am I."

She rubbed the knuckles of his hand, climbing each ridge, kneading the loose skin in the depressions with her forefinger and thumb.

"Do you want to leave now?" he asked.

"Let's finish our drinks," she said, her eyes partly on her watch, wondering when the next contraction would come. It came seven minutes later. She drained her glass: "All through," she said.

David smiled, breathed in his Drambuie and drained it. "Let's go," he said.

He helped her on with her coat. "Where are we . . . ?"

"A friend lent me his studio."

"Where?"

"Rowayton."

"That's an hour."

"Fifty minutes. And it's a nice Indian summer. We'll drive with the windows down. Sea smell's an aphrodisiac."

"I don't need an aphrodisiac." Her voice was surprisingly soft and quiet.

David nodded to the maitre d´, and pushed the door open; she went out. "It's a great place—this place—this studio."

Lynn breathed the late September West 52nd Street smells, and felt another contraction coming on.

When they cloverleafed onto the Merritt Parkway, the tugs were coming regularly, just under five minutes. Both the front windows were down. David had the heater on, her coat off. She had her face against his neck, her jaw pressed there. She'd worn no bra—she didn't really need to—and he was moving the tips of his right middle fingers over the nipple, under her burgundy knit.

"You're perspiring," he said, trying to make it sound playful.

"Yes." She bit at him. "It's the heater. The blower's going right up my dress." She knew, in fact, it was probably lactating.

"Rowayton?" There was a hum in her voice.

"There are fourteen–foot ceilings," David traced her neck. "And a fireplace."

"Had you planned on using the fireplace?"

"For a fire, sure; not for us."

"I don't know if I can wait." Lynn felt her body tightening again, watched the speedometer climb from 70 to 85.

"You'll love it," David said to her; "it's on the shore. You can hear the ocean. Waves. It's a great rhythm. Great keeping time to. Natural. Nothing rushed." He let his hand slide slowly down to her leg. She picked it up, kissed it. She looked at her watch: three minutes and twenty seconds; she picked it up and kissed his hand when she felt the next contraction again; three minutes and fifteen.

"How long until we get there?" she asked him.

"Twenty—twenty–five minutes." He played with her nipple again. She held her breath. "You're really remarkable," he told her. "I've been clawing half New York's concrete for three months."

"Me too," she said. "I've been having the most amazing fantasies."

"I'm not very good at waiting," David told her, then smiled.

"Nor am I." She thought about it; it was true. "I wait for very few things."

"Waiting fantasies are strange." He began to slide his hand down to her abdomen. "They make you feel almost adolescent." She picked his hand up again, kissed it, checked her watch. "Your heart's jumping."

"There's a motel in Mamaroneck," she said.

"One quarter hour, *max*," he told her. The pains were coming every two minutes plus.

When they pulled in beside the studio and cut their lights, Lynn's spasms were only a minute, or slightly more, apart. Like a schoolboy, David started to undress her in the car; she put two hands against his chest: "Let's go inside."

He smiled; "O.K.," then kissed her eyes, let himself out, and walked around to her door. She could smell the sea, as he'd predicted, and it smelled as though her own body had become huge, grown unlit and infinite and moved outside to become anatomy in the night around her. She became her own child briefly—undelivered though dependent and scared. She thought of when she was fourteen, parking out near Coney Island with a boy named Arnold, the "Tennessee Waltz" on the car radio, how her whole mouth had trembled, how her thigh muscles had gone slack. She heard the door button click, felt the sea wind against her hair, smelled the blown redolence of herself.

Lynn didn't like being aggressive. She had always hated that role, it ruined everything; but she pulled David inside and when he wanted to get a fire going, she said *no*.

"Why?"

"Please."

"Lynn, that's the whole . . ."

"Afterward!"

"I may want to sleep."

"Please!"

"O.K."

She pulled him to the bed.

She had continually fantasized David's undressing her, three months lived it in her mind: its being gentle, slow; kisses, where he placed them, breast, belly, hip; when they came. And so against her better judgment she let him, let it work out, let the mind come true. True: she stood there, in the dark, arching, moving, turning slightly for him on the balls of her heels. And David carried it off: it was worth the concealment, worth the pain. The hands played, the kisses came on time, in form. She felt the zipper on her dress move down, slipped her arms out, felt the dress fall around her hips. She felt her water break. "David," she said, and pulled him in.

She dug at him, made his shoulder bleed, bit his face. It helped to get the pain out. He was trembling, "Jesus! Jesus-

God! Jesus, Lynn," he said. "God, come on! Off our feet! Off
our feet! Talk about adolescents! God!"

"Then get undressed," she told him.

"You!"

"David . . ."

"Do it. You—"

His jacket was already off. His neck was moving on its base;
his breath, heavy, wet. "Christ, you're incredible! You're incredible!" he said.

She couldn't help it. They were somewhere between twenty
and thirty seconds apart now, and the pain and pressure was
too much. She grabbed the collar of his shirt and tore, ripped it
down, spread it, snapping all the buttons in a line. They
landed, light as crickets, on the rug. "Fantastic!" David was
moaning. "Oh fantastic! Wow!" She yanked his belt. "Oh,
God!" She felt it uncinch. She broke the button above the fly
and heard the zipper whine. The pants fell past his knees.

"O.K." she managed, her voice strained and tight, "you do
the rest."

"No. Please." He was rocking. "You. The shoes!"

"David . . ."

"O.K. I'm sorry." He stepped out of things. "I'm sorry." He
let other things drop. She saw his shape sit on the bed's edge,
pull his shoes off. She didn't know how she was going to make
it as she removed her panties and came close.

He pulled the bedspread down. She found a wastebasket and
slid it beside the bed. She moved against him, kept his hands
on her back, pressing her whole anatomy hard, violently
down, against, trying to create hard enough pressure to dis-
place some of the pain. She screamed. She dug in. She fought
against him with her fists and knees. He kept bellowing sounds
to match hers, saying things like: *God*—he thought his fantasies
were pretty advanced, but—*Jesus*—he realized now that they
were—*Christ*—naive. But as they tore and fought against each
other, Lynn felt herself giving way and knew what she'd

hoped for was impossible. She could not last. She could not hold out.

She slid down his body slowly, marking it with her teeth, clearing herself as where she could. When the baby came, it came easily and she was able crudely to slice the cord, get everything in the wastebasket and cover it with the bedspread without really losing much of the rhythm of the foreplay. She submitted to David pulling at her, at her shoulders, slid back up along him, joining, both of them, three minutes later, coming almost together under the bloodsoak of sheets.

David lay with his head off the far edge of the bed, making sounds. Lynn played one hand over his ribs, blew breath gently against his sweat. She could smell herself—herself, the ocean and her own birth, but could not keep them apart. She thought she heard a steamer, way out in Long Island Sound. Shortly afterward, when David showered, she took the basket out to the small pier of the studio front and emptied it into the sea. Standing there briefly, she tasted herself again, her own fetality, felt the darkness—warm, salty, moist, in membranes layered out and out around her. The moon, real and untelevised above, seemed a strange opening in space, a place she might ultimately move to, go. She ached, but could not feel her body. It was an abstract ache, one in air.

Inside, they came together one more time: much quicker, less violent, more studied, more synchronized. David did not shower. Instead, he dressed himself hurriedly and lit a long cigar.

"Did I hurt you?" he asked. "I'm always afraid . . ."

"No," Lynn reassured him from the bathroom. She stopped herself with toilet paper, pulled on her panties, and dropped her dress over her head. "No." Somehow it was true.

"Hey—you start?"

"What?"

"Your period start?"

". . . Yes."

In the car, on the way back to Manhattan, they talked enthusiastically about St. Croix.

Her husband, Jack, was sitting on the long couch going through briefs in his blue bathrobe when she came in. There was a small snifter of crême de cacao on the coffee table to his right. They said hello. She kissed him on his forehead and hung up her coat.

"Where you been?"

"Theater."

"What'd you see?"

"*Long Day's Journey.*"

"How was it?"

"Fantastic." She straightened her hair.

"Great play." Jack wrote a sentence in the margin of his brief. "There's some triple sec there, if you want."

"Thanks."

"Picked it up on the way home."

She poured a cordial glass half full. The smell of orange reminded her somehow of Christmas, kumquats from Florida fruit packages she had bitten into in lost distant Decembers as a child. She crossed the room. She stood in front of their window wall, looking out. The lights beyond, below, all the bunched thousands of them, looked like perforations. She stared at the reflected milk stains on her dress, her reflection seeming to spread out across the perforations to surround her until, searching the distance, she was gone.

"Did you find it?"

"Hmmm?"

"Find the triple sec."

"Yes. Fine. Thanks."

"See the letter from Ad?"

"No. What's he say?"

"They beat Taft 21 to 20. He pulled a ligament in his knee. He's been having whirlpools. Nothing serious. They took X rays at the Sharon Hospital. He's seeing Cynthia Kaufmann this weekend. Listen—do you want to?"

"Hmmm?"

"You at all horny?"

She pressed the cordial glass against her lips. The fruity taste rose up, viscous, wet; it made orange seeds of her eyes. "Maybe later," she said.

"Can't hear you."

She took the glass away, wet her lips. "Maybe later."

"Sure, O.K."

Her eyes watered. She experienced the only moment akin to incest she had ever felt. She thought of her son, Adam, in the whirlpool. Her knee hurt.

THE HORSE

Lynda Schor

SHE NOTICED WITH TERROR that he'd gotten rid of her car. She could no longer see it through the picture window where it was always framed, sometimes a bit to the left or the right, but always there, giving her a real sense of security. It was a symbol of escape and he must have sensed that. He always sensed what would cause her pain. She looked again to make sure the car hadn't materialized in the second that she hadn't been looking, but the only thing she could see was the clean edge of the grass, trimmed neatly, not one blade growing out onto the small suburban sidewalk, tidily crew-cut by the high-school kid whom Marvin accused her of making love with. They hadn't spoken to each other in a week. Marvin always thought the sounds the birds made were special code messages of assignations with her lovers, all the birds in the neighborhood having been enlisted as messengers for that cause. Not having spoken to Marvin in a week, she had no idea what he was thinking; she only knew how much she hated him. She feared speaking and not being answered. The whole house was adapted to Marvin's stifled rages. Taciturnity surrounded him like an amnionic sac filled with venom, making it possible, merely by a change in atmosphere, to know whether Marvin was anywhere in the proximity of herself or the house. She feared that one word from her might cause everything to burst all over, contaminating the Autumn Warmth Armstrong carpet, and the Drexel One-of-a-Kind furniture with fleur-de-lis furniture covers. She wandered about the house like a caged animal, caged by Marvin's feelings about her, her inability to fathom what he would do next, and how it related to her. Marvin wasn't ugly at all, but to her every detail about him was enlarged to the point of hideousness. She'd notice that one hair of his dark beard had slanted and grown inward and there was a bit of transparent skin growing over it, and she'd look at it and look at it until it assumed gargantuan proportions, and be triumphant over the ugliness of it. If one of his jowls trembled, she'd feel revulsion. Then triumph.

In the space where her car should have been parked, a horse rode into view. Marvin was on it. She didn't know that Marvin could ride. He rode the horse into the garage and in a few moments came out without it. I wonder if he got the horse to replace the car, she thought, but he must know I don't ride. The thought of it terrified her. She looked up at him as he entered, as if by his having done something she expected the heaviness of his anger to have dissipated. Certainly she expected some sort of explanation for the horse, but there was none.

She watched him morbidly masticate his dinner, his lips framed in glowing grease. He finished the last spoon of chocolate pudding; he smoothed it over his tongue in slow motion, while she watched with absorption and repulsion. When he felt the food drop onto his tongue he'd close his mouth, not without some of it dripping out. She was tempted to take the spoon and wipe it across his lips, collecting the pudding from one side of his mouth to the other. It was a relief to have him leave quickly. She sat there in the company of all the dirty dishes. Actually, his leaving made her angry. Not that he ever did the dishes, but if he sat there while she cleaned up it bothered her less, even though she enjoyed the cleaning more, or didn't have to hate it as much, when he wasn't there.

She began to wonder where he was. She herself never left the house anymore, as he could construe it as suspicious. On the other hand, Marvin was never home anymore. In the morning he'd be out by the time she awoke. Then she'd see him riding the reddish horse past the close houses of the development. Maybe he had a lover. Here she was, locked in the house, and he had a lover. He didn't want her to have one and now he had one. All she did was think about who, where, and when. When she thought the birds were sending messages, she thought, How crazy, I've turned into him.

Isobel never went to see the horse, she never went to touch it. She never went near the garage. It was, she felt, Marvin's very private property, even more so than his underpants, which, though they were exclusively his, she washed, handled, folded, put away—with resentment when she hated him, and proprietarily when she loved him. Even more than his pipes, she had the feeling she shouldn't look at the horse, it was so private it was illicit. One night, late, Marvin wasn't home yet. Isobel was lying in her twin bed with extra-firm Sealy mattress and box spring, with matching Springmaid sheets of Yves St. Laurent design percale, when she heard a faint sound that brought her out of her beginning sleep. It sounded like Marvin having an orgasm. She looked on top of herself for a moment, and he wasn't there, nor was he in his bed. The night was quiet again, except for the scratchy sound of a cricket at sparse intervals. Since there were just high, tiny casement windows in her room, she walked down the carpeted stairs and pulled the large curtains aside slightly at the center of the picture window and looked out. It was an aimless gesture since the sound had seemed to come from the backyard, more force of habit than anything else. Before she got up close to the window she saw a gossamer reflection of herself, transparent, like a ghost, moving gently in her nightgown and peignoir set. She looked lovelier to herself than she'd felt lately, but the fact that she was transparent filled her with terror, since she'd been feeling transparent and now it seemed to have become a reality. She thought that if she didn't do something that involved action immediately, she'd go mad that very instant, so she put on her boots, which were the only shoes she had downstairs, and went outside. She thought of going around the back, but she felt she should keep away from the garage. Her friend Marge, looking out of the window that night from across the street, saw Isobel in her nightgown, sitting on an aluminum outdoor chair in the middle of the lawn, staring into space.

Marvin began to sleep out the whole night, from that night on. If he's going to have a lover, she thought, why can't he eat there too, and why can't she do his laundry? Why do I have to cook his dinner, and then be left alone with the dishes? Yet she herself was afraid to break the last contact. One night she was woken by a loud moan. It really sounded like Marvin having an orgasm, but how could that be? It was louder than the last time. Maybe she was going insane and it was haunting her that he had lovers. She should go to a shrink. You should go to a shrink when you hear your husband having orgasms all the time. But she was afraid to go to a shrink, so she tried to think up more logical solutions. For instance, maybe Marvin was next door with her neighbor Rosalie. Certainly their house was close enough to hear a loud orgasm in the deep silence of the night. Maybe that was Rosalie's husband. Maybe all men sound alike. She really didn't know. If it was Marvin with Rosalie, how come he had louder orgasms than with her? She thought of calling up Rosalie and asking her whether that was Marvin at her house having orgasms all the time, so at least she wouldn't think she was going crazy. But Rosalie wouldn't tell her, so it didn't matter. She could say, "Hi, Rosalie. Good morning. How come you sound so refreshed this morning?"

"Well, I just had a fantastic night's sleep."

"Listen, I've been hearing strange sounds at night; do you?"

"Like what?"

"Just a weird noise."

"I haven't heard anything, but I sleep very heavily."

"Look, Rosalie, was Marvin at your house last night?"

"If he was he sneaked in."

"I thought I heard Marvin having an orgasm in your house last night."

"Don't be silly. Charles was home. You know he'd never stand for Marvin having an orgasm in his house when he was home."

The next day she asked Charles whether he'd been home at around two o'clock in the morning.

He said, "Where else would I be at two o'clock in the morning? I was sleeping because I have to get up and go to work."

"Are you sure?"

"Of course I'm sure, unless my astral body left my physical body and took a journey somewhere, but I try not to because I don't trust Rosalie with my body while I'm gone. She'd nudge me and when I didn't respond she'd pummel me, having no respect for my body. She'd say, 'How come you're always so unresponsive?' and when I didn't respond she'd kick me. Then she'd realize there was something wrong, and, not wanting to waste me before I was cold, she'd get on top of me, and gently rape me, and after she'd come and was still lying on top of my soulless, cooling, unbreathing body, she'd cry sleepily, then that same night she'd call the funeral parlor and have me carted out because she hates to keep things around the house (she's exceptionally neat), and the next day, when my soul returned to my body and I opened my eyes, I'd be wearing powder and rouge and lipstick and staring up into the eyes of my mother-in-law and all my other relatives, and all my stuff would be given away, including my car."

Isobel smiled. "Well then, have you been hearing any strange noises?"

"Like what? Wait, I have been hearing a sound like a bull in heat, but I just assumed it was your new horse. Fantastic replacement for the second car. No gas . . . but then it eats hay. And if it gets sick the vet can rip you off just like the garage, unless you get a home-care manual. And those were probably banned by the American Veterinary Association. No, there's no answer for us suburbanites." His voice ripped across the lawn cheerily, then muffled as he entered his car.

Isobel returned to the kitchen, thinking that he wouldn't tell her if he was away or if there was any fooling around, especially in the morning on the front lawn. Maybe Marvin gets into bed with both of them when Charles is asleep, so Charles never knows. But that would be taking an incredible chance, having to keep the bed from moving, and not making any noise, and what about the orgasm? Rosalie and Charles would be in bed, Rosalie waiting for Marvin, Charles fast asleep, slightly pressed against Rosalie. Marvin uses a key and tiptoes into their room, having left his shoes downstairs. He's also stripped off his clothes before entering their bedroom so that he won't make extra noise. Rosalie opens the covers for him on the other side of her. She has to press closer to Charles in order to have enough room for Marvin. Even so, Marvin has almost no room, so he moves on top of Rosalie. His naked body, slightly cool, gives Rosalie goose bumps in her thin brushed-nylon Ohrbach's nightie, but he warms up almost immediately. They kiss without moving the bed; for a second Marvin leans over to look with trepidation at Charles. He's very fearful that Charles will wake, he can't forget Charles for one moment, yet he's excited by the fact that Charles is there and might wake up, like making love without birth control when you know you're ovulating. It's fun to make love without moving, like a challenge, superexciting. Rosalie doesn't move at all, or slightly, slowly, around, and Marvin, on top, has a bit more leverage if he doesn't move the mattress or the blanket covering the three of them. As he holds Rosalie, his arm is against Charles, who feels warm, as he slowly and subtly moves his whole organ into Rosalie and out, each of them enjoying the enforced resistance against becoming frenetic. Rosalie chokes back noises; they stop and look at Charles, who is still sleeping. Rosalie's more careful and buries her head into the pillow. They both come in a suspended tension of the body, externally still, slightly raised off the mattress. Then Marvin bellows. As soon as he hears himself he becomes silent and they both suspend breathing, not even daring to look over at Charles. After what seems to be an enormous lapse of time, Marvin, without looking around, slides off Rosalie, kisses her goodbye as she pulls down her uncomfortable nonabsorbent nylon nightie, and crawls out of the room, dragging his clothes with him to the stairs like a retriever.

Marvin rode up to the door on the horse and sat down for his silent breakfast. Isobel was tempted to burn the toast to see whether that would get him to say something—for instance, "The toast is burnt"—but maybe he'd do something violent, silently, like look at the toast, walk over to her, put his thick, square-fingered, reddish hands around her neck, and begin to press passionately—but with a restraint similar to that which he used on Rosalie and which would save her life. After Marvin finished he wiped some egg and crumbs off his mouth, crumpled the napkin next to his dish, and, outside, lifted himself onto the horse. Isobel watched him mount the horse. Even while she hated him, his getting on the horse had a sensual quality that made her very jealous of him and his life. She almost desired him again. For an instant it was like being in love with him again. Certainly it was a new Marvin, not the same slovenly movement of slipping heavily down into the low front seat of the car. Then she realized that now he was riding the horse to work.

Maybe he's hiding his music students in the basement and making love with them there while I'm asleep, thought Isobel. She pictured herself descending the cold stairs to the basement in the dark of night. It was mostly dark and very cold, but a slight light shone from the laundry room, lighting her way. She knew she never left a light on in the laundry room. She padded quietly in, her feet totally noiseless on concrete. It felt cold and scrapy, like pumice, as she approached the room from the side so that she could just peek around the corner of the doorway. She almost tripped on the music stands, then adjusted her eyes and made sure she saw all their metallic lines. Terrified to get her head far enough into the doorway in order to be able to see something, finally she did, and saw that no one was looking at her. The light from the bare bulb in the ceiling hurt her eyes and threw a cold, harsh light over the whole laundry room with its cold white Sears Kenmore washer and dryer, and white meat-club freezer. Marvin and his music student were lying on the damp concrete floor on some towels they'd removed from the dryer and thrown down. She was angry that they were using her clean towels. Is that what she washed towels for? The girl was lying on her blue-and-olive Picasso-print velvet-pile towel with her sweater on and her skirt pulled up around her waist. Her nylon stockings lay beside her, limp and deflated like a pair of oversized used condoms. Marvin was lying next to her, with his shirt on and his pants down around his thighs. His skin looked incredibly white in the harsh light, in between the dark shirt and pants, and showing through his dark body hair. He appeared more naked than he'd ever been, even though he was wearing clothes. The girl was moaning because Marvin had his hand up her vagina and every time he jiggled his fingers there was a sucking sound, as if the washing machine was going on WASH. She had her hand around his penis, which was limp and yellow, its head peering over her clenched hand like a newborn kitten. Perspiration poured down Marvin's body and onto her towel as his body clenched with the effort of obtaining an erection. The girl, moaning louder now, looked down at her hand and opened it, watched the tiny thing drop to one side, and murmured in a frenzy of passion and frustration, "Marvin marvin marvin marvin . . ." Marvin removed his hand from her vagina, looked around for a second, and picked up her alto recorder from the floor where it lay beside her music book and shoes. He looked at it for a moment, as though trying to decide which end would be best, and moved it gently toward her as if it were an extension of himself. She lifted her head, leaned on one elbow, and grabbed his wrist. "No, no, Marvin, Marvin, no." She held his wrist in a deadlock for a moment, then pulled his hand toward her, lay down again, and Marvin masterfully inserted the recorder, mouthpiece first, into her vagina. By that time Marvin had an erection, but the woman was coming so Marvin considerately rammed her with the recorder while she writhed and panted. Then, the recorder still sticking out of her vagina, Marvin put his whole body over hers, but way above, held up by his hands, with elbows stiff, and on his toes. She put her hand around his cock once again, and moved it up and down like a piston, never releasing her hold. Marvin became stiffer and stiffer. Over her, he looked like the Verrazano Bridge. He gave two grunts, then his great bellow, as his sperm shot first way up between her breasts and then on her abdomen, falling on her doubleknit sweater and suede skirt, respectively. All of a sudden the bridge collapsed. His hand over her fell into the sperm. He looked into her eyes for a moment and said, "I'm sorry . . . . Lucky this is the laundry. You can wash them."

Marge came over. "I thought I saw you out on the lawn the other morning at about 3 A.M."

"Maybe it was me. I'm going crazy, Marge, I think I hear Marvin coming all the time. It even wakes me up from sleep. I didn't want to tell anyone, because Marvin doesn't sleep here anymore and I don't know where he is, but I must be haunted by it because I hear him having orgasms all the time, and I don't know where the sound is coming from."

Marge said, "Maybe it's the horse. You know, there's not much difference between the sound of a man and the sound of a horse neighing." Isobel offered Marge a piece of cake. "No, thanks, I'm not eating Entenmann's cake today. I ate fourteen in the past three days, so I'm trying to fast today. There's a new swami who comes to the house and gives private yoga lessons. Everyone's been using him, but I have to clean out my system first. It would be a waste of money to have that swami come and do yoga with fourteen Entenmann's cakes floating around my body."

Isobel made up her mind to check out the horse. She got out of bed at about three that night, not knowing why she went to bed at all, except that that's what she always did at night. She put on Marvin's bathrobe because she felt suddenly chilled in a deep way that pervaded her entire body internally through all her organs and left her hands glowing white and her lips tight and blanched, and a pair of green fur slippers Marvin had given her one Christmas, and went out through the side door and slowly up the driveway, toward the garage, trying not to crunch the gravel, which was damp with the night air. It was not a clear night, it was foggy. There was a nimbus of moisture around everything, with a faint rainbow aura. Strings of hay scattered all about reflected the moonlight. Funny she never noticed it before. A slight odor of horse and hay emanated moistly from the closed garage. She was panicky as she bent down for the garage door handle, not knowing how quiet she could be, how quiet she had to be. It depended on what was going on in there. For instance, when she opened it, Marvin could be just sitting there, watching her open it. As she gently lifted the door a few inches—and it made hardly any noise (it must have been oiled recently)—a faint light, reddish, exuded through the crack, shining garishly on the grass. She waited a moment and pulled the door higher. Fearful and impatient, she tried to peer under it without raising it more, but without success. She just got an incredible whiff of barn smell that was staggering. Pausing another moment in the silence she could hear a very gentle breathing that calmed her because it was not the breathing of someone who was waiting for the door to open but the breathing of someone who was sleeping. She took a chance and raised it more. The reddish glow from the light assailed her, along with the smell, before any visual image assimilated. Then she saw that the glow came from a red bulb in a rough socket in the unfinished garage interior. There was hay all over, cobwebs, bags of feed, a pile of horseshit, and, in the corner, on a large pile of hay and some filthy quilted horse blankets, lay Marvin, naked, partially covered with purplish-gray and greenish-purple blankets, the exposed portions of his body pink and red in the glowing light. The horse was lying against him, nearly cradling him, one heavy foreleg over Marvin's body, hair reddish brown, semi-retracted penis gently resting against Marvin's leg, gleaming whitely, as it was shielded from the light by his own upper thigh. Isobel's first thought was that she didn't know horses lay down when they slept. She stepped back out of the garage and just looked at the scene without thinking, just let it sit there, an image. Then it occurred to her what a ludicrous scene was displayed to the people who lived across the street, if they happened to be up, gazing through their picture window; scrupulously and silently she closed the garage door and padded back to bed.

She looked at Marvin with new eyes, as if she didn't know him. He became more interesting to her and even strangely sexually attractive. At the same time, she felt power over him, having seen him—without him seeing her—revealed in an unguarded moment of truth. When he ate his meals in silence she could almost laugh at his pretense of dignity. She was losing her fear of him, yet she was in awe of him for expanding into other realms of living without her. Suddenly life, which was such a drag, became very exciting. She couldn't wait to spy some more on Marvin and the horse. She had to figure out some way to observe Marvin when he was awake to see what exactly he did, but that seemed pretty impossible. She couldn't very well open the garage door while Marvin was awake. She could hide somewhere before he came in, but even if Marvin didn't sense her presence, the horse would. She could go in and meet the horse now to get him used to her. She considered asking Marge's advice, but didn't want to tell her yet. She walked to the garage feeling the same fear she felt when she got her first air conditioner, and she had to relate to it herself, without anyone else to adjust it for her. She decided to call on the horse first, but if Marvin rode the horse to work, how could she? She thought that at least she'd go into the garage and leave her smell around during the afternoon, and sometime right after dinner she'd hide in the garage till Marvin finally came in for the night. As she walked to the garage this time, her high heels crunched in the gravel and her ankle twisted. She felt a strange excitement and a sensation of doing something wrong. Even though she wasn't doing anything actually wrong, she was fearful of being discovered. But Marvin was at work and so was the horse. She realized that she thought of the garage not as Marvin's but as the domain of the horse. Marvin was a guest, just as she was. The garage smelled like a horse—it was furnished with horse stuff right down to the horseshit in the corner. The hay tickled her ankles. It had a rich smell that was almost unbearable. She lay down on it to test it out and it prickled, so she put one of the funky blankets under her. When next she opened her eyes it took her a moment to orient herself, then she realized that she'd fallen asleep in the garage. Having slept there, she was more at peace there, more like she belonged. With the door closed, she felt she could die of the fumes—but at least they weren't carbon monoxide. She wanted to go back to the house and recover for a while, but she had no idea what time it was and resolved not to miss her chance tonight. Chance at what she wasn't sure. There was a flavor of evening in the air even though the garage had no windows. She piled some hay behind two monster bags of feed and covered most of herself with a blanket. She couldn't understand why it didn't bother her to lie in all the junk and get her clothes dirty. She felt a great sense of abandon. Suddenly the garage door opened with a giant proprietary swing on its runners and the whole door was up. There was a rush of cool air. Isobel felt exposed, but apparently no one suspected that she was there. Almost immediately Marvin slammed the door shut behind him and came over to a feed bag. He seemed to be removing some of the stuff—perhaps it was oats—but she didn't see what he was doing because she wanted to remain hidden. She was more titillated and stimulated than nervous.

When next she had the courage to look up, Marvin and the horse were picnicking. The horse was eating oats or something out of her kelly-green Melmac garbage pail, and Marvin had three bags from MacDonald's sitting next to him and all his food spread out: a Big Mac cheeseburger, two packages of french fries, a Coke, and coffee. She felt a surge of anger that Marvin didn't even miss her the first time she wasn't in the house to make his dinner. He wasn't cursing or anything, he just bought his own whatever he liked. Certainly she wouldn't serve him that. The realization that she was getting out of preparing a meal didn't assuage her anger. He seemed to prefer eating with the horse also. He almost looked happy. She watched every motion carefully. She watched him squeeze his ketchup out of those soft plastic containers, which he opened with his teeth then manipulated from the bottom up until every drop of ketchup was spread on the cheeseburger. Then he opened five more and methodically poured them out all over the two packs of french fries. He's really going to the dogs, she thought. He had ketchup on the corners of his mouth. He wolfed everything down and reclined on a bunch of junk. The horse ate slowly. She watched his mouth move, fascinated.

She'd never watched a horse so closely before. The only horse she'd ever seen was in *National Velvet*. She realized that she never really looked at the horses even when she saw other horse movies. The horse seemed to gather up a mouthful of the oats by gently manipulating them into his mouth, using only his soft lips, then raising his head slowly, as if swallowing a pill, he allowed the oats to slip beyond his enormous front teeth, which he exposed for a moment between each bite. Then he chewed carefully, his jaw moving slowly from side to side, and back again, once in every few chews tossing his head like a woman throwing long hair out of her face with a shrug. After a while the horse sniffed around, his nostrils opening and closing like a jellyfish propelling itself along the Caribbean Sea. He sniffed the McDonald's bags, the leftover french fries, and began chewing them up. He masticated all the remains, including the bags and cardboard hotcup. He even gets the horse to clean up after him. Men really have it made, thought Isobel. Then the horse hovered over Marvin himself, looked into his eyes, shot out his tongue, and gently licked the ketchup from the corners of his mouth, and remained there for a moment, hovering over Marvin lovingly. Marvin seemed to be aroused by the horse's hot breath and began to respond. He gazed lovingly into the horse's eyes. Isobel was embarrassed at witnessing that exchange. They both began to breathe heavily, like the grating of onions on the fine side of a grater. Marvin got up and, delicately removing his gaze from the magnetic stare of the horse, swiftly undressed. He lay his clothing over the grain sack that Isobel was hiding behind. She saw them hung over her side, piece by piece. A tiny bit of Marvin smell emanated from them, if she could smell anything over the stable smell, but she seemed to be adjusting, as she almost didn't smell that anymore. Now that Marvin was totally naked, she had no idea what he was going to do, but all he did was lie down again, almost exactly where he'd been reclining when the horse licked his lips. Wasn't he going to do anything? It was becoming damp and chilly in this garage. Marvin's penis lay across his thigh like a cucumber in a bed of chicory. She was shivering, but Marvin naked, didn't appear to be cold at all. The horse moved closer to him again. For a moment the horse's head, glowing redly, obliterated Marvin's face from view, so she watched his penis, which slowly tumesced. It began to fill out all the loose skin very leisurely, at one point it jerked upward a bit on his thigh; then it got larger still, until it stood straight up, almost black in the red light, and pointed navelward. Marvin gently patted the horse's head, and turned it at the same time, in the gentlest way, so that the horse saw Marvin's enormous erection. Isobel saw the horse inhale deeply, his nostrils flaring sensuously as he stood there and looked. Then he looked at Marvin for a moment and slowly unfurled his tongue, like a flag rolling out on a windless day, bits of saliva dripping from the sides of his mouth. Marvin lay there totally passive, melting into the sacks under him, practically two-dimensional, while the horse gently snuffled his nose against Marvin's penis, and a drop of horse saliva fell on the underside and slowly dripped down until it was trapped in his pubic hair like a bit of semen. With utmost delicacy, the horse, beginning at Marvin's pubic hair, lay his thin, flat tongue against his penis and licked upward, the flatness of his tongue practically surrounding the whole cock like a pig in a blanket. Marvin closed his eyes as if in pain, sucked in his breath, and raised his hips in immediate ecstasy. Then suddenly Isobel became cognizant of the horse's penis, swelling between his red legs, white and veiny, enormous as a club. She experienced a strange, momentary, ripping jealousy that Marvin himself should have found the most likely lover. The horse continued his sensuous licking of Marvin's organ, saliva spraying all over, Marvin moaning and writhing around, his eyeballs rolled up into his head. Isobel was becoming extremely excited. She didn't know who she desired, Marvin or the horse. She was becoming breathlessly appetitive watching the movements of the gradual soothing tongue, incredibly wrapping and licking and moistening Marvin's fat purple penis, and she touched her own vagina. With great difficulty she pulled down her underpants, trying to maintain silence, and felt the dirty blanket and some stray straw under her behind. Just as she touched her clitoris, some saliva spray from the horse dropped on it, feeling cool for a moment. That drop of liquid from the horse's mouth drove her wild in itself, but when she moved her hand it lubricated her and she came immediately, frenetically silent. She had the feeling that the horse was aware of her presence and of the sexual thing between them too. She suddenly felt compelled to pull up her pants and rearrange her skirt. She was able to observe more objectively now. The horse stopped for a moment, licked Marvin's balls, then the insides of his thighs and then ran his flat tongue all over Marvin's straining body like a vacuum cleaner; there wasn't a part he missed. Then he gently nudged Marvin at the small of his back, where Marvin's skin was soft, smooth, and white, and at that ever-so-slight touch, Marvin turned over onto his abdomen. The horse licked his slightly hairy ass, the center of his tongue entering the crack slightly. Marvin's back began to arch more and more, until the horse stood over him and gently nudged Marvin's ass with the thick head of his own white penis, and at the touch Marvin let out a soulful moan. Then the horse moved over Marvin until Marvin was completely cradled between and beneath the horse's legs, as if in a house. Breathing heavily, Marvin rubbed his back and head in a very loving way along the horse's chest and underbelly, which were right above him; and then, now and again balancing his body on his two knees and one arm, he caressed a foreleg, running his hand stretched out, as if to achieve the maximum sensual area, along the whole flank and down the leg, from outside in and inside out, in a very loving way. Then, bracing himself for the pressure from the horse, Marvin, arms trembling as they held up his weight, hands making marks in the crusty dirt of the floor, nearly fell forward, but remained up on his hands and knees, and a silent scream was emitted from his wide-open mouth and bugged-out eyes, a look of pain and pleasure both, as Isobel saw that somehow the horse had inserted part of his penis. Incredibly gentle, the horse didn't thrust powerfully but, in order not to hurt Marvin, just moved so tenderly around and around, never forcing. Marvin was still on his trembling arms, moving his behind gently around and emitting moans and cries incessantly, his own organ, swelled to an incomparable size for it, was there in front of him, and Isobel thought for a moment, What a waste. She pictured a smaller animal under Marvin, and in fact it could go on like that forever, until at the bottom a dragonfly was making it with a roach. She watched as if hypnotized, his penis moving closer and closer to the floor with every movement, until it finally touched one of the sacks, and at that instant, as if it were a signal, Marvin and the horse both neighed loudly and came together, Marvin's sperm spurting out and some of it hitting his chest, where it hung in the hair for a moment as the reddish light lent the milky drops a pinkish halo. Suddenly Marvin dropped off his arms and lay, exhausted, where he fell on top of his own sperm. Isobel got up to leave the moment Marvin fell asleep, and she didn't have to wait long. Lying exactly as he'd fallen, he remained and began snoring. The horse lay down next to him without moving away, so Marvin lay cradled between the horse's limbs. For some reason, Isobel no longer feared that the horse would give away her presence. As she walked on tiptoe to the garage door, she looked at the horse and saw his deep, expressionless gaze follow her until she was outside the garage. The last thing she saw as she quietly pulled down the garage door was the horse's one large, dark eye that was still visible over Marvin's slumped body, looking at her, a sharp dot of reflected light emanating from it. As she continued to close the door the dot of light disappeared, but the eye remained steady. When the door shut completely, shocked with the sweet smell of the air, she found herself alone in the dark, moist evening.

Marvin stopped riding the horse to work. Isobel wondered why and suspected that he'd seen her in the garage that night.

She feared that he was planning some sort of plot to discover her in his domain, with his horse, which in itself shouldn't seem suspect, but in view of her own desires, it was, since she thought day and night of that scene, and of herself taking Marvin's place. After the morning she saw Marvin leave for work without the horse, she didn't dare go near the garage. Feeling very uneasy, she decided to call Marge and tell her about the horse.

"Hello, Marge, how's your yoga?"

"Just beautiful, I'm finding my center."

"Where is it?"

"I can't describe it. Why don't you come over for some banana bread?" asked Marge. "I bake my own bread now, and only with organic ingredients."

"Okay, but don't you have your lesson today with the swami?"

"I can't take it today because my system is full. I already ate six banana breads today."

Marge's house smelled sweet and delicious from baking. Marge herself was wearing a transparent Indian shirt which exposed the outlines of her girdle, rolled down at the waist, where, at its boundaries, it absolutely lost the power to contain the waves of flesh that rolled over it. Her legs stuck out from under the shirt like two white, sticky loaves of unbaked bread left to rise under a moist towel, and made a comforting, rhythmic flapping sound as Marge walked about the kitchen, preparing Mu tea (from sixteen herbs) and slicing banana bread for Isobel.

"It's too moist. I like it moist, but this is too moist, don't you think?"

"No, it's just perfect, I love it moist. It's more like a dessert than bread, but I like it."

"It's like banana-bread pudding," laughed Marge as she delicately dropped a tiny tablet of saccharin into her Mu tea from a tiny silver spoon. Isobel watched it bubble ominously until it disappeared and then she was confronted by Marge's enormous nipple, which rested on the edge of the table and was clearly visible through her shirt.

"I think I've fallen in love with the swami," Marge confided. "And I think he loves me too, he just believes in patience. I told Fred and he says I have his blessings as long as I continue to cook meat for him."

"Now what makes you think the swami loves you?" asked Isobel, sinking into the soporific sauna-bath sensation of Marge's kitchen and their conversation.

"Because he said to me, and he looked strangely and deeply into my eyes as he said it, and his eyes emanated love . . .

> 'Serve thou the true guru, lovingly and with single-minded
>   devotion;
> Know that the true guru is the holy of holies,
> Who fulfills all the desires of thy mind.
> Thou gatherest the blessing, the fruits thy heart longs
>   for.'

"That means that if I love him he'll fulfill all the desires I have in my mind."

"I think it means all the desires *of* thy mind . . . not of the body," said Isobel; then she recalled the enormous, dark, expressionless eye of the horse, and felt sudden fear and desire.

"Listen, Marge, I think I'm in love also."

"With who? Marvin?"

"No, no, with the horse."

"With the horse." Marge just repeated the last words.

"I'm not sure what love is, Marge, whether I just desire him sexually or whether that's what falling in love is, because I don't know him, but I can see that he's the most loving per— . . . animal I've ever seen, and I really desire him. I think about him all the time. I'm going mad. But I think he likes me too."

"Well, go ahead, do what you like. It's never wrong to love. This is interesting. Maybe the horse is between incarnations.

He'll probably be human in his next life. But you probably won't, so if not now you may never get together."

"I know," Isobel said, "but I'm afraid Marvin suspects. He's not like Fred. He's very possessive and capable of violence. I'm not sure if he'd be possessive of me or the horse, but I'm scared. He doesn't take the horse to work anymore and I'm afraid it's a trap."

"Oh, no, Fred told me that they just don't like the horse waiting outside the Curran Building in Hempstead all day, and the owners of the building asked him to leave the horse home."

With that explanation, Isobel felt a sudden surge of joy and relief. She went home to visit the horse.

This time when she opened the door to the garage it was with a fear of relating to the horse, not so much the fear of being discovered. She was fearful of being rejected. She opened the door swiftly—after all, it was her garage too. Who had worked to finish putting Marvin through music school . . . and then law school? She was wearing something that exposed her midriff and her navel, which she felt was the most sensuous part of her body, and she had rubbed some musk body oil into it, and rubbed it into her hair. The garage still stank, but the stench had sexual implications to Isobel by this time. One quality the horse possessed that Isobel loved, as she saw him turn his head and look at her without surprise, was his acceptance of everything. He had such a totally open expression. She felt she could be perfectly free with him, be herself for once. There was nothing he expected of her, or an image he seemed to have of her which he projected, and that she had to fulfill or else risk his love being withdrawn. She had the feeling that with this horse she could be as passionate as she liked or do anything she liked, without turning him off. She rolled the garage door down behind her and turned to face the horse, who was standing there looking bored, nudging a pile of hay but not eating. He looked directly into her eyes and she felt as if she were floating and her whole body was being absorbed into his through those orbs, and when his nostrils twitched she felt a mad feeling of love and desire. She realized that it was the angle at which his nose swept down from his brow, and the way it flared out a bit at the bottom, that was so incredibly sensual to her, almost as if that simple aesthetic combination could, like magic, be the whole cause of this passion. She stood there for a moment before walking over to him. With great joy, she saw that he was walking over to her first, and she was pleased that he was making some kind of move. The fact that he was was like all her fantasies of the past days come true. As if aware of her attempts to be seductive, the horse sniffed her navel with his moist, quivering nostrils. Isobel was too happy to feel anything more than just elation at being there with the horse. She looked more closely at him, touched his face gently, snuffed his mane with her nose. When he lifted one thin black lip for one moment, she noticed that his large front teeth weren't even, one stuck out in front of the other. As she was having dental work done, and had temporary jackets on, one of her front teeth stuck out in front of the other too. She whispered goodbye to the horse. It seemed extremely symbolic that they had similar teeth. As she walked down the driveway she wondered why, after all those sexual fantasies, she didn't actually feel like having sex with the horse when she was with him. She recalled what Marvin had said when she first met him: "I like to get to know someone before I go to bed with them. Do you?" And the horse didn't press her either. She was glad he felt the same way.

The next day, when Marvin went into the garage before he left for work, Isobel felt an unexpected twinge of jealousy, since he'd already spent the night in there. As soon as he was gone, she rummaged around for some kind of offering or gift she and the horse could enjoy together. For a moment she couldn't think what horses liked besides sugar, which was no good for his teeth and which she wouldn't be able to partake of with him, then decided on two magnificent reddish-black apples. This was the first time in a long while that she felt really excited to be alive. She experienced a strong sense of release and abandon. She went out in her nightgown, barefoot, an apple in each hand, like Eve. She thought, as she opened the garage door, that maybe she should clean it up a bit, tidy it, and get rid of that odor, and then she realized that she didn't want that kind of relationship again. She wasn't willing to have her ability to clean be one of her desirable traits. If he didn't like her this way, too bad. The horse looked up when she entered, but he never looked surprised. That was one of the qualities she found fascinating about him. She held the apple out to him and he nudged it for a moment with his soft mouth closed, then he raised one of his lips in a weird way and Isobel saw his crooked tooth. For one horrible moment she thought, What am I doing here with this ugly creature? but in a second that passed. The horse took one bite of the apple, which nearly obliterated it, core and all, except for a tiny piece left sitting in her hand which revealed a glaring whiteness in contrast to the almost-black skin, and two tiny capillaries of maroon. In surprise, she handed over the second apple, which at first he only sniffed, as he was still chewing the other, with sideways motions of his head and some slobbering. She watched him with wonder, realizing how well she knew Marvin and how strange this was. The horse stopped chewing for a moment, looked into Isobel's eyes, wrapped his mouth around her whole apple, and remained that way, with his soft lips touching her palm. For the first time since she'd watched Marvin and the horse, she felt sexually excited. As the horse finished her apple too, she said, "You pig!" and laughed. Marvin was a slob, and a hog too, but this horse was even worse. Somehow, she felt all her standards for men or lovers drop away. She felt flexible, able to accept, to find out, free. It doesn't matter, she told herself, I can afford this relationship now. She touched the horse all over his soft face with its coating of short fur, like suede, ran her fingers across his eyelids, causing him to close his eyes and flare his nostrils in that way that appealed to her so much. She put her nose against his and felt his warm breath surround her face like a General Electric facial sauna, and an enormous feeling of desire and abandon overcame her. She began kissing the horse wildly, all over his gentle furred protuberances and concavities, all new to her, grabbed his soft, silky mane, and, clutching the light brown hair tightly, buried her fists in it, while the horse, his nose becoming hot, nuzzled her all over. She collapsed where she'd been standing, not caring whether it was clean or not, and closed her eyes. For an instant she reminded herself of Marvin. The horse took her nightgown between his teeth and lifted it. He pressed his lips gently all over her sentient body, just a soft pressure with gentle furred edges that drove her wild. He pressed, gently pressed, into her pubic hair and along the insides of her thighs, which she spread for him in abandon. She could never picture doing this with Marvin—though she'd felt like it once in a while—as Marvin would think she was lewd. She had the feeling that it would frighten Marvin. The horse continued his gentle pressure all over her body, and again and again she felt his hot nose and lips press her pubic hair and her hidden clitoris. She raised her hips off the garage floor, and felt the horse's large, flat tongue, with a firm muscular pressure, press in between her labia, felt its wet heat encompass her clitoris for a moment before sliding down its length, giving her the most voluptuous sensation she'd ever imagined, and press slightly into the opening of her vagina, and return slowly upward again. She had a desire to move her hips but, wanting to prolong everything, and enjoying the horse, who needed no assistance in pleasing her, she allowed—even consciously trying to remain still—the horse to repeat his slow, endless licks from one end of her labial opening to the other, penetrating subtly, increasingly deeper into her vagina each time he passed it. And she, allowing the waves of sensation, which she felt all over her body and deeply into her thighs, to sweep over her until they became greater and greater, too much to bear—no, she couldn't bear them, she began to moan, but the horse retained his slowness, and she began to grunt and shout, "No, no, no, no, no," as she felt her body contract endlessly. The walls of her vagina clenched tightly around the horse's whole trembling tongue, she felt her eyes roll into their sockets, and then she relaxed. The horse began nudging her on the side. For an instant she felt annoyance and no desire to do anything more, until she saw the horse's penis floating toward her, bobbing up and down lightly, as in water. Defying gravity, it hung there, not down but almost parallel with the horse's underbelly, its thick tip practically staring her in the eye. She allowed the horse to push her limp body over as he might one of the empty sacks, and she lay there on her stomach, her nightgown across her neck and through one armhole like a banner worn in a Miss America pageant. She lay there for a moment and found herself not relating to him at all. She was lying on some coarse muslin sack and gently brushed her fingers along one spot as she often did while falling asleep, feeling the soft brush of the fabric with the very tips of her fingers. She looked up a moment and saw, glowing like a pink fluorescent light bulb, the horse's cock. Then she felt it move under her from behind, until it rubbed her clitoris, as the tip pushed all the way in front, touching her belly. She became excited again, but was slightly terrified by the size of the horse's organ, which she hadn't realized was that enormous. She had an urge to run, then thought it wouldn't be fair to run off without satisfying the horse. She raised herself onto her hands and knees, as she'd seen Marvin do, and she could see, by looking down under herself, the horse's bulbous organ, now appearing dark against her own white skin, lying under her, almost reaching to her breasts. Then she watched it moving away slowly, like being in the last car of a train and watching through the tunnel as the train begins to move, and she felt its whole length move back along her vaginal opening. The horse repeated this movement a few times and Isobel watched from underneath as the penis came toward her and retreated, until she had to close her eyes and strain her whole body back. She no longer cared how large his penis was, she could absorb it. She pushed back more and more, and felt him insert the tip, just the tip, gently into her vagina, where it remained still, stretching her tightly, and feeling heavy, an incredible weight, like a pressurized balloon. She pressed back more, until her whole vagina felt filled—no, her whole body, like a turkey ready for the oven. The horse never tried to insert the full length of his cock. He allowed her to move softly, however she wished, until she came again, and still the horse hadn't had an orgasm. Then he began moving harder, harder and harder, being gentle but still hurting somewhat, a hurt that she knew she was enjoying, as she cried and cried with pain and pleasure, and the horse neighed as he came. Then she realized that she'd forgotten her diaphragm. She wondered whether horse sperm fertilized human eggs. Could she give birth to a centaur? Even the horse's detumescent penis fitted her so tightly it made a small pop as he removed it, like the swollen cork in vintage wine. She caressed his underbelly lovingly, amazed at the incredible consideration and gentleness he'd shown restraining the major portion of his strength not to hurt her. She lay for a moment inside the C shape that he made when lying on his side with his four legs straight out, protected as if in a cave, a warm cave, and she had no idea how much time had passed. She began to feel panicky. She arose, feeling dirty and scrubby for the first time, and brushed herself off. She felt she should say something to the horse since they'd just made love and she didn't want him to think she wanted him only for sex. She looked at the horse, wondering whether he expected anything, and it appeared as if he didn't. He still had his blank, open expression, but warmer, tired, lids hanging lower, relaxed, slicing his eye in half. She noticed some grit in the corner of each eye and, for want of any other expression of tenderness, picked it out with great pleasure, and scraped the little bit of dried moisture that looked like an old tear from underneath the grit, stroked his silky nose, and departed. Her neighbors saw her running down the driveway in her nightgown, hopping gingerly through the gravel, in midafternoon.

Rosalie stopped her as she opened the screen door. "What are you doing in your nightgown at this time of day? You sure have a leisurely life."

"Oh, I was just cleaning out the garage for the horse," said Isobel, blushing. "I began in the morning and got so involved I hadn't realized what time it was." It was true that now, outside the barn, her life had the aspect of a dream. She couldn't get everything connected, and felt strangely discombobulated. Standing there talking with Rosalie, she felt all the horse's seminal fluid running thickly down one leg, past the bottom of her white permanent-press cotton batiste nightgown, then, as if once begun it couldn't be contained, it began running down the other leg too, tickling annoyingly. Isobel said, "I think I left the oven on," and ran inside. Rosalie watched Isobel close the door behind her, the back of her hair and nightgown covered with straw.

Isobel realized that the horse was the best lover she'd ever had. Yet her life and his were so different, he could never become part of hers. She couldn't think how to integrate this affair with the rest of her life. She wondered whether the horse liked her. She'd been so passive, but she really'd felt free to enjoy herself for the first time.

"How is it?" asked Marge.

"He's the best lover I've ever had! It's just incredible."

"Really?"

"Yes. Why don't you try it, Marge?"

"No, thanks. I can't see it," said Marge.

Isobel pictured Marge with the horse. She'd waddle up the driveway, with her shopping cart, full of provisions, bobbing along the gravel behind her. She'd roll up the door, push the cart in, then enter herself. "I wish you had a refrigerator here," she says to the horse. "I don't want these cream puffs to get spoiled." The horse watches as she bustles about, removing groceries from the cart and setting up a picnic on his favorite blanket. Then she relaxes in between the pastries and a dish with ham, capicola, headcheese, and bologna. "Whew," she says as she begins to slice some Jewish rye. Still the horse watches silently. "Have a sandwich," says Marge. "What would you like on it?" She holds up the dish so that the horse can see the choices, and she looks on amazed as he gobbles everything on the dish in one minute, leaving just a morsel of something unrecognizable that goes flying off into a corner.

"It's so nice to cook for someone who enjoys food," she says, ceasing her now-useless bread slicing and proceeding to eat some cake. She picks up a cannoli delicately with two fingers, transferring it to her other hand, where she holds it from underneath and moves it toward her mouth that way, as if it were a loving offering, only she puts it in too far, in her hurry to eat it before the horse does. In her effort to chew too much at one time, some thick cannoli cream creeps out along her lips, which the horse, who is standing over her, immediately licks off. Marge is immobile for an instant while she seems to be deciding whether she wants to continue eating or look into the feeling she got when the horse licked her lips, and then she gets up and removes her clothing, heavily and methodically, including her girdle. She starts by rolling it down over itself at the waist and then continues to roll until, when she takes it off, it's like a thick rubber band, which she throws on top of her other clothes with the agility of a cowboy with a lariat. She lies down right on top of all the food, wriggles in comfortably, and begins emptying éclairs and cannoli on herself, rubbing the cream all over. The horse obligingly begins to lick it off. "Ohhhhhhhh," says Marge. "You smell so male. Like avocado. With garlic. Ohh, that feels good!" She continues frosting herself with various types of creams, marbleizing her body in egg cream, whipped cream, and cream cheese, plastering it expertly into her pubic hair, moaning as the horse licks it off. Then she notices his erection. "My god," she says, "it's as big as a banana bread!" To protect herself she begins stuffing cannoli, cherries, and nuts into her vagina until it looks like the horn of plenty. Gathering up her courage, she takes the horse's penis in her hand and rubs cream all over that. She licks it off in a flurry of activity, while the horse attempts to eat all the goodies out of her vagina.

"Wouldn't you be jealous if I made love with your horse?" asked Marge.

"You don't understand," said Isobel. "Because I love him it doesn't mean that he's mine. We're having a very successful nonexclusive relationship. You forget that Marvin is also the horse's lover." Then she asked, "Whatever happened with the swami?" as she realized that Marge was eating a bologna sandwich.

"He's afraid. Afraid of me, and of strong feelings. Finally, I couldn't stand it any longer and I tried to seduce him, and he absolutely refused to be seduced. He doesn't know what love means or how to give it or receive it, and yet he talks about it all the time. How can he teach it if he's incapable of it? Since he rejected me I've gained fifteen pounds," she pouted.

"Love isn't only sexuality," said Isobel.

"Yes, but if you do love, how can you deny someone that last expression, the most intimate? That's running. And that's what he did—he ran. So fast."

Isobel smiled as she pictured the swami, gnarled and robed, running down Maple Lane, and felt glad to be spared analyzing about love. She felt a sense of superiority about her relationship with the horse.

One morning when she went to the garage she found the horse lying listlessly. His ears didn't even retract slightly as they did when he was exhausted but wanted to acknowledge her presence. His eyes showed no life whatsoever; they seemed to be turned inside out. For a moment she though he was dead, but his body was rising and falling rhythmically as he breathed. She was in a panic . . . afraid that Marvin would blame her if anything happened to his horse. She listened for a rasping in his breathing, as the only horse illness she had heard of was pneumonia. Had Marvin ridden him in the rain? She felt his head, which was moist with perspiration but not at all feverish, and patted him. She kissed him all over his face. He squinted when she kissed him, as if he had a fly on his face, but he didn't respond to her. She was terrified. She couldn't imagine what was wrong and she couldn't do anything until Marvin came home and discovered it himself. And what if there was nothing wrong with the horse, but he was just rejecting her? After all, he also had Marvin, and she never felt too secure with nonexclusive relationships. All along she'd imagined that she had a complicity with the horse that excluded Marvin, and somehow she felt that the horse preferred her to Marvin, as she preferred the horse to Marvin. Yet now she faced the possibility that perhaps his relationship with Marvin had reached an intensity that was going to exclude her. She walked around the house drinking wine and weeping, not daring to even check on the horse. She wept as if the horse had left her forever, though she reminded herself from time to time that that wasn't the reality, only a small possibility. By the time Marvin came home, she was nauseated with fear and sorrow. As soon as she heard the garage door roll up, she ran to the mirror to try to pull herself together. She looked like a dried apricot. She quickly obliterated any sign of emotion and waited in a panic for Marvin's reaction.

After a few moments, Marvin came in and walked right past Isobel. He began riffling through the Yellow Pages. He picked up the phone. "Hello, Dr. Kologna? I have a problem with a sick animal. Could you come right over? . . . Can you recommend someone who does make house calls? Nobody? . . . No, I can't wrap him up and bring him over, he's a horse. No, I haven't got a horse transport, it was shortsighted of me. . . . Okay, thanks. I'm at One–twenty Horace Harding Lane." When Marvin got off the phone he walked back and forth aimlessly but quickly, like a caged wildcat, his Hush Puppies squeaking slightly each time he turned. He seemed suddenly more human, more approachable. She offered him a cocktail and he accepted, looking at her as if he hadn't seen her in a long time. He seemed more calm and sat down with his Dewar's on the rocks.

"What's wrong?" she asked.

"The horse is sick," answered Marvin. "He just lies there."

"Maybe he's just resting."

"No, I can tell it's not that. He doesn't want to eat or look at me or anything. I've never seen him like this. His lethargy is beyond lethargy."

"Is the vet coming?"

"The vet doesn't make house calls, but he's sending over a special Long Island horse doctor. That vet I called doesn't do horses, anyway. He specializes in gerbils with goiter."

Isobel laughed. At least he was capable of joking. The bell rang. Isobel looked out the window and saw a large truck. She wondered whether they had a towing charge. She waited inside, staring at the vet's truck in the dusk, wishing the picture window faced the back, and then swishing her drink back and forth over the ice until it looked like rapids. She watched the vet get into the truck without the horse, hoisting himself into the high seat. She heard the motor, and was still staring out when Marvin came in.

"He says he can't find anything wrong. It look like exhaustion to him." Marvin blushed.

"But you hardly ride him," said Isobel.

"But when I do, we ride far," said Marvin. "Besides, who knows what he does during the day. Maybe he moves around a lot in the garage."

Isobel wondered whether he suspected, but doubted it. Like a child, he was making a quick, unlikely alibi. It was nice to be able to talk to him again.

She waited a week before going to see the horse again. It was a bright day, and cooler. Isobel was fully dressed. Although her appearance was calculated to please the horse, she had no intention of initiating anything, still fearing for the horse's health. She pulled up the door. The place seemed neater. Marvin must have cleaned up. The horse was standing so that she got a complete sideways view of him. He turned his head toward her slowly, with a gaze so large that there seemed to be nothing in the garage but the horse's eyes; still they showed no sign of emotion, surprise, or happiness. She watched his pupils contract with the light. For a moment she considered leaving, then she saw—the horse's penis beginning to move out of its velvet sheath, like an eyeglass case with a tiny beard, and she watched it tumesce slowly, like a Wonderbubbles plastic balloon, and as if by Pavlovian signal, she experienced a surge of warmth and desire, bringing back all her old feelings of previous days. She moved farther inside, rolled the door down behind her, and began to remove her clothes, the horse licking and sniffing her impatiently. So he had missed her! Yes, yes, as she felt and smelled him she realized how much she'd missed him. They patted and licked each other in a frenzy, the horse's fat, flat tongue pressing her breasts, as she lay down on one of the blankets that Marvin had washed and folded in an excess of hygienic zeal. She felt the sensation in her nipples spread all over her body like instant nondairy Cremora in a cup of hot coffee. Still, he continued licking her breasts and nothing else until she became frantic, then angry. Was he teasing her? She expected to see a smile on his face, but she saw only his eyes and his breathing was so heavy that miniature drops of moisture shot from his nose when he exhaled. He continued to stand over her that way, looking at her, until she couldn't stand it any longer and straddled him from underneath, her arms and legs around his sides and back. She hung there under him, belly to belly, a cool breeze washing over her exposed vagina. As she clung like an infant marsupial, she could feel the tip of his penis. As she edged herself farther back on the horse, still hanging there, he thrust forward and inserted the very tip of his penis. She tried, but couldn't move any further back and the horse seemed to enjoy teasing her. Then, as she was becoming angry again, he thrust forward and filled her, ever more, with his enormous organ, and held still. As she let out a deep moan, the garage door rolled up. Looking almost black with the late-afternoon sun behind him creating a sharp brightness around his ominous body, stood Marvin. For a moment there was total silence, nothing moved. His hand still on the handle of the door, he remained outside and rolled it down. Instead of disembarking from the horse, she surprised herself by continuing to make love with him more passionately than ever before, with an excess of abandon coupled with a sense of doom that drove her even faster, and she and the horse made the most violent love until both of them, lathered with sweat, came, her high-pitched shout mingling with his deep unearthly hoot, and, limp, she dropped off of him. Lying there under him, she saw that he had a line of hair down the center of his underbelly, sticking out, like the waves at Coney Island, when, going in opposite directions, they meet and crest. She stroked the length of it gently and then felt his long, soft penis, which hung there, very long, but soft, like the plastic liner of an Evenflo Nurser when it's three-quarters full of milk, one drop hanging from the tip. Then she let go of it, wiped her legs, and put on her clothes. She kissed the horse on both eyes and left. Marvin never mentioned anything.

The next day, arriving home in time to make Marvin's dinner, she thought she saw the horse standing on the front lawn. Marvin was nowhere in sight. Wondering, she walked faster until she was standing on the neatly shaved lawn next to the horse, who hadn't moved a hair. Looking closer, she noticed that his eyes seemed to be marbles, looking at nothing. She put down her Ohrbach's and Korvette's bags and boxes, leaning them against the horse's stiff leg so that they wouldn't spill, and felt the horse. He was hard as a rock. Leaving her bundles there, she ran back to the garage and found no horse. The garage had been cleaned, and she could almost believe there hadn't been a horse there if it weren't for the blankets still piled in the corner and still smelling of horse. She went to get her packages and felt the horse again. It was stuffed. Marvin met her in the foyer with a vermouth on the rocks with two cherries. She looked at the horse through the picture window while they had their cocktails.

THE CONSULTATION

Richard Selzer

HE WALKED THE CENTER AISLE of the convention hall, past stands of textbooks on *Surgical Anatomy, Complications of Surgery, Peripheral Vascular Diseases—Their Diagnosis and Treatment*. Other stalls gleamed with instruments—rows of proctoscopes, bronchoscopes, gastroscopes, rigid with potential, awaiting on one end a palpitating orifice, on the other a knowing eye. Here were forceps, clamps of the finest dentition. He tried one in his hand, listening to the impeccable click as the ratchets locked tight, tighter, tightest, a sound that had both frightened and comforted him all his professional life. There were scalpels of superior edge, their silver bellies as diverse as tropical fish, and retractors for holding open incisions, retractors of such cleverness as to match the ingenuity of a royal armorer.

Suddenly he was bored with it, the lectures, the instruments, the whole gadgetry of surgery, the rooms full of well-dressed men who all looked forty–five years old. . . . He would call her up.

She had a shockingly virtuous telephone voice which placed the brief arrangements over price in the grossest ill taste.

"Shall I pick you up at your hotel?"
"Fine."
"Oh, yes. Dinner first?"
"I'd love to. Where?"
"You choose it."
"What time?"
"Seven-thirty be all right?"
"Fine. Looking forward. . . ."

Gloria Snurkowski was the name he had been given to look up. He had laughed then at the idea of a Polish prostitute. Still, she had to be *something*. He was reassured when he saw her an hour later in the lobby of the hotel, serpentine, icy, impeccably dehumanized. Except for one thing—a gesture. Now and then she would place the third or fourth fingers of her hand to the corner of her mouth and press them against the underlying teeth. It was a Polish peasant's move. He was certain that her grandmother had done it a thousand times in the middle of her wheat field. But that was the only thing she had overlooked. The rest was perfect.

In the morning he had awakened first. One eye was buried in the pillow but with the other he followed the tide of her breathing. She was lying on her side, part of her back resting against him. A golden stripe of sunshine appeared abruptly between two slats of the Venetian blind and lit up the range of her shoulder. His eye moved down her neck to the ridge of her clavicle, and descended to the upper slope of the breast in a squinting shower of light. His vision paused for a moment at the foot of the slope, then moved on up the smooth ascent, slowly, gradually, passing through a small shaded declivity, then up again into the sunlight toward the nipple. He held it there until the strain of looking so far to the side made itself felt, then relaxed, and sped down the far side. Halfway down, his vision was jarred by a small rise. Automatically, he backed up the hill like a rewinding movie, then flicked the switch and let it go again. There, where the bump was on the trail, the skin was different, pitted by a shallow dimple. He raised his left arm to bring his hand around to the breast, and palmed it carefully. When she did not stir, he moved his fingers to the southern slope, sounding the depths as he went. He was moving over the rough spot now, his fingers growing exploratory, aggressive, deft. He picked up tissue between thumb and fingers, rotating it, fathoming. She moaned in discomfort, still asleep.

A cold white knowledge drifted into his mind like a snowfall, each flake of which was a bit of evidence. The lump was hard. It was discrete. It was irregular in shape. It was fixed to the overlying skin, fixed as well to the underlying muscle. It was immovable. It was tender. And his palpating fingers fled from her body like frightened fish in a pond. The suddenness of their departure was what fully awakened her.

He swung his feet to the floor and padded across the carpet to the bathroom, where he showered long and deliberately. He dried himself and went back to the bed, where he sat down and reached for his socks on the floor. She turned, and one of her hands reached around his waist, dipping.

"You're getting dressed?"

"Yes, I've got to be going."

With his back to her, he said. "I've got to talk to you."

"It's a hundred dollars."

"No, no, I don't mean that. I mean, that's O.K., a hundred dollars. Here." He reached for his wallet, counted out a fifty and five tens, and held it out to her.

She raised up on one elbow, watched this very carefully, and said, "Put it on the table." Then she sank back and watched him dress.

"You're buttoning your shirt wrong. You missed one."

He unbuttoned it and started again from the bottom. "There's something I've got to tell you," he began again.

"You're not sick, are you?" She was paying attention now.

"No, I'm not." . . . A pause. "But you are."

"What do you mean?"

"Listen. I'm a doctor, as you know." His voice took on a deeper, more professional tone, but his armpits were wet. "I couldn't help but feel . . ." Her open naive mouth, her eyes wide and waiting . . . "You've got a lump in your breast." He couldn't turn away from her.

Her face stayed vacant.

"A lump. I felt it. Right side."

She moved from her elbow to her back, settling onto the bed.

"Here." He picked up her hand as though it were a cup of coffee, and guided it to her breast. Holding the fingers, he led them toward the spot and pressed them down, moving them in a circular fashion. Her face changed slowly, tightened around enlarging eyes. Her lips were closed and dry.

"Do you feel it?"

She nodded slightly. "Yes."

"You've got to see a doctor. It must be taken care of."

"What is it?"

"I don't know." He shrugged and turned away. "Maybe it's nothing."

"It's something, isn't it?"

"I don't know. You can't tell until it's removed."

"You know."

"I don't know, I tell you."

"You're a doctor. You know. If it is, what do they do?"

He hadn't meant to go this far. "If it isn't, there's only a small scar. It won't show."

"And if it is? They will take off my breast." It was said as an announcement, flatly, without inflection. "I won't do it."

"You have to. It's important."

She covered her breasts with her arm, protectively, the palm of one hand gripping the opposite shoulder.

"Doctor." She was strange to him, formal, as though she had not just a few hours before felt him explode against her. "I can't do that."

"Look, I'm talking about your life, not your livelihood."

Their voices were low, surreptitious. They knew only words of one syllable. It was as though they kept them that way, afraid that if they raised them, spoke out loud, their sentences would crumble into meaningless noises.

"What is it? Tell me."

"I don't know."

"You ought to."

"But I don't."

"What should I . . . ?"

"It needs to come out."

"No!"

"Be sensible. It might be . . ."

"Cancer."

She had said it first. All along it had been a game, not unlike choosing sides by gripping a baseball bat to see who wins first choice. He had won; she had said it first. She reached for her slip and shyly lowered it over her head, then with small furtive movements she put her arms through the strap holes. There was about her the caved-in look of the victim. It made him vaguely nauseated. Not the strangeness of the word; certainly he knew it over and again in his daily work. Nor the translation of it into suffering. But rather what sickened him was the thought that he and the lump had been rivals, each feeding on her flesh, reaching within her, that they had been competing for her in a kind of race to have her before the other could use her all up, leaving none.

His fingers scuttled to the doorknob and locked around it like pincers. He turned to find her eyes fixed on his hand now palming the doorknob.

"Well, good-bye. Be sensible, now. You can only tell under the microscope. Anyway, it's a small price to pay in exchange for your life."

Her eyes never wavered from that doorknob, which was a hard lump in his hand. With sudden violence he twisted it as hard as he could and pulled as though to avulse it from the wood.

"Wait!" She walked to the table and picked up one of the ten-dollar bills. "Here. Thanks for the consultation." She was smiling just a little now.

He matched her smile, but his mouth was dry. "Sorry," he said softly then. "I don't make house calls."

NARCOTIC

Joyce Carol Oates

I

THE THOUGHT OF HER brushed against him, flimsy as a whiff of some faint, faintly disturbing odor. It came and went, somehow in rhythm with his walking quickly along the hospital corridors or taking the stairs down, fast, two or three steps at a time when he was really in a hurry. It was not quite a thought of her—he stopped himself before he mouthed her name—but the idea of her, the abrupt unsettling image of her face, which he did not really know well. In a crowd she might not be recognizable to him. He did not know her at all.

At five o'clock he hurried outside, thrusting his arms into the sleeves of his coat, anxious to get ahead of the crowd of nurses and orderlies who were leaving. They left by the rear exit, which was also the Emergency Entrance. He saw that one of the ambulances had been left at the door, parked hastily, its big rear doors still flung open. The ambulance was empty, the stretcher taken out. The door on the driver's side was still open, as though the driver had jumped out in a hurry.

He was an orderly, himself, but he walked apart from the

others, avoiding their conversations. They emerged into the queer, orange-toned air of a winter afternoon that was really a twilight, premature twilight; already the Christmas lights that had been strung loosely upon evergreens in front of the hospital had been turned on, so that the day seemed cruelly abbreviated, cut short. He glanced at the sparse yellow lights irritably. All that day—in fact for several days—he felt jumpy, disoriented, irritable. He kept thinking of *her*, his mind turning mechanically toward her as toward any distraction, any comfort. Yet he did not want to know her.

"Pretty, aren't they?" one of the older nurses said, meaning the Christmas lights.

"Yes," Neil said.

He was always lying; it had become an art. Working with the sick was itself an art.

At first he had liked his work. He had liked it well enough. Then, after the first several months, which had passed quickly, a kind of dizziness had begun to bother him: not a physical but an intellectual dizziness, a sense of disorientation, a rejection of certain ideas. Yes, he was jumpy, nervous, but he didn't mind that—it was the inability to understand certain things that disturbed him. The idea of health; the idea of sickness. *Health. Unhealth.* Living tissue and dead tissue. *Tissue.* The names of patients and their problems, which were also names, some of them very complex, in fact a secret language. *A secret language.*

It was a shock to keep remembering that the hospital was run by people, and that its dreary corridors and rooms and offices and laboratories were populated by people who shared certain ideas of health and unhealth. These people were states of mind. Together, they were an intricate organization of states of mind; he was one of them. When he tried to comprehend this he felt that his mind was breaking down. Then he felt that it did not matter, all this thinking; then he found himself thinking of the girl, even allowing himself to think her name, and a kind of warm, reckless indifference passed over him. He would be all right. It did not matter.

He was one of a small army of orderlies, young men with strong arms and strong stomachs. Not all young: there were two older men, very efficient and cynical. The orderlies were all called by their first names, which were simple, one-syllable names like his, Neil, and the interns and doctors were called Dr., so there was no confusion between them. Neil wore a uniform that was never white for long. His name was *Neil Myer*. He knew this name was not important, but sometimes he discovered himself repeating it, over and over, mechanically fascinated by its sound. *Neil Myer*. A combination of shrill shrieking sounds that were muffled by the "N" and the "M" but were not really silenced.

Then he rejected his thoughts angrily. "Come off it. Forget it. Get to work," he said, and forced his attention upon other people: patients wheeled down for X-rays and brought back again, patients whose bodies had to be kept clean outside and in, or they would break down and someone would be blamed. He had to talk to these people, in spurts of good-natured bantering, a lot of joking. They liked him. He was careful not to like them too much, that might be bad luck. In the beginning he had liked all the patients on his floor and had regretted it; now he knew better. But though he kept himself busy, that dizziness bothered him. Even while he talked and laughed with other people his mind worked rapidly against him, accusing him: *You are still Neil Myer.*

He decided to walk, not wait for the bus. He didn't want to share in their camaraderie and odd, defensive cheerfulness. They were all good people, the nurses and the orderlies, sturdy and hearty and brave, and he felt that he could not manage himself with them. He could not respond normally. At the same time he hated this in him, this fastidiousness, this disdain for other people. Terror was like a message in code. If you didn't try to decode it, you didn't know that it existed.

He thought of her face again, stark and pale. It had seemed an accusing face, but why should it have been accusing? It had been turned away from him, the face of a near-stranger, a girl lying in a hospital bed like any other bed.

Paula Shapley.

His lips shaped her name, involuntarily. Something was going to happen to him, he thought suddenly, it was time for good luck. For health, for exuberance. For life. You didn't work in a hospital for long without believing in good or bad luck; it was as simple as that.

But nothing was going to happen. He didn't know how to make it happen.

He walked the mile and a half into the city. Traffic rushed past him, most of it headed out. The peculiar orangish twilight had darkened into a true twilight. The air smelled cold and slightly gritty, soiled; in a way it pleased him after the disinfectant of the hospital, all that cleanliness, that sterility. He washed the unresisting bodies of patients all the time. He washed the heavy, cold, lardish bodies of the dead, which did seem to resist; even turning them over was sometimes a struggle, getting them out of the beds that no longer belonged to them and onto carts, ready to be rolled down the corridor and to the elevator and downstairs. He washed them with strong disinfectant on his hands. It burned everything clean and sterile. Germs could not grow where it touched: nothing could grow.

The most disturbing thing that had happened to him that day was the sight of a new admission, a twenty-six-year-old boy, really a "boy" because he was so slight, so ravaged. Brought in for tests, partly paralyzed already; he had collapsed on the street somewhere, his legs had given out. The boy's thin, angular, shadowed face had looked to Neil like the face of death, and he had turned away with tears in his eyes. He was twenty-six himself. But that was not why he felt so agitated. He didn't know why. He didn't want to think about it. He felt a peculiar envy for the boy, who was doped up already with a legal, powerful narcotic. What could he find to narcotize himself?

The girl had been brought in because of an "accident," an overdose of narcotics. Neil had recognized her name because he had known her husband slightly and had met her, once. After a session in the emergency ward she had been brought up to the fifth floor, where she was kept for ten days in a room with two other patients, both old women. Neil had asked about her from time to time and had gone up to look in at her, to walk past her door. He didn't know her well enough to go in. And he feared seeing her up close, feared the ghastliness of her face. She was about twenty-two or twenty-three, but small as a child, very thin, silent. Neil asked one of the nurses about her and the girl said, with a look of repugnance, "Nobody came to visit her. Not one person."

Then she was discharged from the hospital and he believed he would forget about her. It was pointless to think about her: he did not approve of her life, he did not want to get near her. He wished her well, yes, but he feared her. He had not even wanted to recall that her name was Paula Shapley and that she lived only about twelve blocks from his parents' home.

His hands felt heatless, clammy, as if covered yet with those loose-fitting rubber gloves.

If he did not go directly home he would have to telephone his mother. By a coincidence he saw a telephone booth just ahead, adjacent to a drug store. So it was decided! He would telephone his mother, make an excuse. . . . "I won't be home for supper tonight," he said. "I'm working late." His mother believed anything. She believed anything he told her, any excuse, just as she believed anything Neil's father told her: late at the yard, an overnight trip to Toledo, complications. She had never learned to read more than simple signs and familiar advertisements, she was easily hurt and easily confused, accustomed to being laughed at by Neil's father. Neil loved his mother, but he thought of her only with reluctance, guiltily. He did not love his father. He liked him, maybe, as an idea. His father made money out of scrap iron and other junk, enough to support a family of six children. At a distance, as an idea,

Neil's father was excellent. Neil could admire him. But in person he was bullying, rather hateful, always a little drunk. His father always asked, "Why don't you work for me? Why at that hospital with all the sick people?" He teased Neil about wanting to be a doctor, though Neil had explained to him many times that you didn't get to be a doctor that way. But he was blustering, he didn't listen to other people. He went around with a foolish, aggressive, dazed grin, not listening to what people said. Neil explained that he worked at the hospital for the same reason he lived at home—to save money. "It's the only work I can get. *I need the money.*" That seemed to set him apart from the hospital, to mark him as untouched, free. For years his father had taunted him about saving money, half-arguing with him about working at one of the junk yards, or driving a truck; he'd even lend Neil the money for college, he said, if Neil would ask. But Neil wouldn't ask. He had had to drop out of college in his second year, but he wouldn't ask his father for money.

His mother said she would leave something in the oven for him.

"No, don't bother," Neil said.

"It's no bother. . . ."

He felt a thrill of anger at her acquiescence.

"No," he said.

He left the telephone booth and walked over toward the Shapley apartment. It was strange how crazily eager his body was, now! Yet he did not want to see her, he dreaded seeing her. She had been brought back from the dead. What she had done was sick, ignorant, selfish, stupid. . . . He could imagine what she'd looked like, brought in the ambulance, dying from an overdose of barbiturates. He had seen other young people dying like that. He did not want to remember them. Yet his legs carried him swiftly along and his arms swung easily at his sides, as if he were going to meet an old friend, someone who would give him comfort. He had played basketball in high school, and he'd never been able to forget the extreme satisfaction of those evenings when he had performed, his limbs coordinated and shrewd, his fair, handsome head raised nobly in a crush of opponents. He had played well enough. But now there was no time limit to the exertions he had to endure. He had to perform, to force himself into performances, yet there were no rest periods or audiences or scoreboards.

No one was keeping score.

II

"Who? What did you say your name is?"

"Neil. I'm a friend of—I was a friend of—"

She stood very close to him, peering out over the latched chain. The door was open only a few inches.

"Neil Myer . . . ?" she said.

"Yes. I was a friend of Fred's . . . I didn't think you would remember me."

She was silent, looking at him. He wondered why he had said that: *I didn't think you would remember me.*

"You don't have a message from Fred, do you?" she asked after a moment.

"No."

"Did you know him from night school? Those business courses? I can't remember when he brought you over here . . . . I'm a little mixed up but I remember you." She paused, but because of the light behind her he could not make out her expression. "It's because of the way you look; you look polite. It's that night school politeness," she said oddly, as if taunting him. "What did you say you wanted?"

"Just to visit."

"You haven't heard from Fred . . . ?"

"No. I don't know him very well."

"You know he went to California?"

"I heard he left town . . . he went somewhere. . . . I didn't know him very well."

He was standing in a dark, unheated corridor while she

stared at him, studying him. It had been a mistake to come here. His face stiffened with resentment for her slow, almost sluggish manner. This slight, plain, pathetic girl, someone's cast-off wife!

Yet he felt he had carried something heavy, an invisible crippling weight, all the way to this door, and he must set it down on the other side of the door.

"Could I talk with you for a few minutes?" he asked.

He was pleased at the sound of his voice, its unhurried, undisturbed authority. His voice never betrayed him, never showed any nervousness or panic. The girl looked at him, thinking. Her hair fell to her shoulders yet was wavy all over, even frizzy, illuminated by the strong light behind her. Like feathers, like the fluff of milkweed. She was shorter than he remembered. He wondered if she were barefoot—she'd been barefoot the evening her husband had invited him back for coffee—but he did not dare glance down at her feet.

Finally she unlatched the chain. Her movements were abrupt and reckless.

She let the door swing open and backed away. Neil entered shyly. He felt suddenly very tall and awkward. The girl was barefoot, yes, and very small—a head shorter than Neil. He stared at her, his eyes leapt eagerly to her face. There was something in her face he yearned to see. As if knowing this, she allowed him to look at her, her smile small and perfunctory and mocking.

"You're very confident, to come here," she said. "To think I'd remember you after a year and a half—or two years, however the hell many years—"

"I didn't think you would remember me," Neil said.

"Maybe I don't. Sometimes I remember names but not people. I remember names that don't even have people attached to them. . . . But your face, your polite face, you look like someone I met once. Someone Fred dragged home. From night school, huh?"

"Yes. Introduction to Business."

"Oh yes. Introduction to Business. Fred tried that for a while, then he left town. He yearned for a milder climate, he said. Sorry he isn't here tonight."

She folded her arms tightly across her chest. When she raised her eyebrows mockingly there were sudden, deep lines on her forehead. Her face was still pretty but it was going to wear out soon. "So you heard Fred walked out. What else did you hear?" she asked slyly.

"That you've been sick."

"Oh. Sick."

"I worked at the hospital—where they brought you. I'm an orderly there."

"Oh. You work at the hospital. I didn't remember that."

"I've only been working there a few months. I wasn't working there when I knew you before."

"Knew me before," she repeated. "Knew me before. But did you know me before?"

Her smile was insinuating and mocking. But he faced it, he didn't let his disappointment show. And she stepped back as if acquiescing to some priority about him, an authority he shared with her ex-husband—also very tall, also an ex-high school athlete. She seemed to do this unconsciously.

"Well, sit down. If you don't mind the mess in here. This is a kitchen, underneath everything. See the sink? See the table? Sit down, please, you're so tall you make me nervous."

They sat down at the table, Neil thanked her, self-consciously, and saw that she had taken for herself a chair that had a rough, splintering back. The table was cluttered with dishes and silverware and a small pile of newspapers. An extra-large carton of cereal, with a giant panda on its front; tweezers, a soiled hairbrush with nylon bristles, books, with yellowed plastic covers, from the neighborhood library. *The New England Beach: Drawings & Photographs. A Pictorial History of the Adirondacks.* She saw him glancing at the books and said with a smirk, "I need healthy images in my head. It's the first step toward rehabilitation."

"You look all right," Neil said. It was abrupt and clumsy, but he had to continue. "You look good. How do you feel?"

"Take my pulse if you're so interested," she said, thrusting her arm out at him, and then jerking it back. She laughed. He felt pity for her, for her sad shapeless unclean dress, for the straggly hair, the meekness of her shoulders and head. He had not remembered her hair so light: it had looked darker on the pillow, almost black. But it was really a light brown, his own color. Her forehead seemed rather low, perhaps because of her jumble of hair and because of her continual mockery; her eyebrows were raised into those premature wrinkles. "Yes, I'm better. They discharged me. All the laboratory tests agree that I'm better."

She drew her feet up under her, mechanically, unembarrassed. Neil saw the immediate coarse tension of her leg muscles. It was a little shocking, this unconscious and intimate movement of hers; he looked away. "Does Fred know about it?" he asked.

"What? The laboratory test? Their agreement about me? No, he doesn't know. He doesn't even know about the tests and their initial reports, all that fuss," she said ironically. "Since he didn't send me back any address, I couldn't very well let him know the good news, let alone the bad news. Could I?"

"I don't know. No."

"Why did you come here?" she asked bluntly.

"To see you."

"But why tonight? I mean, why tonight especially? Is it maybe my birthday and I forgot? Sometimes I forget things like that."

"I just wanted to see you."

"To see what I look like, come back from the dead?"

"I see dead people all the time. It doesn't mean much to me, anymore," he said.

She drew her breath in sharply, as if this remark surprised her. For a while she did not speak. Neil watched her; he was excited by her, the easy reckless intimacy of her talk, her behavior, even the way her hair looked, as if she'd just gotten out of bed. But at the same time he was a little disgusted, repelled. His mind raced freely ahead as if anxious to get to a time when he would not be *Neil Myer* but an anonymous young man, twenty-six-years old, in anonymous good health, making love to an anonymous young woman.

"Then what does mean much?" she asked slowly.

"Everything else. Life. Health. Control." He spoke in the same frank, open voice. He had learned to imitate the older doctors at the hospital, who answered the most hopeless questions in brief sincere replies, always looking the questioner in the eye. Everything frank, open. Healthy. It was important to make connections, fearless connections.

"Control, fine. I'm in control," she said. "If I'm not, someone else will be; I'm not worried. I might never worry about anything again. . . . Were you there when they brought me in?" She straightened some of the things on the table, suddenly, as if she were alone; Neil understood that she was very serious. "Tell me what I looked like. Don't spare me."

Neil had not been on duty then. He had not seen her until the next morning, and then he'd seen her only from the doorway of her room.

"You didn't look bad," he said slowly. "Very pale. You were breathing hard. You looked very . . . very defenseless, like a child. . . . Very delicate. . . . Everyone wanted you to live."

She had picked up the large cereal box as if distracted by it, and she reached around to set it near the sink. As she turned Neil could see the movement of her skin over the small bones of her throat.

"Everyone wanted me to live . . . ?

"Yes."

She smiled evasively, nervously. Neil felt a sudden, unmistakable sense of authority here, at this table, with this young woman: as if he had come home.

"So they brought me back by magic," she said.

"No, not by magic. By the usual methods."

"Is there much change in people, when they're brought back? I mean, people who are very sick, almost dead . . . can you see the change in them as they're brought back? As the life comes back into them?"

"Yes."

"It must be like magic," she said softly.

"But there's no secret to it. It's mechanical—it's very easy, in fact, if the doctor has the equipment he needs. A stomach pump, fluids to be hooked up to the patient, a few shots of some chemical solution—and the person begins to look better, sometimes in five minutes, his color returns, he begins breathing normally—It's mechanical. It's very wonderful to see," Neil said.

"It wasn't my fault that it happened," she said.

"No."

"You believe me, don't you? It wasn't my fault. It was an accident. It won't happen again. He got me on drugs, you know, Fred, he could handle them all right, he got me started and then he ran out. He said I was too emotional. He said I was sloppy and that I dragged him down, I spoiled his mood. Did he complain to you about me?"

She didn't seem to understand that he had not known her husband well; but he said, "No. Never."

"He could handle them. He only took light doses. It wasn't until he left that I got really bad, I felt sorry for myself. Jesus, I'm such a. . . . I'm a natural addict, it's in my blood. I knew that before the doctor explained it to me. It's in my blood to need things . . . like I used to smoke a lot, and when I was a kid I liked chocolate candy, and I always needed . . . well. I needed people, I mean friends, I needed a close girl friend all the time I was in school, I mean I really needed a girl friend, and then I . . . I needed a boy friend. . . . I need things. I can't control it. In the beginning we were both the same, I mean emotionally, Fred and me, we were both in love, and then it started to change . . . it was like a teeter-totter . . . when I needed him more he needed me less . . . and it kept going that way. He got me started on drugs. Then he ran out," she said bitterly.

Neil thought of her husband, the burly dissatisfied young man who had sat near him in that night school class. He had answered the instructor's questions in an alert, falsely humble voice, though he told Neil and others of his contempt for the man. So much love, so much sorrow, expended on that man? She had wanted to die, because of Fred Shapley? His expression had always been petulant, expectant, as if he were passing judgment on everyone. Neil had not liked him. Yet he had wanted to be friends with him; for some reason he had wanted Shapley's approval.

"Your husband was a cheap bastard," Neil said.

She laughed. She laughed too quickly, too eagerly.

"You wouldn't say that to his face."

"I would."

She smiled so her her lips drew back from her teeth, an oddly exaggerated, starved smile, as if she were alone, grinning unconsciously. Neil wanted to stop her, to caution her— don't twist your face around like that, don't make youself ugly! He squirmed with desire for her. He did not want her to destroy that desire.

"Why did you do it?" he said.

"Because there was no reason not to. Because I watched my hands getting it all ready and I was curious, to see what my hands would do; to see if I was serious or just bluffing . . . And you were there in the hospital, you were there, all the time . . . but you didn't come to see me, not once. No one came to see me, did you know that?"

"No."

"Why didn't you come? Because I looked so bad, I looked so sick?"

"I didn't think you would want to see me."

". . .When I saw myself in the mirror, the first time, I started to cry, when I saw what I looked like . . . because then I knew that I was in for it, the rest of my life behind that face. I am about a teaspoon of protoplasm somewhere inside my skull, and I can't get that protoplasm out and into any other skull. I'm stuck here. I even failed at destroying the protoplasm because it's hard to kill. I discovered that. It must be a scientific fact that other people know, but I had to discover it myself. It's very hard to die."

"How are the nights now? Can you sleep?"

"No, but that's all right. I'm not taking anything now—you know—I promised the doctor I wouldn't. Did you know that no one came to see me, while I was in the hospital? That must be a record of some kind."

Neil thought of his nervousness, the strange despair of the last several weeks; that taunting voice in his head that told him he was *Neil Myer* and could not escape. A teaspoon of protoplasm? He wanted to tell her about his own fears. He wanted to confess to her. But he hesitated as if confessing to this girl would contaminate him.

"Dr. Kohler—do you know him?—gave me a solemn lecture. It was based on God, it was about the ethical commitment to life, and all that," she said with an ironic smile. "Lots of references to his children; he has three children. I don't know what that had to do with me. He told me I had no right to destroy life, even my own. I had a duty to maintain life. What do you think about that?"

"I believe that," Neil said.

"My brother sends me money but he didn't come down to see me. He owns a farm up north, he's thirty-nine, almost doesn't seem like my brother; he's so much older than I am. He doesn't want me to visit him, maybe he's afraid I'll contaminate the children or something. Why do you look surprised?"

It was the word *contaminate* that had surprised him. But he said, "That he would . . . wouldn't come to see you. What about your parents?"

She shrugged her shoulders.

He wanted to ease the tension in her face. "I live with my parents, still," he said. "In the same house I was born in.

I'm trying to save money, trying to get started again in school. . . ."

There was a long silence. He saw that her gaze was evasive, that she was a little confused. Probably she was wondering about him. And his own composure began to grow as he sensed her confusion. He was a healthy young male of six-foot-three, with a stong, intelligent face and clear skin. Always his skin had been clear, never bumpy or marred. That had been good luck. He felt himself humble in his attractiveness, chiseled as a figure made of ice or stone, his eyes on the girl, watchful, cautious, shrewd. His mind spoke bluntly to him as if daring her to overhear: *You don't need this. You don't need her. You are Neil Myer, sitting here, Neil Myer here instead of somewhere else, that's all. You can't change anything.*

But he wanted to put his arms around her and press his face against her, he wanted to burrow himself into her. And then perhaps she would fold her arms over him, her small childish hands on the back of his head.

"He said . . . he said to be careful of living alone, of thinking too much," she went on, slowly. "Of thinking about myself. He said I should avoid emotional things, getting involved emotionally. I laughed and said I was an addict that way, couldn't keep clean, other people were like narcotics to me: like Fred was. Then I got serious and said O.K. I'd try."

She got to her feet, staggering a little, off-balance. She smiled shyly at Neil. "I got an idea: I'll make us something to eat. I'd like to do that."

"That would be too much trouble," Neil said.

"I'd like to do that, please, I haven't made anything to eat for a long time . . . I mean for someone else besides myself, a real supper. . . . All right?

He was very hungry. Yet he hesitated, staring at her.

"I'll make supper for the two of us. Oh, I'd like to do that," she said excitedly. She opened one of the cupboard doors and stood on her toes, peering inside. She was breathing quickly and Neil wondered if she was a little drugged, in spite of what she had said. She was slight, thin, and yet she seemed now energetic, her face coloring with pleasure. She fascinated him— there was something trim and sullen about her body, even a tough attractiveness he had always noticed in girls of a certain type, city girls, hanging around the streets in the slum neighborhood near his own. They were boyish, quick with insults, sometimes pretty and sometimes ugly, but always quick, clever. With soiled, knowing faces. Sullen and joking. He had noticed them for years, knowing himself superior to them. Yet he had been attracted to them, as if wanting to submit himself impulsively to their judgment, their cynicism, the way he had courted Paula's husband.

"Oh, this will be a party. This will be a private party," she said eagerly. "Here's a can that says 'fancy pink salmon,' how do you like salmon? . . . I have four eggs left in the refrigerator, somewhere in here in all this mess . . . and some bread . . . and for dessert peaches, canned peaches . . . yes, there's a can back there. . . . Can you reach it?"

Neil got up to reach into the cupboard. He handed her the can. Then he put his opened hands on her, on either side of her body; he felt the stark ribs beneath her thin dress and the rapid pounding of her heart.

She drew away from him. "Don't touch me. Please," she said.

"I'm sorry."

"Sit down, please. I'll make us supper. I can make a nice supper out of these things. . . ."

He sat down again, embarrassed. He wanted to apologize but he dreaded the sound of his voice.

"It makes me confused to be touched. I'm not ready for that," she said.

And then she began to prepare supper: to perform. Her cheeks colored as she worked. Neil was reminded of the color that flowed back into the faces of the near-dead at the hospital. She moved slowly about the small, cramped kitchen, but very competently, as if performing a ritual she knew well. Her movements had a kind of rhythm that was very pleasing to watch. Himself, he sat quietly and watched her. He knew there was a humility in his sitting like this, a valuable humility, because she had rebuked him and he had accepted it. And this pleased her, his obedience. As she stirred the ingredients together into a large frying pan and held it over the burner, her face was closed, concentrated, warm. She might have been any woman, cooking in any kitchen, being watched by a man— Neil's mother, cooking for him or for his father, in a trance of peace, of certainty, because she was safe in this performance and could not be criticized.

III

They were silent as they ate. Neil was very hungry, surprised by his hunger. And she had been so efficient, suddenly, absorbed in her role, so competent, she had surprised him as well. He had knocked on her door, a near-stranger, and she had opened the door: and he had walked through the doorway and sat down in the center of her life. Now she had prepared food for him. She had given him more of the meal than she had taken for herself. Her face was warm, still abstract from the performance she had just completed.

"Do you like it? Are you sorry you stayed?" she asked, raising her eyes to his, still a little mocking.

He told her it was very good; he was embarrassed not to have spoken sooner. But she had forced him into a kind of awed silence.

He felt overlarge at the table, and was afraid of knocking something over. She was so slight, so close to him; her intimacy was unsettling. He could not quite interpret it. He studied her, the sallow tone of her skin, the slight hollows beneath her eyes, the frizzy, curly brown hair, the deep fleshly pink of her lips, which were full and rounded. . . . He was strangely close to her and could not think if she was attractive or not, as if he were trying to assess his own face, or the face of one of his sisters. *You don't need her. You don't need any of this.* Suddenly he remembered how she had looked in that hospital room, seen from the door: a slight body, a face that seemed almost featureless, hair spilled against the glaring white pillow. Too much white in that room, white reflecting white. Paula Shapley, a young woman who had almost died: she had shot a solution of barbiturate powder into her vein, something Neil had never even heard of before, and she had almost died. But she had not died. They had brought her back to lie there, ordinary and conscious again, in one of the hospital's hundreds of uniform beds.

He wanted to tell her about the young man who had been admitted that morning, partly paralyzed. A dying young man his own age. He wanted to tell her about his own alarming thoughts, the mocking voice in his head. But he hesitated.

They ate the canned peaches out of coffee cups, because she hadn't any more clean dishes. The peaches were almost tasteless. Suddenly Neil had no more appetite; his mouth was dry.

"Do you know Dr. Kohler?" she asked.

"No. I mean yes, a little, not very well."

"When he talked to me I started to cry and embarrassed him. At first I laughed, then I started to cry. I said I didn't want to cry for the rest of my life because it hurt so much. So he told me: '*Pull yourself together.*' "

Neil laughed sharply, in surprise. "*Pull yourself together . . .?*"

She laughed with him, shrilly.

Then they fell silent and she rose to clear the table. Neil got to his feet at the same time. He embraced her, at first experimentally, his mind racing with questions and little taunting shouts: *Now what? Now what are you doing?* She pushed him away, weakly.

"I don't want—"

He held her and pressed his face against hers, bending so that his cheek was flat against hers. He would say nothing. He would say nothing at all.

He felt the tension in her rise, and he caressed her, stroked her, all in silence. She could not draw away from him, not now. He sensed that the time for that had passed and that she was now surprised, baffled, by its passing, not having recognized it. Not quite having recognized it. As he embraced her he saw in his mind's eye the boy, admitted for tests, so pale and doped-up, and the image faded to Paula herself, one body among many. Then he saw nothing at all.

He urged her into the other room, half-walking with her, half-carrying her. She moved along with him, unresisting. She was very warm. The bedroom was darkened but they left the door to the kitchen open; Neil was aware of closeness, clutter, a narrow room with a window near the bed. He felt a draft on the back of his neck.

Her flesh resisted him, then gave in. He sank himself deeply into her.

Then he became aware of himself again, the draft from the window, the girl's damp, heated flesh, his own breathing. The room was chilly. *What are you doing here, what do you want?* He could sense her mind racing, beating like his own. The space between them was suddenly cold.

After a short while she pushed herself up from the bed. She picked up her dress from the floor. There was something defiant in the way she put back on the same dress she'd been wearing, as if canceling him out; she tugged it down impatiently over her head. Turned from him, still silent, she brushed her hair back from her face in brief, hurried gestures.

"You can leave now," she said.

He stared at her back. Stooping to get his own clothes he stared at her rigid back. She had folded her arms tightly across her chest again, still turned from him.

"Get out," she said in a flat, toneless voice.

"Why—What do you—" he began.

He dressed quickly, watching her. She would not look at him. And he would not go over to her, not like this.

"Why are you angry?" he asked.

He was careful to keep his voice neutral, innocent.

"You can leave now. Please. It's all right to leave," she said. Her voice was toneless and might have come from anyone.

He felt a dark, sudden glow deep in his stomach, an echo of the sensation he had felt a few minutes before, sinking himself into this girl. It came back to him strongly. In his mind this same glow unfolded, a certainty about something, a sense of peace. He did not quite understand it. His face was open, questioning, innocent, as he waited for her to look at him. He would let her speak, he would not touch her. He watched her as if obedient to her, staying where he was.

"Get the hell out," she said.

"You won't . . . won't do anything . . . ?"

"Just get out."

He did not move at once, as if testing her. Then, obeying her, obeying that harsh flat voice, he went out into the kitchen. The air there was warmer. The odor of food was warm and pleasant.

"Just get the hell out and don't come back," she said.

She stood in the doorway to the bedroom, hugging herself, her shoulders raised. Everything about her was stiff, ugly. Her face had become rigid.

"I can take care of myself," she said. "Don't worry. Don't worry about me."

Again he felt that surge of dark, abrupt joy. He groped for the doorknob, watching her cautiously. She was forcing him out of here, out into the corridor—very well, then, he would obey her, he would leave! His own expression was composed, grave. He said, "You won't do anything to yourself . . . ? You promise you . . . ?"

"Get out," she said.

He left. Going down the stairs he listened for the slam of her door, but wasn't sure if he heard it or not.

The door had opened to admit him, and now it had closed.

Out on the street he felt a smile distort his face. His mind played back what he had said, lightly and mockingly: *You won't do anything to yourself, you won't do anything? Anything? You won't do anything?* He did not understand his exhilaration. Everything had changed: the world itself had changed. He felt very free, very pleased. "All right, then, I will get out, I won't worry about you, all right," he murmured, as if giving voice to a certain rhythm in his head. "All right, Paula, the hell with you." It was the first time he had spoken her name out loud: it was an abrupt, pleasing fact, like the closing of that door.

THE CONSOLATIONS
OF PHILOSOPHY

John L'Heureux

MR. KIRKO WAS TAKING HIS TIME DYING in bed number seven. He just kept lying there week after week.

"Not even getting any worst. At least not to the naked eye," said his daughter Shelley. "Look, I've got obligations, the children," she said.

"Obligations we've all got," her brother Mervin said. "You've got obligations. Angel's got obligations. And my obligations you know. I'm the son. So forget your obligations sometime. It's Papa."

"It's too true. It's Papa," said Angel, who was unmarried and had nothing. "He's all I've got," Angel said.

"And *he's* dying," Shelley said.

The orderlies came hollering, "Beds number seven and eight," and pulled the curtains around to make tents. Then they staggered off with Mr. Kirko and bed number eight to give them baths. These were old orderlies and their backs didn't straighten much anymore, so they just put Mr. Kirko and bed number eight in the water and let them sit there. Then these orderlies broke out the old Camels and smoked while sick people sat in hot water till their behinds shriveled.

"This is how it is when you're one of the masses," one said.

"Rome wasn't built in a day," the other said.

Then one said a lot and the other said a lot and they checked to see if Mr. Kirko's behind was shriveled, and it was, so they got their hooks under his armpits and dragged him out of the tub. He groaned and his eyes rolled up, but at least he didn't die on them. They sat him on a three-legged stool to dry him. The stool scraped on the tile floor.

"Hear that noise?" Mr. Kirko asked.

"They stopped toweling him because he never spoke and now he was speaking.

"That's the springs in my behind, breaking."

He threw up then, yellows and browns, and most of it went into his slipper.

"Goddamned pigs when they get old."

"There's no fool like an old fool."

These orderlies slammed his foot into the slipper and propped him against the wall. His face was all red from his bath and his foot was yellow and brown.

They checked to see if bed number eight's behind was shriveled, and it was, so they got their hooks into him and started to drag, but he wouldn't give. They let him have a little punch in the head to show they meant business, but it didn't do any good because he only gave a moan or two and died.

"Well, naught is certain save death and taxes."

"We'll let this sleeping dog lie."

They staggered back to bed number seven with Mr. Kirko. The son, Mervin Kirko, was pacing up and down outside the room, looking at his watch. Angel Kirko, who had nothing, was standing in the corner twisting her handkerchief. Shelley Kamm was looking through her purse and sighing a lot.

"Did we have a nice bathie-poo?" Shelley said to her father as these orderlies pulled the curtains.

"It's little enough to have," Angel said.

Inside the tent the orderlies rested for a while and then they each took an arm of Mr. Kirko and counted down. "Three, two, one, GO!" And he went up onto the bed, head first. His head went shlunk into the wall. He wailed for a minute, then tuned down to a whine.

They threw back the curtains and approached the weeping women.

"It's an ill wind that blows no good," one said.

"It's too true," Angel said.

"It's a mercy some of them go when their time has come," the other said.

"I know you're doing everything you can," Shelley said.

On the way out these orderlies nodded at good old Mervin.

"You can just pace around," they said. "Up and down, back and forth, you name it."

Angel and Shelley didn't know what to do next.

"He doesn't look any worst to me," Shelley said.

"Not to the naked eye, he doesn't," Angel said.

"Oh, nurse, nurse," Shelley said, calling Nurse Jane. "He doesn't look any worst, does he?"

"Well, he's going to be," Nurse Jane said. "They don't just go in and out of here unless they're seriously, you know. What he need is some needles and bottles, some pickies and pokies, and a tube up his nose."

Nurse Jane returned with everything she promised.

"Bed number eight," she said to Angel. "Where is he?"

"Personally, I don't know," Angel said. "I haven't the slightest."

"She hasn't the slightest," Shelley said. "She's never had anything and now she's losing her papa."

"It's a matter of professionalism," Nurse Jane said. "There are lists to be filled out, tags, markers, numbers, identity bands, indicators, thingumabobs, you have no idea. So you can't just have bed numbers disappearing. So you've got to tell me everything you can about this case. Now you, Miss Kirko, when did you last see bed number eight?"

"Well, I'll do my best," Angel said. "He was last seen by me personally when they staggered him off for his bath."

"Bath," Nurse Jane said and stalked away, kachung, kachung. "Very good," she said a few minutes later. "Very good, Miss Kirko. We found him dead in the bath and so he's accounted for." She leaned across Shelley and put her hand gently on Angel's bosom. "It's just so we know," she said tenderly. "We have to know."

"It can't be easy," Angel said.

"It's the children I worry about," Shelley said.

"When the doctor comes, you'll see," Nurse Jane said, and wheeled the empty bed out of the room.

The doctor appeared at seven o'clock on the bonker. He had a clipboard in his hand and he kept looking from it to the place where bed eight used to be.

"I see they've dispatched bed eight," he said. "You must be the Kirkos. You belong to bed seven."

"Yes, we're the Kirkos," Mervin said. "I'm the son and these are the two daughters. Angel Kirko and Shelley Kamm. Shelley was a Kirko before she was a Kamm."

"How do you do," they all said, shaking everything.

"I'm Doctor Robbins," Doctor Robbins said.

"Doctor Robbins," they all said, grateful as anything.

Angel and Shelley took a good long look at Doctor Robbins while he took a good long look at Mr. Kirko. In each arm old Kirko had needles that ran down from bottles full of yellow, and there was a tube up his nose that went somewhere and another tube that ran from his winkler into a bottle under the bed. Mr. Kirko was getting the full treatment.

"You're very young for a doctor," Shelley said, taking in the little bulge in his white pants.

"But competent," Doctor Robbins said.

"Oh, I didn't mean," Shelley said.

"We never meant," Angel said.

"Of course, of course," Doctor Robbins said, and he bit the inside of his face so they'd know.

"I'll wait outside," Mervin said.

"You can pace up and down," Doctor Robbins said. "Or back and forth."

The doctor stood for another while looking at Mr. Kirko. He plucked at Mr. Kirko's leg; it looked like turkey.

"I think that leg's going to have to come off," the doctor said.

"Oh no!" Angel said, fainting.

"Oh, God in heaven!" Shelley said.

Angel kept on fainting.

"Mervin! Mervin! We've got to make a decision. This Doctor Robbins here says the leg has got to come off. It's our duty to decide," Shelley said.

Mervin came back in from his corridor.

"These are the moments one dreads, Doctor," Mervin said.

"Oh no!" Angel said, fainting some more.

"Before we decide," Shelley said, "I think I should have a word with the doctor in private."

"I've never had anything," Angel said as Mervin dragged her from the room.

Shelley shut the door and leaned against it, her head thrown back. Outside she could hear them pacing up and down, back and forth.

"I thought we should have a word alone," Shelley said.

"Most understandable at a time like this, Mrs. Kamm," he said, reaching for his zipper.

"Yes, it's difficult for all of us, Doctor. It's the children I worry about." She slipped off her panties and in one graceful motion scooped them up from the floor and tucked them into her purse.

They stood for a moment looking at bed number seven.

"We could put him on the floor, Doctor. He wouldn't mind."

"It's better the patient not be disturbed," he said, and gave a little tweak to a tube here and a tube there.

"Oh, dear," Shelley said.

"Now if you will please step over to the door and lean your back against it, so," the doctor said. "Very good. And now we'll lift this skirt and—yes, you'll have to bend your knees as if you were sliding down the wall, that's right—and then I'll just slip this in here. Um, we need a little wiggly, then oomph, there we are."

"Yes, that does do nicely, Doctor Robbins," Shelley said.

They stood there like a Rorschach.

"Perhaps, Mrs. Kamm, you'd prefer to put your purse on the floor."

"Oh, silly of me."

"Just drop it. That's right. And then you can put your hands right here."

"Oh," she said. "Oh."

"I think you'll find, Mrs. Kamm, that once your father's leg comes off, you'll be more than pleased you agreed to it."

"Oh, I'm sure you're right, Doctor Robbins. It's just that, you know, we've known him so long, Doctor, and always with the leg."

"Yes, yes, of course. These feelings are natural. There would be something wrong if you didn't feel them."

"Oh, yes," she said.

"Could you move that knee out a little, and away?"

"Like this?"

"Fine," he said. "Well, at least we're having marvelous weather . . . for this time of year."

"Marvelous," she said. "Doctor, I want to thank you sincerely for giving us your valuable time. We truly appreciate it."

"A doctor does his best," he said. "Comfortable?"

"Mmmmm, yes. Doctor, I hope you won't think me overly personal, but I couldn't help noticing what an enormous jum-jum you have."

"Oh, I don't know," he said, shrugging modestly.

"Oh, you do, you do. Truly."

He gave her a little jab to the left.

"Thuth thuth thuth," they laughed.

"You must have gone to a wonderful medical school," she said.

"Harvard," he said. "They teach you everything."

"It must be wonderful," she said.

"Philosophy," he said. " 'Every proposition is true or false.' Langer."

"That's deep," she said.

"Heidegger," he said. " 'Listen to what is not being said.' "

"That's deep too," she said.

"Bucky Fuller," he said. " 'Everything that goes up must come down.' "

"I've heard that one," she said.

"Human behavior is a language," he said.

"Yes," she said.

"If the material of thought is symbolism, then the mind must be forever furnishing symbolic versions of its experiences," he said. "Otherwise thinking could not proceed."

"Ooh," she said, moving her right hip forward and backward in a new way.

"Perhaps I'm being too technical, Mrs. Kamm?"

"Oh no, Doctor, no. Those are beautiful thoughts," she said.

"Very well," he said. "Now, Mrs. Kamm, if you would just move this foot forward and in a bit."

"Oh!"

"You see?"

There was a banging outside the door, bonka bonka bonk.

"It's Angel," Shelley said.

"If you'll concentrate, please," he said.

"Oom, oom," she said, and her feet rose from the floor.

Their bodies began to shake like dustrags, and then she bit his neck, and then he punched her ribs to make her stop. Finally she shook uncontrollably and he tore at her hair.

Bonka bonka bonk at the door.

"Hungh," he said, pulling her loose and dropping her in the corner. "Hungh," he said again and stood looking down at the ruined jumjum.

Bonka bonka bonk at the door again.

"It's me," Angel's voice said. "I want to come in."

"I'm just pacing," Mervin said from down the corridor.

Shelley brushed off her dress and patted her hair into place. "It's not bad enough about Papa," she said. "They have to make a scene in the corridor."

"It's the tension," Doctor Robbins said, all zipped and polished. He opened the door. "Come in," he said. "Your sister has reached her decision."

"The leg has got to come off," Shelley said. "Doctor Robbins is right."

"What's all this?" Angel said, pointing to the chunks of Shelley's hair with blood on the ends.

"That's my hair," Shelley said. "These decisions are never easy, Angel."

"Whatever the doctor says," Mervin said.

"I'll tell Nurse Jane," Doctor Robbins said.

In a moment the two orderlies came hollering, "Bed number seven," and wheeled out the last of Mr. Kirko. It was a sad noise going.

"Man proposes, God disposes," one said.

"Every cloud has a silver lining," the other said.

Angel and Shelley and Mervin stood in the empty room looking at one another.

"Once that leg is gone it will be different."

"That leg was the trouble."

"He never looked any worst. Not to the naked eye."

"He looked worst with tubes and needles."

"And the thing in his winkler."

"There's nothing left to do but pray."

"It's too true."

A storm broke outside the window. They all went and looked at it. Rain fell like swords.

"Well, at least he's not out in that storm."

"Oh, nature is terrible," somebody said.

"True, true," everybody agreed.

WAITING FOR CARL

David Huddle

THE INSANE WINTERS in New York, particularly the days when the wind on Seventh Avenue became very nearly unbearable, brought Partridge his best business. So even though he was southern and therefore especially despised the cold, he nevertheless found it necessary to be outside stomping up and down the sidewalk, shivering and hunching his shoulders, to make appointments and to advertise. True, he rented a second-floor office across from the Taft Hotel, but he could afford to go there only when he had made appointments for the afternoon, because if he didn't advertise, he got no business and then had to sit alone playing solitaire. It was also true that he wore a good wool suit, a tasteful tie and a Harris Tweed topcoat that gave him a spiffy appearance, but these had been bought and sent to him by his mother in Athens, North Carolina, along with a stern note about what to wear and what to eat during the cold weather. Even with Partridge's bald head and thirty-five years, his mother still considered him more or less a college boy, and it irked Partridge considerably that he could not be completely independent of her. His business simply did not prosper him. The hand-lettered signs he wore, front and back, were the only advertising he could afford. They read as follows:

KINDNESS
FOR
MONEY.
I WILL BE
GENTLE TO
YOU FOR
FIFTEEN
MINUTES
OR A HALF
HOUR.
REASONABLE
PRICE.

"How much?" a dumpy-looking girl asked him. She was cold and miserable. Her nose dripped so that Partridge wanted to reach over and wipe it for her. She looked like she had been on the street gritting her teeth against the wind for a long time.

"Not much." Partridge hitched up his signs and straightened his shoulders to try to cheer up the dumpy-looking girl. As usual he found himself feeling sorry for someone.

"How long have you been in New York?" he asked her.

"Oh God!" she said and blew her breath into her hands to warm them. "Almost three weeks!" she said.

Then she burst into tears. Brisk citizens passing quickly along the sidewalk craned their necks to look at the miserable girl; one or two of them smiled. Partridge felt his heart give its customary lurch of compassion, and he observed himself ridiculously patting the girl on her lumpy shoulder.

"You'd better come upstairs right now," he said. "It won't be but a dollar. There's a special rate today."

He took her arm, or rather her elbow, and guided her into the building where his office was. He actually lifted some of her weight to help her as they went up the shabby stairway. Sometimes Partridge felt like he could just kill himself he was so mushy. "You mushy son of a bitch," he muttered to himself. So far that morning he had made only one other appointment for the afternoon, and he knew from the look about the man that he would not pay more than five dollars for Partridge's services. You just couldn't stay alive in New York on six dollars a day, though you could live for a week on it in North Carolina, he thought.

"What did you say?" the girl asked. Still she sniffled and gave a dreary appearance while they walked down the dim, musty-smelling hallway, but Partridge thought she had better control now. He took his hand away from her elbow and let her walk by herself.

"I said you talk like somebody from Michigan," he told her.

She brightened a little. "No, but that's pretty close. I'm from Toledo." She unraveled the scarf she had wrapped all around her head and neck and shoulders. Her hair, a dishwater blond color, sprung out from her head at various angles. It's a shame she's not pretty, thought Partridge while he fumbled with the rickety old lock of his office door. Still, she might have a good figure, he hoped, because he could see only the lumpy outside shape of her long, brown, sheepherder's coat. He decided that if the girl had even a halfway decent figure, he would compliment her on it to make her feel better.

"You don't have any heat in here," she informed him when they got inside his office; she wrapped her arms around herself and shivered visibly to show him what she meant. Also, she looked as though she might cry again. Partridge had to agree that his office did appear fairly bleak when you first walked into it, plaster crumbling from the ceiling and walls, nothing in it but a window, a used cardtable, and two mismatched, straight-back chairs.

"I'm from North Carolina myself," he said. He decided not to address himself to the problem of no heat unless she insisted on getting something out of him about it. Certainly it was true that he was from North Carolina, and occasionally he blamed his damnable mushiness on the facts that he was southern and that his mother was such a severe lady, a member of the DAR.

Partridge had a deadly envy of people who had that good, abrasive Yankee toughness of a Massachusetts or a Brooklyn or a Connecticut upbringing.

"Do you mind telling me what's wrong?" he asked the girl. He smiled in a kindly way at her while he lifted his sandwich board up off his shoulders and over his head, then leaned them carefully against the wall. He pulled out one of the straight-back chairs for the girl and then sat himself down in the one closest to the window. The girl was fiddling inside her purse for the dollar. Finally she fished it out, wadded up like an old gum wrapper. She dropped it on the cardtable in front of Partridge, sniffled, and sat down with a heavy clunking noise. She unbuttoned the top buttons of her thick coat, so that Partridge could see the blouse she wore, colored a bright, fire-engine red. Unfortunately, Partridge noted, the blouse contained a regrettable lack of bosom, and he knew that he could not compliment her on her figure without hurting her feelings. Partridge knew that if the girl had been pretty, it would have been easier for him to lift her spirits. He knew a little bit about the despair that fogs up the hearts of people who are not attractive; he himself had a rather egglike face and a bad color about him, so that in his childhood members of his family had predicted that he would become a minister. He picked up the dollar from the cardtable, put it in his jacket pocket, and began shuffling the deck of cards he kept to entertain himself during the long hours when he had no business. A certain smell of the girl came across the table into Partridge's nostrils, and it wasn't good. She needs a bath, among other things, he thought.

"Well," the girl said, "in Toledo I was always respected by everybody as being a person who is deeply devoted to art." The girl looked him squarely in the eyes as she talked to him. "But since I have been in New York, I have had nothing but hideous things happen to me, from the time I got off the train until this morning when a man on Broadway spat at me and called me 'scum of the earth.' "

The girl pressed her lips together to keep from crying, and

Partridge could tell that the man had hurt her feelings. He dealt out a hand of solitaire for himself while he considered the girl's plight. Anybody who does not look like a movie star and who is sensitive ought not to come to New York, he thought. Then he looked out the window beside him and watched the traffic spurting down Seventh Avenue. "I see," he said finally.

"But that isn't my problem," the girl went on. "The worst thing is that I didn't have any money, and so I signed this contract to work in this film about the Pittsburgh Ax Murders, and now I don't want to do it any more." She smiled at Partridge when she told him this, and he saw a certain vivaciousness in her expression that might have led someone to sign her up to do an ax murder or two.

"I see," Partridge said again. He thought that the girl seemed considerably happier now. He could have sworn he noticed a swelling of bosom inside the fire-engine red blouse.

"Why don't you just go on back home to your mother in Toledo and ask for her help," he suggested pleasantly to her. Partridge had the weird southern sense of home and family, which he hated when he thought about it but which he had not got rid of in fourteen years of living in the city.

The girl laughed merrily, a good peasant kind of a laugh, deep and healthy in her chest. "Well, I could, I suppose, but I don't think I'd be happy that way." She leaned across the table toward Partridge so that he could smell her closer, and this time it was quite a good smell to him a musky, hair-spray kind of fragrance. "You see," she said, "I have already completed the first half of the film, and now I sort of have a taste for the thing. You know how sometimes you hate things, but at the same time you kind of like them?" She smiled at Partridge fully, and he had to admit that she appeared seductive to him now, her hair glistening a soft blond color that set off her green eyes in an attractive way.

"Yes, I know," he said. He had the ridiculous urge to reveal something of his secret, innermost self to her. So he blurted onward, "I'm like that about the kindness I sell. I don't really like to give it out the way I do, but I can't help myself. I just can't stop myself from doing it, if you know what I mean." He looked at her pleadingly. Then he added as an explanation for it, "I think it's because I'm southern and because of the way my mother is."

They looked at each other and smiled openly. It was a beautiful moment in Partridge's life, because even considering all the people to whom he had been kind—and there had been a great many—he could not remember one who had understood him so closely as he thought this wonderful girl from Toledo did now.

"Do you mind if I take off my coat?" the girl asked. "By the way," she said, "my name is Cynthia." She took a splendid-looking, long-handled ax from the inside of her coat and leaned it against the wall beside Partridge's sandwich board. Her figure, Partridge now saw as she stood up, was no less than magnificent, a tiny waist, good hips, beautiful balloon-like breasts, and slender legs like those of a seventh-grade girl. All of these qualities gave her the appearance of being a genuine star of the cinema.

When she sat back down across the cardtable from Partridge, he simply could not stop looking at her, except to make a play now and then in his game of solitaire. Across the cardtable an electricity generated back and forth between them that seemed to be warming the entire room. Cynthia put both her hands on the table, and Partridge had to restrain himself to keep from reaching across and taking them into his own hands. The two of them sat staring at each other for a long time, with Partridge occasionally playing a card and with both of them savoring the silence together. They were disturbed by some kind of clamor outside his office, clattering noises of equipment being moved, preparations being made, men yelling at each other, and heavy things being dropped, but this stopped and the pleasant quiet came again. Partridge genuinely regretted it when the time came for his other appointment. He looked at his watch several times before he said anything to her, but finally he had to.

"I'm awfully sorry, Cynthia but I have another client coming here now. He should be here any minute. Maybe, if you don't mind waiting until I've finished with him, we could . . ."

Cynthia smiled gently at him. "Is this client a short man with a bald head and a kind of convict look about him?"

"Yes," Partridge said, "that's him. Why? Do you know him?" A knock came at the office door, and he got up, reluctantly, to answer it.

"Yes, I think so," said Cynthia. She got up from her chair, too, rising with Partridge. She touched his arm as he passed her, going toward the door. "Thank you so much," she said to him. "You've been a great help to me." She brushed his cheek with her lips and the lurch Partridge's heart took was not one of feeling sorry for anybody on the face of the earth.

"You're very welcome," he said. Then he turned and opened the office door for his client. There in the hallway outside his office door, he found an entire camera crew, complete with microphones and sound equipment, carbide lights set up on stands and ready to go, and a huge, triple-lensed sixteen-milli-meter camera on a tripod facing him like a three-eyed Cyclops. His client, the short man with a bald head and a convict look about him, sat a little farther back in the hallway, slouched in a canvas folding chair and puffing impatiently at a cigar.

"Ready, Cynthia?" the short man barked.

"Ready, Carl," she said. Partridge watched her sweep the cardtable clean of his game of solitaire and then come toward him, ax in hand. He had to admit that she looked radiant.

"Lights," said Carl.

BREAKFAST

Joy Williams

THE PHONE RANG at five in the morning. Clem woke with a grunt. Liberty rolled away from Willie's arms and went into the kitchen and picked up the phone.

"Hello, Mother," she mumbled. Clem, a large white Alsatian with one blind eye, took a long, noisy drink from his dish.

"I want to explain some of the incidents in my life," her mother said. Her voice was clear and determined.

"Everything is all right, Mother. I love you. Daddy loves you."

"I had a terrible dream about penguins tonight, Liberty."

"Penguins are nice, Mother. They don't do any harm."

"There were hundreds of penguins on this beautiful beach and they were all standing so straight, like they do, like children wearing little aprons."

What can she do about her mother, Liberty thinks. Drive up and take her out to lunch? Send her tulips by wire?

"That sounds nice, Mother. It sounds sort of cheerful."

"They were being clubbed to death, Liberty. They were all being murdered by an unseen hand."

"You're right, Mother. It was just a dream and it's gone now. It's left you and I've got it." Liberty rubbed Clem's hard skull.

"Liberty, I have to tell you that I had another child, a child before you, a child before Daddy. She was two years old. I lost her, Liberty. I lost her on purpose."

"Oh, Mother," begged Liberty, "I don't want to know."

"Can you remember youself as a child, Liberty? You used to limp for no reason and sprinkle water on your forehead to give the appearance of fevers. You used to squeeze the skin beneath your eyes to make bruises."

"Mother, I didn't."

"You were suicidal. You were always asking me suicide riddles like, 'What would happen if a girl was tied up in a rug and thrown off the roof? What would happen if you put a girl in a refrigerator alongside the eggs and the cheese?' "

"None of those things are true," Liberty said uncertainly.

"I believe that one can outwit time if one pretends to be what one is not. I think I read that."

Clem took a few disinterested laps from his water bowl. He drank to keep Liberty company.

"It's almost Thanksgiving, Liberty. What are you and Willie going to do for Thanksgiving? I think it would be nice if you had turkey and made oyster stuffing and cranberry sauce. It broke my heart when you said you ate mullet last year. I don't think you can do things like that, Liberty. Life doesn't go on forever, you know. Your sister was born Thanksgiving Day. She weighed almost nine pounds."

Liberty was getting confused. The fluorescent light in the kitchen dimmed and brightened, dimmed and brightened. She turned it off.

"I fell so in love with Daddy. I just couldn't think," Liberty's mother said. "He was so free and handsome, and I just wanted to be with him and have a love that would defy the humdrum. He didn't know anything about Brouilly. I had kept Brouilly a secret from him."

"Brouilly?" Liberty asked, not without interest. "That was my sister's name?"

"It's a wine. A very good wine actually. She was cute as the dickens. I was living in New York then and when I fell in love with Daddy, I drove Brouilly eighty-seven miles into the state of Connecticut, enrolled her in an Episcopalian day-care center under an assumed name and left her forever. Daddy and I sailed for Europe the next day. Love, I thought it was! For the love of your father, I abandoned my firstborn! Time has a way, Liberty, of thumping a person right back into the basement."

"You've never mentioned this before, Mother."

"Do you know what your father says when I tell him I'm going to tell you? He says, 'Don't start trouble.' "

Liberty didn't say anything. She could hear a distant conversation murmuring across the wires.

"I chose the Episcopalians," her mother was saying tiredly, "because they are aristocrats. Do you know that they are thinner than any other religious group?"

"I don't know what to say, Mother. Do you want to try and find her?"

"What could I possibly do for her now, Liberty? She probably races Lasers and has dinner parties for twenty-five or something. Her husband probably has a tax haven in Campione."

"Who was her father?" Liberty asked.

"He made crepes," her mother said vaguely. "I've got to go now, honey. I've got to go to the bathroom. Bye-bye."

Liberty hung up. The room's light was now gray, and Clem glowed whitely in it. A particularly inappropriate image crept open in her mind like a waxy cereus bloom: little groups of Hindus sitting around a dying man or woman or child on the riverbank, waiting for death to come, chatting, eating, behaving as though life were a picnic.

Liberty opened the refrigerator door. There was a jug of

water aerating there, and a half-empty can of Strongheart. She poured herself a glass of water and spooned the Strongheart into Clem's bowl.

The phone rang. "I just want you to know," her mother said, "that I'm leaving your father."

"Don't pay any attention to this, Liberty," her father said on another extension. "As you must know by now, she says once a month that she's going to leave me. Once a month for twenty-nine years. Even in the good years when we had friends and ate well and made love a dozen times a week, she'd still say it."

Liberty could hear her mother breathing heavily. They were both over five hundred miles away. The miracle of modern communication made them seem as close to Liberty as the kitchen sink.

"Once," Daddy said, "why, it couldn't have been more than six months ago, she threw her wedding ring out into the pecan grove and it took a week and a half to find it. Once she tore up every single photograph in which we appeared together. Often she gathers up all her clothes, goes down to the A and P for cartons, or worse, goes into Savannah and buys costly luggage, boxes her books and our French copper, makes a big bitch of a stew which is supposed to last me the rest of my days, and cleans the whole damn place with a vacuum cleaner."

"It's obviously a cry for help, wouldn't you say, Liberty?" her mother said.

"I don't know why you'd want to call Liberty up and pester her and worry her sick," Daddy said. "She has her own life."

"That's right," her mother said. "Excuse me, everything's fine here. I made some peach ice cream yesterday."

"Damn *good* peach ice cream," Daddy said. "So, Liberty. How's your own life? How's that Willie treating you?"

"Fine," Liberty said.

"Never could get anything out of Liberty," her mother chuckled.

"You're getting to be old married folks yourselves," Daddy said. "What is it now, going on almost four years?"

"That's right," Liberty said.

"She's a girl who keeps her own witness, that's a fact," her mother said.

"I want you to be happy, honey," Daddy said.

"Thank you," Liberty said.

"But, honey, what is it you two do exactly all the time with no babies or jobs or whatever? I'm just curious, understand."

"They adore one another," Liberty's mother said. " 'Adore' is not in Daddy's vocabulary, but what Daddy is trying to say is that a grandson might give meaning and significance to the fact that Daddy ever drew breath."

"That's not what I'm trying to say at all," Daddy said.

"They're keeping their options open. They live in a more complex time. Keep your options open, Liberty! Never give anything up!" Her mother began to sob.

"We'd better be signing off now, honey," Daddy said.

Liberty went into the living room and looked out the window at the light beginning its slow foggy wash over God's visible kingdom, the kingdom being, in this case, an immense banyan tree that had extinguished all other vegetative life in its vicinity. The banyan was so beautiful it looked as though it belonged in heaven or hell, but certainly not on this earth in a seedy, failed subdivision in Florida.

She didn't know about the "adore." "Adore" didn't seem to be in Willie's vocabulary either. She supposed she could have told her daddy about Willie's saving people, making complete his incomprehension of his son-in-law. "He's going through a crisis," Daddy would say. "I wouldn't rule out an affair either." Once one got started saying things, Liberty knew, there were certain things that were going to get said back.

In the last six months, Willie had saved three individuals, literally snatched them from Death's Big Grab. It was curious circumstance certainly, but it had the feel of a calling to it. Willie was becoming a little occult in his attitudes. He was beginning to believe that there was more to life than love. Liberty didn't blame him but wished she had his vision.

The first person Willie had saved was a young man struck by lightning on the beach. Liberty had been there and seen the spidery lines the hit had made on the young man's chest. Willie had administered cardiopulmonary resuscitation. A few weeks later, the man's parents had come over to the house and given Willie a five-pound box of chocolate-covered cherries. The man's mother had talked to Liberty and cried.

The next two people Willie had saved were an elderly couple in a pink Mercedes who had taken a wrong turn and driven briskly down a boat ramp into eight feet of water. The old woman wore a low-cut evening gown that showed off her pacemaker to good advantage.

"You've always been a fool, Herbert," she said to the old man.

"A wrong turn in a strange city is not impossible, my dear," Herbert said.

To Willie, he said, "Once I was a young man like you. I was an innocent, a rain-washed star. Then I married this bat."

"A 'rain-washed star' is nice," Liberty said when Willie told her.

Willie smiled and shook his head.

"Well, I guess I've missed the point again," Liberty said.

"I guess," Willie agreed.

Willie was making connections that Liberty was finding harder and harder to bypass. She believed in love and life's hallucinations, and that every day was judgment day. It wasn't enough anymore. Willie was getting restless with her, she knew. He felt she was bringing him down. His thoughts included her less and less, his coordinates were elsewhere, his possibilities without her becoming more actualized. This was marriage.

Liberty turned on the television without sound and picked up a piece of paper. She sat on the sofa and drew a line down the center of the paper and on the left side wrote *things i would like* and on the right, *things i would never do.* She looked at the television, where there was a picture of a plate with a large steak and a plump baked potato and some asparagus on it. The potato got up between the steak and the vegetable, and a little slit appeared in it, which was apparently its mouth, and it apparently began talking. Liberty turned on the sound. It was a commercial for potatoes and the potato was complaining about the fact that everyone says steak and potatoes instead of the other way around. It nestled down against the steak again after making its point. The piece of meat didn't say anything. Liberty turned off the television and regarded her list. She was sweating. She had closed all the windows late the night before when she had heard the rain. Now she cranked them open again.

Deep inside the banyan, it still dripped rain. On one of its trunks, Teddy had carved I LOVE LIBERTY with his jackknife. Teddy was seven years old and fervently wished that Liberty were his mother. He often pointed out that they both had gray eyes and dark hair and a scar on one knee. She could easily be his mother, Teddy reasoned. He and Liberty had been friends for several years now. In the beginning, she had been paid by his mother for taking care of him, but now such an arrangement seemed inappropriate. Teddy lived nearby in a large, sunny house in a far more refined area of swimming pools and backyard citrus, but he preferred Liberty's more gloomy locus. It was also his mother's preference that he spend as much time as possible away from his own home. Janiella was a diabetic who did not allow her disability to get her down. She was a slender, well-read, and passionate, if not nymphomaniacal, woman who enjoyed entertaining while her husband was away, which he frequently was. With Teddy she enforced a rigorous mental and physical schedule and was not very nice to him when he wet the bed.

When Teddy first began to wet the bed, Janiella had long discussions with him about the need for him to accept responsibility for his own bladder. When Teddy continued to refuse responsibility, Janiella began smacking him with a Wiffle bat every time she had to change the sheets. Then she decided on an alarm that would awaken him every three hours throughout the night. All the alarm managed to do was increase the number of Teddy's dreams. Teddy dreamed more frequently than anyone Liberty knew; he dreamed and dreamed. He dreamed that he stole the single candy bar Janiella kept in the house in the event she had an attack and had to have sugar. He dreamed of Janiella crawling through their huge house, not being able to find her Payday.

When the phone rang again, Liberty walked quickly past it into the bathroom, where she turned the water on in the shower. She stood in the small stall beneath the spray until the water turned cool. She turned off the water and stared uneasily at the shower curtain, which portrayed mildewed birds rising.

"Hey," Willie said. He pushed the curtain back. His lean jaws moved tightly, chewing gum. Willie made chewing gum look like a prerequisite to good health. He was wearing faded jeans and a snug, faded polo shirt. His eyes were a faded blue. They passed over her lightly. Communication had indeed broken down considerably. Signals were intermittent and could easily be misread. Liberty didn't know anything about him anymore, what he did when he wasn't with her, what he thought. They had been together for six years. They had a little money and a lot of friends. There didn't seem to be a plan.

"That was Charlie," Willie said. "We're going to have breakfast with him."

They could never refuse Charlie when he wanted to eat. Charlie was an alcoholic who seldom ate. He was currently sleeping with Teddy's mother and between his drinking and this unlikely affair, Charlie was a busy man. Liberty thought that Janiella was shallow and selfish and chic. She felt that it was ridiculous for her to be jealous of this woman.

As Liberty was dressing the phone rang again. It was Teddy, whispering.

"Is that tree still outside your house?" Teddy whispered. "Because I'm sure it was here last night. It was waving its arms outside my window, then it flopped away on its white roots. It goes anywhere it feels like going, that tree."

"Trees aren't like people," Liberty said. "They can't move around." She felt her logic was somewhat insincere. "Dreams sometimes make you feel you can understand everything," she said. Liberty herself never dreamed at night, an indication, she believed, of her spiritual torpor.

"Can I come over today, Liberty? Our pool is broken. It has a leak."

"Certainly, baby, a little later, okay? Bring your snorkel and mask, and we'll go to the beach."

"Oh that's great, Liberty," Teddy said.

Liberty imagined him sitting in his small square room, a room in which everthing is put neatly away. He jiggles a loose tooth and watches his speckled goldfish swimming in a bowl, swimming over green pebbles through a small plastic arch. Once, he had two goldfish and the bowl was in the living room, but his mother gave a party and one of her friends swallowed one. It was a joke, his mother said.

Willie and Liberty got into their truck and drove to a little restaurant nearby called The Blue Gate. Clem sat on the seat between them, and from the back he could have passed for another person, with long pale hair, sitting there. At the restaurant they all got out, and Clem lay down beneath a cabbage palm growing in the dirt parking lot. The Blue Gate was a Mennonite restaurant in a little community of frame houses with tin roofs. Little living petunia crosses grew on some of the lawns. The food was delicious and cheap and served in large quantities. Sometimes Liberty and Teddy would go there and eat crullers.

Inside, Charlie was waiting for them at a table by the pie display. He wore a rumpled suit a size too large for him and a clean shirt. His hair was combed wetly back, his face was swollen, and his hands shook. Nevertheless he seemed in excellent spirits. The last time Liberty had had the pleasure of Charlie's company at table, he had eaten three peas separately in the course of an hour. He had told her fortune in a glass of water and then taken a bite out of the glass.

"Been too long, man," Charlie said to Willie, shaking his hand. "Hi, doll," he said to Liberty.

Charlie ordered eggs, ham, fried mush, orange juice, milk, and coffee cake. "I love this place, man," he said. "These are good people, these are *religious* people. You know what's on the bottoms of the pie pans? There are *messages* on the bottoms of the pie pans, embossed in the aluminum. Janiella got a pineapple cream-cheese pie here last week and it said WISE MEN SHALL SEEK HIM, man. Isn't that something? The last crumbs expose a Christian message! You should bring a sweet-potato pie home, Liberty. Get a message for yourself."

"There are too many messages in Liberty's life already," Willie said. "Liberty is on some terrible mailing lists."

"Yeah," Charlie nodded. "Yesterday, I got a letter from Greenpeace. They're the ones who want to stop the slaughter of the harp seals, right? Envelope had a picture of a cuddly little white seal and the words KISS THIS BABY GOOD-BYE. You get that one, Liberty?"

"Yes," Liberty said.

"You know what those Greenpeace guys did one year? They sprayed green dye all over the seals. Fashion fuckers don't want any green baby seal coats, right?" Charlie laughed his high, cackling laugh. The Mennonites glanced up from their biscuits and thin pink gravy.

Liberty ordered only coffee and looked at Charlie, at his handsome, ruined face. He was a Cajun. His mother still lived in Lafayette, Louisiana. She was a "treater" whose specialty was curing warts over the telephone.

"Janiella has a fur coat," Charlie said. "She has lots of lousy habits. She never shuts doors, for example. I have to tell you what happened. I was there yesterday, right? I'm beneath the sheets truffling away, and her kid comes in. He's forgotten his spelling book. His spelling book! 'Mommy,' he says, 'have you seen my spelling book?' I'm crouched beneath the rosy sheets. My ears are ringing! I try to be very still, but I'm *gagging*, man, and Janiella says sweetly, 'I saw your spelling book in the waste-basket,' and the kid says, 'It must have fallen in there by accident,' and Janiella says, 'You are always saying that, Ted. You are always placing things you don't like in the wastebasket. I found that lovely Dunmore sweater I gave you in the wastebasket. That lovely coloring book on knights and armor from the Metropolitan Museum was in the wastebasket also.' 'I'm too old for coloring books,' the kid says. Picture it, man. They are having a *discussion*. They are arguing fine points."

Liberty did not want to picture it. Breakfast had been placed before them. Charlie looked at the food in surprise.

"Well?" Willie said.

Charlie seemed to be losing his drift. He kept looking at his food as though he were trying to read it.

"So what happened?" Willie insisted. "Finally."

"Well, I don't know, man. The future is not altogether scrutable."

"Janiella and Teddy," Willie said, glancing at Liberty. "The spelling book."

Charlie giggled. "I fell asleep. The last thing I heard was the kid saying, 'I thought Daddy was playing in Kansas City.' I passed out from the heat, man."

"Playing in Kansas City?" Willie asked. He poured syrup on his fried mush. Liberty reached over and scooped up a bit for herself with her coffee spoon.

"He's a baseball player. He catches fly balls and wears a handlebar moustache and spits a lot. I think he suspects something. They've got this immense swimming pool wherein Janiella and I often fool around, and there was this little rubber frog that drifted around in it, trailing chlorine from his bottom. Cute little frog with a happy smile, his rubber legs crossed and his rubber eyes happy? Well, Mr. Mean came home last weekend and took his twelve gauge and blasted that poor little froggy to smithereens."

Liberty grimaced. Willie asked Charlie, "Who does Teddy think you are, a visiting uncle?"

"We've never met. I've only laid eyes on him in a photo cube. Janiella wants to keep him out of the house and she's got him busy every minute. He has soccer practice, swim team, safe-boating instruction. He's hardly ever at home. After school, he takes special courses in computer language, calligraphy, back-gammon. Poor little squirt comes staggering home, his brain on *fire*. I think of myself as a fantastic impetus to his learning."

"Liberty's not happy with this situation at all," Willie said.

"Liberty's all right," Charlie grinned, showing his pale gums. "Liberty's a great girl." The waitress arrived and warily placed a pint carton of milk by Charlie's right hand. The carton of milk had a straw sticking out of it. "Oh, look at that!" Charlie ex-claimed. "I love this place. You gotta get a pie, Liberty. Bring it home to Clem. He'd scarf it down and get some words. BE ZEALOUS AND REPENT. Dog'd go wild!"

Liberty reached across to Willie's plate and spooned up another piece of mush.

"That's extremely irritating," Willie said. "You never order anything and then you eat what I order."

Liberty blushed.

"Liberty!" Charlie cried. "Eat off my plate, I beseech you! Let's mix a little yin and yang!" He speared a piece of coffee cake with his fork and fed it to her.

"It's just one of those things," Willie said, "that has been going on for years." He looked unhappily at his plate.

"Really, man, you're losing energy with these negative emo-tions. You're just going dim on us, man," Charlie said.

"All right," Willie said to Liberty, "let's talk about you for a while. Tell me something you've never told me before."

"She's going to say, 'David,' " Charlie said. He brushed his fingers lightly across the veins in Liberty's wrist.

"David?" Liberty asked. "Who is David?"

"David is the boy you never slept with," Willie said. "David is your lost opportunity."

"I think we're talking too loud," Charlie yelled. "These are polite, God-fearing people. Their babies come by UPS. Big brown Turtle Waxed trucks turn into their little lanes. They have to sign for them, the babies. The babies grow up to be just like these old geezers here. Nevertheless, it's better to get babies by UPS. The sound of two bodies yattering together to produce a baby is a terrible thing, really."

"With David you would be another kind of woman," Willie said. "At this very moment, you could be with David, cuddling David. After you cuddled, you could arise, dress identically in your scarlet union suits, chino pants, ragg socks, Bass boots, British seaman pullovers, and down cruiser vests and go out and remodel old churches for use as private residences in fashionable New England coastal towns."

"But David," sighed Charlie, "is missing and presumed at rest."

"Change the present," Willie said. "Through the present change the future, and through the future, the past. Today is the result of some past. If we change today, we change the past."

Charlie shook his head. "Too much to put on a pie plate, man. Besides, it doesn't sound Christian."

"If you were another kind of woman," Willie said, "you could be married to Clay, the lawyer, dealing in torts. You'd have two little ones, Rocky and Sandy. They'd have red hair and be hyperactive. They'd be the terror of the car pool. Clay would have his nuts tied."

"Oh, please, man," Charlie exclaimed.

"You and Clay would fly to your vacations in your very own private plane. You'd know French. You'd gain a small reputation as a photographer of wild flowers, really bringing out the stamens and pistils in a studious but quite improper way. Women would flock to the better department stores in order to buy the address books in which your photos appeared. With menopause would come a change in faith, however. You'd get bored with your recipes and your BMW. You'd stop taking dirty pictures. You'd divorce Clay."

"I knew it, I knew it!" shouted Charlie. "There he'd be with his useless nuts!"

"You'd become a believer in past lives. You'd become fascinated with other forms of intelligent life. You'd see that Christ had returned as a humpback whale. You'd study whale language."

"Oh, I love whales too, man," Charlie said, spilling coffee down the front of his pink button-down shirt. "They are poets in tune with every aspect of their world. They sing these songs, man."

"You'd curse the house in Nantucket Rocky and Sandy had spent so many happy summers in."

"Ahhh, Nantucket, built on blood. Let's abandon this subject," Charlie said. He looked sadly at his shirt. "I've got to throw up, man. The happy vomiter has got to leave you now." He sighed and remained seated. "God is unrelenting and bitchier than a woman, I swear. What do you say, Liberty?"

"Liberty's song is a little garbled," Willie said.

"Aren't ours all," Charlie said graciously. "Ubble-gubble." He smiled at Liberty, who tried to meet his thoughtful, thickened gaze. She wished that she could watch him without being seen. The considerable fact that she was attracted to him made her feel morbid. *Things i would like,* she thought, *things i would never do.* She had to get started on that list.

"Except for Clem's song," Charlie was saying. The dog was visible from their table, lying beneath the palm tree, his paws crossed, yawning. A sheriff's deputy sat nearby in his cruiser, looking at him as though he'd like to write out a ticket. "Clem's song is serene. How'd you get such a great dog, Liberty?"

"He came in on the night air and settled on her head as she slept," Willie said.

"Gubble-ubble," Charlie said.

"He was in the envelope with the marriage license," Willie said. "He puffed up and was made soul."

"Leave this creep and come away with me," Charlie said.

Willie said, "We got him from the Humane Society. He ate a child. The police impounded him but what could they do? After all, this isn't the Middle Ages. We don't hang animals for crimes. And he was an innocent, a victim himself, belonging to a schizophrenic, anorectic, unwed mother who kept leaving her infant son alone with him, unfed, in her fleabag apartment."

Charlie said, "I mean it. I love married women. I treat them right. Your blood will race, I'm telling you. I'm also a cook. I make great meat loaf. No, forget meat loaf, I'll make gumbo. I'm third in line for two acres of land in Saint Landry Parish. Only two people have to die and it's all mine. It's got a chinaberry tree on it. We'll go to cockfights and pole the bayous and drink beer and eat gumbo."

"Actually," Willie said, "she found him sitting in the road. He'd been hit by a car. His eye was in a ditch of water hyacinths, being examined by two ducks. Blood all over the place. What a mess."

"Everything's so relative with you, man. I don't know how you make it through the day," Charlie said. He gazed at Liberty, absorbed.

"A linear life is a tedious life," Willie said. "Man wasn't born to suffer leading his life from moment to moment."

"I love quiet married women," Charlie said. "Their lack of fidelity thrills me. But I am coming to the conclusion that Janiella talks too much. Even in situ, she's gabbing away. And she's into very experimental stuff. There are not as many ways of making love as people seem to believe. Janiella may not be for me, actually."

"I'm splitting," Willie announced.

"I think you're making a fetish out of the real world," Charlie said, looking at Willie glumly. He rubbed his face hard with his hands. Liberty knew he wanted a drink. He had that look in his eyes. "And seriously, man, about these people you've been saving, I don't know. I mean about those *old* people particularly. I would allow them to go under if I were you. They might buy another Mercedes and take the wrong turn this time right into school recess. See them! Barreling through shrieking groups of shepherd-pie-stained Bubble Yum T-shirts, hand-tooled pointy-toed cowboy boots and small rucksacks stickered with hearts, flattening little hands holding hamsters, little sunburned arms . . ." He shook his head. "And that bugger you saved . . ."

"Bugger?" Willie looked rattled.

"You saved a bugger, you know," Charlie said morosely.

"He saved someone who had called his mother a 'bugger' is what I said," Liberty said. "That's what the mother told me."

"You're so literal," Willie said to Liberty. "What the young man said to me was that getting struck by lightning didn't feel like getting laid."

"Well, now *that's* expected," Charlie said. "It's well known that people say mechanical things under certain circumstances."

"Liberty prefers not to read between the lines," Willie said. "The clearly visible is exhausting enough, she feels."

"Liberty's a great girl," Charlie said. "A girl of romantic sensibility. She's a girl who cares."

"Liberty is a highly depressed individual," Willie said.

"Whatever," Charlie said cheerfully. "Building, building."

Willie stood up and leaned slightly toward Liberty, his hands on the table. His hands were tanned and strong and clean. His wedding band was slender. Liberty remembered the wedding clearly. It had taken place in a lush, green tropical forest in the time of the dinosaurs. "I've got to shake myself a little loose," he said. "Do you want the truck?"

"No," Liberty said.

"Just a few days," Willie said. "Later," he said to Charlie. He left.

"A butterfly vanishes from the world of caterpillars," Charlie said.

Liberty saw Clem get up and look after the truck as it drove away. He trotted over to the restaurant and peered in, resting his muzzle on a window box of geraniums. Liberty waved to him.

"He can't see that," Charlie said. "Animals live in a two-dimensional world. For example, like with roads? To a dog each road is a separate phenomenon which has nothing in common with another road."

"That sounds about right," Liberty said. She watched Clem nibble on a pink geranium. His bad eye was like a smooth stone.

"There are lots of roads," Charlie said. He picked up her hand and kissed her palm. "I love you," he said.

Liberty smiled. "Janiella's your married woman."

He shook his head and blew softly on her palm. "There's only you," he said.

"You're a bottle man," Liberty said.

"Liberty!" A child's voice called. It was Teddy, standing by the bakery counter. He hurried over, shoelaces flapping, holding a waxed bag. "Mommy sent me here for rolls because Daddy's home and they're fighting."

He sat on Liberty's lap while she tied the laces. Charlie closed his eyes.

"Who is that?" Teddy demanded.

"My man," Charlie said, "we were just discussing running away together."

"I want to go too," Teddy said. "You won't make me memorize poetry, will you?"

"What kind of monsters do you think we are?" Charlie said.

"My mother makes me do a lot of memorizing. I'm going to go to boarding school next year. 'Marriage needs room,' she says." Teddy pointed to a shelf of items for sale on the far wall—palm canes, dolls, cream pitchers in the shape of cows. "I bought my mother one of those for her birthday," Teddy said, pointing at a cow.

Charlie's long face looked sad. "That touches me," he said.

"I have been touched. I have been reached now for sure and I suddenly see things clearly. This is us," he said, touching their arms. "We should do something about us."

"Did this ever happen before?" Teddy asked, his arms lightly encircling Liberty's neck. "It seems like it happened before."

"A very common feeling in childhood," Charlie said. "Stuff that should have happened but didn't has to keep trying to happen until it does."

Liberty shook her head and smiled.

"Look at this pretty lady smile," Charlie said to Teddy. "I love this lady. I've loved her for a long time. It's been a secret just between us, but now you know too."

"I want to run away with you and Liberty and Clem," Teddy said.

"A beautiful woman, a smart dog, a little kid, and yours truly," Charlie said. "We can do it! We will become myths in the minds of others. They will say about us," he leaned forward and lowered his voice, "that we all went out for breakfast and never returned."

"Good," Teddy said.

"So where shall we go?" Charlie said. He kissed Liberty's face. The line of people waiting to be seated, old women in bonnets, holding one another's hands, looked at them in alarm.

"There's no place to go," Liberty said.

"There are many places to go," Charlie said. "Hundreds."

"Let's make a list, I love lists!" Teddy said.

"We're the nuclear unit scrambling out, the improbable family whose salvation is at hand," Charlie said. "We'll go to Idaho, British Columbia, Cancún, the Costa del Sol. We'll go to Nepal. No, forget Nepal, all those tinkly bells would drive us crazy. What do you say, we'll go to Paraguay. That's where Jesse James went."

"That's where the Germans went," Liberty said. "Jesse James just died."

"You're right," Charlie said. "It wasn't Paraguay. It was

Patagonia where Butch Cassidy and the Sundance Kid went."
He was fidgeting now. His dark eyes glittered.

"They were outlaws," Teddy said.

"They were outlaws," Charlie said. "Successful outlaws."

"Why are you crying?" Teddy asked Liberty. "Are you crying?"

"We've got to move along, it's later than we think," Charlie
said. "How about some lunch?"

ELENA, UNFAITHFUL

Gloria Kurian Broder

ALEXEI SAZEVITCH leapt out of the barber's chair and looked into the mirror after his haircut, and when he saw that he was exceptionally handsome for his age, he decided to retire. From his office he placed a call to his childhood friend, André, who lived in Paris, and said, "I'm stopping this nonsense, André. From now on I intend to spend all my time with Elena.

"She's getting younger and prettier," he told André, though in fact he thought she was getting older and homelier. After that, he descended a long flight of stairs to the office of a man he knew only slightly, but who was also a Russian by birth and an engineer, and leaning on the man's desk with the palms of his hands, he confided, "Rothkovitch . . . Rothkovitch . . . I have four children—Arianne, Eva, Ilya, and Katya. They are all grown and out of the house now, thank God, and my wife is not growing any younger or thinner; she's not like you and me"—he punched Rothkovitch in the stomach and planted a cigar in Rothkovitch's pocket—"so I've decided to stop all this and retire."

Finally, Alexei gave his secretary a silk scarf, a scarf unusual for being so long. After she had unwound it and wound it up again, Alexei noisily kissed her on the mouth and tossed her in the direction of the radiator. Forcefully he grasped and shook the hands of the rest of his staff and at last went down in the elevator carrying his framed diplomas; a silver plaque for designing the Elgar Bridge; two brass cups for jumping overboard and saving lives at the scene of that bridge; a wedding picture of his mother and father; and a large, embossed, half-eaten box of Ghirardelli chocolates. He put all of these in the back seat of his Bentley and drove through Detroit, cruising one-handedly through streets arched over with dust-laden trees and factory-filtered sunlight, past tight rows of brick-faced houses offering their ancient, cracked, cement porches, out into the raw, bleak avenues of tire and automotive supply stores, and finally beyond, to his own neighborhood of wide and utterly isolated lawns.

"Elena, Elena," he shouted at the front door. And when his wife appeared, he greeted her: "From this moment on, my darling girl, I will spend each and every moment at home with you!"

At these words it seemed to him that Elena's eyes started up and that she turned peculiarly pale. But he was altogether unprepared when, two days later, she took ill and died. The entire family went to the funeral and the priest read a eulogy.

Alexei could not believe anything like this had happened. He caught a cold and felt numb. All the same, grief—which he did not like, which he had always hid from—threatened to visit him, while terrible questions pushed their way into his clogged mind, such as, had he, during his and Elena's forty-five years together, treated her well enough for a European husband of average morality who was the head of his house and irresistible to women? On her last birthday, had he written a large enough check to Products for the Blind? And why had he gone fishing with his friend, Vassily, and their redheaded, then their brunette, mistresses on the very day that his second daughter, Eva, was born? the following year when Ilya was born? two mornings after the premature arrival of Katya, and exactly one week later, on the Fourth of July?

Alexei blamed his naiveté most of all. He had thought, initially, that his children would somehow look better. But no, in the early years he had always seemed to come upon them sitting on the linoleum in the pantry in wet snowsuits, holding out their swathed and dripping arms. "Papa, Papa," they would urge, while he would take a few steps back and as a young father observe that they had features he had not wholly counted on, mannerisms he was not prepared for. From the very beginning, Arianne was too awkward, Eva too mean, Ilya too pulling, and Katya unaccountably squashy and low to the ground.

"Think of the poor," Elena sang to them in their cradles, training them for good deeds. "Think of the poor," she warned them, each time he took off for a weekend. Busily, she sent forth baskets of fruit and new shoes, mailed out letters to the city council, and steadily brought in painting after painting of hefty-looking fruit, which she bought from starving artists. Nor was he, Alexei, exempt either, for each time he headed for the door, carrying suitcases, Elena would unlock his fingers, take hold of both of his hands, gaze into his eyes and say, "Alexei Mihailovitch, think once more about the poor." On these occasions he understood she spoke about herself.

Had it been all his fault then, he wondered. Was there time to start anew? His cold got better, his head cleared, and for a brief time he faced the fact that Elena had died; but he was a man who had always hid from unhappiness, who now grew aware that a terrible horizon of pain waited in the distance for him like a bank of fog. Massing together, it thickened and inexorably moved closer. In his sleep he moaned; he called out for Elena, and awoke each day feeling drugged and dizzy. Then in the middle of one night Birdie, the old housekeeper, brought him ice water, and after drinking it he fell asleep and dreamed of love, of youth, of bands of handsome, free, unfettered people moving along the banks of a rich, green river. Violets and poppies embroidered the meadows and a scent of lilac inundated the air while he—only he could not be certain it was he—and Elena danced, wandering amidst it all. In the morning he woke up feeling sensual, played upon, vulnerable to desire; and with the idea that something miraculous had happened, he got out of bed, crossed the carpeted bedroom, thrust open the windows, and, looking light-heartedly out onto Elena's garden, understood in the sweet, wild, and pungent summer air that Elena Petrovna had not died after all: she had simply run off with another man—very likely with a man who still worked—and she was happy.

Tears of gratitude glistened in Alexei's eyes. A photograph of Elena stood on the dresser. "Look at you!" he exclaimed, pressing the cardboard between his fingers. "Fifty pounds overweight, hair in braids like my great-grandmother, bags under your eyes, forever taking your shoes off and leaving them where I can trip—unable to wear a pair of shoes comfortably for more than five minutes—talking on and on about Congress, the war, the poor—and yet . . . yet I've misjudged you, I've never fully known what you are!"

He kissed the photograph, leaving wet marks, put it down, opened Elena's closet and looked in. Except for a strange umbrella and a folding chair, it was empty. She had taken all of her clothes, he thought, which was just as well since she did not own very many. His own wardrobe exceeded hers by ten times.

Alexei went to the phone. He wanted to ring up people and tell them his news. He would say to Vassily, "Vassily, just think of it—Elena's going off like that. Isn't it unusual, isn't it ironic!" But as luck would have it, he had recently kicked Vassily out of his house. And then, he debated, if he placed a call to André, there was a good chance André might misjudge his marriage—after all, they had not seen each other in thirty years. As for his children, they doted and depended on their mother much too much: finally he did not wish to cause them any pain.

His hand still on the phone, for a moment Alexei considered

telling the lady in the bakery whose blue, fractured eyes already held the knowledge of hundreds, perhaps even thousands, of different lives. Unfortunately, he thought, he did not know that lady. He took the umbrella from Elena's closet and went downstairs, still wearing his robe. Through the double glass doors that led into the living room he saw Birdie dusting the furniture with a feather duster, her hand moving like a pendulum as she mechanically turned here and there, touching the worn, rose-colored satin setee and couches, the samovar on the coffee table, the mended china lamps and clocks. He opened the glass doors and stepped in, then stepped out as a smell of stale oranges and apples rushed at him from the framed pictures of fruit on all the walls. Stepping in again, he shut the glass doors behind him.

"Birdie," he said, thinking perhaps she should be the first to know. After all, she had helped diaper and she had stuck pins, he conjectured, into all four of his children. For that alone she deserved something: should he clap her on the back and shout into her good ear, "Birdie, you old vixen, you demon! Just guess what your mistress has gone and done!"

He decided not. She would not believe him; worse still, she might say nothing at all. "Birdie, whose umbrella is this?"

She took it from him and looked at it for a long time. "It's Arianne's. She left it here last week, when it rained." Then she walked past him with the umbrella, which she put in a closet in the front hall.

"Arianne!" he exclaimed; Arianne, he thought. Why hadn't he singled her out from the others? She was his eldest daughter, the only one at whose birth he'd been present, the only child who had grown up as tall as he, with shoulders practically as broad; who beat him at badminton, who was more of a son to him than his other daughters or his son, and who could match him drink for drink at family gatherings until late in the night, when they would smile at one another, clasp their arms about each other's powerful shoulders, and loudly chorus "Auld Lang Syne."

He rushed to the phone in the den, and when she answered in the familiar, hearty voice that cracked in between syllables due to hoarseness and the headlong intensity of her goodwill, he leaned way back in the swivel chair behind the desk, stretched out his legs, and to the ceiling trilled out, "A. .ri. .anne, A. .ri. .anne!"

"Papa, I'm glad you called. I was just about to call you and ask you how things are."

"They're wonderful."

"I'm glad to hear that."

"Yes, they're perfect," he offered again, happy with such an exchange. Arianne, he thought, smiling broadly, was always cheerful. Unfortunately this virtue had also become her failing and he conceded that it even showed on her, physically—for although up to the neck she stood as proudly as a colt or soldier, her head with its close-cropped, curly dark hair tended to droop, and on her gaunt and pleasant face loomed the resigned and tragic expression of one who can never publicly come up with any but jovial things to say.

"How are your husband and children?" he asked her.

"We're all first rate."

"Excellent. How is the dog?"

"Getting much better. Thank you very much for asking."

"How is the cat?"

"Papa, uh . . . we don't have a cat."

"Never mind then; forget that I asked you." He leaned into the phone. "Arianne, I have something to tell you." A surge of anticipation welled up inside of him. "Your mother's gone . . . she's gone . . . shopping." His heart sank; he felt that he had failed. He let out his breath.

There was silence for a few moments and then Arianne shouted with no crack in her voice this time, "Papa, what did you say?"

"I said she's gone shopping." The statement sounded plausible enough to him except, of course, that everyone knew Elena never went shopping: it was always he who spent his spare time riding escalators in search of the latest, most elegant accessory from Italy or France.

"Papa, what did you say?"

"She's gone . . ." unsuccessfully, he tried again, "she's gone shopping."

"Listen, Papa, don't think about it. You have a point. Don't think about it and I'll come see you at two this afternoon. You have a point. There are good sales all over town. There are excellent sales in all the shopping centers." She hung up.

Downcast, Alexei remained seated at the desk, thinking that if only he had been able to tell Arianne the truth about her mother, he might have been able to tell her more—such as the differences between some of his competitors' work on bridges, and his own work; and how Vassily, after marrying a dreadful woman too late in his life, had forgotten the names of all their mistresses. Subsequently he and Vassily had had nothing to talk about; they'd quarreled over cards; at last Alexei threw him out of the door.

Brooding stonily in the swivel chair, Alexei turned prey to old irritations. Why, he wondered—as he had often wondered— why had Arianne, on the morning before her marriage, jumped into her mother's lap and remained there for half an hour when she was twice the size of Elena and might just as easily have jumped into his? Rehearsing these tales, Alexei's eyes began to flicker, his fingers to touch and move an ashtray, a letter opener on the desk, until all at once he grew impatient, jumped up and ran into the front hall.

"Breakfast, Birdie," he called, "right after my shower." He climbed the stairs, turned on the water in the bathroom, went into the bedroom and slid open the doors of his wall-to-wall, beloved closet. At this instant, the phone rang.

"Father?"

"Eva?"

"I hear that mother's gone shopping."

Eva's voice, suspicious and complaining at best, now snapped and accused. Alexei held the receiver a distance from his ear and inured himself by gazing at the orderly array of suits, trousers, jackets, vests, and coats that hung from wall to wall, harmoniously arranged by color. It was a sight he found soothing and peaceful, but which angered Eva, for whenever she visited the house, after she had eaten up all the scraps in the icebox, opened and searched in every drawer for childhood mementos, stormed abstractly through the basement and sniffed into the attic, she invariably ended up by confronting his clothes.

"Fifty-one suits," she would declare pointing to them with a long, ink-stained, crooked finger. "It's disgusting! Give some to the poor!"

"But they're not for the poor," Alexei would inform her, very simply, "they're for me."

Sometimes Katya would follow her sister to Alexei's closet. Katya was the baby. She was plump, with chubby upper arms Alexei liked to pinch. She had a small, cupid's face with hair planted on top of her head like a robin's nest; she had short legs and wore long dresses with uneven hems; and instead of becoming a ballet dancer, as Alexei had hoped, she had gone petulantly, yet unhesitatingly, into social work. Hair pins fell from her head, and like Eva, she said, "Give some to the poor."

And on occasion Ilya would wander in and, standing with his nose comfortably inside Alexei's closet and his hands on his hips, would inquire with a show of great kindness and concern, "Papa, what are you trying to prove? Why do you have so many clothes?" Alexei would answer, "Why do you have a moustache? Why, in these ecologically troubled times, do you have nine children? Why do you always only act in plays by Gorki?"—to which Ilya would raise his head high and, with heartfelt sincerity and the voice projection of an actor, solemnly intone, "At least I don't have so many clothes."

"What," Eva now pursued, as she liked her facts to fit, "what did mother go shopping for?"

Alexei frowned into the phone. *"For?"* An expression of pride—self-loving and stubborn—chiseled itself onto Alexei's face. He lifted his chin and reflected. "For shoes. Stockings. A dress. A purse." He paused. He leaned against the bedroom wall and crossed his ankles. "A hat. Some gloves. A bottle of perfume. You ought to go shopping yourself." He referred, as he knew she understood quite well, to the fact that she always wore an old serape and sandals and drove a camper truck with a broken muffler, and beyond that to the greater facts: that she taught in a ghetto school with hungry, angry dedication; that she stared glassily at him through thick lenses while clutching an enormous guitar; that she was bowlegged, vast-hipped, militant about women's rights, middle-aged, and had never married; and that more than any of the others, she had been influenced by her mother, but did not have her mother's grace.

Yet the tone of her voice suddenly softened. "Listen, Papa, tell me something. Have you been feeling yourself? How have you been feeling? Father . . . Papa, I think I'll come sleep home tonight. Tell Birdie to put out fresh sheets."

"No, no, no, no!"

"Why not?"

"No, no!"

"I'd like to."

"I think . . . it occurs to me," he recovered from her offer, "there's no need to." He smiled and murmured gallantly into the phone, "After all, my dear, you have your own apartment, your own little kitty cats, your guitar . . . "

"What I think," Eva said, "is that I'll pick Ilya up at the airport at one. That's when his plane comes in."

"Ilya?" For an instant he panicked. "Where's Ilya been?"

"Chicago. Don't you remember? In a play. He's been there for two weeks."

Alexei felt both relief and annoyance. "Gorki again. Why

does Ilya only act in plays by old Russians? Why doesn't he act in something modern, up-to-date?"

"Right after that," Eva went on, ignoring him, "I'll stop by for Katya at her work and we'll come to you around two."

"All of you?" Alexei objected.

"All of us," Eva confirmed, and added before hanging up, "Arianne said she'd drive over at the same time."

This plan depressed Alexei. He showered and dressed, thinking that his children were coming to see him. What could he do with them? He came down the stairs, shouting, "Breakfast, Birdie, breakfast!" and went into the living room to wait. Opening the double glass doors, he stepped on figured rugs that lay on top of the heavy carpet. He glanced about. Pictures of glossy fruit—one of peaches and pears, one of plums and pears, one of plums and apples, and one simply of bananas—painted by artists, each one more poor, he guessed, than the others—hung on three thick, ivory walls, while at the window heavy drapes kept out the light, the air. He had never liked this room. He had often told his family it was too old-fashioned, too Russian, and they had answered that they were Russian. Each time he came home from an illicit weekend, he had wanted to tear out walls, put in a bold expanse of vinyl floor and a sleek, white, modern couch. But Elena pleaded that he had his office and his outings and that this was her room. She began to go out less and less. She grew heavier, closer to life, less willing to keep on her shoes. Neighbors, teachers, other Europeans, and her own four children came to see her—brought her their troubles—as she sat on the worn, rose-colored satin settee, listening through long winter afternoons, her shoes paired next to her and two bunions on her toes. While she listened, her fingers peeled and divided an orange, and he remembered that her lips would first purse together as if they could taste each trouble and then grow round as if they were labeling and judging the trouble as "pretty good" or "pretty bad." After that, her manner changed. She gave advice. Handing around sections of the fruit, she tossed her head, her black eyes gleamed like a girl's amidst their bed of wrinkles, a high color rose to her flat cheeks, and even her chins—her grand and battered chins—jumped about with a certain ebullience and style.

Watching her in those last few years, Alexei's throat had closed; he had wanted those bursts of animation for himself. At the same time he eyed her audience, wondering if her opinions had come to be more respected than his own. How could that be? He, after all, had built fifteen bridges and designed six exhibits in the 1939 New York World's Fair where, whenever he turned around, one hundred beautiful women seemed to be concentrating raptly on him. And yet just this past spring, unable to make his presence felt, he had shouted into a group of acquaintances and strangers, "Let me talk, let me talk!" and then, overcome with shame, with chagrin, had quit the room, fled up the stairs, and placed a call—for no good reason—to André in Paris.

Alexei gazed at the rose-colored settee. It was empty; Elena was not there; and yet he seemed to hear her say, "Alexei, let's not eat cake; let's eat bread." She said it liltingly, with humor and in the voice of her youth, the same voice that had promised him a sweet, unjudging, shrewd frivolity forever—and then betrayed him.

At breakfast, Alexei ate in the dining room, alone, his eyes fixed on the buffet opposite him. Lifting his spoon, he reflected that inside those carved and massive drawers, both his and Elena's family silver was stored and lay together, rested side by side—a fact that struck him as so peculiarly intimate and fitting that briefly he faced the idea that Elena had died. But he got up at once and went into the den. Like the other rooms in the downstairs of the house, the den was dark and heavily carpeted. Drapes and venetian blinds hung at the windows. Two brown leather couches, a charcoal drawing of mangoes, and a desk lined the walls. In the center of the desk stood an immense world globe, its roundness and airiness, its light-blue color, and the fact that it so easily revolved making it a focal point in the room. Spinning the globe, Alexei's fingers caught at Rome, St. Tropez, at Venice, and impulsively, as though he were proposing some marvelous vacation by the sea, he urged out loud, "Elena, let's be young again!" The sound of his voice shocked him and he retreated up the stairs.

There, looking out the window over Elena's garden, he again smelled honeysuckle, saw fresh primroses, orchids, and daisies, and was once more reassured that Elena had run off with another man and was happy. He phoned the bakery and requested that they send up a cake. Then he lay down on the bed and fell deeply asleep.

When he awoke, he remembered that his children were coming to see him, and he felt pleased. He changed his shirt and brushed his hair. On the landing he met Birdie and she inched her way up for an afternoon nap, her bald head ringed round with ancient markings. They exchanged awareness of each other but no words and Alexei continued down, saw in the kitchen that his cake had arrived and transferred it to a crystal platter.

At two o'clock, he stood outside the front door and heard Eva's broken muffler in the distance. Presently the camper came into view and Eva maneuvered the vehicle up the driveway, her head craned out one window of the cab, Ilya's head protuding out the other window, and Katya in between them, staring straight ahead. A few houses down, Arianne parked her VW by the curb and ran at a gallop until she joined the others. The four of them headed up the path. They called, "Papa . . . Papa."

Eva confronted him first. Clasping her guitar with one hand, she removed her glasses with the other and lunged at him, timing her kiss so that it landed in the air. At this she looked wounded and angry, as if it were somehow all his fault. He gazed closely at her, struck as always by the beauty, not of her features, which were coarse, but of her translucent, pearly skin. She had, if nothing else, inherited his grandmother's complexion. He said to her, "Try again."

Surprised, Eva obeyed and then stepped back, tripping on her guitar. Katya took her place. She, too, appeared surprised by Alexei's order. Katya stood on tiptoe. Delicately she bestowed on her father a sweet and prissy peck, then turned her head away. As she was still his baby, this greeting—ambiguous though it was—pleased and undid him a bit. "Katya," he said. "But why are you so thin?"

"I've lost weight."

"Ah, Katya," he mourned, wondering if her husband beat her. He felt in his pocket for a piece of candy and at the same time noticed that her hair had turned entirely gray. "Ah, Katya, you've lost too much weight. You look like a cobweb."

"I've lost," she corrected him, proud and plaintive at once, "the right amount."

"Then never mind," he told her, comforting them both and dismissing her, for behind Katya, Ilya pushed for his turn, and behind Ilya he saw his tall and self-effacing Arianne, a brown paper bag in her hand—doubtless it contained brandy—who registered his awareness of her by signaling above the heads of the others in a voice that croaked like a frog's, "It's a most beautiful day, Papa—it's a most beautiful day in summer!"

"Arianne . . . Ilya . . . Katya . . . Eva . . . I'm so happy to see all of you!"

"And we're so happy to see you," said Ilya, stepping forward. He took both of his father's hands in his and stared intently into his father's eyes as if trying to glean from them something vital and unknown. His moustache quivered.

Uncertain as to what Ilya wanted, Alexei said, "Your mother isn't home."

"We understand," said Ilya.

"She'll be back quite late. But what I have for you is . . ."

"We understand," Ilya said. "She's gone shopping."

"She's gone shopping," said Katya.

"She's gone shopping," Arianne confirmed.

Alexei felt uncomfortable, but overcame it. "Come in, come in," he said, holding the door open. "What I have for you is

... I have some very excellent cake. Birdie didn't make it. Your mother didn't make it either. I got this exceptional cake by ordering it from the bakery." He led them through the front hall, the dining room, turned to face them by the kitchen. "As you will see, it is chocolate and has icing out of spun sugar and flowers and other such decorations." Flute-like, his fingers gestured in the air to convey the ambience of such a cake: its roses, its sugared avenues and lanes, the possibility of castles. "Now who will help me? Katya, put on coffee. Eva, bring out cups and plates. What else do we need? Napkins. Did I forget napkins? Ilya, see if you can find some napkins."

Alexei carried the cake into the living room, carefully set it down on the dark wood of the inlaid coffee table and sat down in the center of the rose-colored satin settee in what had always been Elena's place. He bent down to remove his shoes, but straightened up again, feeling foolish. His children arranged themselves in a semicircle around him and appeared fascinated. They had an air of being welcome strangers. Conscious of their mood, Alexei sliced the first piece of cake and meticulously placed it in the perfect center of a plate. He sliced a second, third, and fourth piece and handed these around. He had, he supposed, never served his children before and yet now, in Elena's absence, it seemed absolutely proper and what he wanted.

He watched as they began to eat: Eva avidly gobbled, Katya licked, Arianne chewed awkwardly, getting crumbs caught between her teeth and claiming she had never tasted anything better. As for Ilya, his cake went into his mouth and simply disappeared. Alexei smiled. A sense of satisfaction and fulfillment swept subtly over him. He decided he would call in his children's spouses, even all his grandchildren, despite their bad manners and unkempt hair.

To pave the way, he said, "I think . . . it occurs to me . . . I have something to tell you. Your mother's run off . . . with a lover."

"Oh, Papa!" all of them scolded at once and Katya added, "Stop it!"

"Don't worry, Katya. It will be a nice change for her; it will do her good.'"

Arianne objected, "Papa, she wouldn't do such a thing."

Ilya said, "I thought you told us she went shopping."

Katya cried out indignantly, "Listen to that! Have you ever heard such a thing! It's too much! I can't bear it!"

Through thick glasses Eva eyed him steadily and warned, "You'd better be careful, Father. You'd better stay off that track. Go back to shopping."

"But I don't understand," Alexei told them, shrugging, "you act as if your mother isn't capable of having a lover when, after all, she's like everyone else in this world; she's capable of carrying on . . . of enjoying herself . . . as you and me."

"No more, no more!" Katya wailed. She stamped her foot. "One more word and I'll scream."

But Alexei could not stop himself. "Most likely this is not her first lover. Indeed, there is good reason to think," he went on, lifting a speculative finger into the air, "that your mother has had many different lovers in the past. Perhaps some of them were social workers, community workers, teachers, even psychologists—yet they were lovers all the same." But even as he said this—even as he recognized its hollow sound—he knew he had gone too far.

Ilya stood up and faced his father. A sound of muffled choking issued from his throat. From his moustache came a whistle like a train's. Yet all he could utter was, "Cad!" A few minutes later he managed, "Bounder!" Katya fell out of her chair, sideways, and began to sob. Dragging her guitar behind her, Eva started to pace, agitatedly marching up and down the length of the room in a cold, even voice summing up: "You never deserved her. You never thought of anyone but yourself."

Of the four, only Arianne approached her father. She put a long, large-boned arm around him and tried to chuckle. "You're mistaken, Papa. She wouldn't do that, you know. She *couldn't* do that." But then, as if suddenly overcome, she moved off to a corner behind the fireplace, dropped into an armchair and covered her face with her hands.

Eva continued pacing and narrating, "You never tried to understand her. She was a saint, a free spirit." From the floor Katya sent up sharp yelps. Eva stepped over her and went on, "You never cared enough for her . . . or for us. You were always too vain, too arrogant, too unfeeling." Ilya, who had remained rooted to the same spot, his face pale, his neck livid, now grabbed hold of the cake knife, brandished it in the air, gnashed his teeth violently, and cut himself another piece of cake. He then left the room and went into the den to phone his wife. Katya crawled after him; she phoned her office.

Reentering the living room together, the two of them looked about, preparing to resume their angry postures. But in that dim, enclosed room—crowded with the clocks and china of their childhood, the pictures, upholstery, and samovars of their lives—they could not bear the violence of the fury and the anguish that they felt, so that, with a shriek, Katya opened the double glass doors and tumbled through the back hallway. One by one the others followed after her, squeezing through the narrow door and catapulting out into Elena's garden. And there, surrounded by the green spread of lawn, and under the splendor of the sky, they seemed more easily able to breathe. They said, "Ahhhh . . . ahhhh."

Ilya stretched out on a chaise, lifting his face to the sun. Eva uncovered her old guitar behind a rose bush, and gently administered to it. On her hands and knees, Katya picked herself a bouquet of small flowers, and Arianne, her mighty shoulders bent, emerged from the garage with the lawnmower. At once she sent the tall weeds flying.

Alexei isolated himself from them. Pulling a chaise a good distance away, to the other side of the cement path, he lay down and shut his eyes, his head also seeking the summer sun. Instead, in his mind's eye, he saw the brown, chill winter before snow. He stood on the frozen lawn while his small children ran toward him from the candy store, clasping white paper bags and sticks of licorice in their hands; calling him, while he, aloof and detached held off, waited until the last minute when they reached him before embracing and claiming them for his own.

Now it was all over, he thought. They could have nothing more to do with one another; he had waited too long. For the first time he wondered whom Elena had run off with, and where they'd gone. A powerful jealousy invaded him, and almost vengefully he decided he would phone Vassily and say, "Vassily, do you remember those wig models we met in New York City, in that restaurant on 57th Street? They were eating cannelloni and had ribbons in their hair?" Vassily's memory, he knew, was worth nothing these days, but he would prod it, stir it up. "Remember you had veal parmigiana and I had saltimbocca and those girls were done up just like gift packages? Vassily, my friend, let's go to New York and look for them. I'll take the taller of the two and since you're so very much shorter . . ."

But he did not feel like, going on. He let his hand drop over the edge of the chaise and plucked a blade of grass, which he put to his mouth. Once, at the beginning of his marriage, he had lain in a field with Elena and tasted one of her toes. He had never done that again, not having particularly liked it; yet the memory came back to him in the deep, bitter taste of the grass, this time telling him that what he wanted, more than anything else, was to take Elena from her lover and bring her back—beautiful and black-haired—for himself.

Quickly he went into the house and up the stairs, pulled out two suitcases from a closet and opened them on his bed. He chose underwear, shirts, handkerchiefs, and socks. On the way he planned that he would run into a shop and buy Elena a necklace, a new wedding ring. He would buy himself a tie. From down the corridor he heard a banging and Eva's voice that said, "Wake up, Birdie, wake up. There are a lot of things to do. We're taking inventory, and Ilya wants to see you."

Alexei glanced at his watch, thinking that Birdie had slept long enough. He went on packing, elaborately folding his clothes, taking fresh pleasure in his skill.

But when he descended the stairs half an hour later, he found his way to the front door barred by a carton of books, a samovar, the world globe from the den, and Arianne's umbrella. Behind these, three large paintings stood lined up against a wall. Setting down his suitcases, he followed voices to the dining room.

There, Katya and Eva leaned over the open drawers of the buffet, Katya with a pad and pencil in her hand. They were counting silver. Above them, where a picture of avocados always hung, was an empty space. Everything, Alexei thought, seemed odd. He sensed something—some strange current in the air, some bewildering change that he could not identify. Fear and suspicion seized him. His pulse began to pound.

"Twelve spoons," Katya said, "leaf pattern."

"No, ten," said Eva.

His two daughters stopped when they noticed him. But Ilya and Birdie, who were playing cards at the dining-room table, did not look up even after he had entered and demanded, "What's going on?" His fear grew stronger, became a kind of panic. Then suddenly he thought he understood: he had been duped. His children had been in on Elena's plan from the very beginning; all along they'd known where she'd gone off to, and with whom.

A false smile stretched across Alexei's face—a wheedling, over-intimate expression so alien to him it cut his cheeks. "You might as well tell me. There's no point in hiding it. Where has Elena gone?"

Eva strode over to him. It was then that he started to feel the other fear, the other terror. Eva lifted her face close to his and, looking down at her, he knew what she was going to say. More than ever before, he was aware of her extraordinary complexion, inherited from his own family. And indeed the skin on her face appeared so milky-white, so translucent, that for a moment he believed in the possibility of seeing right through her to some preferable object—such as bridges, even trees—but was stopped by the stubborn, owl-like challenge of her nearsighted eyes, by her brooding nose, by her chin as she said, "Mama has not run away. She is dead. She died six weeks ago."

Even as Alexei's head cleared, his mouth opened in a cry of pain. "A. . .ri. . .anne!"

Eva told him, "Arianne's busy drinking. She's drinking because, on top of other things, the house is too big. It's too big for you alone. We're closing it up."

He found Arianne in the den, sitting in the dim room with a bottle of Scotch, a bottle of bourbon, and an ice bucket at her side. Still disoriented and with no exact motive in mind, he tried out his grotesquely unconnected smile on her, but was relieved when she did not see it in the dark. She said, "Come sit down next to me, Papa, and have a drink. I'm way ahead of you, I've finished the bourbon. It was wonderful bourbon. First rate, really. Let me fix you a Scotch."

He drank from the glass she handed him, taking comfort from it and from her hoarse, warm, cracking voice. "Do you remember, Papa," she asked him, "all those games of badminton we used to play? Do you remember all those nights we ended up drinking brandy in the garden at two o'clock in the morning and singing 'O Tannenbaum' and 'Auld Lang Syne'? Those are first-rate songs. I love those songs." She poured them each another drink.

But he would not touch his. Something was stuck in his mind, in his heart. He fought both to locate and to control it, and presently he said, "Arianne, I think . . . it occurs to me . . . your mother died."

Through the slats in the venetian blinds he could see Eva carrying one of the large paintings down the front path. She loaded it into the cab of her camper. Alexei waited for Arianne to answer. But Arianne, as always unable to think of any but jovial things to say, stared straight ahead in her sorrow.

THE UGLIEST PILGRIM

Doris Betts

I SIT IN THE BUS STATION, nipping chocolate peel off a Mounds candy bar with my teeth, then pasting the coconut filling to the roof of my mouth. The lump will dissolve there slowly and seep into me the way dew seeps into flowers.

I like to separate flavors that way. Always I lick the salt off cracker tops before taking my first bite.

Somebody sees me with my suitcase, paper sack, and a ticket in my lap. "You going someplace, Violet?"

Stupid. People in Spruce Pine are dumb and, since I look dumb, say dumb things to me. I turn up my face as if to count those dead flies piled under the light bulb. He walks away—a fat man, could be anybody. I stick out my tongue at his back; the candy oozes down. If I could stop swallowing, it would drip into my lung and I could breathe vanilla.

Whoever it was, he won't glance back. People in Spruce Pine don't like to look at me, full face.

A Greyhound bus pulls in, blows air; the driver stands by the door. He's black-headed, maybe part Cherokee, with heavy shoulders but a weak chest. He thinks well of himself—I can tell that. I open my notebook and copy his name off the metal plate so I can call him by it when he drives me home again. And next week, won't Mr. Wallace Weatherman be surprised to see how well I'm looking!

I choose the front seat behind Mr. Weatherman, settle my bag with the hat in it, then open the lined composition book again. Maybe it's half full of writing. Even the empty pages toward the back have one repeated entry, high, printed off Mama's torn catechism: GLORIFY GOD AND ENJOY HIM FOREVER.

I finish Mr. Weatherman off in my book while he's running his motor and getting us onto the highway. His nose is too broad, his dark eyes too skimpy—nothing in his face I want— but the hair is nice. I write that down, "Black hair?" I'd want it to curl, though, and be soft as a baby's.

Two others are on the bus, a nigger soldier and an old woman whose jaw sticks out like a shelf. There grow, on the backs of her hands, more veins than skin. One fat blue vessel, curling from wrist to knuckle, would be good; so on one page I draw a sample hand and let blood wind across it like a river. I write at the bottom: 'Praise God, it is started. May 29, 1969," and turn to a new sheet. The paper's lumpy and I flip back to the thick envelope stuck there with adhesive tape. I can't lose that.

We're driving now at the best speed Mr. Weatherman can make on these winding roads. On my side there is nothing out the bus window but granite rock, jagged and wet in patches. The old lady and the nigger can see red rhododendron on the slope of Roan Mountain. I'd like to own a tight dress that flower color, and breasts to go under it. I write in my notebook, very small, the word "breasts," and turn quickly to another page. AND ENJOY HIM FOREVER.

The soldier bends as if to tie his shoes, but instead zips open a canvas bag and sticks both hands inside. When finally he sits back, one hand is clenched around something hard. He catches me watching. He yawns and scratches his ribs, but the right fist sets very lightly on his knee, and when I turn he drinks something out of its cup and throws his head quickly back like a bird or a chicken. You'd think I could smell it, big as my nose is.

Across the aisle the old lady says, "You going far?" She shows me a set of tan, artificial teeth.

"Oklahoma."

"I never been there. I hear the trees give out." She pauses so I can ask politely where she's headed. "I'm going to Nashville," she finally says. "The country-music capital of the world. My son lives there and works in the cellophane plant."

I draw in my notebook a box and two arrows. I crisscross the box..

"He's got three children not old enough to be in school yet."

I sit very still, adding new boxes, drawing baseballs in some, looking busy for fear she might bring out their pictures from her big straw pocketbook. The funny thing is she's looking past my head, though there's nothing out that window but rock wall sliding by. I mumble, "It's hot in here."

Angrily she says, "I had eight children myself."

My pencil flies to get the boxes stacked, eight-deep, in a pyramid. "Hope you have a nice visit."

"It's not a visit. I maybe will move." She is hypnotized by the stone and the furry moss in its cracks. Her eyes used to be green. Maybe, when young, she was red-haired and Irish. If she'll stop talking, I want to think about trying green eyes with that Cherokee hair. Her lids droop; she looks drowsy. "I am right tired of children," she says and lays her head back on the white rag they button on these seats.

Now that her eyes are covered, I can study that face—china white, and worn thin as tissue so light comes between her bones and shines through her whole head. I picture the light going around and around her skull, like water spinning in a jar. If I could wait to be eighty, even my face might grind down and look softer. But I'm ready, in case the Preacher mentions that. Did Elisha make Naaman bear into old age his leprosy? Didn't Jesus heal the withered hand, even on Sunday, without waiting for the work week to start? And put back the ear of

Malchus with a touch? As soon as Job had learned enough, did his boils fall away?

Lord, I have learned enough.

The old lady sleeps while we roll downhill and up again; then we turn so my side of the bus looks over the valley and its thickety woods where, as a girl, I pulled armloads of galax, fern, laurel, and hemlock to have some spending money. I spent it for magazines full of women with permanent waves. Behind us, the nigger shuffles a deck of cards and deals to himself by fives. Draw poker—I could beat him. My papa showed me, long winter days and nights snowed in on the mountain. He said poker would teach me arithmetic. It taught me there are four ways to make a royal flush and, with two players, it's an even chance one of them holds a pair on the deal. And when you try to draw from a pair to four of a kind, discard the kicker; it helps your odds.

The soldier deals smoothly, using his left hand only with his thumb on top. Papa was good at that. He looks up and sees my whole face with its scar, but he keeps his eyes level as if he has seen worse things; and his left hand drops cards evenly and in rhythm. Like a turtle, laying eggs.

I close my eyes and the riffle of his deck rests me to the next main stop where I write in my notebook: "Praise God for Johnson City, Tennessee, and all the state to come. I am on my way."

At Kingsport, Mr. Weatherman calls rest stop and I go straight through the terminal to the ladies' toilet and look hard at my face in the mirror. I must remember to start the Preacher on the scar first of all—the only thing about me that's even on both sides.

Lord! I am so ugly!

Maybe the Preacher will claim he can't heal ugliness. And I'm going to spread my palms by my ears and show him—this is a crippled face! An infirmity! Would he do for a kidney or liver what he withholds from a face? The Preacher once stuttered, I read someplace, and God bothered with that. Why not me? When the Preacher labors to heal the sick in his Tulsa auditorium, he asks us at home to lay our fingers on the television screen and pray for God's healing. He puts forth his own ten fingers and we match them pad to pad, on that glass. I have tried that, Lord, and the Power was too filtered and thinned down for me.

I touch my hand now to this cold mirror glass, and cover all but my pimpled chin, or wide nose, or a single red-brown eye. And nothing's too bad itself. But when they're put together?

I've seen the Preacher wrap his hot, blessed hands on a club foot and cry out "HEAL!" in his funny way that sounds like the word 'Hell" broken into two pieces. Will he not cry out, too, when he sees this poor, clubbed face? I will be to him as Goliath was to David, a need so giant it will drive God to action.

I comb out my pine-needle hair. I think I would like blond curls and Irish eyes, and I want my mouth so large it will never be done with kissing.

The old lady comes in the toilet and catches me pinching my bent face. She jerks back once, looks sad, then pets me with her twiggy hand. "Listen, honey," she says, "I had looks once. It don't amount to much."

I push right past. Good people have nearly turned me against you, Lord. They open their mouths for the milk of human kindness and boiling oil spews out.

So I'm half running through the terminal and into the café, and I take the first stool and call down the counter, "Tuna-fish sandwich," quick. Living in the mountains, I eat fish every chance I get and wonder what the sea is like. Then I see I've sat down by the nigger soldier. I do not want to meet his gaze, since he's a wonder to me too. We don't have many black men in the mountains. Mostly they live east in Carolina, on the flatland, and pick cotton and tobacco instead of apples. They seem to me like foreigners. He's absently shuffling cards the way some men twiddle thumbs. On the stool beyond him is a paratrooper, white, and they're talking about what a bitch the army is. Being sent to the same camp has made them friends already.

I roll a dill-pickle slice through my mouth—a wheel, a bitter wheel. Then I start on the sandwich and it's chicken by mistake when I've got chickens all over my back yard.

"Don't bother with the beer," says the black one. "I've got better on the bus." They come to some agreement and deal out cards on the counter.

It's just too much for me. I lean over behind the nigger's back and say to the paratrooper, "I wouldn't play with him." Neither one moves. "He's a mechanic." They look at each other, not at me. "It's a way to cheat on the deal."

The paratrooper sways backward on his stool and stares around out of eyes so blue that I want them, right away, and maybe his pale blond hair. I swallow a crusty half-chewed bite. "One-handed grip; the mechanic's grip. It's the middle finger. He can second-deal and bottom-deal. He can buckle the top card with his thumb and peep."

"I be damn," says the paratrooper.

The nigger spins around and bares his teeth at me, but it's half a grin. "Lady, you want to play?"

I slide my dish back. "I get mad if I'm cheated."

"And mean when you're mad." He laughs a laugh so deep it makes me retaste that bittersweet chocolate off the candy bar. He offers the deck to cut, so I pull out the center and restack it three ways. A little air blows through his upper teeth. "I'm Grady Fliggins and they call me Flick."

The paratrooper reaches a hand down the counter to shake mine. "Monty Harrill. From near to Raleigh."

"And I'm Violet Karl. Spruce Pine. I'd rather play five-card stud."

By the time the bus rolls on, we've moved to its wider back seat playing serious cards with a fifty-cent ante. My money's sparse, but I'm good and the deck is clean. The old lady settles into my front seat, stiffer than plaster. Sometimes she throws back a hurt look.

Monty, the paratrooper, plays soft. But Flick's so good he doesn't even need to cheat, though I watch him close. He drops out quick when his cards are bad; he makes me bid high to see what he's got; and the few times he bluffs, I'm fooled. He's no talker. Monty, on the other hand, says often, "Whose play is it?" till I know that's his clue phrase for a pair. He lifts his cards close to his nose and gets quiet when planning to bluff. And he'd rather use wild cards but we won't. Ah, but he's pretty, though!

After we've swapped a little money, mostly the para-trooper's, Flick pours us a drink in some cups he stole in Kingsport and asks, "Where'd you learn to play?"

I tell him about growing up on a mountain, high, with Mama dead, and shuffling cards by a kerosene lamp with my papa. When I passed fifteen, we'd drink together, too. Applejack or a beer he made from potato peel.

"And where you headed now?" Monty's windburned in a funny pattern, with pale goggle circles that start high on his cheeks. Maybe it's something paratroopers wear.

"It's a pilgrimage." They lean back with their drinks. "I'm going to see this preacher in Tulsa, the one that heals, and I'm coming home pretty. Isn't that healing?" Their still faces make me nervous. "I'll even trade if he says. . . . I'll take somebody else's weak eyes or deaf ears. I could stand limping a little."

The nigger shakes his black head, snickering.

"I tried to get to Charlotte when he was down there with his eight-pole canvas cathedral tent that seats nearly fifteen thousand people, but I didn't have money then. Now what's so funny?" I think for a minute I am going to have to take out my notebook, and unglue the envelope and read them all the Scripture I have looked up on why I should be healed. Monty looks sad for me, though, and that's worse. "Let the Lord twist loose my foot or give me a cough, so long as I'm healed of my looks while I'm still young enough—" I stop and tip up my plastic cup. Young enough for you, blue-eyed boy, and your brothers.

"Listen," says Flick in a high voice. "Let me go with you and be there for that swapping." He winks one speckled eye.

"I'll not take black skin, no offense." He's offended, though, and lurches across the moving bus and falls into a far seat. "Well, you as much as said you'd swap it off!" I call. "What's wrong if I don't want it any more than you?"

Monty slides closer. "You're not much to look at," he grants, sweeping me up and down till I nearly glow blue from his eyes. Shaking his head, "And what now? Thirty?"

"Twenty-eight. His drink and his cards, and I hurt Flick's feelings. I didn't mean that." I'm scared, too. Maybe, unlike Job, I haven't learned enough. Who ought to be expert in hurt feelings? Me, that's who.

"And you live by yourself?"

I start to say "No, there's men falling all over each other going in and out my door." He sees my face, don't he? It makes me call, "Flick? I'm sorry." Not one movement. "Yes. By myself." Five years now, since Papa had heart failure and fell off the high back porch and rolled downhill in the gravel till the hobblebushes stopped him. I found him past sunset, cut from the rocks but not much blood showing. And what there was, dark, and already jellied.

Monty looks at me carefully before making up his mind to say, "That preacher's a fake. You ever see a doctor agree to what he's done?"

"Might be." I'm smiling. I tongue out the last liquor in my cup. I've thought of all that, but it may be what I believe is stronger than him faking. That he'll be electrified by my trust, the way a magnet can get charged against its will. He might be a lunatic or a dope fiend, and it still not matter.

Monty says, "Flick, you plan to give us another drink?"

"No." He acts like he's going to sleep.

"I just wouldn't count on that preacher too much." Monty cleans his nails with a matchbook corner and sometimes gives me an uneasy look. "Things are mean and ugly in this world—I mean *act* ugly, do ugly, be ugly."

He's wrong. When I leave my house, I can walk for miles and everything's beautiful. Even the rattlesnakes have grace. I don't mind his worried looks, since I'm writing in my notebook how we met and my winnings—a good sign, to earn money on a trip. I like the way army barbers trim his hair. I wish I could touch it.

"Took one furlough in your mountains. Pretty country. Maybe hard to live in? Makes you feel little." He looks toward Flick and says softer, "Makes you feel like the night sky does. So many stars."

"Some of them big as daisies." It's easy to live in, though. Some mornings a deer and I scare up each other in the brush, and his heart stops, and mine stops. Everything stops till he plunges away. The next pulsebeat nearly knocks you down. "Monty, doesn't your hair get lighter in the summers? That might be a good color hair to ask for in Tulsa. Then I could turn colors like the leaves. Spell your last name for me."

He does, and says I sure am funny. Then he spells Grady Fliggins and I write that, too. He's curious about my book, so I flip through and offer to read him parts. Even with his eyes shut, Flick is listening. I read them about my papa's face, a chunky block face, not much different from the Preacher's square one. After Papa died, I wrote that to slow down how fast I was forgetting him. I tell Monty parts of my lists: that you can get yellow dye out of gopherwood and Noah built his ark from that, and maybe it stained the water. That a cow eating snakeroot might give poison milk. I pass him a pressed may-pop flower I'm carrying to Tulsa, because the crown of thorns and crucifixion nails grow in its center, and each piece of the bloom stands for one of the apostles.

"It's a mollypop vine," says Flick out of one corner of his mouth. "And it makes a green ball that pops when you step on it." He stretches. "Deal you some blackjack?"

For no reason, Monty says, "We oughtn't to let her go."

We play blackjack till supper stop and I write in my book, "Praise God for Knoxville and two new friends." I've not had many friends. At school in the valley, I sat in the back rows, reading, a hand spread on my face. I was smart, too; but if you let that show, you had to stand for the class and present different things.

When the driver cuts out the lights, the soldiers give me a whole seat, and a dufflebag for a pillow. I hear them whispering, first about women, then about me; but after a while I don't hear that anymore.

By the time we hit Nashville, the old lady makes the bus wait while she begs me to stop with her. "Harvey won't mind. He's a good boy." She will not even look at Monty and Flick. "You can wash and change clothes and catch a new bus tomorrow."

"I'm in a hurry. Thank you." I have picked a lot of galax to pay for this trip.

"A girl alone. A girl that maybe feels she's got to prove something?" The skin on her neck shivers. "Some people might take advantage."

Maybe when I ride home under my new face, that will be some risk. I shake my head, and as she gets off she whispers something to Mr. Weatherman about looking after me. It's wasted, though, because a new driver takes his place and he looks nearly as bad as I do—oily-faced and toad-shaped, with eyeballs a dingy color and streaked with blood. He's the flatlands driver, I guess, because he leans back and drops one warty hand on the wheel and we go so fast and steady you can hardly tell it.

Since Flick is the tops in cards and we're tired of that, it's Monty's turn to brag on his motorcycle. He talks all across Tennessee till I think I could ride one by hearsay alone, that my wrist knows by itself how far to roll the throttle in. It's a Norton and he rides it in Scrambles and Enduro events, in his leathers, with spare parts and tools glued all over him with black electrician's tape.

"So this bastard tells me, 'Zip up your jacket because when I run over you I want some traction.' "

Flick is playing solitaire. "You couldn't get me on one of them killing things."

"One day I'm coming through Spruce Pine, flat out, throw Violet up behind me! We're going to lean all the way through them mountains. Sliding the right foot and then sliding the left." Monty lays his head back on the seat beside me, rolls it, watches. "How you like that? Take you through creeks and ditches like you was on a skateboard. You can just holler and hang on."

Lots of women have, I bet.

"The Norton's got the best front forks of anybody. It'll nearly roll up a tree trunk and ride down the other side." He demonstrates on the seat back. I keep writing. These are new things, two-stroke and four-stroke, picking your line on a curve, Milwaukee iron. It will all come back to me in the winters, when I reread these pages.

Flick says he rode on a Harley once. "Turned over and got drug. No more."

They argue about what he should have done instead of turning over. Finally Monty drifts off to sleep, his head leaning at me slowly, so I look down on his crisp, light hair. I pat it as easy as a cat would, and it tickles my palm. I'd almost ask them in Tulsa to make me a man if I could have hair like his, and a beard, and feel so different in so many places.

He slides closer in his sleep. One eyebrow wrinkles against my shoulder. Looking our way, Flick smokes a cigarette, then reads some magazine he keeps rolled in his belt. Monty makes a deep noise against my arm as if , while he slept, his throat had cleared itself. I shift and his whole head is on my shoulder now. Its weight makes me breathe shallow.

I rest my eyes. If I should turn, his hair would barely touch my cheek, the scarred one, like a shoebrush. I do turn and it does. For miles he sleeps that way and I almost sleep. Once, when we take a long curve, he rolls against me, and one of his hands drifts up and then drops in my lap. Just there, where the creases are.

I would not want God's Power to turn me, after all, into a

man. His breath is so warm. Everywhere, my skin is singing. Praise God for that.

When I get my first look at the Mississippi River, the pencil goes straight into my pocketbook. How much praise would that take?

"Is the sea like this?"

"Not except they're both water," Flick says. He's not mad anymore. "Tell you, what, Vi-oh-LETTE. When Monty picks you up on his cycle" ("sickle," he calls it), "you ride down to the beaches—Cherry Grove, O.D., around there. Where they work the big nets in the fall and drag them up on the sand with trucks at each end, and men to their necks in the surf."

"You do that?"

"I know people that do. And afterward they strip and dress by this big fire on the beach."

And they make chowder while this cold wind is blowing! I know that much, without asking. In a big black pot that sits on that shipping fire. I think they might let me sit with them and stir the pot. It's funny how much, right now, I feel like praising all the good things I've never seen, in places I haven't been.

Everybody has to get off the bus and change in Memphis, and most of them wait a long time. I've taken the long way, coming here; but some of Mama's cousins live in Memphis and might rest me overnight. Monty says they plan to stay the night, too, and break the long trip.

"They know you're coming, Violet?" It's Flick says my name that way, in pieces, carefully: Vi-oh-LETTE. Monty is lazier: Viii-lut. They make me feel like more than one.

"I've never even met these cousins. But soon as I call up and tell them who I am and that I'm here . . ."

"We'll stay some hotel tonight and then ride on. Why don't you come with us?" Monty is carrying my scuffed bag. Flick swings the paper sack. "You know us better than them."

"Kin people," grunts Flick, "can be a bad surprise."

Monty is nodding his head. "Only cousin I had got drunk and drove this tractor over his baby brother. Did it on purpose, too." I see by his face that Monty has made this up, for my sake.

"Your cousins might not even live here anymore. I bet it's been years since you heard from a one."

"We're picking a cheap hotel, in case that's a worry."

I never thought they might have moved. "How cheap?"

When Flick says, "Under five," I nod; and my things go right up on their shoulders as I follow them into a Memphis cab. The driver takes for granted I'm Monty's afflicted sister and names a hotel right off. He treats me with pity and good manners.

And the hotel he chooses is cheap, all right, where ratty salesmen with bad territories spend half the night drinking in their rooms. Plastic palm bushes and a worn rug the color of wet cigars. I get Room 210 and they're down the hall in the teens. They stand in my doorway and watch me drop both shoes and walk the bed in bare feet. When Monty opens my window, we can hear some kitchen underneath—a fan, clattering noise, a man's crackly voice singing about the California earthquake.

It scares me, suddenly, to know I can't remember how home sounds. Not one bird call, nor the water over rocks. There's so much you can't save by writing down.

"Smell that grease," says Flick, and shakes his head till his lips flutter. "I'm finding an ice machine. You, Vi-oh-LETTE, come on down in a while."

Monty's got a grin I'll remember if I never write a word. He waves. "Flick and me going to get drunker than my old cousin and put wild things in your book. Going to draw dirty pictures. You come on down and get drunk enough to laugh."

But after a shower, damp in my clean slip, even this bed like a roll of fence wire feels good, and I fall asleep wondering if that rushing noise is a river wind, and how long I can keep it in my mind.

Monty and Flick edge into my dream. Just their voices first, from way downhill. Somewhere in a Shonny Haw thicket.

"Just different," Monty is saying. "That's all. Different. Don't make some big thing out of it." He doesn't sound happy. "Nobody else," he says.

Is that Flick singing? No, because the song goes on while his voice says, "Just so . . ." and then some words, I don't catch. "It don't hurt"? Or maybe, "You don't hurt"? I hear them climbing my tangled hill, breaking sticks and knocking the little stones loose. I'm trying to call to them which way the path is, but I can't make noise because the Preacher took my voice and put it in a black bag and carried it to a sick little boy in Iowa.

They find the path, anyway. And now they can see my house and me standing little by the steps. I know how it looks from where they are: the wood rained on till the siding's almost silver; and behind the house a wet-weather waterfall that's cut a stream bed downhill and grown pin cherry and bee balm on both sides. The high rock walls by the waterfall are mossy and slick, but I've scraped one place and hammered a mean-looking gray head that leans out of the hillside and stares down the path at whoever comes. I've been here so long by myself that I talk to it sometimes. Right now I'd say, "Look yonder. We've got company at last!" if my voice wasn't gone.

"You can't go by looks," Flick is saying as they climb. He ought to know. Ahead of them, warblers separate and fly out on two sides. Everything moves out of their path if I could just see it—tree frogs and mosquitoes. Maybe the worms drop deeper just before a footstep falls.

"Without the clothes, it's not a hell of a lot improved," says Monty, and I know suddenly they are inside my house with me, inside my very room, and my room today's in Memphis. "There's one thing, though," Monty says, standing over my bed. "Good looks in a woman is almost like a wall. She can use it to shut you outside. You never know what she's like, that's all." He's wearing a T-shirt and his dog tags jingle. "Most of the time I don't even miss knowing that."

And Flick says, disgusted, "I knew that much in grammar school. You sure are slow. It's not the face you screw." If I opened my eyes, I could see him now, behind Monty. He says, "After a while, you don't even notice faces. I always thought, in a crowd, my mother might not pick Daddy out."

"*My* mother could," says Monty. "He was always the one *started* the fight."

I stretch and open my eyes. It's a plain slip, cotton, that I sewed myself and makes me look too white and skinny as a sapling.

"She's waking up."

When I point, Monty hands me the blouse off the doorknob. Flick says they've carried me a soda pop, plus something to spruce it up. They sit stiffly on two hard chairs till I've buttoned on my skirt. I sip the drink, cold but peppery, and prop on the bed with the pillows. "I dreamed you both came where my house is, on the mountain, and it had rained so the waterfall was working. I felt real proud of that."

Ater two drinks we go down to the noisy restaurant with that smelly grease. And after that, to a picture show. Monty grins widely when the star comes on the screen. The spit on his teeth shines, even in the dark. Seeing what kind of woman he really likes, black-haired as a gypsy and with a juicy mouth, I change all my plans. My eyes, too, must turn up on the ends and when I bend down my breasts must fall forward and push at each other. When the star does that in picture, the cowboy rubs his mustache low in the front of her neck.

In the darkness, Monty takes my hand and holds it in his swelling lap. To me it seems funny that my hand, brown and crusty from hoeing and chopping, is harder than his. I guess you don't get calluses rolling a motorcycle throttle. He rubs his thumb up and down my middle finger. Oh, I would like to ride fast behind him, spraddle-legged, with my arms wrapped on his belt, and I would lay my face between his sharp shoulder blades.

That night, when I've slept awhile, I hear something brushing the rug in the hall. I slip to my door. It's very dark. I press myself, face first, to the wood. There's breathing on the other side. I feel I get fatter, standing there, that even my own small breasts might now be made to touch. I round both shoulders to see. The movement jars the door and it trembles slightly in its frame.

From the far side, by the hinges, somebody whispers, "Vi-oh-LETTE?"

Now I stand very still. The wood feels cooler on my skin, or else I have grown very warm. Oh, I could love anybody! There is so much of me now, they could line up strangers in the hall and let me hold each one better than he had ever been held before!

Slowly I turn the knob, but Flick's breathing is gone. The corridor's empty. I leave the latch off.

Late in the night, when the noise from the kitchen is over, he comes into my room. I wake when he bumps on a chair, swears, then scrabbles at the footboard.

"Viii-lut?"

I slide up in bed. I'm not ready, not now, but he's here. I spread both arms wide. In the dark he can't tell.

He feels his way onto the bed and he touches my knee and it changes. Stops being just my old knee, under his fingers. I feel the joint heat up and bubble. I push the sheet down.

He comes onto me whispering something. I reach up to claim him.

One time he stops. He's surprised, I guess, finding he isn't the first. How can I tell him how bad that was? How long ago? The night when the twelfth grade was over and one of them climbed with me all the way home? And he asked. And I thought, *I'm entitled*. Won him a five-dollar bet. Didn't do nothing for me.

But this time I sing out and Monty says, "Shh," in my ear. And he starts over, slow, and makes me whimper one other time. Then he turns sideways to sleep and I try my face there, laid in the nest on his damp back. I reach out my tongue. He is salty and good.

Now there are two things too big for my notebook but praise God! And for the Mississippi, too!

There is no good reason for me to ride with them all the way to Fort Smith, but since Tulsa is not expecting me, we change my ticket. Monty pays the extra. We ride through the fertile plains. The last of May becomes June and the Arkansas sun is blazing. I am stunned by this heat. At home, night means blankets and even on hot afternoons it may rain and start the waterfall. I lie against my seat for miles without a word.

"What's wrong?" Monty keeps asking; but, under the heat, I am happy. Sleepy with happiness, a lizard on a rock. At every stop Monty's off the bus, bringing me more than I can eat or drink, buying me magazines and gum. I tell him and Flick to play two-handed cards, but mostly Flick lectures him in a low voice about something.

I try to stop thinking of Memphis and think back to Tulsa. I went to the Spruce Pine library to look up Tulsa in their encyclopedia. I thought sure it would tell about the Preacher, and on what street he'd built his Hope and Glory Building for his soul crusades. Tulsa was listed in the *Americana*, Volume 27, Trance to Venial Sin. I got so tickled with that I forgot to write down the rest.

Now, in the hot sun, clogged up with trances and venial sins, I dream under the drone of their voices. For some reason I remember that old lady back in Nashville, moved in with Harvey and his wife and their three children. I hope she's happy. I picture her on Harvey's back porch, baked in the sun like me, in a rocker. Snapping beans.

I've left my pencil in the hotel and must borrow one from Flick to write in my book. I put in, slowly, "This is the day which the Lord hath made." But, before Monty, what kind of days was He sending me? I cross out the line. I have this wish to praise, instead of Him, the littlest things. Honeybees, and the wet slugs under their rocks. A gnat in some farmer's eye.

I give up and hand Flick his pencil. He slides toward the aisle and whispers, "You wish you'd stayed in your mountains?"

I shake my head and a piece of my no-color hair falls into the sunlight. Maybe it even shines.

He spits on the pencil point and prints something inside a gum wrapper. "Here's my address. You keep it. Never can tell."

So I tear the paper in half and give him back mine. He reads it a long time before tucking it away, but he won't send a letter till I do—I can tell that. Through all this, Monty stares out the window. Arkansas rolls out ahead of us like a rug.

Monty has not asked for my address, nor how far uphill I live from Spruce Pine, though he could ride his motorcycle up to me, strong as its engine is. For a long time he has been sitting quietly, lighting one cigarette off another. This winter, I've got to learn smoking. How to lift my hand up so every eye will follow it to my smooth cheek.

I put Flick's paper in my pocketbook and there, inside, on a round mirror, my face is waiting in ambush for me. I see the curved scar, neat as ever, swoop from the edge of one nostril in rainbow shape across my cheek, then down toward the ear. For the first time in years, pain boils across my face as it did that day. I close my eyes under that red drowning, and see again Papa's ax head rise off its locust handle and come floating through the air, sideways, like a gliding crow. And it drops down into my face almost daintily, the edge turned just enough to slash loose a flap of skin the way you might slice straight down on the curve of a melon. My papa is yelling, but I am under a red rain and it bears me down. I am lifted and run with through the woodyard and into the barn. Now I am slumped on his chest and the whipped horse is throwing us down the mountainside, and my head is wrapped in something big as a wet quilt. The doctor groans when he winds it off and I faint while he lifts up my flesh like the flap of a pulpy envelope, and sews the white bone out of sight.

Dizzy from the movement of the bus, I snap shut my pocketbook.

Whenever I cry, the first drop quivers there, in the curving scar, and then runs crooked on that track to the ear. I cry straight-down on the other side.

I am glad this bus has a toilet. I go there to cool my eyes with wet paper, and spit up Monty's chocolate and cola.

When I come out, he's standing at the door with his fist up. "You all right, Viii-lut? You worried or something?"

I see he pities me. In my seat again, I plan the speech I will make at Fort Smith and the laugh I will give. "Honey, you're good," I'll say, laughing, "but the others were better." That ought to do it. I am quieter now than Monty is, practicing it in my mind.

It's dark when we hit Fort Smith. Everybody's face looks shadowed and different. Mine better. Monty's strange. We're saying goodbyes very fast. I start my speech twice and he misses it twice.

Then he bends over me and offers his own practiced line that I see he's worked up all across Arkansas, "I plan to be right here, Violet, in this bus station. On Monday. All day. You get off your bus when it comes through. Hear me, Viii-lut? I'll watch for you?"

No. He won't watch. Nor I come. "My schedule won't take me this road going back. Bye, Flick. Lots of good luck to you both."

"Promise me. Like I'm promising."

"Good luck to you, Vi-oh-LETTE." Flick lets his hand fall on my head and it feels as good as anybody's hand.

Monty shoves money at me and I shove it back. "Promise," he says, his voice furious. He tries to kiss me in the hair and I jerk so hard my nose cracks his chin. We stare, blurry-eyed and hurting. He follows Flick down the aisle, calls back, "I'm coming here Monday. See you then, hear? And you get off this bus!"

"No! I won't!"

He yells it twice more. People are staring. He's out of the bus pounding on the steel wall by my seat. I'm not going to look.

The seats fill up with strangers and we ride away, nobody talking to anyone else. My nose where I hit it is going to swell—the Preacher will have to throw that in for free. I look back, but he's gone.

The lights in the bus go out again. Outside they bloom thick by the streets, then thinner, then mostly gone as we pass into the countryside. Even in the dark, I can see Oklahoma's mountains are uglier than mine. Knobs and hills, mostly. The bus drives into rain which covers up everything. At home I like that washing sound. We go deeper into the downpour. Perhaps we are under the Arkansas River, after all. It seems I can feel its great weight move over me.

Before daylight, the rain tapers off and here the ground looks dry, even barren. Cattle graze across long fields. In the wind, wheat fields shiver. I can't eat anything all the way to Tulsa. It makes me homesick to see the land grow brighter and flatter and balder. That old lady was right—the trees do give out— and oil towers grow in their place. The glare's in my eyes. I write in my notebook, "Praise God for Tulsa; I am nearly there," but it takes a long time to get the words down.

One day my papa told me how time got slow for him when Mama died. How one week he waded through the creek and it was water, and the next week cold molasses. How he'd lay awake a year between sundown and sunup, and in the morning I'd be a day older and he'd be three hundred and sixty-five.

It works the other way, too. In no time at all, we're into Tulsa without me knowing what we've passed. So many tall buildings. Everybody's running. They rush into taxis before I can get one to wait for me long enough to ask the driver questions. But still I'm speeded to a hotel, and the elevator yanks me to a room quicker than Elijah rode to Heaven. The room's not bad. A Gideon Bible. Inside are lots of dirty words somebody wrote. He must have been feeling bad.

I bathe and dress, trembling from my own speed, and pin on the hat which has traveled all the way from Spruce Pine for this. I feel tired. I get out into the loud streets full of fast cars.

Hot metal everywhere. A taxi roars me across town to the Preacher's church.

It looks like a big insurance office, though I can tell where the chapel is by colored glass in the pointed windows. Carved in an arch over the door are the words "HOPE OF GLORY BUILDING." Right away, something in me sinks. All this time I've been hearing it on TV as the Hope *and* Glory Building. You wouldn't think one word could make that much difference.

Inside the door, there's a list of offices and room numbers. I don't see the Preacher's name. Clerks send me down long, tiled halls, past empty air-conditioned offices. One tells me to go up two flights and ask the fat woman, and the fat woman sends me down again. I'm carring my notebook in a dry hand, feeling as brittle as the maypop flower.

At last I wait an hour to see some assistant—very close to the Preacher, I'm told. His waiting room is chilly, the leatherette chairs worn down to the mesh. I try to remember how much TB and cancer have passed through this very room and been jerked out of people the way Jesus tore out a demon and flung him into a herd of swine. I wonder what he felt like to the swine.

Ater a long time, the young man calls me into his plain office—wood desk, wood chairs. Shelves of booklets and colored folders. On one wall, a colored picture of Jesus with that fairy ring of light around His head. Across from that, one of His praying hands—rougher than Monty's, smoother than mine.

The young man wears glasses with no rims. In this glare, I am reflected on each lens, Vi-oh-ETTE and Vii-lut. On his desk is a box of postcards of the Hope and Glory Building. *Of* Glory. *Of* Glory.

I am afraid.

I feel behind me for the chair.

The man explains that he is presently in charge. The Preacher's speaking in Tallahassee, his show taped weeks ahead. I never thought of it as a show before. He waits.

I reach inside my notebook where, taped shut, is the thick envelope with everything written down. I knew I could never explain things right. When have I ever been able to tell what I really felt? But it's all in there—my name, my need. The words from the Bible which must argue for me. I did not sit there nights since Papa died, counting my money and studying God's Book, for nothing. Playing solitaire, then going back to search the next page and the next. Stepping outside to rest my eyes on His limitless sky, then back to the Book and paper, building my case.

He starts to read, turns up his glitter-glass to me once to check how I look, then reads again. His chair must be hard, for he squirms in it, crosses his legs. When he has read every page, he lays the stack down, slowly takes off his glasses, folds them shining into a case. He leaves it open on his desk. Mica shines like that, in the rocks.

Then he looks at me, fully. Oh. He is plain. Almost homely. I nearly expected it. Maybe Samuel was born ugly, so who else would take him but God?

"My child," the man begins, though I'm older than he is, "I understand how you feel. And we will most certainly pray for your spirit. . . ."

I shut my eyes against those two flashing faces on his spectacles. "Never mind my spirit." I see he doesn't really understand. I see he will live a long life, and not marry.

"Our Heavenly Father has purpose in all things."

Stubbornly, "Ask Him to set it aside."

"We must all trust His will."

After all these years, isn't it God's turn to trust mine? Could He not risk a little beauty on me? Just when I'm ready to ask, the sober assistant recites, " 'Favor is deceitful and beauty is vain.' That's in Proverbs."

And I cry, " 'The crooked shall be made straight!' Isaiah said that!" He draws back, as if I had brought the Gideon Bible and struck him with its most disfigured pages. "Jesus healed an impediment in speech. See my impediment! Mud on a blind man's eyes was all He needed! Don't you remember?" But he's read all that. Everything I know on my side lies, written out, under his sweaty hand. Lord, don't let me whine. But I whine, "He healed the ten lepers and only one thanked. Well, I'll thank. I promise. All my life."

He clears his long knotty throat and drones like a bee, " 'By the sadness of the countenance the heart is made better.' Ecclesiastes. Seven. Three."

Oh, that's not fair! I skipped those parts, looking for verses that suited me! And it's wrong, besides.

I get up to leave and he asks will I kneel with him? "Let us pray together for that inner beauty."

No, I will not. I go down that hollow hall and past the echoing rooms. Without his help I find the great auditorium, lit through colored glass, with its cross of white plastic and a pinker Jesus molded onto it. I go straight to the pulpit where the Preacher stands. There is nobody else to plead. I ask Jesus not to listen to everything He hears, but to me only.

Then I tell Him how it feels to be ugly, with nothing to look back at you but a deer or an owl. I read Him my paper, out loud, full of His own words.

"I have been praising you, Lord, but it gets harder every year." Maybe that sounds too strong. I try to ease up my tone before the Amens. Then the chapel is very quiet. For one minute I hear the whir of many wings, but it's only a fan inside an air vent.

I go into the streets of Tulsa, where even the shade from a building is hot. And as I walk to the hotel I'm repeating, over and over, "Praise God for Tulsa in spite of everything."

Maybe I say this aloud, since people are staring. But maybe that's only because they've never seen a girl cry crooked in their streets before.

Monday morning. I have not looked at my face since the pulpit prayer. Who can predict how He might act—with a lightning bolt? Or a melting so slow and tender it could not even be felt?

Now, on the bus, I can touch in my pocketbook the cold mirror glass. Though I cover its surface with prints, I never look down. We ride through the dust and I'm nervous. My pencil is flying: "Be ye therefore perfect as your Heavenly Father is perfect. Praise God for Oklahoma. For Wagoner and Sapulpa and Broken Arrow and every other name on these signs by the road."

Was that the wrong thing to tell Him? My threat that even praise can be withheld? Maybe He's angry. "Praise God for oil towers whether I like them or not." When we pass churches, I copy their names. Praise them all. I want to write, "Bless," but that's *His* job.

We cross the cool Arkansas River. As its damp rises into the bus and touches my face, something wavers there, in the very bottom of each pore; and I clap my rough hands to each cheek. Maybe He's started? How much can He do between here and Fort Smith? If He will?

For I know what will happen. Monty won't come. And I won't stop. That's an end to it.

No, Monty is there. Waiting right now. And I'll go into the bus station on tiptoe and stand behind him. He'll turn, with his blue eyes like lamps. *And he won't know me!* If I'm changed. So I will explain myself to him: how this gypsy hair and this juicy mouth is still Violet Karl. He'll say, "Won't old Flick be surprised?" He'll say, "Where is that place you live? Can I come there?"

But if, while I wait and he turns, he should know me by my old face . . . If he should say my name or show by recognition that my name's rising up now in his eyes like something through water . . . I'll be running by then. To the bus. Straight out that door to the Tennessee bus, saying "Driver, don't let that man on!" It's a very short stop. We'll be pulling out quick. I don't think he'll follow, anyhow.

I don't even think he will come.

One hundred and thirty-one miles to Fort Smith. I wish I could eat.

I try to think up things to look forward to at home. Maybe the sourwoods are blooming early, and the bees have been laying-by my honey. If it's rained enough, my corn might be in tassel. Wouldn't it be something if God took His own sweet time, and I lived on that slope for years and years, getting prettier all the time? And nobody to know?

It takes nearly years and years to get to Fort Smith. My papa knew things about time. I comb out my hair, not looking once to see what color sheddings are caught in the teeth. There's no need feeling my cheek, since my finger expects that scar. I can feel it on me almost anywhere, by memory. I straighten my skirt and lick my lips till the spit runs out.

And they're waiting. Monty at one door of the terminal and Flick at another.

"Ten minutes," the driver says when the bus is parked, but I wait in my seat till Flick gets restless and walks to the cigarette machine. Then I slip through his entrance door and inside the station. Mirrors shine everywhere. On the vending machines and the weight machines and a full-length one by the phone booth. It's all I can do not to look. I pass the ticket window and there's Monty's back at the other door. My face remembers the shape of it. Seeing him there, how he's made, and the parts of him fitted, makes me forget how I look. And before I can stop, I call out his name.

Right away, turning, he yells to me "Viii-lut!"

So I know. I can look, then, in the wide mirror over a juke-box. Tired as I am and unfed, I look worse than I did when I started from home.

He's laughing and talking. "I been waiting here since day-light scared you wouldn't . . ." but by then I've run past the ugly girl in the glass and I race for the bus, for the road, for the mountain.

Behind me, he calls loudly, "Flick!"

I see that one step in my path like a floating dark blade, but I'm faster this time. I twist by him, into the flaming sun and the parking lot. How my breath hurts!

Monty's between me and my bus, but there's time. I circle the cabstand, running hard over the asphalt field, with a pain ticking in my side. He calls me. I plunge through the crowd like a deer through fetterbush. But he's running as hard as he can and he's faster than me. And, oh!

Praise God!

He's catching me!

LAST NIGHTS:
I. MEDICINE

Pat Rotter

THEY WALKED in hot and dirty, Artie and Tommy and Frank, and more of them than that, their hard hats parked and bottles of beer soon in their hands. Shelly was at the bar, waiting. Playing with her drink, talking to the guys, but looking past them to the door each time it opened.

Then he came in, Big John. Walked the way he walked, to the back, where they all stood. Where she sat. A flash of red, a feather, was attached to the back of his hard hat. He smiled at her and took off his hat, hanging it on one of the coat hooks.

He was the one she wanted. He was the one who in some way invited her, though it was hard to find that behind his shyness, behind that closed Indian pride. On the street, talking to her, he was polite yet friendly. Quiet. And she never really could read him through his silvery mirrored sun glasses.

"Hey, John," she called out to him, "I never saw you wear a feather before. Is that new?"

"It's medicine," he said. "My mother sent it from the reservation."

"What kind of medicine?" she asked.

He grinned. "Good medicine."

"Of course," she said, "but what for? What does it do?"

"It keeps me on the iron," he said, his face closed again, and serious.

His broad Indian face was strong. And he was big, though not quite as big on the ground as he looked up there on the iron where she'd found him. She'd watched them putting up iron from her typewriter window across the street. Another skyscraper. And she got to know them pretty well, by sight before she started to talk to them, lunch times on the street. And Shelley found out where they drank. And looked for him.

"I could use some medicine," she said to him. "Can you get me some of your medicine? Some Indian medicine?"

"I'll give you some medicine," one of her friends teased, and they all laughed. "Yeah, c'mon over here, I'll give you some of my medicine." And Shelley laughed with them.

Still, she was glad when John made his way over to her, put himself between her and them and put his money down on the bar in front of him. "You want a drink?" he asked, as he ordered his beer.

"No, I'm all right," she said.

"What kind of medicine you want?" he said between drinks of his beer. "What do you want it for?"

"Can you get some for me?" she asked. Why not serious? She needed anything that might help.

"That depends," he said, "on what it's for. What do you want it for?"

"I don't know," she said. "There are so many things, I'll settle for promotion, I guess. There's something coming up. Let me just get that, that job as an office manager and I guess I'll be happy. I've been a typist for so long."

"I'll see if I can," he said. "I can write my mother. I'm not sure it'll work, though. I'm not sure it works unless you're an Indian." But he bought them both another drink, then put his hand on her arm. Touching her with some of his medicine.

Always before, Shelley had dated young executives, assistant d.a.'s, and men on the rise. Unlike them, these men were up there where they wanted to be. To hear them tell it. She listened as they talked of how many pieces they'd made that day. How many beams connected, and how tough that last son of a bitch was to get into place.

"You should'a seen it," John said to her. "I was pushing, trying to get the damn thing to line up, and the muscles in my neck got so swollen up it busted my chain with that arrowhead I wear. You've seen it. Lucky I got it. It fell right inside my shirt."

Shelley liked to hear them brag, talking of the ease with which they walked the iron. "Just like walking to the candy store," John would say, lying. "Just like walking to the candy store."

The more John drank, the more he bragged. And when he bragged, the timbre of his voice roughened, deep and hoarse. When he and Shelley talked though, his voice was smooth and low. She asked him about the reservation where he'd been raised, wanting to know about him.

"I don't go much anymore," he said. "Not since I split with my wife."

"What happened?" Shelley asked.

He shrugged. "I found her with another man," he said. "What did you do to him?" she asked. "What did you do to her?"

"Nothing," he said, and shook his head. "Walked out and just kept going."

"I used to travel a lot back then," he said. "Before I worked in New York, I boomed out all over the country. California, Colorado. All over. Hardly ever got home. Once, my mother asked my kids who that man was. I had just come home. They were real young. Real young. You know what they said? They said, 'He's the man who comes to visit sometimes, but he always leaves.' They didn't even know I was their father."

Shelley didn't know what to say. This was more of the man than she'd guessed at. "I'm sorry," she said, and she rested her hand on his arm. "Is there medicine for that?"

His black eyes narrowed, his mouth softened, as he studied her, gave in a little. Then he turned back to the others, to shop talk and bragging. And drinking more.

Then they were leaving, Shelley glad to go with him til she found they were going with others to some Indian bar out in Brooklyn. "Stay here," she said. "I don't live far away. We can go to my house. All of us if you want. Though I'd rather just be with you."

"Don't worry," John said. "We'll get there. I'll take you home. When you're with Big John, you're taken care of. You don't have to worry." And the four of them got in a cab.

All Shelley knew in that cab on that wild ride to Brooklyn, was how drunk the others were, John and Rick, and that girl Rick was with. But Shelley felt so good close against John, she relaxed some. And he kissed her the way she wanted. And again, 'til they were in Brooklyn, Rick and John laughing and drunkenly giving the driver directions. They were down right near the water, no lights to the streets, and the place they said was the bar looked closed, with a metal gate across the front. Behind them was lower Manhattan and rising from it, the World Trade center, bigger than anything.

"Did you build that?" she said to John, hanging onto his arm.

"No," he said, "I wasn't here for that one."

There was a side door to the bar, and they went in, the big room bright-lit but dead. A jukebox played though, and two guys were playing pool, balls clicking. John looked glad to be there even if Shelley wasn't. She leaned against the jukebox, studying the songs, then asked John for money to play them, drinking from the drink he gave her. She was too sober.

John was moving around the place, talking loud to people he knew in that rough, sensual, voice, almost gravelly now. Then he settled with his drink on the bar stool next to Rick and his girl, Rick already falling off the stool. Shelley played her songs and stood there to listen, wondering what she'd got into. She liked John. She wanted him. But this wasn't quite what she figured.

Her back to the rest of them, she began to move to the music: "Scotch and soda, jigger of gin. Oh, what a spell you've got me in. Oh my, do I feel high. . ." Then John came up behind her, turning her to him. He moved against her, touching more than dancing, though he did dance well. Up against his chest, his arms around her, she felt how muscular and hard he was. How strong. Maybe it would be all right. They kissed for a very long time.

They were in that bar too long, played a little pool, and those funny pinball type machines in the back. But Shelley just couldn't get drunker. They did.

And John kept disappearing into the back with Fat Rose, the lady who owned the bar. She was from his tribe, he said. And he almost fought that pool hustler who was trying to hit on her. She was almost family, he said.

Whenever Shelley'd get impatient though, John would move to her, knowing what she'd need. He'd hug her and kiss her. And she would try teasing him out of there. He was funny though. Shy. And when she asked him once, close against him, what he wanted to do when they got home, he shook his head, serious black eyes, lank black hair. "We just will," he said. "I don't like to talk about that."

By now Rick had passed out. On the stool. And his girl friend was ministering to him, though hardly in much shape to do so. John made sure that they'd get home all right, then called for a car. No cabs would move on these streets. And then they left.

In the car back to Manhattan, they necked some, or Shelley just rested her head up against John. Finally, she thought, she would have him. She hadn't yet noticed that Big John was flagging. In the restaurant, though, down the block from her place, John seemed to nod right off between french fries, then come back to it. They were starving though, and ate fast. Paid, and left that place, Shelley still hoping.

Halfway down the block to her house though, John just

stopped. "How far are we going?" he said. "You better get a cab. I don't think I can walk anymore."

"It's only half a block," she said. "We're almost there." And she got them there. Inside, and on the couch. He was awake enough to want her, and to try at it. Kissing her, and touching her, along the way to where they'd be, to where they'd get to. She wanted him. Had wanted him. Still wanted him. But John kept sliding off, between kisses. Finally she said, "Look, why don't I just get you a pillow and you can sleep here on the couch? I'll just go to bed."

"No," he said, and again he kissed her. "No," and he fell asleep.

She got John a pillow. Tried to get him up on the couch so he'd be comfortable, struggling with his legs, pulling hard at his boots though she couldn't get them off, and trying to lift his heavy, muscled torso so his head would rest on the pillow.

She started to laugh, doubling over with it. One thing for sure, she guessed she'd never be able to look at that picture, that picture of him on the iron, without also thinking of this. Beautiful Big John passed out on the couch. And Shelley. She thought she was laughable too. Making something of iron, when flesh was there. She put on her nightgown, and went into bed.

It was light when John woke her, just sitting on the side of the bed. "I didn't know where I was until I found you," he said.

"Are you all right?" she said.

He nodded. Quiet. "Can I kiss you?" he said. "I want to kiss you."

She nodded, not sure that she still wanted him. She still wanted him. And John kissed her, and touched her. And it felt fine. He felt fine, over her.

She opened her eyes and looked up at him, closed them and felt what he felt. Still she told herself, arms round his back, body glued to him, he was a man like any other man. Skin as fine, muscles as smooth, hands no harder, no rougher, no more capable of imparting what she wanted than any other man. A remedy beyond this pleasure.

Lying there after, she remembered the med student she'd gone out with so long ago. They were driving somewhere, and she, looking for a match, pulled a syringe out of his glove compartment. "What are you going to shoot me full of this week-end?" she'd said, then blushed furiously.

What he had shot her full of, what John had just given, there was no medicine in that. Was there? She'd have to find her own medicine. She guessed he would too.

II. COITUS INTERRUPTUS

ONE DAY, Bo Charon walked into the art department of *Vogue Magazine* and suddenly his eyes opened revealing Valerie Brand to him as a glowing sexual creature, and not simply the attractive and competent art director he had known and worked with over the last few years. As a cat wants cream, he wanted her.

She knew. When his usual chair stood cold and he, instead, warmed the cushion next to hers, she knew. He moved slowly, subtly—only casually touched her shoulder, then her hand. Smiled a bit more than usual, but she kept talking. About his assignment, and what had to be done before he again came back to town.

They stood at the elevator when he said it to her. "You know," he said, "it's not just work I'm after this time." He walked her to her next appointment, trying not to touch her, giving her time to get used to the idea of him as a lover. Had his eyes been open before that day, he'd've known she'd wanted that all along. Or perhaps he had always sensed it.

"I know this isn't the place for philosophical discussions," the writer said to her editor, "and I'm not sure yet how I'd use it, but was his sensing her desire of him the spore of their affair? Did it lie dormant there, in his loins, or in his heart, for romantics, all that time until one morning the sight of his wife, a not necessarily tiresome women, made him tired. And so, the spore ripened and he went to the woman he always knew, without knowing, would have him.

"And does that mean that her desire for him, which she'd kept so carefully disguised—or so she thought—was the primary factor? Or not a factor at all? Or was it simply his abrupt virus of lust for her, to which she, of course, succumbed?"

"Why of course?" he asked.

"Are you an editor or a psychiatrist, for Cris'sake? This is a story. She just did."

"She or you," he interrupted.

"The story is in the third person. Besides, most women would have. He's a very attractive man. And extremely talented."

"Does talent play a large part in getting women into bed?" he asked.

"Yes, with some women. But wait, that's not important. I don't know where you're trying to lead me, but your digressions are getting out of hand. You have to read more of the story. I have to write it. Then if you still think that's important, we can talk about it later. . ."

When they met that evening before going together to a dinner party, they kissed. Speaking desire unspoken. At dinner, they sat and stood apart, as if afraid they would touch. But each one heard each word the other spoke, though they barely spoke to each other.

In the privacy of their departing cab, they could only grip the other's hand, could barely look at one another. Inside her door, and they sank into one another, onto the rug, laughing and then, she, crying. She saw the end before the beginning, but wouldn't tell it. He dried her tears with kisses, then led her to her bed. They knew each other so well, or so it felt.

In the gray light of their first night's ending, she sat above him, tracing his face, the dawn's city sounds filtering up from the street.

"You know," she said, "you look like Michelangelo's 'Dying Slave' when you're in the throes of love. Your face takes on a twisted, tortured look, but beautiful. Are you in such pain? Giving to me?" She paused. "Perhaps it is I who should be in pain," she said softly, "that this will soon be over."

"I will have to go home," he said, his words carefully spaced. "But it's not the end. There are two days left to have each other, and all of this city. You can take off from work, and we can. . ."

"And after?" she asked.

"We'll see each other," he said. "You know I come to New York for work, and you're my work. You'll be my excuse and my reason." He touched her cheek, and she shuddered imperceptibly.

"You needn't worry," she said in a smile more near to a grimace. "I'll find someone to fill in for you when you're home with your wife."

"Don't," he pleaded, and he kissed her. She kissed him back, harder, her fingers digging into his arms. Then she went to his sex, taking it hungrily into her mouth. . . .

"You don't have to describe their touching and kissing. Their love making," the editor said. "Not in a short story. The reader just assumes that goes on. And perhaps the reader would be even more aroused by the intimation of sex within the context of everything else that goes on."

"But that's all that goes on, isn't it? This is a story about sex."

"Is it?" he asked in his infuriating way, flinging the question back at her.

"No damn it, I suppose you're right. It's about love, among

other things, but I can't bear that. Cynics can't write love stories. Besides, then he'd know. They'd know. The bastard doesn't deserve it."

"Are you angry?" he asked, smug in the knowledge of response.

"Yes," she said. "Even if Valerie doesn't have the sense to be angry at Bo, I do. Like Spinks to Ali—and I didn't even like that dead end kid, Spinks—I just want to bust him in his superior mien. Ruffle up his pretty, pouty face a little.

"There's lots more to it than that, but wait. I want to give you more. . ."

Then Bo was above her, touching her, teasing her, finally burying himself in her. Stroking slowly, he kissed her breasts, then buried his head in the hollow of her neck. She tried to wipe away the tears that came pushing out of her eyes so that he wouldn't see, but it was no use.

"Don't stop, Bo," she said.

"But you're crying."

"I know, damn it. And there's nothing more boring than a woman who cries during sex. Look, it doesn't mean anything. I just can't help it."

Bo was fine then. Talking to her, stroking her, kissing away the tears. You're making me love you, she thought, but pushed that aside. He was still inside her, and they finished together. Then slept.

Later that morning, she rode with him in a cab up to Walter's where he was supposed to be staying. He wouldn't take her upstairs. Walter was an old friend, and Walter couldn't care. But Bo did.

"I just want to check in," Bo said. "I don't expect to hear from Claire, but it can't hurt to be sure. And there could be other calls."

I'm just along for the ride, Valerie thought, as the taxi caromed up Third Avenue. I'm just along for the ride.

"Do you really believe that?" her editor said.

"Believe what?" she asked.

"That part about just being along for the ride?"

"Not really," she said, making a face. "I'm too old to get away with that. And so is Valerie Brand. No. I don't think so. I suppose we get what we want. What we're asking for, that is. Not what we think we want."

"Well then," he went on, "why that sentence? With the taxi 'caroming' up Third Avenue. It's damn corny, anyway."

The writer laughed harshly. "Yeah, it's corny. But damn it, that's what it feels like when you let yourself get carried along like that. Fall in love."

" 'Let yourself get carried along?' Is that what you said?"

"Yes, that's what I said. God, I don't know about Valerie Brand, but I fell in love once for a day and a half because I thought he was possible. Really in love. You're right, though," she said. "It's not 'let yourself get carried along.' You're the one that's doing it.

"Look," she said, "we're talking too much. "I want to get back to them. . ."

Dinner again was in company. Their second night. They'd have three. It was Bo's gallery owner this time, and the woman he lived with. Valerie knew them, of course. And she had a right to be there, professionally. They were friends to Bo's wife, though, and she had to be on good behavior. Not touch him. Not look at him that way. It put her in her place. A reminder of who she wasn't. And besides, this pompous deacon of the arts was attacking her friend, another artist who she was inordinately soft on.

"He lives off women," the fat man said, sniffing as at something gone bad.

"What does that have to do with his talent?" Valerie said. "He's a genius with color, and you show him. I hardly think that that's relevant. Even if it were true."

She hated it. Wanted not to be there. Not to be so polite. She wanted to be alone with Bo. In bed with Bo. But she drank too much, and Bo left her off to go and sleep back at Walter's, worried and certain his wife would call in the morning.

"We'll have tomorrow," he said. "The whole afternoon, and on throughout the night." And he held her close there inside her door, nuzzling his face against her neck like a cat, before he turned to leave.

"There's something I don't understand," the editor said.

"What's that?" she asked.

"Well," he said, "there are all these clues. All along the way. Doesn't she know she should stop? Stop herself falling in love at least."

"It's not that easy," the writer answered. "A woman always has hope. That's what makes her a woman, I think. And since I'm writing this, there's hope there in Valerie."

"False hope," her editor said. "She's a damn fool!"

"Yes, maybe," she said. "But there's something else, too. The story. Not this story, but their story. Her story. She has to play it out. Let it run its course. Let it finish. If she stops it, interrupts it, she won't have what was there. What would be there. She won't have anything."

The editor groaned. "All right," he said. "I can see I'm not going to get anywhere with that one. So let me ask you an easier question. About talent. Tell me about talent. I wouldn't have brought it up except that you did again, in Valerie's conversation about her artist friend. At dinner, with Bo's gallery owner. Is talent an important part of it? Is that why a woman goes to bed with a man?"

"No, I don't think so," the writer said. "Valerie never went to bed with her other talented artist friends. And I don't think that's why she went to bed with Bo. She liked him. They liked each other. Besides," she added, sounding annoyed, "she's too far along for that. Quite successful herself, you know. It happens more with younger women, I think, falling in love with a man who is what they want to be. Valerie's close to thirty-four when all this happens. Same age as Bo.

"Still, he is the artist, and she the art director. He, the creator. And she *does* admire his work. Maybe. Maybe, but not here. Not in their story. I don't want that in there. . ."

That next afternoon was lost to them. Lost to meetings with Valerie's editor on future projects. And drinks for Bo with buyers of his paintings. But after, he met her at home. Walked in with a bag full of groceries. Walked in with that same good-natured sexuality, that sexual generosity, that he'd beamed at her two days before. And she, still caught in those rays.

They put away the food, laughing and planning what they'd later cook. Valerie made them drinks, and they took to the couch. Close together, drinking and talking and touching, she thought that the way he touched her, the way he held and stroked her feet and her legs and her hands, was so intimate, so natural, as if it was his own body, not hers. They made love.

In that night it seemed, they always made love. Before during and after everything. And it was the way it is when it's good. More than good.

It was in the kitchen, though, that Valerie said it to him. Not what she might have said. "I've never done this," she said. "Cooked with a man. Isn't that funny? Sex is one thing. Coin of the realm, if you will. But this is special. This is really special."

He hugged her, the garlic on his hands so near her face, and she felt giddy. She laughed. "You've taken my virginity," she said.

"Her virginity?" the editor said, raising an eyebrow.

"You're interrupting," the writer said.

The editor laughed. "I thought that's what this was about."

"Yes, all right," she said. "Now what is it you want to know?" ,

"Virginity," he said. "What's that all about?"

"Yes, virginity," she said. "That's the bloody miracle. That everything is new, every time. We do the same things over and over again, falling in love. Every man we fall in love with, every man we make love with, brings us something new. And takes, in a sense, our virginity."

She laughed. "I know that's far-fetched," she said. "And ghastly romantic. But it's true. God knows it was true for Valerie. Sure Bo was special for her. And yes, he did take her virginity. But so had every man she'd ever had, and every man she'd be with. The needs are the same. And the answers. But each time different. . ."

Valerie had fallen in love with Bo. In their long night of loving, in their long night of talking and cooking and eating, and loving, she fell in love. And she believed Bo when he said he'd be back. When he said he'd come back. She didn't believe that there'd be much more than that, but Valerie did believe that.

But Bo was gone. Bo was gone and never did come back. There were letters. Letters disguising what they felt. What she felt, because she never did know what he felt. They were letters Bo's wife, Claire, might read, that talked of Bo's assignments and Valerie's projects, that talked around everything else.

And there were phone calls. Those few phone calls when Claire was out and Valerie could tell Bo what more she'd left out of those letters. Too much more. More really than Bo wanted to know. And then there was his letter. Bo's final letter.

"Wait a minute," the editor said. "What the hell did she expect with a married man?"

"There's no logic in love," the writer answered. "Besides, if you've got a story called *Coitus Interruptus*, you haven't many choices. Well, more than a few. A married man is one."

"That's cheap," he said, shaking his head. "No. That's not good enough."

"Well, maybe Valerie likes married men. Some women do, I'm told."

"Why?" he asked.

"Jesus god, I don't know," she said. "Ask her psychiatrist. Maybe she just liked Bo. Single men leave too, you know."

"Yes," he said, "but the risks aren't as high. Are they? Yes, she liked Bo. She could still have gone to bed with him. She could have had an affair with him without falling in love."

"Some women can't," she said. "Some women can't go to bed with a man without falling in love. Still. But you're right. It goes back to something deeper. Need, I guess. What does a woman want when she goes to bed with a man? Something more than sex. I still believe that. I don't know about men, but I still think it's true of a woman."

"Well then," he said, "why would Valerie sabotage her own desires by falling in love with a married man? With any man impossible to her?"

"I can't answer that question," she said. "I don't think I can answer that. Except there is one thing I mentioned before. And I believe it, I guess. That you get what you really want. Even if it isn't what you think you want. There are no accidents."

"Well, did Valerie get what she wanted?" the editor asked, raising an eyebrow.

"I don't know," the writer answered. "The story doesn't go that far. Stops in the middle, like their relationship. *Coitus Interruptus.*"

"What about Bo's letter?" he asked. "What did his letter say?"

"Oh, the usual," she said. "About how much he loved his wife and how he didn't live well with secrets and couldn't risk hurting her. You know. It was a beautiful letter though, and she cried over it.

"There was one thing he said, though, a quote from Vonnegut: 'Everything was beautiful and nothing hurt.' Then added Bo, 'Not altogether true, or nearly complicated enough, but I try to think of it that way. Please, Valerie, you try, too.' "

"Did they ever see each other after that?" the editor asked. "Work together?"

"He sent in a lot of his work," she said. "And when they did get together, it was business as usual for him, business uncomfortable for her. There was something still there though, and they slipped once. It was a parody, though, of what they'd had before. Then Valerie left *Vogue,* and they didn't see each other at all after that."

She shook her head. "You know what I find so sad about all this?" the writer said to her editor. "About Valerie and Bo. Whoever. . . . Fucking is hardly ever a beginning. No, what I mean is, it usually is the beginning, but only of the end. And when it does end that way, it usually just stops completely, since one of you is too angry or embarrassed or guilty or hurt to keep it going at all. In any way. What was there besides sex, that made you want to be that way to each other, is lost. That person you found, the Bo that Valerie found, in the close quiet after sex, is also lost. The fucking can be replaced. But not the other."

She thought a minute. "Unless you believe that memory saves you," she said. "I guess I have to."

"You wouldn't need the memory if you had the man," the editor said. "What are memories but fantasies? What are fantasies but stories? It's a good thing you're a writer."

III. CLEANING HOUSE

SHE TURNED on her bar stool and glared at him. "She what?" Dottie said to him there in Rakehell's. "You're kidding. Your ex-wife cleans your apartment?"

Bear shrugged, his sheepish smile turning kind of smug. "She wanted to," he said. "Besides the divorce isn't final yet. She likes to, I guess, and I didn't want to hurt her feelings. I do pay her. What could I do?"

"You could say no," Dottie said. "You could say no. Jesus, you're crazy. She's sick and you're crazy. What does she do? Smell your sheets?"

Bear drank down his beer. "Well, I was going to fire her," he said, "but she does such a good job. Eddie, you know, my roommate, he talked me out of it. Anyway, at least we can trust her. There's stuff all over the place. Grass. And Eddie's guns. Him being a detective and all. We can't just hire anyone. Besides, she does such a good job."

Dottie choked on beer going down wrong, coughing like hell, her eyes watering. Bear thumped her on the back and handed her a cocktail napkin. She wiped her eyes, shaking her head. "You're right," she said. "You're not crazy. What have you got to lose? She's the one who's crazy. She's crazier than I am! I mean that girl needs a psychiatrist. That's the weirdest thing I've ever heard. I know about hanging on. But what a way to hang on!"

"She did go for a while," Bear said. "After we separated. To a psychiatrist, I mean. He just fired her though."

"What do you mean he fired her," Dottie asked.

"He fired her. Said she didn't need it anymore." Bear was straight-faced. Dead-pan.

"Doesn't need it? Jesus, he's the one who's crazy. He's crazier than you and me and her all together. That's one crazy psychiatrist."

"He's not that crazy," Bear said. "He got me in there once. We got on great. Then he told my wife she should never come near me again."

"Well, he's right about that," Dottie said. "He sure was right about that."

Bear looked at her, and grinned through that beard they'd named him Bear for. "Never mind," he said, and he ran his big hands up and down her thighs right there in Rakehell's, turning her on.

He didn't have to even touch her to turn Dottie on. Just sitting in a bar on a bar stool next to Bear, and Dottie got all heated from the bar stool up. Whatever they were talking on. Whatever asshole thing he'd done he was making up to her for. None of it mattered. None of it seemed to matter. She just hotted right up.

That's where they spent most of their time though, most of their time together. Right there on bar stools next to each other. In Rakehell's or some other nearby bar. They hadn't met there, and sometimes they'd end up somewheres else. Her bed, not his. And once, maybe twice, he actually took her to dinner, on a real date. But mostly it was Rakehell's, and bar stools.

She'd only just stopped by to see her brother's friend on a job site nearby her house. That's when Bear'd glommed his

372   PAT ROTTER

eyes on her. Sashayed right over. Charming as a sonofabitch when he wanted to. He sure was then. And mostly.

Except when he wasn't. And he wasn't when he wasn't. Just took himself right out of focus. Took himself away. Which was too damn much of the time. Made Dottie so damn mad she had to come back for more. Always thinking she just might get something back. Wore her out, not quittin'. Just coming back for more.

Dottie figured she was lucky not to love him. Liked the hell out of him, but nothing more than that. They did have a good time, though. Laughing and drinking like they did. And when they'd go home. Take turns climbing on top of each other. She sure liked the hell out of that. Still, she should've known right there at the beginning that she ought to stop and step back away from that. Didn't need much smarts to have a sense of that.

Charming, yes. Bear sure had come on strong. Offering to show her 'round the job. Buying her drinks and turning it on, that charm. Then just about when Dottie'd bought his message, Bear kind of started pedalling back. Treading water. He was talking to her still, there in the bar, but Bear wasn't making any offers. So Dottie did. Invited Bear for drinks one day, back at her house. "I'll buy you dinner," he'd said. "Monday?"

Well, Bear stood her up. First date, and he stood her up. Never even called to explain, or apologize or nothing. That sure should'a given her a clue. Anybody sane would have quit it then. Not Dottie.

A week later or so, she was standing on the corner waiting for the light to change. Bear standing there across from her. She could've turned, gone down the street away from him. Around the corner, anywhere but where she finally did. Knew she would. Seeing him just made her mad, and being mad just made her want him. First time, in fact, she really did.

But it was the "mad" made her cross to him. She'd tell that man a thing or two. Bear flinched when she came near to him, like he thought Dottie might hit him. And she might have if she'd thought it would do something. Break her fingers though, and never make a dent. Bear was built like the side of a shit house. So Dottie just hit him with words.

"If I was smart," she said, "I'd just walk right past you. You shit. I don't know what your excuse is, but the least you could have done was call. Didn't your mother teach you any manners? Women are people like you, 'ya know. How do you think that made me feel? You had some reason? You could at least have called."

Bear lowered his head, looking sorry, and kind of shamed. He almost was blushing, if a man like Bear could blush. "I'm sorry," he said. "I just got drinking. And when I get drinking like that, I don't stop. I meant to call, but well I never did."

"That's for sure," she said.

"Then afterwards, I just couldn't. I hoped I would see you," said Bear. "Come have a beer with me now. I'll try to make it up to you."

Dottie'd just felt herself turn more and more on, then and there yelling at Bear. And she couldn't turn him down. So they had a few at Rakehell's, and made a date for real. Her friends told Dottie she was crazy, going out with Bear after that first time around.

But it was worth it. Bear took Dottie out to a real nice restaurant. French. And he was all dressed up in a jacket, big body looking trim in that navy blazer. But he always did look, well solid, in those shirts he wore. Those plaid shirts. Of one color or another.

They go on real well, Bear and Dottie. Always did. That night, talking and laughing. They drank some after dinner, then went home to Dottie's bed. Bear was big, so warm and cozy, and Dottie felt lovely so high off the ground. Atop him, wrapped 'round him, then cuddled up tight. Bear stayed all night. He must'a liked it.

He did like it. Liked her, Dottie. Told her she'd given him something that night something special he needed, something special he'd lost that she'd given him back. Though he wouldn't explain what he meant.

It worked pretty good for a while. They drank together, loved together, and went out some around town. Only thing always missing was weekends. He'd disappear. Talk about taking her away places, lying there in bed with her, but he just never did. And never took her home to his bed.

Bear had those other girls. That was all right. She knew about them. That was some of what they talked about. Like she was his buddy, not a lover. And she guessed that's what she mostly was. "Fucking buddies," that's what he'd say about her and him. Then he'd fill her in on those others.

There was Rae, the one he'd left his wife for, who then had left him for another man. She wanted him back now, and Bear took great pleasure in playing her, like she was a big fish on his hook. Laurie was the little one, the nurse, naive and big-eyed. What had he told Dottie she'd said to him? Made her think, "Poor thing." Something about she didn't want any of the Sunday paper, she was happy just watching him read it. Lord, was poor Laurie in trouble.

The funny thing, ass-backwards, Dottie thought all those months later, was that she could sit there on that bar stool and laugh like hell at those stories he'd tell. Like she was on Bear's side and not one of them. Not jumping through hoops just like they was.

"Jesus," Bear said one day, looking weathered. "What a night I spent last night!" Dottie had spent hers alone.

"Out drinking again?" Dottie said.

"Not me," he said as he lifted his Sambuco, 4:00 in the afternoon. "I'm cutting down. No, it started out really quiet. Laurie took me to the movies. Then she came over afterwards. You know. We were in bed after, practically asleep when the phone rang. It was Rae. She had to see me. Had to be with me. I tried to talk her out of it but she was near hysterical. I had to say yes."

"What do you mean you had to? What did you do with Laurie? Jesus, how can you do that to people?"

"Oh, it was all right," Bear said. "Laurie understands. She knows about Rae. She just got dressed and went home."

"Yeah," Dottie said. "You got to keep her in line. Don't want her falling in love with you. Or do you?"

Bear shrugged. "What do you think it is?" he said, patting his belly. "My body? They just can't resist me." He shook his head. "I don't know if my body can take it though. Two in one night." He grinned, loving it.

"Yeah, I know what you mean," Dottie said. "I could wear these contacts I have instead of glasses. Spent enough for 'em. But then I'd be so glamorous, I'd have to fight 'em off. You can handle it. I can't. One's enough for me."

"I like a woman in glasses," Bear said, ignoring what she really said. "They turn me on." He came closer, kissing distance, his hands again on her thighs there in the bar. Turning her on. They made a date. Dottie would cook.

The date was for a Thursday, and when she called to ask him when he'd get there, she couldn't track him down. The guys in the shanty always covered for him. Never did know where he was. And Bear never did show.

She hadn't cooked that meat she bought, but Dottie was mad as hell. This time the son-of-a-bitch for sure wouldn't get anymore. No more Dottie. She was quittin'.

Quittin'? She couldn't quit. Monday morning she found that meat in her fridge, startin' to go. She laughed like hell, put it in an old manila envelope, wrote up a note to go with it, then took it over to the shanty, leakin' already, and dropped it on that desk he used. "The meat's a little rotten," she'd said, "but then, my dear Bear, so are you." Then to close: "Just 'cause you've got a little bull stick between your legs (those big things they used to turn the derricks), you think you can piss on anything in a skirt. Well, you can't."

Couldn't he? He came back to her some. But for that time then, it was more drinking than loving. More breaking than dating. He loved her note, though, he, and his roommate Eddie. Thought they'd put it up on the wall. And she was more distanced than distancing. Settled to it, but not happy with it. It inspired her though, to great flights of wicked wit.

Another time he'd stood her up, or hadn't done what he said he might, she delivered to the shanty a box of Saran wrap. "To the biggest prick in the world," she'd said. "You!" And that college tee shirt he asked that she buy on a visit out of town. Only 'stead of buying one, Dottie'd had one made up. "Fuck U," it had said. Was Dottie clever? Clever and still caught.

This had been going on for months now, and they saw each other drinkin' quite a lot. Once in a while for the other stuff. Once in a while, rare and rarer, did Dottie get some of that. Some lovin' straight from Bear. By now, it had filtered down to never.

But she was drinking there in Rakehell's on that warm Friday there at the beginning of summer's end. Looking good, Dottie was. New shades, hair tousled, trim in those red hot shorts. Waiting for Bear.

Bear came in, and, like the first time, glommed his eyes right on her. He parked his hat on its hook, and set right down beside her. Grinning at her. Touching her without touching. He bought them a round. Then another, seducing as if it was necessary. Then laughing, he started to tell a new story about his wife.

"She called me the other day," Bear said. "Saturday it was. Asked me if I wouldn't make love to her. It'd been over three months, and she was needin'. So," he shrugged, "I said yes."

"You said yes?" Dottie said. "I didn't know that was part of your duties as a divorced husband. You are divorced now."

"Yeah," he said. "But, well, I felt bad for her. So I said I'd come over. She sure pulled one on me. I came out of the bathroom, after . . . She said, 'I just gave you crabs.' I looked down and sure enough. . . ."

Dottie was laughing. Laughing like hell. Bear lookin' hurt he'd got no sympathy. He didn't think it was that funny. But

Dottie just couldn't stop laughing. Laughing, eyes tearing, and coughing, 'til she finally stopped herself and took a long, long drink from her beer, finishing it.

"I don't think tonight's such a good idea," Dottie said, and she slid off her stool there at Rakehell's before Bear might have put a stop to it, and walked right out. Finally cleaning house.

ACKNOWLEDGMENTS

I'd like to thank my editor for her encouragement, her support, and for liking the stories that I liked and letting me win when she didn't. And especially I'd like to thank the writers here, who, like all writers, do sometimes accept less than they are worth. Thanks to them for their stories, the ones that never leave us. Thanks to them, and to their agents and previous publishers who allowed us to publish their work in *Last Night's Stranger*.